The Jade Bracelet

A NOVEL

WILMA WALL

Kregel
Publications

The Jade Bracelet: A Novel

© 2006 by Wilma Wall

Published by Kregel Publications, a division of Kregel, Inc., P.O. Box 2607, Grand Rapids, MI 49501.

Library of Congress Cataloging-in-Publication Data
Wall, Wilma.
  The jade bracelet: a novel / by Wilma Wall.
    p. cm.
1. Chinese Americans—Fiction. I. Title.
PS3623.A3597J33   2006
813'.6—dc22   2006018961

ISBN 0-8254-3948-5

Printed in the United States of America

06 07 08 09 10 / 5 4 3 2 1

In memory of my father and mother,
John S. and Tina Dick,
faithful missionaries until the
very ends of their lives.

Acknowledgments

MY HEARTY THANKS TO ALL those who shared their memories and writings about China. Special thanks to my sister, Verna Richert Enns, whose recollections are greater than mine. To cousins Adina Robinson, who made her book *China Beckoning* available, as well as granting me interviews; Linda Gerbrandt for answering questions; and Ann Wiens, who with her husband, Roland, wrote *China Then and Now* and filled me in on changes in that wonderful country.

Posthumous thanks to my mother, Tina H. Dick, for her story, "My Heart Looks Back," and brother Vester Dick for his fabulous pictures; my uncle, missionary F. J. Wiens, for *Fifteen Years Among the Hakkas of South China*; A. K. and Gertrude Wiens for their book, *Shadowed by the Great Wall*; and for Pauline Foote's memoirs. The list of other books I've devoured while immersing myself in Chinese culture would fill a whole volume.

A gold medal to Dave Borofka for introducing me to the fascinating world of writing and not letting me defend my blunders.

Thanks to Mildred Ewy for nursing-school info from the era, and Reedley Pharmacy for pharmacy-school details. Any errors on those subjects are mine, not theirs.

Thanks to Becky Durost Fish for her insightful editing while preserving Elsa's voice. My appreciation to Kregel Publications and their hardworking staff, especially Steve, Amy, Janyre, and Miranda.

Deepest gratitude to my husband and best friend, Dave Wall, for his immeasurable tolerance and patience, and my family—Judi, Don, Jean, Ed, Margie, Rick, Mike, Katye, Jeff, Eric, Robyn, Carrie, Micky, Natalie, Tamera, Terra, and David—for their emotional support.

As always, bouquets to my dear friend and mentor, Elnora King, and the Tuesday afternoon group.

Although many situations in this story are loosely based on actual events, the characters are fictitious. For those who know my family personally, I want to emphasize that Elsa is not me, and Rachel is not my mother.

—WILMA WALL

Not what we give, but what we share,
For the gift without the giver is bare.
—J. R. LOWELL,
Vision of Sir Launfal II

Prologue

Inner Mongolia, 1980

A PILLAR OF SAND SWIRLED ALONG the path toward the mountain, eddied upward, and disappeared overhead. Above, the sky was the color of ashes.

Shiao Yangshan. Little Goat Mountain. In the dim light before dawn, she could barely see its head, its body. If she stretched her imagination, she could make out the haunches.

By those rocks, she'd picnicked long ago, eating boiled eggs and melon slices. In their shadows, she'd waded in the little stream, collecting pebbles, patting the grassy hummocks as though they were fat, furry animals.

The bell tower and the compound walls should have blocked her view. But now there was no tower, no wall. Only the brick house was the same, unmistakable in its shape: nine rooms in a long row, a window for each room. The fifth window to the left of the door had been the classroom, where Mama had given so many assignments and marked the errors with her red pencil.

It was still too early for much activity, so when the front door opened, she caught her breath, her chest tightening with anticipation. So many times Papa had come out that door, walking toward the church, going into the village, or heading for the train station to pick up the mail.

But a stranger stepped out, an old Chinese man scratching his ribs and shivering. He spit in the sand and fumbled with the drawstring of his pants.

She turned away and slipped into the shadow of the old church building. When the door creaked again, she continued on around the house. Here, nothing was familiar. What once had been the back compound now held rows of flat-roofed mud huts, their chimneys exhaling thin wisps of smoke. The housewives must be feeding the brick stoves handfuls of straw to heat water for their husbands' morning tea and the gruel called *yomein huhu.*

She plotted the distances. One of the houses was a little larger than the others; could that be the stable? Farther on would have been the ice pit. On the opposite side, the swings, the garden. The root cellar.

All were gone. Even the trees were no longer there, those sturdy sycamores planted in straight lines beside the paths. Without the wall and the trees, how would she ever find it?

She closed her eyes and counted the steps. *Yi, er, san, sih, wu, liu, chi, bah. Yi, er, san, sih, wu, liu, chi, bah. Yi, er, san, sih.* She repeated the sequence twice more, and then added four extra counts, taking her to where the wall would have been. To one side, the back gate; to the other side . . .

She hurried forward, holding her breath.

So many losses—friends, family, her country, and all her beloved people. Blinded by tears, she dropped to her knees and patted the dry earth, searching for clues. This *must* be where it was.

But it was gone. Even the grave was gone.

Part 1

Chapter 1

Shungtau, South China, May 1933

EXPLOSIONS PEPPERED THE HOT summer air. "Firecrackers!" shouted Elsa Meier.

Perched high in a chestnut tree near the wall of the mission compound, she could see the road leading up from the South Han River. Could it be a parade? She loved the huge paper dragons, tossing their bearded heads and prancing with many human feet, the funny men on stilts, the dancers in ferocious lion masks.

Instead, she saw a peasant woman running barefoot, her carrying pole across one shoulder. At one end a water pail jiggled and sloshed; at the other, a toddler clung to a swinging basket. The woman darted off toward a cluster of huts and disappeared, leaving a curling trail of drops in the afternoon dust.

In the rice paddies beyond the huts, the coolies straightened their bare backs, slogged out of the mud, and fled down the path away from the river, their cone-shaped bamboo hats bobbing.

Puzzled, Elsa peered toward the nearby city of Shungtau. Maybe it was a wedding, the bride hidden in her red-curtained sedan chair carried by bamboo poles on the shoulders of coolies. Elsa waited to hear the wailing two-stringed *pipa*, the gongs and cymbals of the nuptial band, the taunts of children hoping for a shower of dates and candies. But all she heard were more strung-out pops, zooming whistles, and dull thuds. And now shouts in the distance.

The noise seemed to come from across the river, in the lush green mountains where pilgrims climbed the dirt trail to worship the *feng-shui,* the spirits of wind and water. But there, too, the trail to the cave temples was deserted. Except . . . what were those puffs of smoke? And now, she could make out a man darting among the bushes. Then another and another.

Suddenly, Elsa knew. She felt it in her fast-beating heart, in her lurching stomach. Those were gunshots! This was what Papa and Mama had whispered about when they thought she wasn't listening. *Red soldiers. Fighting. War. The Reds want to drive all foreigners from China—especially missionaries.*

Elsa hadn't believed them. This was her home! She belonged here. Tucking her dress into her bloomers, she started down the tree to tell Papa.

Then she remembered: two days ago, he'd left to visit an outstation. He usually rode his bicycle, but this time he was headed up into the mountains so he'd walked, his ivory-tipped cane in one hand and his Chinese Bible under the other arm.

Fear sent a cold chill up Elsa's neck. Would those soldiers find him? What would they do to him?

Mama was nearby, teaching at the girls' school at the north end of the compound. At first, Elsa had wished she could study with the Chinese girls instead of alone with Mama after school hours, but now she was glad she didn't—Mama ruled her class like a Mandarin at court. And she had a strict rule: her lessons must never be disturbed.

Elsa glanced toward the gatehouse where Huang spent his days deciding who could enter the mission compound. He'd know what to do.

But the gateman wasn't in his usual place this time of the afternoon, squatting on his haunches and rolling dice with the houseboy. Instead, he stood outside on the dusty road—and with him were three men in uniform.

Were they Red soldiers, this close to the compound? Would Huang allow them in? Elsa inched around out of sight behind the trunk of the tree and considered the distance to the wide arched veranda of her home. Would it be safe to run there?

A movement behind the red-tiled house caught her eye, and she jerked back, catching her loose sleeve on a twig. There, down in the vegetable garden, among the glistening leaves—

But it was only Ho Fen, the cook, hands full of spinach picked for this evening's supper, hurrying back to the house. Squawking, the ducks scrambled out of the nearby pond and waddled single file to their pen. A flock of chattering sparrows rushed by, not stopping for their usual snack.

Something hit Elsa on the arm. She caught her breath and frantically ripped her sleeve free. Glancing down, she saw it was only three-year-old Jasper under the tree, throwing bristly pods at her. His rompers were crumpled from his nap, and he clutched his brown teddy bear.

"What you doing?" he asked.

"Sh-h-h," she said, and looked around. The soldiers hadn't come through the gate, so she climbed down the branches and jumped to the ground. "Come with me." Grabbing her little brother's hand, she started running with him across the lawn toward the house.

But Jasper pulled loose and ran the other way, to Mama's school. Tugging open the door, he squeezed through without even politely scratching on the wood for admittance. Dreading the sure punishment, Elsa followed and peeked into the classroom. Rows of Chinese girls sat straight as bamboo stalks, each with a black braid hanging down the back of her white shirt. Their shrill voices chanted loudly in unison, "*Go-go, Dee-dee, shiang shan, siah shan*—big brother, little brother, go up the mountain, come down the mountain."

Had Mama heard the shots? Would it be all right to break the rules and ask her?

From the house came the wailing voice of her nursemaid, the amah, calling in Shungtau dialect, "Hoo, hoo! Little Tiger, Eternal Virtue!" She came running, wide black trousers flapping. "*Buh, buh!* No! No! Do not enter," she shouted, "or I skin you alive!"

Tsao Po-Po scolded a lot, but never punished them. Ignoring her, Elsa looked back into the classroom, then clapped her fist over her mouth.

Jasper had gone all the way across the room to the front desk! No matter what, Mama would blame her for this.

Mama sat stern and dignified in a dark blue skirt and white blouse. Her brown hair was pulled up into a smooth coil at her neck, and her dark eyes swept the classroom from behind horn-rimmed glasses. Peeking out from under the desk were her Chinese-style flat black satin shoes trimmed with red and gold embroidered butter-flies. Mama loved pretty shoes.

Little Tiger climbed up into his mother's lap, threw his chubby arms around her neck, and burrowed his mop of golden hair into her bosom.

Elsa waited for his scolding, but without missing a beat in the recitation or taking her eyes off the class, Mama gave Jasper a hug and gently set him down, then glanced toward Elsa.

Elsa wondered: did she dare run and whisper the news to her mother? She lifted her foot to tiptoe in, but Mama's lips twitched. The twitch usually meant Mama was upset with her, and Elsa's moment of courage faltered.

Then she thought again of the soldiers and of Papa out in the mountains. "But Mama!" she blurted. "The shots! Didn't you—"

Mama's eyes darted to the class, then back at Elsa. Her expression was stern, and she flicked her head in the direction of the door. Swatting Jasper's bottom lightly, she pushed him toward Elsa. The class droned on in unison as though nothing had happened, their eyes fixed on the chalkboard, their backs erect.

Jasper scampered back to the door, grinning like he'd been handed a piece of sesame candy.

Didn't Mama care? Elsa felt tightness in her chest, as if her heart were being squeezed by a vise, and she backed out of the door after Jasper, still wondering what to do.

Hands gripped her shoulders, and she spun around. But it was only Tsao Po-Po whispering, "Go to the house. *Kwai, kwai,* hurry, hurry!"

As they ran, her amah grumbled, "*Ai-yah,* I have looked for you everywhere! Eternal Virtue," she clucked, "you are an untamed goat. You should be called Eternal Mischief." She rushed them past the cosmos bed and the climbing nasturtiums that Elsa loved to taste, up the steps of the veranda, through the parlor, and into the dining room.

Ho Fen came from the kitchen with a plate of ginger cookies. He smelled of dried salt fish, and his white apron was spotted with reminders of breakfast and lunch.

Just as Elsa reached for a cookie, another string of shots crackled through the air, this time much closer. Ho Fen's hand jerked, and the cookies jumped straight up from the plate, then settled back down. He pushed the plate at the amah, and ran back to the kitchen.

Tsao Po-Po froze, clutching the plate to her chest, her free hand covering her mouth. Worry wrinkles creased her eyes.

"What's happening?" whispered Elsa, her heart racing.

Tsao Po-Po bent and picked up two cookies that had fallen to the floor, blew off the dust, and put them back on the plate. When she looked back at Elsa, her eyes had turned clear and calm again. "It is nothing. Target practice in the hills."

Unconvinced, Elsa studied Tsao Po-Po's face. If that was target practice, why was everyone afraid?

"You stay inside now," said the amah. "Understand, Yung-det?" She reached for the teapot waiting on its dish of coals, poured them each a cup of pale green tea, and sat down on a low stool. Taking her small, bamboo shoe-making frame off a shelf, she began pasting scraps of fabric onto a coarse cotton base to be cut and stitched into soles for whoever needed the next pair of shoes. "And never, *never*, leave the compound alone. *Ai-yah*, what *mafang* you always make. Such trouble."

Elsa sat on the floor with Jasper, the cookie plate on her lap. She chewed slowly, remembering. Last week, from up in the tree, she'd seen a group of Chinese children walking along the riverbank. Thoughtlessly, she had slipped out the front gate, followed them home, and stayed to play.

When Elsa had returned to the compound, Mama had spanked her. But it wasn't the spanking that kept her from sneaking out again. On the way back, she'd noticed a dark round object set on a high stake. A real human head with matted hair, empty black eye sockets, and a mouth twisted in a silent scream.

One of Papa's books had pictures of the terrible Boxer Rebellion— missionaries fleeing, hiding behind rocks, half naked and bloody— and stories about the Chinese who had helped them and who had been executed for their kindness.

It all fit, she realized. The soldiers, the shooting, the gruesome head. It must hurt an awful lot to die. If Papa died, he would go to heaven. But she wasn't good enough for heaven. Would she ever see Papa again?

Elsa watched as her amah dabbed more flour paste onto a sole. Over that, she smoothed another scrap of material. Tsao Po-Po's high cheekbones tapered down to a pointed mouth, her lips barely covering her large, protruding teeth. Mama had said the woman's jaw was deformed, but Elsa thought it was an elegant face, like that of an imperial princess. Sometimes she sucked in her own cheeks to make her mouth tiny like that.

More than anyone in the world except for Papa, Elsa loved Tsao Po-Po. She couldn't remember a time when her amah hadn't been there, keeping her warm and safe, protecting her from harm while her parents did the work of the Lord. But could her amah protect them from this new danger? Her stomach ached, and she slid the plate across the floor to Tsao Po-Po's feet.

The amah set aside the shoe frame, picked up the plate, and set it on the table. She pulled out a needle tucked into her white tunic, threaded it, and squatted down. Holding Elsa tight, she mended the torn sleeve.

Elsa looked past her and through the window, watching for Mama's class to march outside for calisthenics. They would count, chanting: *"Yi, er, san, sih, wu, liu, chi, ba,"* arms up, arms down, turn left, turn right. Always to the count of eight, a magic number, or so Tsao Po-Po had said. Elsa had believed that when she turned eight she would become beautiful and good and deserve the name Eternal Virtue. And then Mama would be proud of her.

But last Tuesday had been her eighth birthday. Papa had given her a beautiful doll ordered from the "Monkey Ward" catalog, and she'd named it Glory after the angels in the highest.

Mama had scolded Papa. "Porcelain? That's much too expensive a gift for a tomboy. It'll be broken before the week is over." And Elsa had realized the magic number hadn't turned her into Eternal Virtue after all.

Now she heard a noise and turned, startled to see Mama coming up the veranda steps and through the parlor door.

Mama said, "I've sent the class home."

Elsa stared at her. School had never been dismissed early before. Something *was* terribly wrong. Silently, she prayed: *Please, God, bring Papa safely home.*

Then she heard Mama whisper to Tsao Po-Po, "Bolt the doors."

Chapter 2

BY EVENING, PAPA STILL WASN'T HOME. Elsa felt a rock settle in her stomach, and she hardly touched the supper Ho Fen had set out.

She watched him clear the dishes and light the kerosene lamp on the dining table. Mama took her journal from a padded box on Papa's lacquer desk, moved near the light, and began writing. In a dark corner of the room, Tsao Po-Po settled on a low stool, lifted Jasper and his teddy bear onto her lap, and rocked back and forth while crooning a lullaby.

Sitting next to Mama, Elsa tried to read, but her worries kept getting mixed up with the words. She asked, "When will Papa get back?"

Mama glanced over the lines she'd written and sighed. "I've told you three times." Her voice sounded angry. "He will come when he can." She closed her diary, placed it and the pen back into the box, and slid the ivory hasp in place.

Suddenly, the air burst with a loud string of gunshots that wouldn't stop. Jasper screamed and Mama jumped up, sending the box clattering to the floor. An explosion shook the house, and a strong, bitter smell floated in through a broken window.

Tsao Po-Po slid from the rocker, still holding Jasper to her chest, and scuttled under the table, grabbing Elsa on the way. Elsa buried her face into her amah's shoulder, then peeked out and saw Mama's legs standing stiff beside the table.

Tsao Po-Po reached out and touched Mama's ankle, whispering, "*Lai, lai,* come, come." Elsa was shocked to see her dignified mother crawl under the table with them as if she was playing a game. But her face shone pale in the shadow, and she didn't smile.

Elsa remembered the head on the stake and asked, "Are we going to be killed?"

At first, Mama didn't answer, and Elsa thought she hadn't heard. But finally, Mama said, "Ask God to protect us."

Elsa huddled back against her amah and whispered, "Now I lay me down to sleep, I pray the Lord my soul to keep—" She stopped, her throat tight, unwilling to finish. *If I should die before I wake . . .*

Her prayer was interrupted by shouting and scuffling at the front door. She heard Huang's familiar voice, and watched as Mama crawled out from under the table and let him in.

"Soldiers march to the city!" he whispered hoarsely, gasping for breath. "Many, many."

Mama asked in Chinese, "Is it the Red Army?"

"Reds or Nationals, all the same," Huang said. "All make bad trouble. Smash, steal, kill, or worse. Danger, danger. You must hide."

Mama said, "When Pastor Meier returns—"

"No, no, no." Huang's voice grew louder. "You cannot wait for Mai Mushih. Go now."

"But where?"

He looked down. "People here are afraid to hide you. Foreigners are bad luck."

Elsa had wondered why the faithful Mandarin teacher had stopped coming for her parents' language lessons. And lately, at Sunday services, instead of the usual full benches and loud singing, only Tsao Po-Po and a few other people sat huddled together. Papa's messages had been short, and there'd been a lot of praying and crying. Now she knew why.

Tsao Po-Po, still under the table and holding Jasper, looked out and spoke softly. "Maybe flee to the mountains. There is a pagoda—"

Mama looked horrified. "We can't go into a heathen temple!"

Huang shrugged. "Maybe it is the safest place. No idols now. Nobody goes there. People say it is haunted. But Mai Mushih does not believe in ghosts."

Before Mama could answer, the shooting started again. Tsao Po-Po pushed Jasper close to Elsa and scrambled out from beneath the table. She and Mama rushed around, packing food and clothing into baskets, rolling bamboo mats into tight cylinders and tying them. Huang began collecting the baskets as Ho Fen filled a clay pot with charcoal and wrapped it with oilcloth. Elsa stayed under the table and held Jasper, watching and wondering what was waiting outside.

A monstrous explosion blasted the air, and the wooden floor shuddered. She suddenly remembered her doll, let go of Jasper, and darted toward the stairs.

Mama swung around like a flash, catching her arm. "Where are you going?"

"I have to save Glory!" cried Elsa.

"Stay right here," Mama said firmly. "There's no time for toys." She rolled up a length of mosquito netting and pushed it into a basket already stuffed with extra clothes.

Tsao Po-Po quickly tied the last bundles together, slung them over her shoulder, and whispered hoarsely, "We go now." She whisked off the tablecloth, folded it into a sling, and tucked Jasper into it. She then lashed it onto Huang's back and grabbed Elsa's hand.

Elsa jerked loose. "No! We have to wait for Papa!"

Just then, they heard scratching at the front door. Er-dze, the house-boy, yelled from outside, "Soldiers at the north end of the city!"

Mama opened the door. "Go find Mai Mushih," she told him.

Er-dze's eyes were wide, rings of white showing around the edges. He gulped, then turned and ran off into the dark.

Tsao Po-Po cried, *"Kuai, kuai."* She arranged the cloth bundles dangling from around her neck, grabbed Elsa's hand again—this time extra tightly—and pulled her toward the back door. Huang pushed past them, a large filled basket on each arm and Jasper bobbing on his back.

Looking around, Elsa saw her mother snatch up an armload of packages and Ho Fen gather up the rest. She wondered how far it would be. And could they get there before the soldiers caught them?

Only a sliver of moon peeked through troubled clouds. Elsa clung to her amah's hand, stumbling along in the half-darkness; first through a bamboo grove, the stalks rustling in protest, then across open rice fields in mud up to her ankles.

Finally, Tsao Po-Po helped her step up to a dirt path twisting away from the city. People rushed past in both directions, their straw sandals slapping. With baskets and cloth bundles lashed to their backs, they frantically pushed handcarts loaded with bedding and kitchenware, dragging along a pig or two, dangling chickens on carrying poles. Some of the Chinese spit at Elsa; others hissed, *"Yang kweidze." Foreign devils.*

Elsa shuddered, feeling the bitterness behind the words. She'd heard people called that before, but no one had ever said it to her face. She loved the Chinese people! Why did they suddenly hate her so much?

From behind, she could hear screams of *"Sha! Sha!" Kill! Kill!* along with the gunfire, and wished she could cover her ears. They passed little stone huts with boarded-up windows. Behind one such hut, a man hurriedly dug a hole, and Elsa saw him drop in a small sack. *It must hold his most precious treasures,* she thought, and she wondered what would happen to all the nice things in the mission house.

Not long ago, Papa had taken her for a ride on his bicycle, and they'd stopped by a street vendor with a tray of ornaments. The man had held out a pair of pale green bracelets with carved dragons curling around the outsides. "Jade," he'd said proudly. "Very good luck. Dragon is royalty."

He'd slid the bracelets onto Elsa's thin arm, and they felt smooth and cool.

Papa had haggled on the price, and to her delight, he'd bought them. But then he'd said they were for Mama's birthday. "She deserves something nice. Life is hard for her."

Elsa had taken the bracelets off slowly, biting back tears, not wanting him to see her disappointment. Mama had other pretty things; how could her life be hard?

Papa must have seen her sadness, because he'd said gently, "They're too big for you now, Dumpling. I'm sure someday when you're grown, she will pass them on to you."

Now Elsa wondered if she'd ever see those bracelets again.

They reached the South Han River, where a flight of wooden steps led up to a planked footbridge on stilts, without a railing, high above the water. Huang had already started across, Jasper clinging to his back like a hump. From the top of the stairs, Elsa watched the boards sag in rhythm to his steps.

She squirmed, pulling loose from her amah. It was getting dark, and what if the soldiers were on the other side?

Tsao Po-Po hissed, "You want the river dragon to swallow you? Come. Don't waste time. Hold onto my *pow-dze,* and follow my feet." Elsa swallowed hard, grabbed the back edge of her amah's tunic, and pattered across after her.

After they had scurried down the steps at the end, a fresh burst of gunfire tore through the air, louder this time. Elsa looked back and could barely make out her mother's form slowly inching across the swaying bridge. She wanted to call out, to tell her to hurry, but Tsao Po-Po grabbed her hand again and led her up a winding road through the rain forest. Ferns and bushes whipped and scratched her arms. She tripped over a root, but her amah's grip kept her from falling. Her legs hurt, her side ached, and she was so tired.

They reached the top of a hill. All was quiet again, except for the swish of leaves and a stealthy crunch of pebbles under their feet.

Another explosion thundered across the valley, echoing against the mountain, followed by a violent storm of gunfire. Looking down, Elsa saw columns of smoke far below. Dots of light, hundreds of them, bobbed around crazily like stars playing leapfrog.

Shouts rang out, and anguished screams ended suddenly. Outlined in flashes of lights, tiny figures that looked like toys crouched, leaped, and fell to the ground.

Tsao Po-Po's hand tightened, and Elsa stumbled on. Drops of water pecked at her head, and soon a heavy rain swallowed them up. She couldn't see Huang and Jasper ahead and wondered if they were all lost in the mountains. Were Mama and the cook still behind them?

Oh, Papa, where are you? Dear Jesus, please keep him safe. And help us all!

Chapter 3

ELSA WOKE TO THE TWITTERING of birds. Rubbing her cramped legs, she opened her eyes and pushed aside the mosquito netting. Through the dimness of early morning, she saw a round room with high slits for windows and stone steps that led to the higher levels. Reaching out, she felt Jasper sleeping nearby, curled into a ball, clutching his teddy bear.

The smell of a charcoal fire drifted through the room, and slowly what seemed a bad dream trickled into Elsa's memory. Shooting, screams, and all those soldiers, tiny in the distance, staggering and falling. The long frantic scramble up the mountain. Papa—

She sat up suddenly, clapping her hand over her mouth to stifle the cry. In the pale light of dawn, she saw her father lying on the floor, snoring softly, wrapped like a mummy in a light blanket, with just a few red curls sticking out. At his feet slept Er-dze. How had he ever found Papa? Her sore legs forgotten, Elsa's joy bubbled over.

Mama sat on a mat nearby, leaning against the curved wooden wall. She didn't look dignified now. Her clothes were muddy and rumpled, her hair loose, her feet scratched and swollen. Tsao Po-Po squatted next to her, rubbing something smelly onto Mama's feet. Then she slid them into a pair of straw sandals.

Elsa wondered where the beautiful embroidered shoes were, but she knew it was better not to ask. Instead, she whispered, "Where did Er-dze find Papa?"

"He was hiding in a cave with the mountain people," said Mama.

Papa woke then and smiled, his green eyes calm and comforting. He rubbed his grizzled chin.

Elsa went to him and hugged him, laughing with joy, and he squeezed her. Now that he was here, she thought, everything would be all right. Not smiling, Mama watched, twisting her hair up into a neat bun.

Tsao Po-Po brought steaming bowls of *juht*, and Papa gave thanks, praying for God's continued protection. Elsa smacked her lips over the rice gruel, but Papa seemed to inhale his food and held out his bowl for more. He said he hadn't eaten for two days.

After breakfast, Papa sent Ho Fen and the houseboy back to their families. He and Huang went up the pagoda's winding stone steps, and Elsa listened to their footsteps circling overhead, then tapping up another set of stairs to a third floor. When they came down, Elsa heard Papa whisper to Mama, "Smoke in the sky."

Mama mouthed, "Shungtau?"

He nodded.

Elsa's throat felt tight. Had the soldiers burned down the city? What about the mission? Her room, her bed, her beautiful doll? She went to the stairs, crept up a few steps, and peeked over the landing.

All she saw was a bare room that was smaller than the downstairs, very dusty and smelling faintly of incense. Just as on the first floor, high, narrow open slits ran around the circular wall. There was a door, and Elsa remembered seeing pictures of pagodas with balconies all around tucked under their curved roofs.

She stole up the next set of stairs; the top floor was also empty and even tinier.

Standing on tiptoes, she could barely reach the window slits. She saw mountain peaks, trees, and the rain forest below. Beautiful red azaleas bloomed among tall ferns as if they didn't know the world was fighting.

Which direction would Shungtau be? Elsa followed the slits around the room until she saw the smoke. Big, horrible black columns billowing up into the sky, so awful she could almost feel the heat.

It was true! Would they have to hide up here for the rest of their lives? She sat down on the dusty floor, dropped her head to her knees, and burst into ragged sobs.

After a long time, Papa came up and found her. He said she

shouldn't worry; maybe that was only a brush fire along the river. Unconvinced, her stomach aching, she followed him downstairs and lay down on a mat beside her amah, resting her head on the woman's lap.

Tsao Po-Po stroked Elsa's hair and asked, "You like to hear a story?"

Her amah knew wonderful, deliciously spooky stories about people who turned into stone, and animals that hid in mountain caves or flew up beyond the clouds. Elsa wiggled into a more comfortable position and said, "Not too scary this time."

Jasper came and squatted on the other side of Tsao Po-Po. The amah glanced at Mama, across the room writing in her journal, and whispered, "There once lived a snow-white jade dragon in a rock cave near the Celestial River. Nearby lived a beautiful golden phoenix."

"What's a phoenix?" asked Elsa.

"A magical bird with long, beautiful feathers. The jade dragon and the phoenix met at a fairy island, where they saw a shining pebble. 'Let us carve it into a pearl,' said the jade dragon."

Elsa was transported out of the old temple. Gone were the explosions and gunshots, the escape up the mountain, the fire at Shungtau. She was the phoenix, gathering dewdrops to mold the pebble into a dazzling pearl that magically transformed the world into a flowering garden.

Tsao Po-Po whispered, "The Queen Mother of heaven became jealous. She waited until the jade dragon and the golden phoenix were asleep, and she stole the pearl—"

Elsa's spirit searched the Celestial River for the pearl until suddenly she saw a bright light—

Mama's voice broke harshly into the story. "Tsao, I've told you many times. Stop filling the children's minds with superstition."

Elsa gasped. Mama always spoiled everything. "But I have to know—did the phoenix find the pearl?"

Her amah looked down and didn't answer. She reached behind her head, pulled a hairpin from the black knot of hair and began picking her teeth with it.

The hairpins were Tsao Po-Po's prized possessions. She'd shown them many times to Elsa—long, sharp silver picks with tiny heads shaped like lions and gargoyles, useful for protection and many other purposes.

Elsa, still the golden phoenix, stared angrily at the ceiling. She would just have to make up her own ending. Her amah turned into a kind empress, and with the jade dragon, they searched through mountain passes and rivers until they found the beautiful pearl high in a tree. The rest of the day they celebrated in a magnificent palace while she wore the pearl on a golden chain.

THE NEXT MORNING, Elsa and Jasper made the upstairs their playroom. Elsa looked out the window slits and saw only small wisps of smoke in the distance. Papa must have been right; maybe their home was safe.

Mama made one rule about the upstairs. "Don't open the balcony door."

The more Elsa thought about that, the more it tempted her. On their fourth day in hiding, it was very hot. While Mama sat reading, Tsao Po-Po knitted, and Papa was outside with Huang. Elsa took Jasper upstairs to play.

It was even stuffier up there. Elsa eyed the door. Nobody would know if she opened it just a crack. The fresh air would feel so good.

She ran her hand over the splintered wood and fingered the latch.

Jasper grabbed her arm. "Mama said no!"

"Sh-h-h." Elsa tugged at the door, and with a tiny squeak it opened.

A breeze cooled her face. Birds sang in the trees, and she smelled ferns, wet earth, and the spicy fragrance of jasmine. Far away, where the smoke had been, white clouds drifted in a clear blue sky. She started to step out on the balcony when a hand gripped her arm. *Evil spirits!*

Slowly, fearfully, Elsa turned, only to see Mama's face red with fury. She felt three sharp slaps on her bottom.

"Why won't you obey?" Mama closed the door and latched it firmly. "Go downstairs and sit facing the wall."

Dejected, Elsa sat cross-legged, listening to the clicking of Tsao

Po-Po's needles and the pages rustling in Mama's book. How could Mama be so mean? Why was it wrong to peek outside? Why couldn't Tsao Po-Po finish her story? And why hadn't Mama allowed her to bring Glory along—Jasper had his teddy bear! It just wasn't fair.

Jasper got by with everything. He only got love pats. If she were pretty and had golden curls instead of a straggly red braid, maybe Mama would love her as much as Jasper.

If Papa had been here, she wouldn't have been spanked. Papa was always cheerful, always kind to her. When he had time, he played games with her. And she loved the rides he gave her on his bicycle.

Elsa stared at the crumbling wall of the pagoda and thought again of the bracelets. Mama would never give them to her!

What if the Red soldiers had gotten into the mission and stolen them? Then Mama wouldn't get them, either. Elsa didn't know if she'd be sorry or glad.

Behind her, she heard Tsao Po-Po chanting a finger play to Jasper, "Raining in the sunshine, the dog paws up the ground. Dug up here, dug up there, dug up all around."

Jasper giggled, and Elsa was jealous, knowing her amah was gently poking him in ticklish spots.

When Papa came back, he had good news: the battle in Shungtau was over. The bad news was that the Communists now ruled the city. Elsa didn't know what a Communist was, but she knew it wasn't good.

"What will we do?" asked Mama, motioning for Elsa to get up and go to her amah.

"They've signed an agreement for our safe passage."

"But will they honor it?"

"I hope so, Rachel. We must trust in the Lord."

Mama and Tsao Po-Po quickly gathered up the bundles, and they all hurried down the mountain. Elsa's heart sang, *We're going home, going home.*

But Papa's eyes looked worried.

Chapter 4

AT THE MISSION, ELSA WAS SHOCKED to see the compound walls torn down in places, the windows of the house smashed, and Papa's beloved bicycle missing. Their books were scattered, their bedding and clothes in dirty heaps, but Elsa found Glory safe and sound in a dark corner of her closet.

When she came back into the parlor, she saw Papa uncovering a secret hole he'd made in the wall. He removed a small bundle and unwrapped it carefully. The jade bracelets were safe!

Papa slid them onto Mama's wrist and kissed her. "An early birthday present," he said. "I don't want to risk having them stolen."

Mama stepped back and frowned. "Philip! They're much too extravagant."

Papa smiled and winked at her. "Pretty things for a pretty lady."

Elsa reached up and ran a finger over the smooth jade on her mother's arm. If Mama didn't want them, she would gladly have them. "I helped pick them out," she said. But Papa and Mama were still looking at each other and didn't seem to hear.

All that summer, soldiers marched through the streets, and only a few Chinese Christians came to the chapel services. In August, two officials came to the mission and pasted a large paper notice on the front door. Elsa heard them shout about military occupation, evacuation, and three days to prepare. Mama and Tsao Po-Po packed up everything, wrapping the bracelets in tissue paper and pushing them deep into a box of quilts. Papa sold his desk, the dining table, and all the beds.

Elsa looked around at the empty house. "Where are we going this time?"

She was surprised to see Mama smile. "To America, where there's no war."

All the way to America? "But we'll be back soon, won't we?"

Papa pulled Elsa close, biting his lips. "Not until it's safe, Dumpling. And that could be a long, long time." His voice trembled, and Elsa knew he must feel as sad as she did. They said tearful farewells to Ho Fen, Er-dze, and Huang, and the few Chinese Christians who dared sneak past the Red soldiers. Elsa went to her beloved chestnut tree and sobbed into its rough bark. The leaves fluttered in the breeze, seeming to whisper, "Good-bye, Eternal Virtue."

UNDER THE CURVED, BAMBOO-MATTED roof of a houseboat, Elsa sat with her family and Tsao Po-Po, watching the coolies lean their shoulders against the long, sturdy bamboo poles they'd planted into the river bottom. Two men in front and one on each side of the boat pushed, chanting over and over: "O-yo-yo." They grunted and strained, their bronze faces streaming with sweat, and the boat moved slowly into the current. Once out into the wide, smooth, brown sheet of water, they relaxed and used the poles to steer.

Elsa's whole world had disappeared and left her heart in pieces. Under the boat's nailed floorboards, crates and barrels held everything her family still owned.

Her mind numb, she watched dully as the burned and crumbling buildings of Shungtau slid out of sight. Fields of spinach and bok choy glided by, and in the shallow ditches bordering them, an occasional water buffalo lay soaking, with only its nose poking out of the murky water. At the river's edge, pink lotus blossoms floated peacefully on their green pads.

Elsa was sure that no country could be as wonderful as China. Would America have such beautiful flowers? Would there be trees to climb? Would Mama teach school there? Would the American children be friendly?

But as long as her amah went along, it might not be too bad. She seemed more like a foreigner than a Shungtau woman, since she didn't have tiny bound feet. Papa said that was because she came from the hills, from the Hakka tribe, who didn't need to truss their little girls' feet into tortured stumps in order for them to be beautiful for their future husbands.

Elsa's legs grew restless, and she wished there was room to run. She jumped up and began pulling Jasper's hands back and forth, chanting an old Chinese nursery rhyme: "We push, we pull, to saw the wood, we pull, we push, to make a fine house."

Then Mama scolded her for making the boat rock, and Jasper tugged loose. He asked, "Are we almost there?"

Papa rumpled Jasper's hair. "No, it'll take two days. Then we'll go on a long train ride to Tientsin, and after that get on a steamship to America."

Now the river grew narrower, flowing faster around big jagged rocks. The coolies pushed their poles against the largest ones, winding a zigzag course between boulders, bouncing over rapids, turning sharply to meet more violent torrents. Foaming waves splashed over the sides, soaking the polers' trousers and flooding the deck.

Jasper screamed, and Mama held him tightly, her face pale. Elsa held her breath, sure they'd all be thrown into the angry water. Then Tsao Po-Po pulled her best hairpin out of her knot and threw it into the river. Elsa watched the glint of sun against the silver as it whirled and disappeared underwater. Astonished, she frowned at her amah.

Tsao Po-Po's lips were drawn over her teeth. She glanced at Mama, then murmured, "We must appease the *feng-shui.*"

Across from her, Papa stared straight ahead, his lips moving silently, and Elsa knew he was praying for safety.

Suddenly, the boat pitched and headed straight toward a huge jagged rock. Elsa screamed, expecting an awful crash, but at the last moment the polers steered the boat aside, and shuddering, it scraped past.

Papa murmured, "Praise the Lord!"

Looking back, Elsa saw chunks of wood littered along the edges of the rock and wondered how many other boats had been shattered there. And whether the *feng-shui* hadn't been appeased for them because Papa hadn't been there to pray.

A few more bouncing rapids brought the boat into calmer water. Papa smiled, Mama collapsed against his shoulder, and Tsao Po-Po took Jasper onto her lap. She drew Elsa close, took several long breaths, and started a story about four dragons that had created rain from the Eastern Sea to save the people's crops, rain that became the four great rivers of China.

Mama glanced over several times and sighed, but didn't stop her.

After a while, when the sun was still high, the men poled the boat to a grove of trees on the shore. One of them jumped out and waded to the bank.

Papa shouted, "What are you doing?"

"We stop for the night," said the head boatman. He tossed a rope to the man on shore, who tied it to a tree.

Papa scolded the men and tried to argue with them, but it was no use. They jumped ashore, ran up the riverbank and disappeared beyond the trees.

"What shall we do now?" Mama asked, her voice weak.

Papa's shoulders slumped. "There's nothing we can do. Except wait. And pray." He sat down at the bow, knees pulled up, his head resting on his crossed arms.

"Death-deserving creatures," muttered Tsao Po-Po. She dipped up buckets of river water, started rice cooking over the clay pot of coals, and helped Elsa and Jasper wash their hands. When the rice was done, Papa asked the blessing and prayed for protection, and they ate in silence.

Later, after the rosy glow of sunset faded, Mama and Tsao Po-Po strung up a quilt at the end of the bamboo roof, making a tiny room. They spread mats on the floor and threw light blankets over them for beds.

Elsa wondered how she'd be able to sleep. She dearly missed her cool, whitewashed bedroom in Shungtau, the shelves full of books, blocks, and spool people.

Jasper's bedspread had a big picture of a boat. One of their favorite games had been to sit on his bed, pile the spools on the boat, and pretend they were all sailing far away to mysterious lands. They'd trot the spools through marketplaces, parks, and zoos, and zoom them up on imaginary flying carpets.

But this trip wasn't fun at all. Papa soberly scanned the mountains along the shore, Mama's face looked pinched, and even Tsao Po-Po seemed anxious. Elsa wondered why—they'd passed the rapids, and Shungtau with its Red soldiers was far away. What was still ahead? She was afraid to ask.

Jasper grabbed his teddy bear and began rubbing his ears with his other hand. Tsao Po-Po took him in her arms, crooning a Chinese lullaby. *"Hualala, baby, don't you cry . . ."*

After Tsao Po-Po settled Jasper on a mat, Elsa lay down beside him, listening to the quiet gurgling and sloshing of the river against the boat until the gentle motion sent her to sleep.

IN THE BLACK OF NIGHT, the houseboat rocked. Elsa woke, lifted the edge of the quilt curtain, and saw a sampan nearby. In it were several men with red scarves over their faces. Long knives and bayonets glittered in torchlight. She watched, horrified, as they tied their boat to the houseboat and jumped aboard.

Quickly, she dropped the quilt, but one of the men leaped to rip it away. She tried to call Papa but couldn't make a sound. Her heart thumping, she hid her face in her hands.

Then she heard Mama gasp. Papa called for the boatmen, but there was no answer.

Elsa peeked out and saw the bandits point guns at her parents, telling them to be quiet. They jabbed and poked at them, looking in their pockets and sleeves, even under Mama's dress. They shouted when they found money in Papa's pockets and Mama's handbag, grabbed Papa's pocket watch and pulled off Mama's wedding ring.

The bandits cursed and grumbled. "There must be more. Rich foreigners have much money and treasures." While one man held a bayonet on Papa, the others took huge hooks, ripped up the floor boards and wrenched open the boxes Mama had packed so neatly. As they lugged out the heaviest one, Elsa heard them say the word *gold.* When they pulled out only books and a box of empty spools, they cursed, threw most of the books into the river, and turned to the other crates.

Carelessly, they tossed the clothes and bedding onto the floor until they came to Elsa's doll. The leader grabbed it and dangled it by the feet.

Glory cried, "Ma-ma!" and the men hooted with high, mocking laughter. One man poked his fingers into the doll's eyes, forcing them open and shut; another drew his knife and chopped off Glory's beautiful golden curls.

Elsa burst into tears. How could anyone be that cruel? She couldn't watch, but couldn't turn away.

Finally tossing the doll aside, the men dug deeper. Tearing pictures from their frames, they poked in the grooves with their knives. Pans clattered to the floor, and Mama's good dishes fell and broke.

One man noticed Jasper holding his teddy bear. The man snatched it out of Jasper's arms, tugged at its little arms, and shook it, holding it up to his ear. Then the men took turns stabbing it with their knives. They didn't stop until all the stuffing had spilled out and the poor creature hung limp, a fuzzy brown rag.

Jasper made an awful face, and then vomited. Tsao Po-Po held his head over the water pail until his shuddering heaves were over; after that, Mama kept him on her own lap.

Suddenly, one of the bandits shouted, *"Ai-yah!"* and held up a jade bracelet.

"No!" screamed Elsa, but Tsao Po-Po's hand clapped against her mouth.

"Sh-h-h," said Papa. "They're only things. We must let the men take what they want." The bandits dug frantically in every box, slinging out the contents. As they pawed through rumpled piles, Elsa held her breath, waiting for them to find the other bracelet.

When the darkness began to fade and the sky brightened over the mountains, other houseboats drifted toward them. The bandits stuffed bedspreads, wall hangings, Mama's stationery box, and pots and pans into gunnysacks and slung them down into their sampan. Grumbling, shouting threats, and waving their knives and guns, they swarmed back into their boat, the leader with Mama's best stockings draped around his neck.

Elsa grabbed her doll and smoothed its ragged hair. One eye was shut, and the other stared sadly at her. "I'm sorry, Glory," she whispered.

Jasper sobbed against Mama's shoulder, and Papa smoothed his hair. "Hush, Little Tiger," said Papa. "The bandits are gone. It's going to be all right."

Elsa picked up the ragged Teddy bear and Jasper grabbed it. "Maybe I can fix it for you," she told him. But the cloth was so full of holes that she knew it was hopeless.

Mama started crying, and Papa hugged her. "Take heart. It could have been worse."

Elsa stared at him. The bandits had all their money, Papa's watch, Mama's ring, and one bracelet. Bedding, wall hangings, and cooking pans were gone. The books were at the bottom of the river. All the rest of their things were broken or scattered around the boat, and Glory and Teddy were ruined. What could be worse?

Then she remembered the pictures in Papa's book about the Boxer Rebellion and understood. She and her family were still alive.

Mama and Papa repacked what was left, and Tsao Po-Po rocked Jasper back into a restless sleep while he still hugged the limp fur of his teddy bear.

When the sun finally peeked over the mountaintops, the boatmen sauntered back from the grove of trees along the riverbank. Papa told them about the raid, and the head boatman said, "Very bad. You must go quickly to the nearest village and tell the authorities."

The other men nodded, murmuring polite concern.

"Do not go," Tsao Po-Po whispered to Papa. "It may be a plot to kidnap you."

Elsa stared at her in horror. Kidnap? What would she do without her papa? Her amah took care of her, but Papa was the strong one, who always knew what God wanted them to do.

Papa turned to Mama. "She could be right. They might think we can bring them more money through ransom." He stroked his cane and looked into the distance. "That's probably what saved us." In

Chinese, he told the head boatman, "We'll wait and report it in the city."

"No, no," said the boatman. "Too late, too late."

"Too late for what?" asked Papa.

The man looked at his crew and shrugged. "Too late . . . uh . . . to find bandits."

"They wouldn't catch them anyway," said Papa sternly. "Nail down those floorboards and then start the boat. It's getting hot, and we still have a long way to go."

The men argued, but Papa said, "You won't be paid until we reach our destination." They started working, whispering, and looking sideways at each other.

Papa nudged Mama and whispered, "I'm sure they were in on the raid."

Finally, the men dug their long poles into the muddy riverbed and began their usual mournful chant. The boat dipped, and a coin slid across the deck. A boatman quietly moved his foot to cover it, and Papa glanced at Mama and nodded.

Tsao Po-Po folded up the bedding and prepared their breakfast *juht* and bits of dried fish over the little clay stove.

Papa watched each sampan that passed. Cuddled against him, Elsa looked too. But they didn't see the bandits again. Relieved, she wondered why the men hadn't found the other bracelet. And without money, how would Papa pay the boatmen? How would they buy food and blankets in America?

Chapter 5

ELSA STARED THROUGH THE TRAIN window, watching green country-side fade into bare yellow plains and rocky hills. It was the middle of August; they weren't going to America after all, and she was glad. At the port of Tientsin, Papa had asked for a visa, but the officials had told him no foreigners could get passage on the ships.

Mama had begged him to send a telegram to the mission board. The board had replied: "Shiao Yangshan, Inner Mongolia, desperately needs help. Stay till way opens." Papa had asked people in the embassy about Shiao Yangshan—Little Goat Mountain—and they'd told him it was a village behind the Great Wall, a mission where the old pastor had become very sick; he and his wife had returned to America for medical help.

Mama had cried all day, but Papa had said God must have planned it this way. "Don't you see, Rachel? It's a double answer to prayer: a safe place for us to stay until travel restrictions are lifted, and an opportunity to shepherd this needy flock."

Elsa thought that was wonderful, but Mama's lips had twitched. Elsa could tell she didn't agree.

The city of Tientsin was huge and bustling, with tree-lined side-walks, and rickshaws pulled by coolies trotting along the wide, clean streets. They'd stayed in a special house for missionaries, and she and Jasper had loved playing with Swedish and American children. In a big store, Papa bought bedding and winter clothes along with a *peshong,* a small lacquered trunk in which to pack them. Elsa asked where he'd found more money after the robbery, but he said the Lord had protected his secret fund and she wasn't to worry.

She looked at him now in the train seat just ahead, leaning back with eyes shut and arms crossed, his mouth slightly open. He wore a new cap, a Russian one, fat and furry with earflaps, and it made a nice pillow. He'd bought one for Mama, too, but she'd told him it made her look ridiculous, and she wouldn't put it on.

The whole car was filled with people in gray padded clothes, shouting and jabbering, their voices drowned out every few minutes by sudden hoarse shrieks from the train whistle. The luggage racks spilled over with packages, poles, and bedrolls. Trapped in gunnysacks in the aisles, live chickens flopped and squawked, their feathers working through the tiny holes and fluttering up in the air.

The wooden car creaked and swayed in rhythm, its wheels clacking, "It won't be long, it won't be long." Squirming on the hard wooden seat, Elsa hoped that was true. It had been hours, and her stomach was growling. Beside her, Mama leaned back against a wadded shawl, staring ahead, one hand rubbing her forehead. Elsa's feet were numb, but she was afraid to move them because she might bump Mama. She looked across the aisle and envied Jasper, sprawled across Tsao Po-Po's lap, both of them sound asleep.

Turning back to the window, she saw tiny mud shacks dotting the sandy fields in no particular order, as if a giant hand had flung them out like Huang's dice. Chickens ran in and out the open doorways, and pigs rooted through piles of melon rinds. Women stood with mouths open, shading their eyes and staring at the train. They wore bulky gray tunics with padded trousers bound at the ankles.

The train rocked more slowly. All the people stood and pushed out into the aisle, dragging their baggage, the chickens flopping wildly and squawking even louder.

Papa got up and nudged a place for himself among the boxes, sacks, and bodies. Swaying with the motion, he pulled down their belongings from the shelf above.

The train jerked to a stop, and everyone staggered against one another, grabbing at whatever was handy to keep their balance. Elsa wiggled into a small space and stamped her feet to get rid of the prickles. She looked out the window to see a sandy yard swarming with life—beggars and vendors shoving, yelling, and shaking their fists; goats bleating and pigs squealing.

Papa motioned beyond the crowd. "Here we are. See the wall with a tower? That must be the mission. Just a short walk from here. And there's Little Goat Mountain behind it."

Elsa looked where he pointed, her heart pounding in excitement. Mama, her face puckered, slowly gathered up their bundles and bags, nudged Elsa into the aisle, and motioned for Tsao Po-Po to bring Jasper.

Before they reached the door, oncoming passengers started shoving their way into the train. The crowd squeezed around Elsa so tightly that she could hardly breathe. She imagined herself as a piece in a moving jigsaw puzzle, shifting inch by inch, forward a little, sideways, back a step, forward again.

A last shove brought her to the open door, and Papa's hand reached out to help her jump down the steps. An icy wind slapped her face, and blowing sand bit her cheeks. Tsao Po-Po buttoned Jasper's wool jacket and wound a long scarf around Elsa's neck and over her head.

Mama told Elsa, "Stay close." Scowling, she reached into a bag, brought out the Russian cap, and jammed it on her head. "If it's this cold in August, what will it be like in winter?" she muttered.

Jasper clutched Tsao Po-Po's hand and stared around groggily, but the fresh air gave Elsa new energy. She charged ahead, pushing through the crowd. She heard her mother's voice but didn't listen to the words.

The people of the village swirled around her, jabbering, poking, and gesturing. Elsa tried to understand what they said, glad for the bits of Mandarin she'd picked up from her parents' lessons. Vendors hawked pet crickets in tiny sandalwood cages, and box lunches that smelled so good they made her even hungrier. Beggars whined, stretching out their crippled and sore-covered hands, and she wished she had coppers to give them.

A loud, metallic *ding-ding-ding* split through the clamor, and she looked up to see a huge brass gong on the station platform. A man struck the rim with a slender rod, his wrist flicking back and forth.

The ground shook, the train snorted and gruffed away, and Elsa looked toward the mud-brick wall with its tower, eager to see what the mission looked like. She took deep breaths of the cold air, glad to be safely away from the Red soldiers and the war.

Papa caught up with her, and a man in a long black gown and skullcap came toward them, bowing. He introduced himself as Deacon Wu Shong, and with him was the gateman, Fung Choi, wearing padded trousers and a tunic.

A crowd streamed from the mission gate, surrounding them, waving banners and flags, singing a hymn, and shooting off firecrackers. In the tower beyond, a bell clanged joyfully.

"Welcome, honorable Mushih," said Wu Shong in Mandarin. He flung his arm toward the wall and its large wooden gate. "We are very happy God brought you here." His speech went on and on until finally he announced: "I will now take you to your home. After that, our humble congregation wishes to invite you to a feast."

Papa bowed several times, saying words of appreciation, and Mama nodded politely, murmuring her thanks. But her face was pale and her lips tight as she followed Papa and the deacon through the large, unpainted wooden gate into the walled compound and up the gravel path. Elsa forced herself to walk slowly behind them with Tsao Po-Po and Jasper, anxious to see the big house that would be their home.

They passed rows of connected gray brick rooms along both sides of the walls, and Wu Shong explained they were workers' apartments. Through a side gate, Elsa could see in a separate compound the square church of the same gray brick, its double wooden doors decorated with peeling orange paint.

Ahead, a lower wall made of open-scrolled brickwork blocked their way. Wu Shong held open its little gate and led them into a small inner courtyard.

"Here is your home," he said.

Elsa blinked her eyes. It was so different from Shungtau's airy, white two-story house with its veranda and arches and red-tiled roof. This one looked just like the workers' apartments—flat, gray brick rooms, each with its own window, stretching all the way across the compound. The only difference was the single door in the center.

Papa pulled off his fur cap, took Mama's arm, smiled at everyone, and marched inside. The people stood back, clapping their hands and saying, *"Hao, hao!* Good, good."

Tsao Po-Po carried Jasper in, his eyes huge and his fingers gripping her shoulder. But Elsa darted in past everyone and ran through the main room to a long, back hallway with doors that opened into one room after another. She counted nine in all and wondered what would go into them and which would be hers.

In the center of the hall, a small, high window gave very little light. A few steps away was a back door. Elsa opened it and looked out into an enormous sandy yard bordered with a high mud wall. Near the house on the right side she saw a well, its bucket swaying in the wind, a clothesline, and behind that, a large shed. On the left side was an outhouse. There were no trees, and Elsa felt a stab of longing for her chestnut perch. But those sandy paths beckoned her—they seemed to stretch for a mile—and she ran all the way to the far wall to look up and beyond at the long, sculptured mountain that Papa had said gave the village its name.

Little Goat Mountain. Hardly noticing the cold sand swirling around her, Elsa tried to make out the outline of a kneeling goat. Then the door opened, and she heard Mama scream, "Elsa's run off again!"

Tsao Po-Po called "Hoo, hoo!" and waved for her to come; she dashed back, panting with excitement, her cheeks tingling deliciously, her legs aching for more exercise.

"It's wonderful," she shouted. "The biggest yard I've ever seen!"

Papa pulled Elsa into a hug. "There'll be plenty of time to play tomorrow. Now we need you to help plan the rooms."

But she didn't get to do much planning. The kitchen had a big iron stove and cupboards. Of course the dining room had to be next to it, and the parlor after that, because it had the front door. Papa claimed the next small room for his office, and Mama said the one after that would be their bedroom, with Jasper's and then Elsa's on the east side.

The only pieces of furniture were a single iron bed frame without springs and a few broken bamboo chairs. Mama said that when their boxes came from the train station she would have Tsao Po-Po spread out comforters and sheets so they could sleep on the floor. Papa said not to worry; it wouldn't take long to build whatever furniture they needed.

Two small rooms were still left, and Elsa peeked into the one next to her own. "Will this be Tsao Po-Po's?"

Mama shook her head. "That's our classroom."

Elsa pointed to the last room. "Then I guess that one."

Mama glanced at Papa and said, "No, that will be a workroom. I'm ordering a sewing machine." Papa looked surprised, but Mama added, "As cold as it is, we'll need more winter clothes. Tsao can stay in the workers' quarters in the front compound. I'm sure there'll be room for her."

Elsa's happy world exploded. "But who will take care of Jasper and me?"

Papa opened his mouth, but Mama touched his arm and said, "Philip, we discussed this before." She turned to Elsa. "We'll be here only a short time. With no mission school, I can spend more time on your care and schooling. Jasper is old enough for lessons now, so he'll join us."

"But what will my amah do?" asked Elsa, blinking back tears. Would there be no more stories about dragons and pearls and golden birds?

"Oh, I'll keep her busy," said Mama. "She can wash, iron, sew— lots of other things. She can even cook until we hire someone else."

Elsa stared at her mother, anger boiling up into her sorrow. How could Mama take away the one person she loved best?

Mama added, "You're too big for an amah now. You'll see. It'll be nice to have a real schoolroom, and we'll have regular study hours."

Elsa didn't see anything nice about that. She *needed* her amah. And with all that studying, when would she have time to run in that wonderful back yard?

Just then, she heard a scratch at the door, and Wu Shong came in with a woman who was carrying a fluffy bundle. "This is my wife, Sen Ying," he said. "She brings you old *mushih's* dog. It cries, wants a friend."

From the crook of the woman's arms, a little gray fluffy dog stared at them, snuffling its pug nose and lifting one small black ear. Jasper shied away, but Elsa looked into its eyes and knew she'd found a friend. She reached out to pet it, and the dog licked her hand.

Sen Ying said, "Old *mushih* kept the dog in a box under the kitchen stove."

Mama looked horrified. "In the kitchen? That filthy Pekingese?" But when the woman leaned down, the little dog ran straight to the stove and jumped into the box, then turned around and peered at them with bright eyes. It seemed to challenge them, saying, "This is my home."

Elsa held her breath and watched her mother anxiously. Mama had never allowed pets in Shungtau, saying they were too dirty, had fleas, and made messes. Would she make this dog leave too?

Finally, Mama said, "It looks like a dirty mop. But maybe a bath will do some good." She glanced at Elsa. "And taking care of it might teach you to be responsible."

Elsa felt a bubble of relief. But looking at the dog, she had to laugh. Its long gray hair did make it look like a mop. "I'm going to call you Mopsy," she told it.

This would be a good place to live. And no matter what Mama said, she would find ways to be with her amah.

Chapter 6

THAT EVENING, SITTING NEXT TO Tsao Po-Po at a long table in the mission chapel, Elsa watched Papa expertly pop a handful of pumpkin seeds into his mouth. Just as the Chinese did, he rolled them around and spit out the shells one by one onto the floor. Next to him, Mama pried open a single seed with her thumbnails and set the hull carefully on her napkin.

There had been endless speeches and long hymns, the people singing as they pleased, some ending long after the others. Elsa became very hungry and flipped a seed at Jasper on the other side of her amah; he laughed and batted it back to her.

Mama's lips twitched. Tsao Po-Po glanced at her, spit a hull out the side of her mouth, and picked up Jasper's hand. She stroked it, whispering a Chinese patty-cake: *"Pai-pai tsoe, Cher go-go, Shao shao dee doo pee, Cher buh doe." Clap, clap, sit down; eat some fruit. The little stomach does not eat much.*

Finally, the servers came in with small plates of sliced pickled turnips and carrots. Wu Shong stood and gave a long blessing for the food, for the *mushih* and his family, for the sick old *mushih* and his wife who had to leave them, and for the whole congregation.

At last, the people urged Elsa's family to, "Eat, eat!" and put the best delicacies in their bowls. Jasper ate only a slice of melon, and Mama picked at little pieces, but Elsa watched Papa try everything—black jellied hundred-year eggs, thin strips of dried turtle, three kinds of melons, sweet and sour fish, fried cucumbers—and she copied him, teasing her appetite for the main dishes she knew were yet to come.

Next, the servers brought in huge, steaming bowls of something that looked strange but smelled wonderful. There were little dumplings swimming in broth, and dishes of hot green vegetables mixed with chunks of pork, bean sprouts, and coils of long, shiny strings that looked like endless worms, all mixed in a brown sauce. Beside that, a cold dish: pencil-thin strips of potatoes, also mixed with bean sprouts and those same slimy strings.

Papa praised the food, and Wu Shong explained that the dumplings were *jaodze,* with a spicy filling of ground mutton and pork. The strings were bean threads. It was a very special dish, he said, usually eaten only on New Year's Day. But the arrival of a new *mushih,* especially after so long a wait, was a great occasion deserving of a feast.

Elsa remembered the church feasts at Shungtau; there, the Chinese had used their chopsticks to pick up rice, carefully plucking out bits of meat or greens. But these people poured vinegar and soy sauce onto their helpings, dipped their chopsticks into little dishes of red paste, and used them to swirl it all together. They then held their bowls up to their faces and shoveled the mixture into their mouths with their chopsticks.

This seemed like a lot less work, and Elsa watched to see what Papa would do.

He glanced at Mama, and then lifted his bowl to his mouth.

Mama turned away. With her chopsticks, she twisted off corners of the dumplings and daintily nibbled at the dough. Tsao Po-Po offered a bit of meat to Jasper, but he clamped his mouth shut.

Elsa picked up a fat little *jaodze* with her chopsticks and tasted it. The flavor was strange but interesting, and she took a bigger bite. A slithery bean thread started down her throat and nearly gagged her, but she couldn't stop now. People were watching, and she needed to show she wasn't babyish like Jasper or fussy like Mama.

Tsao Po-Po poured a few drops of vinegar and soy sauce into Elsa's bowl.

Oh, yes, that was even better. Elsa dipped her chopsticks into the red sauce, and suddenly everyone around was laughing.

Fung Choi waved his hands and shook his head. "No, no, little one. That is *lahdey.* Very hot pepper sauce. Burns the mouth. Not good for little children."

Next to him sat a boy who looked about her age and had a shaved head except for a wide forelock like girls' bangs. He grinned at her.

Elsa glared back. *Little one?* She would show them. Deliberately, she mixed the blob of pepper sauce into her bowl and then lifted it to her face like the others and took a big gulp.

The fire hit her mouth like an explosion. Every nerve in her tongue became alive, and she could feel her gums tingle all over, even the spaces between her teeth. She wanted to get rid of her mouthful, but everyone was watching her. Especially the boy. If she spit it out, she would lose face.

Tears flowed from her eyes, and her nose dripped. She sniffed and wiped her eyes on her sleeve, chewing the burning mass until it finally slid down her throat.

The audience clapped their hands. Papa smiled at her, and the boy gave Elsa a thumbs-up sign. Tsao Po-Po fished out a handkerchief from inside her sleeve and handed it to Elsa. But Mama shook her head, her forehead wrinkled.

Someone whisked away Elsa's bowl and handed her a fresh serving of food. This time she dipped her chopstick into the *lahdey* very, very gently, so only a drop clung to the tip. She mixed it thoroughly, added the flavorings, and triumphantly ate the entire bowlful. From all around the room, she could hear applause and murmurs of approval.

Elsa grinned triumphantly. She had saved face and now was accepted.

After Papa gave a thank-you speech to the people, Wu Shong led Elsa's family through the side door of the church and back to the house. The sun had set, and it was even colder. Dust still blew in the wind. Elsa looked toward Little Goat Mountain and saw lights twinkling here and there up its side.

Inside the house, a fire glowed in a kerosene stove, and the parlor was warm. But Mama shivered. She pulled out more sheets and had Papa cover all the windows, giving him a thick mat for the little hall window. "We don't want anyone watching us," she said.

Elsa was used to the Chinese staring at her and wondered why Mama was worried. But before they all went to bed, Papa had them bow their heads while he thanked God for the safe journey and asked Him for protection and good health here in Shiao Yangshan.

IN THE MIDDLE OF THE NIGHT, Elsa woke with a jolt. She listened, straining to see in the dark, her heart pounding wildly. Something banged and crashed like chairs tumbling over. Was she having a nightmare? No, the dog had heard it, too—she could hear him yipping in the kitchen.

The noise stopped for a few minutes, but then it started up again, like horses galloping from one end of the house to the other.

Now she was wide awake. Had the robbers followed them here? Or the Red soldiers? Was this what Mama had been afraid of? Throwing her blanket around her, she ran into her parents' bedroom, nearly knocking over the chamber pot next to their makeshift bed.

Before she could say anything, an especially loud thud echoed above her head. Papa sat up and switched on his flashlight, and Mama gave a strangled scream, her hands over her mouth. There was a quick patter of feet, and then Jasper appeared and dove into bed with Mama.

Mama tucked Jasper closely under the covers, and Elsa pushed in after him. "What's all that noise?" she asked.

Papa flashed the light around the room and up to the ceiling. "Aha!" he said. "There's the problem."

The ceiling was covered with shiny black dots. Puzzled, Elsa stared at them, then at Papa.

"Rats," he explained. "See their eyes looking through those holes?" He got up, put on his slippers and robe, and lit the lantern. The black dots glittered against the stream of light, and then disappeared in a thundering herd. From the kitchen, Mopsy still barked hysterically.

Elsa climbed back out of the bed. "Only rats? It's not robbers?"

"Oh, they'll rob us, all right," said Papa. "What they want is our food."

Mama muttered, "As if the dirt and ugliness isn't enough, now we'll all die of the plague."

But Papa said, "Don't worry. I'll take care of them in the morning." In the dim light of the lantern, his face looked pale and ghostly.

Elsa looked up at the ceiling. Here and there, little black eyes still sparkled at her. She asked Mama, "If we catch one, could I have it for a pet?"

Mama shuddered. "Certainly not. They're filthy. They spread terrible diseases."

"But Papa could make a cage, and I'd keep it clean."

Suddenly, Jasper gagged. Mama pulled the chamber pot close and held his head over it until he got rid of what little dinner he'd eaten. Papa poured him a cup of water from a covered pitcher on the floor, then wet a washcloth and wiped his face.

Mama helped him down to her own pillow. She told Elsa, "Go back to your room now. It's still the middle of the night."

"But what if the noise comes back?" asked Elsa, looking up at the ceiling. The shiny black dots were gone now.

Papa pulled her up and gave her a piggyback ride down the hall. "I can't do anything now, Pumpkin. I'll leave the lantern on for a while; that ought to quiet them down. Try to sleep. Daylight will come before you know it."

Elsa didn't think she'd be able to sleep, and her legs jerked every time she heard a noise. When she finally drifted off, her dreams were of Red soldiers racing on horses, shouting and waving their guns at her, and when she woke up, her heart was pounding again.

That morning after breakfast, Papa brought in the gateman and his son Ling, the boy who had been sitting next to the man at the feast. They hunted through the rooms until Ling found a hole in the bottom corner of the hall.

They banged on the ceilings and walls with broomsticks, shouting "Ai-eeeh! Ai-eeeh!" in high, screechy voices.

One by one, out came the rats. As each one burst out, the little dog yipped hoarsely and chased it into a corner. Fung Choi whacked them with the stove poker, and Ling scooped them up with a dustpan and ran to throw them in a heap in the back yard.

It took a long time for Papa and his team to fight their battle, but after several days, the night noises finally stopped. All together, they counted 213 dead rats.

Elsa was so proud of her little dog. Now, maybe even Mama

would like it. She picked it up and cuddled it. "You're a good dog, Mopsy."

Mama looked through the door at the big pile of rats in the back yard and shook her head. "They'd never believe this in America."

Papa winked at her, then ran to get his folding camera.

For days, from all around the countryside, people came to see the wonder. And that was when Elsa first saw the *yahbah*.

Chapter 7

THE FRAIL-LOOKING MAN IN RAGGED clothes had skin as pale as an egg, and pinkish eyes squinted below his white eyebrows. Like the other men in Shiao Yangshan, he shaved his head, but it was smaller than most, and he had tiny, crinkly ears like dried apricots. His teeth were yellow and crooked, with gaps between them.

The wind had died down that afternoon, and the sun shone. The back compound swarmed with Chinese, pushing and scuffling around the rat display. Over the noise of laughing and shouting, the strange-looking man's voice shrilled, "Oowah, oowah."

Elsa tugged at Papa's jacket. "What's the matter with him?"

Fung Choi's son, Ling, stood nearby, and when Papa didn't answer, Ling said, "Pay no attention. He is nothing, a little potato. Only a *yahbah*."

Elsa didn't understand. What was a *yahbah?* But before she could ask, Ling and his father took the man by his arms and started toward the gate.

Papa called out, *"Deng-ye-deng.* Wait!"

He questioned the gateman, and Choi stuck out his tongue, making a slicing motion. "Red soldiers torture him."

The *yahbah* pulled away, shaking his head and waving his arms. His eyes looked wild and terrified.

Papa laid his hand gently on the *yahbah's* shoulder, smiled into the man's face, and spoke distinctly in Mandarin. "We won't hurt you." He turned to Choi and said, "Let him stay. I want to talk to him."

"But Mushih, he cannot hear nor speak! He is a *yahbah!*"

Elsa stared in horrible fascination. She'd never seen a deaf mute

49

before, but Tsao Po-Po had told her stories about *fei-hsing,* bad luck people who caused terrible things to those who came near them. Some of the *fei-hsing* had violent fits and foamed at the mouth. She must have meant people like this man.

But Papa didn't seem afraid of the *yahbah,* and after the crowd left, the pale-skinned man stayed behind. With gestures and nods, Papa and Choi talked with him.

Later that morning, Elsa watched as the man shoveled the dead rats into a wheelbarrow and took them out the back gate to burn them. In the afternoon, he was still there, sawing wood.

When Papa and Choi went into the village for supplies to mend the walls and ceiling, Elsa skipped along beside them. She asked her father about Tsao Po-Po's warnings about *fei-hsing,* and he shook his head.

"There's no such thing. The poor man can't help the way he looks. Don't be afraid of him."

A nagging doubt squirmed into Elsa's mind. Papa was very wise, but could this be one thing he didn't know about?

Having a *fei-hsing* around was taking an awful chance. She didn't want terrible things to happen to them. Someone could die—maybe she herself, and she hadn't been baptized yet. She worried quietly until they reached the village.

There was only one street, made of packed dirt and lined with little mud-brick shops showing displays of roots and powders, brushes and paper scrolls, and granite ink boxes. Narrow paths threaded out into the countryside, ending in jumbles of houses no larger than a single room in their mission house.

In the distance, a giant needle jabbed into the sky. Choi said it was the spire of the Catholic mission in the next village. Many little villages lay close by, he told them, and on market days, the people all came together bringing many things to sell, including sheep, chickens, and produce.

A flash of bright blue in an open shop window caught Elsa's attention. Tiny clay birds hung on strings, swaying in the breeze. Bits of tail feathers added to their beauty. It was such a surprise, this sudden color where everything else was gray.

She stared at them, yearning. But Papa went on into the next shop, and pointed to rolls of oilpaper and bags of cement, dickering for a good price. All the way home, he and Choi planned how they would plug up the rat holes and put up a new ceiling.

The next day, and almost every day after that, the *yahbah* worked in the compound. When he came, Mama always locked the back door, her mouth set in a grim line, one corner twitching. Elsa felt as though her big sandy Eden had been invaded by a serpent.

Tsao Po-Po muttered fearful predictions—diseases, accidents, attacks from bandits—and after the man left, she burned incense to clear away his spirit. But Mama scolded Tsao Po-Po and made her throw out the joss sticks and wave away the smell with a tea towel.

Elsa was puzzled. If Mama didn't believe in *fei-hsing*, why was *she* afraid of the *yahbah*?

The strange-looking man worked hard. He helped Papa build a dining table and chairs, beds, dressers, and shelves for their books and treasures. He planted dozens of trees along the paths leading from the mission house to the back gate and along the walls. On the east side of the compound, past an old garden plot, he put up a set of sturdy swings. He also painted the peeling church doors with bright orange lacquer and kept the sandy compound raked smooth.

Papa hired a cook, Fu Liu. He wasn't as friendly as the one in Shungtau. His lips were thick, and the top one curled up as though he was always sneering. Every noon, Papa had Fu Liu take the *yahbah* a lunch of soft, boiled noodles in broth. The deaf mute squatted beside the stable and held the bowl up to his mouth, shoveling the food in with chopsticks he kept in his pocket.

As time went on, the *yahbah* didn't look so frail. His face grew rounder, his shoulders bigger. Whenever he looked at Elsa, he'd smile, his small, tongueless mouth forming an oval and his pink eyes squinting until they looked like slits. But Elsa remembered what Tsao Po-Po had said about him, and she would shudder and run away.

By winter, the sandstorms had turned to muddy sleet, and it was too cold to play outside. Elsa and Jasper read books and acted out the stories, played hide-and-seek from room to room, and built block houses for the spool people.

On Sundays, besides their usual union suits, padded clothes, and wool socks, everyone bundled up in thick woolen coats and caps for the short walk over to the church. Mama, usually so slim and dainty, looked as round as Tweedledee, in layers and scarves and heavy Mongolian boots. In the church, the only warm spot was near the round iron stove and its long, crooked pipe stretching over one side of the platform.

But the people were friendly. They tweaked Elsa's cheeks and marveled over her red hair. She laughed with them and played with their babies. During the service, she imitated their singing, racing loudly through the hymns to finish before the others.

In Sunday school, she and Jasper sat with the village children, but afterward Mama and Tsao Po-Po always examined their clothes and hair for lice and gave them castor oil for worms.

At Christmas, the church was so full that people lined up two-deep around the walls, staring at the bright paper chains, flowers, and lanterns strung up on bare branches. After everyone had recited their verses and poems and sung carols, they yelled *"Yi lu ping an!"* for peace and safety, and then went home huddled against the cold wind, clutching gift bags full of nuts, tangerines, and sesame candy.

The *yahbah* never came to church. Papa told him he must take a day of rest on Sundays, but he often wandered around the compound instead, picking up a bit of stray trash, raking smooth a mound of dirt.

He didn't seem to mind the cold. On the west side of the back compound, behind the stable, he dug an ice pit for Fu Liu to store meat, crocks of *jaodze,* and pickled vegetables. When Papa bought a cow and a donkey and turned the big shed into a stable, the *yahbah* spent hours tending the animals and keeping their stalls clean.

When spring came, he planted two little trees in front of the house, one on each side of the small private courtyard. After patting in flower seeds at the base, he made circular brick borders around them.

The borders were just the right height for sitting, but Elsa liked best to walk on them, round and round, balancing herself like an acrobat. Then Mama would yell at her, startling her and making her fall. "You'll scuff your shoes. Don't be such a tomboy." No matter what Elsa did, Mama always seemed to get mad.

But Mama didn't mind the swings, and they were the most fun. When Elsa pumped high in the air, her braid trailing and then slapping back, her world was perfect—the long gray house, her big play yard, and the Chinese people in their padded clothes. She sang "Praise Him, praise Him," loving God for everything He had done, especially for bringing her here.

In April, Papa planned a baptism for new believers, to be held in the little stream by Little Goat Mountain. Elsa asked if she could be included.

At first, Mama said she was too young, but then Papa took Elsa aside. He talked and prayed with her, and she told him she believed that Jesus was her Savior and she wanted to follow Him all her life.

After that, Papa said she was ready to be baptized, and she felt good all over. From now on, she would be able to stay out of trouble. And if Jesus had forgiven all her sins, she didn't have to be afraid to die anymore, because He would take her to be with Him in heaven, just like He would Papa.

When the big day came, Elsa dressed in a white sheet and stood with the others to take her turn in the stream, now dammed into a little pool for the ceremony. Elsa looked into Papa's reassuring eyes, trusting him to support her.

He spoke softly to her, calming her fast-beating heart. "Be strong and of good courage. The Lord is with you." Then he pronounced: "I now baptize you in the name of the Father, the Son, and the Holy Spirit," and lowered her until the icy water washed across her face. Then it was over. Papa handed her to Sen Ying's outstretched hands, and Tsao Po-Po waited in a tent with towels and dry clothes.

Now, she did feel strong, and ready to follow Jesus, just as Papa did. She really belonged here; she was part of the Chinese church.

She thought of the escape from the fighting in Shungtau, of hiding in the pagoda, the rapids in the river, the bandits, and the stolen bracelet. Papa had searched through all the boxes and never found the other one. Still, through all the fearful times, God had protected them, and now they were safe.

But she was still afraid of the *yahbah*.

Chapter 8

EVERY DAY, THE TRAIN CAME TWICE. Early in the morning, it arrived from the west; at two in the afternoon, it rushed in from the east. The sound was always the same: first the dinging of the gong, then the rumbling—louder and louder until the ground shook.

On Wednesday afternoons, Papa went to the station for the mail. Elsa loved to go along and watch the travelers, the peddlers, and all the beggars from the village. Some of those she already knew by name. She knew which ones were really poor and which ones were fakes. Some of the fakes even had hired helpers.

She waved to the baggage handler who threw out the heavy sack of letters and packages. At the depot, Papa helped the station master sort the mail, easily picking out the ones with American postmarks.

She knew that for a long time he'd looked for a letter from the mission board in America, answering his request for special funds to build a school and clinic. So far, it hadn't come.

Mama hoped to hear that the old missionary had recovered or that a replacement had been found, but she was also disappointed.

Sometimes there were fat envelopes from Papa's brothers, George and Silas, or from Grandpa and Grandma Meier. After Papa read the letters aloud, he'd get out the albums and point out pictures of all the relatives Elsa and Jasper had never met.

He would always insist that Mama show her family, too—the Carlisles, dressed in fancy clothes as if they were going to a party.

Strangely, no letters ever came from them. When Elsa asked about that, Mama said, "Maybe next week." She often talked about America and its wonders, but she wouldn't talk about her family.

In the mail were usually several newspapers and magazines, and Papa and Mama read bits of them to each other. They mentioned somebody called Efty Are, and it was a long time before Elsa realized they were referring to the president of the United States, Franklin Delano Roosevelt, who was known by his initials, F-D-R. There was also something about a depression, and a "new deal" that was supposed to fix it.

None of it made any sense to Elsa, and she couldn't see why it was important. After all, this FDR wasn't president of China.

She hoped her family would stay in Shiao Yangshan forever. She liked dressing like these Chinese—the wide padded trousers folded tight at the waist and ankles and fastened with cords, and the *pow-dze*, a jacket that was padded in winter, and lighter weight in summer.

She loved the church, the people, and the village, with its little shops selling mutton and pottery and woven blankets of camel's wool.

One market day, Papa bought an old bicycle from a peddler, and the *yahbah* helped him repair it, painting it shiny black. From then on, Papa used it for visiting outlying stations. But once, when Mama was busy with the women's hygiene class, he took Elsa along to the next village, bumping over rocks and ruts in an ox-drawn cart. They passed fields of oats, hemp, millet, and opium poppies until finally reaching the grasslands. They greeted shepherds sitting on the rocks, watching their flocks and picking lice from their long, sheepskin coats, cracking them with their teeth as though they were pumpkin seeds. Eagles circled in the sky, and riders in knee-length boots and brightly sashed coats galloped past, their horses' tails decorated with red ribbons.

Papa stopped at little mud huts, cave homes, and round sheepskin tents, called *yurts*, lined inside with bright rugs and hides. He gave blankets to the poor and oat flour to the hungry and read to them from his Chinese Bible. The people, who were very friendly, served them tea with goat's milk. When Elsa couldn't finish hers, Papa drank it, too.

Elsa thought this was a wonderful way to live, with no walls and few rules. She thought about Mama, who was always fussing about dirt and lice, the babies wearing split pants instead of diapers, bandits in the mountains, the Japanese taking over in Manchuria—and always, always, the Red Army. Papa told her not to worry so much, but it didn't seem to help.

What if Mama's complaining could actually make bad things happen, as Tsao Po-Po believed? It would be awful if the Red Army made them leave this beloved compound with its high, mud-brick walls. Elsa knew she was safe here; she wasn't afraid of anything.

Except she still didn't trust the *yahbah*.

On May 16, Elsa's ninth birthday, she knew the next year would be happy. She hadn't changed much: the mirror on her dresser showed the same freckled face and straggly red hair. And when she followed Mama to the classroom after breakfast, her head still barely reached Mama's shoulder.

But she *felt* different. Even Mama noticed that she sat quietly during lessons and didn't kick Jasper under the table.

It was a nice day for a birthday—not very cold, no dust blowing, and the sun shining through new leaves in the sycamore trees. For recess, Elsa and Jasper marched up and down the sandy paths of the back compound, waving scarves for parade banners, counting, *"Yi, er, san, sih,"* four big strides between trees. *"Wu, liu, chi, ba."*

When they reached the stable, the *yahbah* came out and motioned to the open door behind him. "Oowah, oowah."

Elsa shook her head and started away, but the *yahbah* grabbed her arm. "Oowah, oowah," he repeated, a little louder.

"Let me go!" Elsa yanked loose, ready to run. Then she heard a faint cry and turned to see a scrawny yellow cat staggering out the stable door.

The *yahbah* smiled his empty oval smile. "Oowah," he said, pointing to the cat. He reached into his sleeve and brought out a small chunk of steamed bun. Squatting down, he offered it to the cat. Forgetting her fear, Elsa knelt beside him and stroked the cat. Its bony back quivered, then rose up to meet her hand. She turned to show Jasper, but he'd run to the house.

Elsa lifted the cat to her chest. It sniffed her face and licked her nose.

The deaf mute gave the cat another scrap of bread and then went back to his work.

"Your coat is the royal color," Elsa told the cat, rubbing its head. "I'll call you Empress."

Just then, Mama called from the back door. Empress jumped out of Elsa's arms and ran back into the stable.

After supper that day, Mama brought out a sponge cake for Elsa's birthday celebration, and Papa put two packages on the table. Elsa could tell by the shape that one of them was books. She opened that one first and found *Little Women* and *Gulliver's Travels*. She set them aside lovingly to read later.

When she opened the other package, she cried out, "Papa! I didn't think you'd noticed!"

Inside the brown oiled paper were three little blue clay birds, feathered tails and all, attached by yellow braided strings to a wooden bar. The same ones she'd admired in the shop.

Elsa stroked the pretty feathers. "They'll look nice hanging in my window."

Mama's lips twitched. "They'll attract all the sparrows in the village."

Empress would like that, thought Elsa. She turned to Papa. "I had another present today."

"Another one? From whom?"

"The *yahbah*. He gave me a cat. She lives in the stable."

Mama darted a look at Papa, then toyed with her fork. Finally she said, "I don't want you playing with the *yahbah*."

Elsa had no intention of playing with the *yahbah*. But Mama's order made her curious. She asked, "Why are his eyes pink?"

Papa swallowed a mouthful of food. "He's an albino."

"Is it catching?" Jasper's voice trembled a little, and his eyes were wide.

"No, Little Tiger. Don't worry. The *yahbah* was born that way. And he won't hurt you. In fact, I believe he is a Christian."

"Philip!" said Mama. "How can that be? Even if it were true, how could you tell?"

Papa smiled. "I can tell. There are more ways to talk than with words."

"Well, I still don't want him around the children. You just never know."

"Then you'll have to keep them inside tomorrow. He's going to dig a root cellar for me."

Chapter 9

THE ROOT CELLAR NESTLED IN THE east corner of the back compound, between the house and the garden. It was a snug little cave, mostly underground but with a mud-and-straw roof peaked high enough to allow for an open window on each side. The entrance sloped, so Fu Liu could roll down a wheelbarrow and unload the carrots, potatoes, and dried herbs that would fill the packed-dirt shelves.

Elsa claimed the root cellar for a playhouse. Its shelves were layered like steps, and many were still empty. Sometimes she and Jasper brought Empress and Mopsy in and pretended the shelves were their thrones. They stocked the risers with spool people and made grottoes for them in the mounds of potatoes.

Mama didn't seem to mind if they played there, as long as Tsao Po-Po worked outside and the *yahbah* was busy on the other side of the compound.

But then Jasper got sick. Mama and Tsao Po-Po coddled him for days, and one morning he popped out all over with red spots. Measles.

Mama dismissed lessons and told Elsa, "Run along and play."

She asked, "May I go outside by myself?"

Mama carefully poured medicine into a spoon. Not looking up, she murmured, "Go on. Don't bother me."

It was a nice sunny day, and the spring sandstorms hadn't started yet. Elsa was glad that Tsao Po-Po had washed and put away the padded suits and brought out her loose summer trousers and a cool *pow-dze*.

After swinging awhile, Elsa took Empress and the box of spools into the root cellar. It was dim and cool and smelled of garlic and old potatoes.

Empress purred and twitched the tip of her tail. She wasn't bony now, and her fur was thick and glossy. Elsa was reaching to arrange one of the spool families when suddenly the cellar got darker. She looked up.

A man's legs blocked the doorway.

The *yahbah!* Elsa shrank against the shelves.

But when he bent to come in, she saw it was a much larger man, a tradesman she'd often seen talking to Papa in the compound. The man had bushy black hair and huge yellow teeth. When he smiled, it looked like he was saying the word *cheese,* so Elsa thought of him as the cheese man.

Only the cook or Tsao Po-Po used the cellar to get supplies for the kitchen. So why was the cheese man there?

He stared at Elsa, his dark eyes glittering, his big teeth hungry looking. He put his finger to his mouth and hissed, "Sh-h-h."

Empress stirred, pricked up her ears, and made a funny little "merow" in her throat.

The cheese man giggled, a high shrill "hee-hee-hee" that didn't fit his huge size.

Elsa held Empress tighter. The man reached over and stroked the cat, his hand sliding past the cat to Elsa's arm. He fingered her braid, then picked it up and tickled her nose with the end.

Maybe Papa had sent him to get some potatoes. Elsa decided to go around him and out the door. She edged to the other side of the cellar and stepped up on the lowest dirt shelf.

The man sat down beside her, blocking her way. His hand clutched her ankle; his fingers slid up, tickling her shin, stroking her in places that were not to be touched.

Why was he doing that? It made her stomach feel funny; she said, "Don't," and kicked out at him. He caught her foot, slipping off her cloth shoe.

Elsa grabbed the next shelf to keep from falling, accidentally squeezing the cat. Empress yowled and spit, struggling to get away.

The man snickered and said, *"Buh yao pa—*don't be afraid. I'm very nice." His fingers tightened, hurting her, and she cried out. There had to be some way to get away from this awful man! But she was trapped.

Empress stretched out her claws, burst out of Elsa's arms, and streaked out the door like golden lightning.

The cheese man leaned over Elsa, his hot stinking breath filling her nose, choking her. His arm squeezed her waist, and she struggled as hard as she could, but all her strength couldn't break the man's hold.

She spit in his face, but he didn't bother to wipe it away. She scratched his arms and face, but his skin was like leather and it didn't do any good. Her mouth opened to scream as loud as she could, and his wet lips blocked her voice.

Suddenly, she heard a familiar noise. "Oowah, oowah!"

Oh, no! she thought. *Not the* yahbah, *too!*

Then came a loud thump. The cheese man shuddered, and his heavy bulk fell limp against her.

"Oowah, oowah!"

Elsa squirmed, fighting for breath, shoving and whimpering until she'd wriggled out from under the man. Free at last, she dug her fingernails into the dirt and hurdled up the shelves past the potatoes and jars and pushed herself out the tiny, ground-level window.

She ran as fast as she could, stumbling and limping, not stopping to see if the men were following. The back door was locked, and she pounded her fists against it until the cook opened it, his eyes bulging with surprise.

Elsa ducked under his arm, flew into her bedroom, and slammed the door. Then she looked around wildly. Where could she hide? She heard footsteps and dove under the bed, pushing aside the clattering chamber pot, scooting until her head bumped against the far wall. There she huddled, shivering and retching, her knees to her chin, her arms hugging them.

"Elsa? Where are you?"

Her ears were ringing, and the voice was distorted as though from the bottom of a well. She heard a high whining sound, like a hurt dog, then realized it was her own voice. "Elsa, what are you doing under the bed?"

Mama. Now she was in bad trouble. Mama always said she shouldn't play with the *yahbah*, and that big man was even worse. She felt dirty and ashamed and couldn't answer.

"Come out of there, right now!" Mama's voice was harsh.

"I . . . I can't." Elsa could barely get the words out.

Then she heard whispers sounding far away, as though from a different world.

"I don't know. She just came running in—"

Papa's voice asked, "Elsa, are you all right?"

Papa. The person she trusted the most. But would he hate her now? Mama had said never to touch herself there.

"It's all right, Dumpling. Come, come to Papa."

Slowly, blindly, Elsa crept out. Mama held out her hands but it was to Papa that she went, hiding her face in his strong arms. Finally, she felt safe. The little hairs tickled her nose, and his skin smelled salty. She tried to talk but could only sob.

Papa smoothed her hair. "Now, now," he said. "It's all right. Can you tell me what happened?"

"What did you do?" asked Mama.

"I . . . I was in the root cellar—"

"Yes?"

"Then the cheese man, the *yahbah*—"

Mama gasped. "The *yahbah*? Philip, I *told* you to get rid of him." Her voice rose to a screech.

"Go on, Elsa." Papa's voice was low. "Did he hurt you?"

But she couldn't answer. A sour lump choked her, and she could only burrow her head into Papa's chest.

Mama grabbed Elsa's shoulder and shook it. "What did the *yahbah* do to you?" Her voice sounded angry. "Tell me! What did he do?"

Elsa felt Papa's voice rumbling in his chest. "Give her time. Can't you see she's upset?"

"I *told* her not to play with the *yahbah*. I always knew . . . And Philip, if you'd just listened to me and gotten rid of the man . . ."

Elsa covered her ears. Even after her baptism, she still got into trouble. How could she ever earn Mama's love? "His hands . . . ," she mumbled into Papa's neck. "I couldn't stop him."

Papa said, "I can't believe the *yahbah*..." His voice was rough. "But if he hurt her, I'll make sure he gets what he deserves."

"If we'd gone back to America as we'd planned—but no, you had to settle in here, knowing all the dangers."

Papa stood up, lifting Elsa to her feet. She'd never seen his face that furious. "Take care of her. I'll get to the bottom of this. Go on, Dumpling. Let Mama help you." His footsteps pounded down the hall, and she heard the back door slam.

Tsao Po-Po brought a basin of warm water and washed Elsa's face, arms, and legs, hissing in her breath at the sight of several long scratches on her arms, now caked with blood and dirt.

Mama glanced at the flecks of blood on Elsa's *pow-dze,* then back at her arms. "What happened here?" Her voice was softer, but her face looked like thunder.

"Empress scratched me. I was playing with her in the cellar, but she ran away."

"Why didn't you leave too?" Mama opened Elsa's bed and motioned her in.

Elsa snuggled under the covers and pulled them up to her chin. "I tried." She thought of the big cheese man and closed her eyes to block out his picture. "He wouldn't let me."

Tsao Po-Po took the basin out, and Mama turned to leave the room, too. She muttered, "That *yahbah's* going to pay for this."

Elsa slept the rest of the afternoon and half woke to a heavy sensation of dread, ugly visions of the cheese man and "oowah" sounds mixed with wisps of Tsao Po-Po's crooning. Then she heard whispering: "Get rid of him right now!"

"What if he's not guilty?"

"You heard what she said."

Elsa opened her eyes.

Papa asked her, "Was anyone else in the compound today?"

"The cheese man—"

"What do you mean? We don't have a cheese man."

Mama spoke up harshly, "Philip, don't waste time. Just have the *yahbah* arrested and be done with it."

Elsa thought it over. If they got rid of the *yahbah,* she wouldn't have to be afraid anymore. Or would she? She didn't want to remember, but she could almost see the huge man in the root cellar. "Not a *real* cheese man," she said. "That man with the big teeth, like he's smiling for the camera. He—put his hand—" She couldn't finish.

Papa said, "Hong, the merchant? Choi saw Hong here earlier but didn't see him leave . . ." He hit his fist into the palm of his other hand. "Now it all makes sense."

Mama shook her head. "What are you talking about?"

"Hong was the one in the root cellar. The *yahbah* tried to show me, but I didn't understand. I couldn't believe he was that strong. He grabbed a board—" Papa made a hacking motion with his arms. "I don't think we'll see Hong around here again. But to make sure, I'll go to the village and tell the magistrate to arrest him."

Elsa sat up quickly. "The *yahbah*? He—he rescued me?"

"He's a hero today. You don't have to be afraid of him."

"But how could he know where I was? I tried to scream, but I couldn't."

"He wouldn't have heard it anyway. No, it was the cat. He saw Empress flying out of the cellar like a bat out of—"

"Philip!" said Mama.

"—and started running. I guess he knew the cat wouldn't leave you unless something was wrong."

Elsa took a deep, ragged breath. The *yahbah*. He wasn't *fei-hsing*, after all. He was her friend!

A FEW DAYS LATER, ELSA came down with the measles. Papa said that if she had to be sick, now was a good time because the spring windy season had started, with thick whirls of sand dancing in the compound, and it was best to stay inside anyway. She lay in her darkened bedroom while Tsao Po-Po told her stories about tiny dwarfs who lived in the hillside, a magic bell that could tell when people were lying, and wicked men who were thrown into a pit of poisonous snakes.

While Elsa's imagination watched the snakes coiling and hissing their revenge, Mama came into the room. Her lips were tight, and she carried her Bible and a basket full of clothes. "Tsao, these need mending," she said, handing Tsao Po-Po the basket.

Elsa kicked at her blankets, wanting to coil and hiss along with the snakes. Even when she was sick, Mama was mean to her. "Can't I hear the rest of the story first?" she asked. But Mama didn't answer, and Tsao Po-Po left the room without looking back.

Mama straightened Elsa's blankets firmly, then opened her Bible. She read to Elsa about the people who were too scornful to get into Noah's ark, the rebellious Korah and his friends getting swallowed up by the earth, and Joseph helping Pharaoh during the Egyptian famine.

Despite her resentment, Elsa became caught up in the stories. She thought about their own kitchen shelves full of crocks and sacks. All spring, the weather had been dry, and Papa had said if it didn't rain soon, the millet fields would dry up and blow away.

The people of Shiao Yangshan had beaten gongs, set off firecrackers, and even taken idols out of their temples to show them the parched land, reminding them how close the village was to a famine.

What if the mission would have to feed all the people in the compound—even the whole village? Elsa imagined herself as Joseph, standing by the gate, handing out portions of grain in little twists of oiled paper, nobly saving the villagers from starvation. She would ride around in a golden rickshaw, and people would kowtow to her. She would spread her arms out, loving them all, motioning them to get up.

When Jasper came into her room, Elsa asked him to act out the stories with her. They pretended her bed was an ark and crawled together, making the right sounds for each pair of animals. After bouncing around to make waves, they took turns being the dove flying out to find ground. Jasper found a pencil to carry in his mouth, to be the one that came back with the olive branch. But when they played famine, he wanted to be Joseph, too, and wouldn't bow down to her. When Mama came in and found them pushing each other and giggling, she told them to stop making fun of the Bible.

WHEN THE SANDSTORMS WERE over, Mama declared that Elsa was well. The next time Tsao Po-Po went outside to do the laundry, Elsa and Jasper followed her to play hide-and-seek. A sound came from the house, and Elsa looked back to see Mama standing at the door, but then she quickly closed it.

Elsa tried to think of a good hiding place. The root cellar?

Then she remembered the cheese man. Her stomach churned, and she couldn't look in the direction of the dugout. "I don't want to play," she said, choking down a sour taste in her throat.

Jasper tugged at her arm. "Aw, come on."

But Elsa pulled loose, and Jasper ran off to the swings. He draped himself over one of the canvas seats and swung upside down, pushing with his toes, singing "Jesus Loves Me."

Empress came out of the barn, and Elsa picked her up, cuddling the thick yellow fur. In the distance, the station gong sounded *ding-ding-ding*, and farther away, the train whistle wailed hoarsely. Elsa heard the first faint rumble of the engine, getting louder and louder until the familiar thunder echoed around her and the ground vibrated under her feet. Empress squirmed, jumped out of her arms, and ran back to the stable.

A shiver snaked all the way up Elsa's spine and to her scalp. She thought of the cheese man touching her, and felt dirty. If she moved, the earth might open and swallow her just as it had Korah and his wicked friends.

Then the whistle shrieked again, the gong sounded, and the train roared away. The world was silent. Even the sparrows were quiet.

She couldn't help it—her eyes turned to the other side of the compound toward the root cellar.

But there was no root cellar!

Elsa blinked her eyes. Had she imagined the whole thing? The dirt was flat from the house to the swings. Then she noticed that the vegetable patch was bigger, with rows of tiny, new green onions spiking up next to the carrots and cabbages. Papa must have had the *yahbah* fill in the ground. Little dark circles showed where Tsao Po-Po had carefully poured dippers of water. A flock of sparrows swooped down, chittering and pecking at the fresh greens, and Elsa ran to shoo them away.

When she turned back, Mama stood in the back doorway again,

and Elsa wondered why. They were safe enough; Tsao Po-Po was out-side with them, and the *yahbah* was inside the stable.

But she felt little prickles on the back of her neck and went and climbed on her swing. She began pumping, her feet stretching out over the vegetable garden. The next time she looked at the door, Mama was gone, and it was shut.

Chapter 10

IN THE MIDDLE OF JUNE, Papa came back from the train station, and smiled as he handed Mama an envelope.

Mama, sitting at the dining table studying her Bible, looked up at him with wide eyes. "Good news?" she asked. But when she opened the letter, her face sagged.

"What's the matter?" asked Elsa.

Her mother smiled, but her eyes still looked sad. "You'll be happy to hear this. The Moffats are coming to visit."

Elsa clapped her hands and jumped up and down. "When?" She loved the Moffats. She'd never met her own grandparents, but she had always imagined them to be like this older couple. Stationed at a Presbyterian mission in the nearby town of Shendong, the Moffats visited whenever they could get away.

"In two weeks," said Papa. "They'll spend the Fourth of July. Let's have a picnic on Little Goat Mountain to celebrate."

Mama nodded, reached for a tablet, and started making a list. She murmured to herself: "Chicken, boiled eggs, potato salad . . ."

Elsa ran to Jasper's room to tell him.

All winter, Mama had warned Papa not to explore Little Goat Mountain with all its caves and gullies. But finally in the spring, he'd persuaded her to climb to his favorite place, a ledge of boulders halfway up the nearest slope, and now that was their family's favorite picnic spot.

A wide riverbed, dry during the cold weather, wound around the foot of the hill and disappeared under a railroad trestle in the distance. In the summer, it turned into a little stream that gurgled over gravel and rocks, with little hummocks of grayish grass bulging up here and there like plump, furry animals. If the weather was warm enough, Mama let Elsa and Jasper roll up their trousers and wade in the ankle-deep water.

When Jasper heard the plans, he shouted in delight, and for the next two weeks, Elsa helped him mark off the calendar days.

On the afternoon of July 3, Reverend Moffat, small and wiry and sporting a white goatee, arrived with a satchel full of streamers, firecrackers, and an American flag. Mrs. Moffat, chubby and beaming, brought a tin of crisp rice cookies and a new game ordered from America: Chinese checkers.

Mama pulled out a nested set of black lacquered tables that Papa had ordered from Peking, and she served tea, using Mrs. Moffat's cookies and acting very proper.

By evening, the whole house was decorated for their patriotic party. The American flag stretched above the door; chains of red, white, and blue crisscrossed the ceiling; and everyone wore paper hats with red and white stripes and a blue pompom.

Reverend Moffat brought out the Chinese checkers game and taught them how to play. Elsa caught on quickly, fighting for space and squealing with glee when she jumped a marble. To her surprise, even her mother joined in the shouts of triumph and screams of outrage through several games, until finally they all had to admit that Reverend Moffat was the champion.

Later, Papa told stories of how America was discovered and about its struggle for independence from England. Elsa had studied the Revolutionary War with Mama, but Papa made it so interesting that her imagination flew and her brain didn't want to shut off for sleep that night.

Still inspired the next morning, Elsa decided to build a miniature fort in the sandy soil between the trees. Using a pailful of water from the well for moistening, she and Jasper squatted Chinese-style, forming the walls and sticking twig soldiers into the ground to fight the battles and guard the gates. Even Papa and Reverend Moffat got down on their knees and used mud, leaves, and bits of bark to mold little houses and tents. They all pitched in to make a pile of wet sand into Bunker Hill and plant a long pole for the Washington Monument.

Just as they finished and everyone was admiring their work, thunder rolled over the skies and echoed from the mountain. Huge drops of rain plopped into the sand.

"Praise the Lord," said Papa. "The drought has ended, and the crops are saved."

Mama sniffed the air. "I hope we'll get enough to do some good."

It started to rain hard, and they all ran inside. Elsa looked back, wailing, "The fort, the tents, they'll all be ruined!"

Jasper cried, "What about the firecrackers?" But Reverend Moffat promised he would set them off the next day.

Of course, they couldn't have the picnic, but Papa spread a blanket on the parlor floor, and they sat there to eat lunch, pretending the chairs were rocks.

When they finished, Elsa and Jasper dumped out the box of spools and blocks, letting the spool people hike over a bumpy block mountain and eat their own picnic with their little thread notch mouths.

The next day, Reverend Moffat had to break his promise. The rain still came down in torrents, sometimes a steady downpour, then a cloudburst pounding on the roof like thousands of hammers. Fu Liu, grumbling and muttering, set buckets all around the house to catch the leaks.

Elsa, in the parlor playing Old Maid cards with Jasper, halfway listened to the older people talk about operations and sewing, banks, unions, and cars. Papa's mission board had decided against a school but was still considering a clinic. There were rumors of soldiers marching through the mountains.

She listened more carefully when Reverend Moffat said that first the Communists, and later the Nationalist soldiers, had stolen goats and cows and forced people to join their armies, killing those who refused. The Nationalists then had pushed the Communist army back, some thought in the direction of Shiao Yangshan.

Was the war following them here? Elsa looked out the window; the rain still pelted down, and she couldn't sit still any longer. Jumping up, she told Jasper, "Let's play hide-and-seek. Not it!"

But when she darted down the hall to hide in a cupboard, she crashed into Tsao Po-Po carrying a box of sewing supplies. Buttons and pins scattered all over the floor, spools rolling in every direction, and Mama shouted for her to find a different game.

The weather refused to clear, and after several days cooped up in the house, Mama wasn't the only one to be crabby. Reverend Moffat insisted that President Roosevelt's New Deal would solve the depression in America, but Papa argued with him. Tsao Po-Po, knitting a red, white, and blue afghan, mumbled over dropped stitches, and Mrs. Moffat lost her usual smile. Fu Liu overcooked the *yomein* noodles, and when Mama scolded him, he sneered and muttered. Elsa felt as though she would go crazy if she couldn't run outside, and Jasper's cheerfulness made her angry.

On the fifth day, the rain finally stopped. By four in the afternoon, a shaft of weak sunlight broke through the clouds. The men pulled on rubber boots and went outside to inspect the compound.

Elsa was delighted when Mama rummaged in a missionary box for galoshes and told her and Jasper, "Go outside and run off some of your energy."

She found some that fit, and Jasper tugged on an unmatched pair: one yellow, one brown.

Tsao Po-Po sat in the sewing room, still knitting. "Too soon," she grumbled. "Get muddy, make much washing." But Elsa was already outside, Jasper right behind her.

The garden was nearly drowned, and little ponds covered the whole back compound. She looked for the fort, but it was gone, and Bunker Hill was flat. The Washington Monument lay on the ground, just an ordinary pole. Elsa felt like crying.

But not for long. When she saw all the rain worms, she ran to the door and asked Fu Liu for a bucket. Tree limbs had broken off and lay on the ground, and she picked one up to snag the worms and flick them into the bucket. "Come on, Jasper," she shouted. "Let's make a snake pit!"

Papa came out, too, and called workmen to mend cracks in the compound walls. After a while, Elsa noticed him talking to Mama at the back door and went a little closer.

She heard him say something about flash floods. "The river's full and rising. I've never seen anything like it. They say the railroad trestle is washed out and the train can't get through. The village is full of stranded travelers."

Mama glanced behind her, then said, "The Moffats will have to—"

"They can't leave until the bridge is repaired."

"What'll I do? With the railroad down, there won't be a market day. That means no fresh food."

Papa scratched his head, then said, "Send Fu Liu to the next village for supplies."

Mama sighed. "All right. You be careful."

Elsa saw the men walk out the back compound gate. She set down her bucket of worms and ran to the door. "Where's Papa going?" she asked Mama.

"To the river."

Elsa thought of their picnics at the stream and the pleasant swirl of water against her bare legs. The river had always been one of her special places, but she'd never seen it full. "May I go too?"

Mama shook her head and closed the door.

Elsa went back to her bucket and kicked it, dumping out all the worms. Mama never let her do anything interesting!

She wondered what a flash flood was like. Maybe Papa would build an ark like Noah in the Bible. They could take the animals along—the cow, Mopsy, Empress—maybe even goats, pigs, and chickens from the village.

Her branch became a cane, and she pretended she was hiking to the river. But it wasn't enough. She had to see for herself.

Mama hadn't actually said no. Maybe what looked like a forbidding shake of the head was really a yes.

The workmen had left a ladder leaning against the back wall, and Elsa climbed up to look over. She could see Papa in the distance, walking through a valley between the compound and the mountain. If she ran fast enough, she could catch up with him.

She looked toward the house. No one was watching.

"Stay here," she told Jasper. "I'll be right back." She tugged open the back gate just far enough to squeeze through, shut it as well as she could, and ran after the men.

Elsa heard the swollen river before she saw it. The ground under her feet shook with thundering rage, worse than a hundred trains. Little Goat Mountain, looming ahead, didn't look like a peaceful spot for picnics. Its side was slashed with dozens of ravines like the wrinkles on an angry man's face. Water gushed down the crevices, desperate to join in the battle.

Elsa glanced back and was horrified to see that Jasper had somehow pushed through the gate, too, and now trotted after her.

"Go back," she shouted at him. "You're too little."

But the roar swept her voice away, and he kept coming.

Papa was just ahead, climbing a boulder at the foot of the mountain. Elsa dropped her branch and scrambled up after him for a better look.

Instead of the familiar pleasant, bubbling stream, this was a dirty, yellow, violent monster boiling and splashing over the highest banks. A shoe bobbled near shore, caught in the branch of a tree, then spun back into the muddy current and disappeared. A chimney pipe, two goats, and part of a wagon whirled past.

Elsa stared in awful fascination. This was far worse than the Han River rapids near Shungtau. Her stomach heaved with the roiling waters, and she closed her eyes, then opened them, trying to bring the little stream back.

Papa turned, surprised to see her. "What are you doing here? Get down, quickly." His face looked strange and puckered.

Elsa jumped down from the rock and went to meet Jasper. Papa and the others joined them, and as they all started back to the compound, water began trickling from the crumbling bank. A rivulet blocked their way, then another, then several more joined to make larger streams. Elsa and Jasper held the men's hands and were swung over each flow.

The water looked shallow, and once Elsa dipped her toes into the edge. Immediately her foot was seized by a strong, evil force that demanded her whole body.

The *feng-shui!* She pulled back and clung to Papa's arm for safety, shivering violently, her heart pounding. This roaring, greedy monster was alive! They were going to drown—and all because she hadn't obeyed.

Dear Lord Jesus, forgive me. Help us get home, she prayed silently.

Fung Choi found rocks to stand on, and he and Papa swung the others over. But each time they crossed safely, they met still more outbreaks.

Slipping, falling, jumping, and scrambling, Elsa finally stood on higher ground, a mound of earth not far from the compound. She held Jasper's hand and watched Choi help Papa over the last hurdle.

Then Papa stumbled, and the waters dragged his feet downstream. Remembering the awful tug of the water, Elsa screamed but could barely hear herself.

In the distance, she saw the riverbank collapse. Monstrous waves gushed over, turning the wide sheet of water in the valley they'd just left into boiling whirlpools.

Just as Choi and Reverend Moffat pulled Papa up to safety, a tree limb swirled toward them, and Elsa felt Jasper jerk his hand loose from hers.

He shouted, "I want that!" and stooped to pull it from the water.

"No, Jasper, don't!" shrieked Elsa, grabbing his shirttail. But the shirt ripped out of her grasp. Elsa watched in horror and disbelief as her little brother tumbled into the thundering torrent.

His head went under, then surfaced again, his face pale against the muddy foam. Choi grabbed a large branch from the water and held it out to Jasper, but the current swirled him out of reach.

Papa gave a strangled cry and jumped back into the water, but Choi shouted, "Mushih, you will drown!" He stretched the branch to Papa, but Papa fought it away and tried to keep going.

Then a large bush spun toward Jasper, catching him in its tangles; screaming, he grabbed the branches and, with the bush, spun out of sight.

Elsa screamed, "Hold tight, Jasper," but knew he couldn't hear her.

Choi said, "Mushih, maybe the bush will keep him up. We better run for help," and Papa finally let the two men pull him back onto the knoll.

Choi ran to the compound and came back with a crowd of men with ropes, nets, and poles. They lashed barrels to the torn-off compound gate and sailed away down the rushing waters.

Reverend Moffat led Papa and Elsa, stumbling in shock, toward the house, but before they reached it, Mama came running to meet them. She stared at Papa's white face and red eyes. "What happened? I heard shouting—"

His mouth worked, but no sound came out.

Mama looked at Elsa and back at Papa, then screamed, "Little Tiger! Where's my baby?" She started for the gate, but Papa held her tightly, sobbing, "I'm so sorry, I'm so sorry."

Reverend Moffat put his arms around both of them. He said, "Rachel, the best thing you can do is go in the house and pray that we find him." Then he ran back out of the compound.

Chapter 11

ELSA'S LEGS SHOOK, AND SHE could hardly breathe. "I told Jasper to wait!" she sobbed. "Why did he follow me?" Her arms hung limp as her amah helped her change into dry clothes.

Tsao Po-Po pulled her close and rebraided her tousled hair. "The men will find your brother, Yung-det."

"Don't call me that!" Elsa scrubbed at her tears with a corner of the woman's apron, but they wouldn't stop. "I'm not Eternal Virtue! I'll never be good enough for that name." Through the wall to Jasper's bedroom, she could hear Mama weeping and Mrs. Moffat praying. Her *pow-dze* frogs only half fastened, Elsa threw herself facedown on her bed.

After a long while, she heard voices at the back door, and then a loud scream. A voice—was that her mother? "No! Don't give up! He'll be so afraid!"

"We can't get through." That was Reverend Moffat. "I'll wire the next town; maybe someone there will search."

Peeking out the bedroom door, Elsa saw Choi. He told Mama, "People fear storm gods. They will not go out." His face was muddy and bleeding, his clothes torn.

Mama cried, "They *must*. We'll pay anything!" The rain came down again, hammering the roof. She stared out the back door, ignoring the splatters on her clothes.

Elsa stole out of her room, her stomach churning, remembering the terrible, yellow, boiling river. *It should have been me instead of Jasper!* She went to Mama, but Mama pushed her aside, not looking at her, and she felt desperately alone.

Reverend Moffat brought the wet and dirty searchers into the kitchen, and Fu Liu served tea and *juht* to them. Then Choi lit a lantern and went outside again. Papa sat at the dining table, slumped over, his hands covering his face. He sobbed in a strange, thin voice, "My God, my God, why have You forsaken us?"

Elsa went and stood next to him, leaning against his shoulder, but even Papa didn't seem to notice her.

Then Choi was back, scratching at the back door, shouting, "Water pouring through compound walls!"

Papa was still crumpled at the table, and Reverend Moffat told Choi, "Get sandbags." Tsao Po-Po rounded up flashlights and lanterns, and Reverend Moffat set the men to work.

Soon Elsa heard Choi's voice again, his rain-streaked face appearing at the kitchen door. "No good. Walls crumbling. Better go to Catholic mission in next village. Higher, safe there. Go now before roads wash away."

Mama shouted, "No! I must stay here. If someone finds Jasper, if he comes back and nobody's home—"

Reverend Moffat cleared his throat, then said, "You must leave, Mrs. Meier. It's the only way. We men will stay. If the flood gets too high, we can go up into the bell tower."

Tsao Po-Po and Mrs. Moffat packed a basket of rolls and canned meat while the men rolled up rugs and stacked mattresses on the table.

When Choi opened the front door, Elsa saw water swirling into the front compound. Choi uncoiled a length of rope and said, "Everyone, hold on to this."

Elsa stared at him, not understanding. Tsao Po-Po grabbed her hand, curled the fingers around the rope, and pushed her forward. She was barely aware of the blinding sheets of rain, of slogging through ankle-deep mud. Jasper was still out there in the cold dark water, screaming for help. She could hear his voice echoing in her head.

As she pushed away from the rope and turned to go toward the sound, she stumbled over something solid. Tsao Po-Po lifted her up, and Elsa realized they had reached the railroad tracks.

Her amah's arms were still around her, urging her on. "Walk now. Easier here."

Her clothes soaked, her hair plastered against her face, and her hand smarting with rope burns, Elsa staggered mindlessly over the ties until they reached the next village. With the others, she plodded up an incline and entered the square, brick Catholic church.

The building was packed with refugees. Benches had been pushed to one end of the room, and mats laid out. Village families huddled together on them, wailing, tearing at their clothes. Travelers squatted by their baggage, arms hugging their knees. Flickering candles on an altar reflected in their tired eyes.

If Papa were here, he would have comforted them. But Mama turned away from them.

Tsao Po-Po handed the basket of food to one of the black-robed nuns moving among the people, serving hot tea and steamed *baodze* buns and handing out blankets. The sister thanked her and said, "Eat first, then lie down." She pointed to an empty space near the baptismal font.

Elsa took a bun but could barely swallow a bite. Mrs. Moffat helped her to a mat next to Mama and tucked a blanket around her.

She closed her eyes, but horrible pictures flashed through her mind. Papa crumpled at the table, that awful look on his face. Choi, ragged and bloody. Jasper struggling in the water, hanging on to the bush. *Hold tight, Jasper!* Tomorrow, the men would find him, cold and crying, but safe. Wouldn't they? *Dear Jesus, take care of Jasper.*

Pain washed through her like the flooding rain, and she rolled her head side to side. *Please, please, dear Jesus, don't let him die.* She looked for Tsao Po-Po but couldn't see her in the shadowy corner. Needing comfort so badly, she stretched out her hand to her mother, lying straight and still on the next mat.

But Mama gasped and stared at her. Pointing a finger at her, she spit out, "You—"

A dark form rushed to Mama. "Sleep, my dear," said the nun. "Tomorrow will be brighter." She knelt down and tucked Mama into her blanket.

Elsa rolled over and sobbed quietly into her fists. Nobody loved her anymore.

One by one, the lanterns hanging from the ceiling snuffed out, until only one light shone dimly at the other end of the building. Soft breathing and light snores filled the air.

Elsa lay awake, watching the shadows. Along the wall in little niches, small statues bowed their heads, ignoring her. She felt all alone in that building full of strangers. Lightning flickered against a nearby window, bringing out the design. A frosted line, straight up the center. Another line, horizontal. The sign of the cross. But as she watched, rain pounded against the window, blurring the picture.

JASPER WAS BURIED IN THE shadow of the wall near the back east corner of the compound.

The workmen had made a small coffin out of boards, and the *yah-bah* had polished it until it shone. Tsao Po-Po lined it with the red, white, and blue afghan she'd knitted and helped Mama lay Jasper to rest in a quickly sewn white funeral suit. She covered his face with a handkerchief—so evil spirits wouldn't recognize him, she told Elsa—and tucked in a *bao-dze* bun for his comfort, but Mama took both of them away.

The church people brought white paper flowers to cover the coffin. Just like a celebration, except nobody was smiling.

Reverend Moffat preached the funeral message. "Everyone loved Little Tiger, with his smile and cheerful nature," he said. "God will enjoy having Jasper in heaven. Jesus will hold our little friend in His arms and wash away his tears."

Elsa was not comforted by the thought. She remembered the day before, when the flood had receded and they had come back home. She'd heard the faint moaning of many voices in the distance getting louder and louder until the back door banged open—then the shouting, wailing, and shrieking that filled the whole house.

She'd snaked her way through the legs of the searchers until she saw something in the center of the kitchen floor. But it wasn't, couldn't be, Jasper. The body looked like a big rag doll with torn and dripping clothes. An awful waxy-white face, hair matted with silt, an ugly red gash zigzagging across the forehead—why was Tsao Po-Po squatting there, wiping it with a rag?

Why had the search party stopped looking for Jasper and brought in this—this—*thing?* She looked for Papa and saw him standing with his forehead against the wall, his fists hammering against the bricks.

Mama crouched over the body, her hair loose, her face red and crumpled. She blew into its mouth again and again, until the Moffats helped her up and led her away.

Elsa stared at them, then at the still figure on the ground. Couldn't they see it wasn't Jasper?

Then she noticed the boots. One yellow, one brown. Pain clutched her throat; she dropped to her knees and shook Jasper's arm. "Wake up, Little Tiger. Wake up!" she cried. "I'll read you any story you want. You can play Joseph if you like. You can be first in all the games—"

Firm hands lifted her up and patted her shoulder. "He is gone," said Wu Shong's wife, Sen Ying. "It is time to mourn your brother. You must relieve your soul."

Now, at the funeral, Elsa looked up from the coffin and realized that Reverend Moffat had finished talking. One by one, members of the church came forward and spoke. Wu Shong and Sen Ying, Choi and his wife, Fu Liu, many others—even Ling—said nice things about Jasper.

All around, people wept. Papa, Mama, the Moffats, Tsao Po-Po, the whole congregation. Elsa hardly recognized her mother's face, now so white and distant, a mask with stranger's eyes. Those eyes glanced at her, then away. There was no comfort, no sign of love— just an empty look. Didn't Mama know how awful she felt?

She looked around. Even the compound looked strange. In the garden, sparrows boldly pecked at the carrot tops, and no one shooed them away. The swings stirred in the summer breeze, as though Jasper sat on them watching the service. Any time, he would jump down and run up the path to her.

The Chinese sang their version of "Safe in the Arms of Jesus," and the music rang off-key in Elsa's head. She put her hands over her ears and shut her eyes.

When she opened them again, the workers had lowered the coffin into the grave and were shoveling sand and pebbles onto the polished wood.

Oh, no! They mustn't do that! What if Jasper wakes up and is hungry, like Jairus's daughter in the Bible story?

She couldn't breathe. Her eyes blurred, and the ground rocked under her feet. The next thing she knew, she was lying down with Tsao Po-Po squatting beside her, fanning her face with a hanky.

Elsa looked around, confused. Everyone was staring at her. She staggered to her feet, thinking how odd that had felt. She'd have to tell Jasper about it.

Then she realized she'd never again be able to share things with Jasper. They would never run and play together anymore: never act out stories, hunt for rain worms, or sail boats on his bedspread. She hung her head, feeling too tired to move.

The grave was finished now, heaped up like a hummock in the river. The people laid their decorations on the mound. Sen Ying handed Elsa a paper flower, and she stared at it, not understanding. Tsao Po-Po guided her hand forward, and together, they placed the white tissue blossom on the heap.

Then the congregation moved away from the grave in procession, leaving only Mama, Papa, and the Moffats. Tsao Po-Po put her arm around Elsa and held her close.

A breeze whipped up a little sand eddy, and a shadow fell across the swings. Elsa looked up. In the sky, a small dark cloud blotted out the sun. She shivered.

Even God hates me.

Chapter 12

SUMMER PASSED, AND THE FLOODS became a bad memory. Choi reported that the farmers of Shiao Yangshan had reseeded their millet fields and would have a huge crop. Papa opened three new outstations and spent a lot of time visiting them.

With Sen Ying's help, Mama started more women's training classes, even going as far as the next village, and she was gone almost as often as Papa.

Without Jasper, Elsa felt dull and empty, as if someone had scraped out her insides and left her hollow as a dry rain barrel. When she went outside, she stayed close to the house, avoiding the little mounded grave near the back gate of the compound. She followed Tsao Po-Po around, begging for stories.

The amah—no matter what Mama said, Elsa still thought of her as that—talked about opposites: yin and yang, dark and light; about little creatures who lived on the moonbeams and sprinkled moon dust on unsuspecting people; and about a dragon that stole the rooster's comb so roosters could never fly high anymore. She told about a man who saw the reflection of the moon in a well and thought it had fallen out of the sky, and about fox spirits that possessed people and made them act crazy so the authorities had to come and lock them up in a big cage for all the villagers to gawk at and laugh.

While she talked, Tsao Po-Po taught Elsa to sew on the treadle machine, and Glory, her hair trimmed to a boys' cut, gained a whole new doll wardrobe from scraps.

When lessons started up again in September, Elsa couldn't bear to

82

look at the chair where Jasper had sat. Mama never smiled, and her red pencil marked up Elsa's test papers without mercy.

One day while Papa was gone on one of his trips, Mama dismissed lessons early and went to the church to teach a singing class. Tsao Po-Po was busy showing Fu Liu how to bake ginger cookies.

Elsa went into Jasper's old room and lay down on his bed. Her outstretched hand touched something furry. Startled, she pulled away and looked to see what it was. Stuck between the bed and the wall was the empty casing of Jasper's old teddy bear, tattered and dirty. She held it close to her and cried until she had no more tears.

Exhausted, she got up and went to Jasper's toy shelf. She fingered the spools and blocks and leafed through his books. Taking down a notebook and pencil, she turned to an empty page and sat down on the bed. She wrote Jasper's name several times and the Chinese character for Little Tiger, drawing little hearts around them. Then she doodled aimlessly, scribbling circles, then loops. One figure became a long, thin 8 with a lump on its side. When she got up to put the notebook away, she noticed that if she held the page sideways, the drawing looked like the hat on a cowboy she'd seen in her history book.

She drew a circle under it and filled in a face. It was an interesting face, with mischievous eyes and a grin that invited her to come and play.

Elsa couldn't help smiling back. She asked out loud, "What's your name?"

A voice in her head answered, *Mealy Fray.*

She laughed. "That's a funny name."

Mealy Fray said, *Come play with me.*

Elsa took his invisible hand, and he led her to the back compound. Mealy Fray smelled of straw, manure, and fresh milk, and he wore chaps and a blue bandanna around his neck like the cowboy in her book. He was strong and brave and had a horse named Charger.

There was a sawhorse in the barn, and Elsa climbed on. She clung to Mealy Fray's waist while Charger leaped over the compound wall, trotted through the valley, splashed through the stream, and easily climbed Little Goat Mountain.

Beyond the hills, they galloped past golden fields of millet, oats, and opium poppies. On they sped through the grasslands, waving to people watching from the doorways of their little yurts.

"Eternal Virtue, come to supper!"

That was Tsao Po-Po's voice! How did she *get to the grasslands?*

Elsa climbed off the sawhorse and went inside, her heart still pounding from the exciting ride.

After that, she wasn't quite as lonely. Every day now, she rushed through her lessons, knowing that Mealy Fray was in the barn, waiting for their exciting rides.

She added more friends, going down the alphabet and choosing a boy's and a girl's name for each letter. Alice, Barbara, Crystal; Andrew, Benjamin, Charles. But Mealy Fray was still her favorite.

All that year, Elsa played with her friends. They became more real to her than Tsao Po-Po and Mama, even Papa.

On her tenth birthday, she had a big party, laughing and dancing with all her imaginary friends. Some Chinese men working in the back compound watched her, pointing and whispering. Then one of them went to the kitchen door, and soon Tsao Po-Po came out.

"With whom do you speak?" she asked.

Elsa straightened a bow on Crystal's golden curls. "My friends."

"I see no one," said Tsao Po-Po, her eyes bulging.

"Of course not. They have no *hsing,* no form. They're invisible. But I can see them."

The workmen backed away. Some of them spit in the dirt, making little craters with tiny clouds of dust.

Tsao Po-Po cocked her head on one side. "What do they look like?"

Elsa glanced from one friend to the other. "Well, Mealy Fray has on blue trousers and a red shirt." She pointed toward the swings, gently swaying in the breeze. "Crystal's wearing a—"

"Ai-yah!" screamed the workmen, and they fled out the side gate.

"What's the matter with them?" asked Elsa.

Tsao Po-Po's mouth pursed even smaller. "They are afraid. They say you talk to *kwei.*"

Elsa blinked her eyes. She bit her lip and scuffed her shoe in the sand. "They're not evil spirits."

"What then?"

She shrugged. "They're just in my mind."

Tsao Po-Po stared at her and shook her head. "The *mushih* will have a hard time finding other workmen." She went back into the house, mumbling, "What a *mahfang*. Trouble, trouble."

Elsa got on the swing and pushed slowly back and forth, thinking. Could these imaginary friends be fox spirits? No, they were much too nice.

You're not going to send me away, are you?

Elsa twisted around. Mealy Fray looked worried.

"No," she told him. "But we have to be careful now. I don't want to be locked up in a cage for people to laugh at."

At the supper table that evening, while Elsa held her bowlful of noodles to her mouth Chinese style, she caught Mama eyeing her but pretended not to notice.

Finally Mama said, "Tsao Po-Po says you've been talking to yourself."

"I was just pretending." A noodle slapped her chin, and she wiped off the pork sauce.

"Pretending what?"

"Pretending to have friends."

Mama caught her lower lip between her teeth and looked at Papa. "See what's happened? We should have gone home long ago, Philip. Wasn't it enough that Jasper—"

Papa broke in. "I've been thinking. Maybe we should send Elsa to boarding school. She could make some real friends there."

Elsa stared at him. *Boarding school?* "Where? What's that like?"

Papa smiled. "There's one in Peking; you could come home for holidays. A lot of missionary children attend there. I think you'd like it. But first we'd have to save up some money."

Elsa wasn't at all sure she'd like it. Leave Shiao Yangshan, all the people, the big compound where she could play and run freely? Her swings? Maybe if she was extra good, Papa would forget about it. She would only talk to her imaginary friends in her bedroom when no one was watching.

In the next week's mail came Papa's hoped-for letter from the mission board. The clinic had been approved, and two nurses were on their way to Shiao Yangshan.

Papa was able to hire more workmen, and by the time the nurses arrived, he had an apartment fixed up for them and a clinic built next to the church.

Miss Sarah Bergen was tall, heavy, and cheerful. Miss Helen Penner was short, with a red face, and worried about everything. They both talked a lot. Elsa watched, fascinated, as they unpacked huge boxes of medical supplies and equipment.

All that winter, after she finished her lessons with Mama, Elsa would run over to the clinic and watch the nurses treat their patients. Although they'd begun language study, Chinese was hard for them, and Elsa was happy to translate for them.

The nurses praised her, and before long she was running errands for them, helping them with bandages and eyedrops, and unpacking medicines. By the time she was eleven years old, she'd learned how to carefully record the patients' names and medications in a big ledger.

Elsa felt grown-up and important. At the clinic, she wasn't just a little girl to be ordered around and scolded. She was part of a team. When she grew up, she would be a nurse, too, and listen to hearts and lungs and give vaccinations.

She forgot all about the boarding school. She even forgot her imaginary friends.

Chapter 13

ELSA WANDERED AROUND THE parlor, flipping open the cover of a book, pushing at a chair. It was the second week of June, she had finished all her seventh-grade books and passed all the exams, and the nurses had locked the clinic and gone to a weeklong conference in Peking. Now she had nothing to do.

Mama sighed. "Go outside and run off some of your energy. You're making me nervous."

It had been a long time since Elsa had played in the back compound—not since she'd scared off the workers with her imaginary friends. She thought of the swings, the trees now growing tall, the long paths where she and Jasper used to run.

Jasper. She closed her eyes and saw the shovels filling in the little grave. Her throat ached, and she couldn't move. Beside her, Mama stood waiting, her eyebrows raised.

Instead, Elsa turned and went out the front door.

Inside the circular brick borders the *yahbah* had built, red verbenas and black-eyed daisies bloomed around the small ornamental trees. Elsa stepped up onto the bricks just as she had when she was younger, and was surprised to see that with the extra height, she'd grown almost as tall as the tree. She circled around, balancing herself with out-stretched arms, humming a soft, mournful tune that Tsao Po-Po had taught her.

Behind her a voice said, "That is a sad song."

Elsa nearly fell off the bricks. The gateman's son, Ling, had sneaked into the yard. She jumped down, scowling at him. "What are you doing here?"

"So sorry to startle you. It is a nice song. But very sad."

"You have no right to spy on me!"

"I do not spy. I have a message for the *mushih*."

She waved toward the side door of the church. "He's in there. Go on in."

"Yes. Very well." Ling bowed with a flourish of his hand. "Please, sing some more. I will try not to listen."

Elsa squinted at him. Was he making fun of her? His dark brown eyes were clear and direct with just a hint of sparkle.

Ling was fourteen now, two years older and a little taller than Elsa. His whole head had been shaved like a grown man's, and his face had a golden glow like the sun shining through a parchment window.

Ling looked away from Elsa's stare, and scuffed his toes on the gravel path. "I must go now," he said and swaggered to the side door of the church.

He didn't come back, and Elsa knew he must have left through the front door of the church, which led to the outer courtyard. She felt lonely and wished she hadn't snapped at him.

The next day, Elsa went into the front yard and sang the same song, louder, pronouncing the words clearly: "*I hear the river flowing, and I must sail away. But my heart is sick with fear I won't return by day.*"

She peered through the open scrollwork wall into the front public compound and the gatehouse. When Ling didn't appear, she unlatched the connecting gate and walked out. Still singing, she skipped down the path, her eyes on the window of the gatehouse.

Suddenly, she tripped on something hard and solid. She stretched out her arms to break the fall, and her elbows jabbed into the gravel. Pain shot through her arms, and her knees ached. She wanted to cry but was afraid somebody might see her.

Slowly she got up, brushed off the dirt, and examined herself. Her elbows were bleeding, and even through her *kuhdze* she had skinned her knees. She looked around and saw an iron wedge in the path. Elsa scowled at it and the unknown person who had thoughtlessly left it there. With the clinic closed, she'd have to go inside and let Mama treat her with iodine.

"Yung-det! You are hurt?"

Elsa jumped. Ling had come up quietly again. Now he would laugh at her for not watching her step.

"It's none of your—" Then she remembered what had happened the last time she'd been rude to him. She cleared her throat. "I'm all right." But her elbows stung almost as bad as when Mama put on the iodine. Her knees felt stiff, and her toes hurt where they'd caught on the wedge. She chewed her lips to force the tears back.

"I have salve to heal your *maobing*." Ling headed for the gatehouse, motioning with his chin for her to follow. He called, "Ma!" There was no answer, and he opened the door and bowed for her to enter.

Elsa drew back. Mama never allowed her to go into the workers' apartments. Choi was her friend, but she didn't know Ling or his mother very well.

But Ling was waiting, and she couldn't let him think she was scared. She glanced about. No one was watching, so she stepped inside and looked around.

The gatehouse had two rooms: an office and the living quarters. In the office, below a window that faced into the compound, a large gray journal labeled with Chinese characters lay on a desk. Another window, shuttered, faced the street outside the compound.

There were no pictures on the wall except for a small calendar showing Jesus calming the Sea of Galilee. The disciples huddled in terror, their mouths frozen open in silent shrieks.

Ling had gone through an open arch into the living quarters. A large *kang* nearly filled the room, with a stovepipe from a brick cauldron threaded into its side.

Elsa had seen *kangs* in the huts she'd visited with Papa—brick platform beds as high as her waist and wide enough for the whole family to sleep in a row. During the day, with the blankets rolled up against the wall, it became a nice place to sit and work, eat, or play. The hot pipe from the cauldron kept it toasty warm.

Elsa thought that was a very cozy way to live. She wished her family used a *kang* instead of sleeping in separate bedrooms all strung out down the hall, with hers far away at the very end.

Against the opposite wall stood a small chest of drawers, and above that hung an embroidered bamboo scroll: two birds on a single branch of cherry blossoms.

Ling went to the dresser, brought back a square black tin, and motioned Elsa to sit on the *kang*.

She hesitated. He grinned and said, *"Buh yao pah." Do not fear.*

She made a face at him, hitched herself up next to the curled-up blankets, and pulled up her *kuhdze* legs.

Ling cleaned her elbows and knees with a damp rag and smeared on the salve. It smelled like kerosene and sweaty feet, but it felt soothing, much better than Mama's awful, stinging iodine. "Now the *maobing* will go away," he said.

"Thanks. It feels better already." Elsa jumped down from the *kang*, and they started to leave. Then she noticed in the corner of the office three narrow stone steps going up and angling to one side. She pointed and said to Ling, "What's up there?"

Ling glanced over. "The bell tower."

"Are you the one who rings the bell for church services?"

His eyes sparkled. "I am the one."

Elsa laughed. She knew that the word *ling* meant "bell." She asked, "May I go up and see it?"

Ling hesitated. He looked around, and then shrugged. "If you wish."

Upstairs, a huge copper bell hung from a beam, a thick rope dangling from its base. In a corner of the bare floor lay a tablet, an ink pot, and a slender brush. Ling pushed them aside with his foot, but Elsa stooped to look more closely. It was a sketch of a train, with people crowding toward the station.

Elsa asked, "Who drew this?"

Ling's golden skin turned orangey-red. "It is also my duty to watch for strangers coming to the compound. The hours go slowly, and sometimes I sketch."

"I wish I could draw like that."

"My teachers say drawing wastes time. But when—*if*—I can go to the university, I will study painting. For my own pleasure."

"The university? Where?"

"In Peking. This year, I finish classes in the village school. But I wish to study more. In the university there is much to learn, many different things. Who knows? I might even become a doctor."

A doctor! Elsa stared at him in awe. Her thoughts raced ahead. If she grew up to be a nurse, then when Ling was a doctor, they could work together in the clinic. People from villages all around would come and stand in line, waiting to be healed. They would become famous all through China, she and Ling . . .

A small, barred window faced the train station. Elsa looked again at the sketch, then back at the station. He'd captured the whole scene: across the tracks, the road led to the village of Shiao Yangshan, and beyond that, the spire of the Catholic mission stabbed the sky.

The Catholic mission. She shivered, remembering that rainy night, Jasper still missing, Mama's coldness.

"I want to go downstairs now," she said.

Ling flicked the bell with his fingernail, and a dull *plunk* echoed in the tower. He scampered down the steps with the carelessness of habit. Elsa followed more slowly, trying not to bend her sore knees.

Downstairs, Choi had returned to the office. His mouth opened when he saw Elsa. Then he bowed to her, his eyebrows still raised. He said, "Eternal Virtue honors us with her presence."

That was odd. Choi had never talked formally to her before. She glanced at Ling.

His face colored again, and he looked down.

Was she in trouble again? Would Choi tell Mama she'd disobeyed and come into the gatehouse?

"I fell," she explained, pointing her elbows at him. "Ling put salve on them."

"Ah!" Choi nodded. "Very good medicine." He turned to Ling. "Go tell the *mushih* I have hired an oxcart for his journey tomorrow."

Ling sidled past his father and ran toward the church.

Elsa peeked out the door. No one else was in the compound. She walked slowly back to the house, careful this time not to trip on the iron wedge.

THE NEXT WEEK, THE NURSES were back, and the clinic opened again. Elsa kept busy helping them, and the summer passed quickly. When fall came, Elsa studied science and math with Miss Bergen, in addition to her classes with Mama. Miss Bergen was an interesting teacher, not strict like Mama, and she didn't mark all her papers with red pencil.

Every time Elsa walked to the clinic or ran errands, she looked through the open-brick wall to see if Ling was around. Often, he worked in the front compound, raking the sand or whitewashing the workers' apartments. When he saw her, he would come over, and they would talk until Miss Bergen called her into the clinic or Choi called him back. Sometimes he taught her poems or songs from school, and once he brought her a smooth, round stone. He told her to keep it in her pocket and rub it whenever she was troubled. That would ease her spirit.

When Ling came home from the village school, he wore his navy blue uniform with brass buttons straight down the middle of the jacket. With his matching visor cap, he looked as noble as General Chiang Kai-shek.

Sometimes he brought his friends along into the front compound, and they jostled around, laughing, making faces, and mimicking their teachers. They marched and postured like soldiers, pretending to carry guns.

Sometimes they played *jiandze,* using a shuttlecock made from a cloth-wrapped coin attached to sparrow feathers. They would stand on one foot and bat the object up with the side of the other shoe, over and over, counting until they'd miss.

Elsa watched the boys and decided that Ling was the most handsome. She was certain he was the smartest, too.

He could also spit farther than any of the other boys. Elsa, fascinated, watched him hawk until his mouth was full of saliva and mucous and then send a stream shooting through the air in a graceful arch, landing in a viscous little puddle on the sandy ground.

His friends competed with him, but when they measured the distances with a piece of string, Ling was always the winner. Then he would strut like a rooster, his chin up, thumbs under his arms, and the others would laugh and slap him on the back.

Elsa, peeking through the open designs of the wall, applauded silently. He was a prince, her Ling. She envied the boys who were with him in school all day.

One spring afternoon, when Elsa went to get the nurses some tea, Ling came into the front yard with a tiny sandalwood box in his hands. Through slits carved in the frame, she saw something move. Then it chirped, and she realized it was a cricket.

Ling told her, "It is a gift for you."

Surprised, she held the little cage up to let the sunlight shine through. "Thank you. What does he eat?"

"Many things. Leaves, grain, crumbs." Ling opened the cage just far enough to poke his finger in. "If you stroke his back, he will sing to you."

The cricket shrilled, *"Cher-key, cher-key."*

Elsa's insides tickled all the way from her throat to her stomach. "May I pet him?" she asked.

They sat close together on a brick flower border. Elsa could feel Ling's breath on her cheek. He held the cage so she could put in her finger without letting the cricket out.

"I'll call him *Cherky*," she said. "I'll keep him on my windowsill so he can see the first sunbeams in the morning."

"You must not let your cat find him. He would make a very nice meal for her."

Mama was not pleased to see Cherky and told Elsa she'd have to keep him locked up. "If he gets out, he'll get squashed."

Elsa looked down at Mama's sturdy Mongolian boots. "I'll be careful. He won't get out." She put the cage on the windowsill and ran to get the tea for the nurses.

Chapter 14

THE NEXT DAY, AFTER HER CLASSES, Elsa looked through the open-brick wall and saw Ling standing on one foot by the gatehouse, playing a solitary game of *jiandze*. Over and over, he popped the shuttle into the air with the side of his foot. Elsa counted past fifty, then lost track. He still hadn't missed.

She called to him, "Come here and teach me to do that!"

Ling snagged the shuttle with his hand and came to the wall, peering through the curved design. "I must keep watch in the tower today. My father is going to the village. But tomorrow I will show you."

"May I come up to the tower, too?"

Ling looked away. "My father does not allow others to distract the watchman. It would make much trouble."

So that's why Choi had acted so strange when he'd found her in the gatehouse. But if he wouldn't be home . . .

"Just for a little while? I wouldn't bother you."

Ling coughed lightly and tossed the shuttle from one hand to the other. He glanced at the gatehouse and back at Elsa.

Just then, Choi came out of the gatehouse. "Ling! *Gan-kuai!* Make haste!"

"I must go." Ling turned and ran. He shouted over his shoulder, "I will come tomorrow."

Elsa kicked the gravel in gray puffs. Now there was nothing to do. Tsao Po-Po was busy doing laundry. Papa was in his study, planning a sermon. Mama was working out Bible study plans with Sen Ying in the parlor. Elsa called Empress, but the cat was watching a sparrow build a nest and only twitched the tip of her tail.

Elsa remembered the stone Ling had given her, and took it out of her pocket. Was it true that rubbing it would ease her spirit? She rolled it in her fingers, but didn't feel any different. Then she smelled hot oil and followed her nose into the kitchen, where Fu Liu was busily chopping vegetables with a huge, square cleaver.

The cook smiled, but his curled lip sneered. Elsa was still a little nervous around him, especially with that sharp cleaver in his hand. With his high cheekbones, narrow chin, and squinty little eyes, he looked like a fox. Could he be possessed by a fox spirit?

As she started to back out of the kitchen, he said, "Eternal Virtue would perhaps like some carrot?" His voice sounded friendly.

Elsa put her stone back in her pocket, took the piece, and edged away, watching the cleaver bobbing through the vegetables. She realized she didn't know anything about this man. Between crunches she asked, "Do you have a family?"

"Yes, yes." Fu Liu's curved lips widened. "I have two sons." He licked the end of a chopstick, dipped it into the hot oil, and watched it crackle and spit.

Elsa had never thought of him as being a father. "How old are they?"

"My number one son is three, and the second is yet an infant."

Elsa sighed. She'd hoped they were old enough to play with her. "Do you have any girls?"

Fu Liu deftly flipped the chopped vegetables into a colander with the edge of his cleaver. "My brother has two female children. They come next week to stay at our house."

Elsa perched on a stool near the work table and reached for another chunk of carrot. "How old are they?"

"Lihua has twelve years. Her sister Shirhua has ten."

Just the right ages! Fu Liu's sneer seemed less evil now, his face more human. "Can you bring them here sometime?"

He tilted the colander and the vegetables sizzled in the hot fat. "Oh, no, it is not fitting. They are too poor."

Elsa knew that was just Chinese politeness. *Kerchieh* decreed that one mustn't accept an invitation the first time or one would seem too eager.

She asked Mama for permission that night when Papa was there so he'd be on her side. They decided it would be all right if the nurses first examined the girls for lice.

After the third invitation, Fu Liu agreed. His nieces would visit the first Friday afternoon after they arrived.

Lihua, which meant *Plum Blossom*, was slim and graceful, with a pretty face. Shirhua, *Persimmon Blossom*, was short, a little chubby, and had a round, flat face with a snub of a nose. They wore drab gray pants and *pow-dze*, and like Elsa, had single thick braids down their backs.

Elsa politely asked after their health. *"Ni hao ma?"*

They covered their eyes, peeked at each other, and giggled.

She didn't know what to say next, so she skipped around the flower beds, and they laughed harder. When she started singing in rhythm to her steps they stopped laughing.

"I hear the river flowing, and I must sail away. . . ."

Lihua said, "I know that song. *'But my heart is sick with fear I won't return by day.'"*

After that, their shyness left, and they went with Elsa into the back yard and took turns swinging. When their father came to pick them up, Elsa asked if they could come again. After urging, he agreed to bring them the next week.

It became a routine, and the nurses gave Elsa Friday afternoons off to visit with her friends.

Sometimes, Ling joined them, and they played tag. The girls had no trouble talking now. Ling said they chattered like sparrows did in the early morning when he wanted to sleep. He'd tweak their braids and then prance out of their reach.

One day, he brought a handful of small, round pebbles. They all squatted in a circle while he showed Elsa how to cup the stones in both hands, toss them up, then flip her palms over to catch the pebbles on the backs of her hands.

Elsa thought the game was fun, but she always dropped most of the stones. Shirhua wasn't much better. But Lihua's graceful hands turned and flipped, and only a few pebbles fell. Slowly and carefully, balancing the catch, she dipped her thumbs and forefingers down to nip up her losses, flicking them one by one back up to nest with the others.

Then Ling, the prince, the champion, spread his long fingers slightly and caught every stone, winning the game. He arched his eyebrows and grinned before running off to watch in the bell tower.

Elsa called after him, "You forgot your pebbles!"

He waved. "They are yours."

After the girls left, Elsa put the smooth stones in a little tin box with her other treasures. She practiced playing every night, sitting cross-legged on her bed, trying to get as skillful as Ling. But she never could.

When the fall sandstorms came and it was too cold to play outside, Elsa asked the girls to come into her room.

Silently, they shook their heads.

Elsa sighed. *Kerchieh* was such a waste of time. But she obeyed the courtesy rules, gave the invitation two more times, and then they followed her.

They tittered at Elsa's bright clay birds hanging in the window. They giggled when she dumped out her box of spools and blocks and showed them how she made houses and peopled them with the spools. When she turned Glory over and made her cry "Mama," they covered their heads with their arms and shook with laughter.

Shirhua was fascinated by Cherky, sitting in his little cage on the dresser. Elsa took the cage down for Shirhua to hold. They sat together on the bed, talking, and Elsa showed her how to stroke the insect's back and make him chirp.

It was wonderful to have girlfriends. They were interested in everything Elsa said. She told them about Shungtau, how warm and green it was, and described the mission house with its arched veranda and wide lawn, the nasturtiums she'd nibbled on for their nectar, and the chestnut tree she'd loved to climb.

The girls giggled at the idea of a female climbing a tree just for fun.

Lihua talked about their home out on the plains, and about the daydreams she had while she tended the goats. She imagined being a princess with beautiful clothes and carved furniture and ivory treasures. She would own huge fields of oats and millet. But not poppies.

Not poppies? Elsa thought of the miles of beautiful golden flowers and the seed pods that could be split open for miniature dishes.

Lihua shook her head. "Poppies are not so nice. They make opium. People smoke and then sleep and sleep. Always want more."

"Does your father smoke opium?"

Lihua looked sad. "When he has money."

Elsa knew opium was bad. Papa preached about it a lot. But she hadn't realized that it came from those beautiful blossoms.

Lihua whispered, "Sometimes he steals money for smoke."

Elsa remembered the bandits on the river and told her friends about their money being stolen, along with Papa's watch and Mama's ring and best stockings. The books and other treasures had been thrown into the water, her doll's hair ruined, and the teddy bear destroyed. The jade bracelet was taken, one of a pair. She wondered if the men had robbed to buy opium.

"Where was the other bracelet?" asked Lihua. "Did you find it?"

"No. It probably fell into the water with the other things." Elsa stared at nothing, reliving the terrible night. Those bracelets had been so beautiful. Papa said they would be hers someday, but now that would never happen.

Lihua said that once a flood had washed away their house and they'd lost all their belongings. Everything. They'd had to start over with one goat and a borrowed iron pot.

Lost everything? That was much worse than just bracelets and books, even money, and Elsa pressed Lihua's hand. Then her throat tightened. "I remember that flood. My little brother—"

She covered her face with her hands. She hadn't meant to talk about him.

"You have a brother?" asked Shirhua. "Where is he?"

Elsa started to nod, then shook her head.

"Did he . . . drown?" whispered Lihua.

Elsa couldn't stop the tears. "They buried him in the back compound near the gate."

The girls cried with Elsa and told her she must put toys on the grave to make his journey happy.

Elsa brushed away her tears and wiped her nose on the sleeve of her *pow-dze*. She couldn't tell them that it hurt too much to go near his grave.

The next time the girls came over, Lihua said she would soon move to another village.

Elsa caught her breath. She'd just made new friends; how could she bear losing them so soon? "Why?"

Looking down, Lihua said in a whisper, "I am promised for marriage."

Elsa's mouth dropped open. "Why do you want to get married so young?"

"It is not my want; it is custom. Uncle Liu is the go-between to find us both rich husbands."

Elsa imagined Lihua in red-beaded brocade in a bride's sedan chair. "Is the man handsome?"

"I do not know. They say he is old and owns much land. I will be his third wife."

Lihua, twelve years old—her own age—getting married! And to an old man! Elsa couldn't believe it.

Tsao Po-Po had told stories about Chinese marriages. The young brides were practically slaves to the old men and their first wives.

Elsa thought of Lihua's graceful hands tossing pebbles. Now they would get red and chapped scrubbing kettles and stirring laundry in boiling cauldrons. Emptying chamber pots. Sleeping as a family on a *kang* might be cozy, but not if it was with an old man, his other two wives, and all their children.

"Well," she said finally, "I wouldn't want to marry someone like that."

Shirhua said softly, "If she refuses, she will be beaten."

Beaten! Elsa stared at the girls. Surely there had to be a way out. "I'll talk to Papa. Maybe he can help you."

The next morning, Elsa stared out the window, dabbling her spoon in her breakfast bowl of oat gruel.

"Eat your *yomein huhu*," said Mama. "It's time for your studies."

Papa, sitting at the head of the table, turned his head into Elsa's line of vision and narrowed his eyes. "Is something bothering you?"

She tried to form her thoughts into words. "I was just wondering— you know the cook's nieces? Lihua and Shirhua?"

"What about them?" asked Papa.

"Lihua is getting married."

Papa shot a glance at Mama. "Most Chinese girls are engaged when they are little. But usually they don't get married until they're older, maybe fifteen or sixteen. They have to wait for their bridegrooms to grow up."

"But this man's already old. She'll be his third wife."

Mama's lips twitched. She pushed aside her gruel and stood up. "Papa will talk to Fu Liu. He knows the church doesn't allow plural marriages."

Papa looked uncomfortable, as though he had bitten into a peppercorn, but he nodded. "Something must be done."

Elsa felt better. Papa was strong and wise. He could take care of any problem.

Chapter 15

EVEN THOUGH ELSA HAD forgotten about the boarding school, Papa hadn't. In May, the mail brought a fat envelope from Peking. A catalog of classes with pictures of the teachers, the grounds, and the dormitory rooms. Laughing students at parties and concerts, exciting ice hockey games, polo, tennis. Music and drama—real plays to act out.

Papa said people from America had sent donations, and they almost had enough money. If she finished the eighth-grade level by the end of summer, she could enroll there in fall as a freshman.

Elsa tried to imagine what it would be like to go away to school. It might be a relief to get away from Mama's strict rules and red correcting pencil, but she would miss Shiao Yangshan—the house, the big compound, all her friends, and the clinic. Tsao Po-Po's warmth and comfort, her stories. Papa.

Most of all, she'd miss Ling. But if he qualified for the university in Peking, he'd also be somewhere in that city. Maybe they'd find a way to see each other.

Elsa studied the catalog until she knew the pictures by heart. She chose her favorite teachers, decided which students would be her friends. There was even a girl named Crystal—the name of one of her imaginary friends. Surely that was a good sign.

Mama looked through an old Montgomery Ward catalog for fashion ideas, Elsa picked out two sweater patterns, and Tsao Po-Po started sewing and knitting. Along with the sweaters, there would be a skirt, several blouses, and three new dresses, one in green brocade. Mama dug into a box of used clothes from America and found a big, brown coat she said Elsa could grow into.

Elsa sorted through her things, wondering what to take along to the school. Her favorite books, of course; the blue hanging birds; and the Chinese checker game the Moffats had given them.

She put everything in a pile on her bed, then added her treasure box filled with the smooth little pebbles from Ling, some pretty feathers, chestnut tree pods, and seashells from Shanghai.

She looked at Glory sitting on the dresser. No, she was too big for dolls now. The spools and blocks? Mama would never let her take such a big, heavy box.

Cherky. If she left Cherky, who would feed him? She set the cage next to her treasure box.

"Why is your room so untidy?"

Elsa jumped. Mama had sneaked into her room. "I was just deciding what to pack."

"You won't be leaving for three months. Clean it up." Her hand flipped through the pile. "What are all these rocks doing on your bed?"

"Watch out, Mama, the cage—"

But it was too late. Before she could grab it, the latch jarred loose, and the little gate swung open. Cherky sailed out of his cage, leaped through the door, and vanished down the hall.

Elsa ran through the house calling, "Cherky, come back!" She heard Mama's footsteps behind her. *Please God, don't let her step on him!*

Her parents' bedroom door stood open. Had he gone in there? Or maybe the dining room? She looked under the bed, chairs, and table.

His little black body had disappeared.

Mama rushed for the broom, and Elsa followed her into the kitchen. Next to the stove crouched Empress, crunching on something black, her head turning from side to side to get a better grip.

Elsa gasped and pounced on the cat. "Bad girl!" She grabbed Empress by the throat and tried to force her mouth open. The cat growled, swished her tail, and slashed out at Elsa, then struggled loose and ran behind the cupboard.

Mama shrugged. "Well, at least we won't have to listen to that continual squawking."

Shocked, Elsa stared at her. How could she be so heartless?

Mama shook her head. "Don't look at me like that. There are hundreds of crickets outside every spring. And that's where they belong. Outside."

Tsao Po-Po came into the dining room to see what all the fuss was about. She stroked Elsa's hair and said, *"Muh yu guang shir.* Never mind. If your little friend was not eaten, he would soon die of loneliness. Much better for him to play with other crickets in the night."

Sadly, Elsa put the empty cage back on her windowsill. How could she tell Ling that Cherky was gone? Maybe Lihua could help her find another one so he needn't know.

But the next Friday, the girls didn't come over, and Elsa wondered if she'd offended them in some way. She asked Fu Liu, and he said, "Who can tell what females think?"

Elsa sighed. Cherky was dead, and now all her friends had deserted her.

Then through the window, she saw Ling strutting into the front courtyard and ran to meet him. Before she could stop herself, she'd blurted out Cherky's sad ending.

He sat down beside her on one of the little brick enclosures. "So sorry. I will find you another one." He thought a little, waggling his thumbs back and forth. "When I was small, my mother told me stories to make me happy. I will tell you a story."

"About a cricket?" Elsa felt better already. The sun felt warm on her back, the little trees were in full leaf, and around their trunks bloomed a wreath of petunias.

Ling shook his head, staring beyond the mission house at Shiao Yangshan Mountain. "It is an old legend. There once was a warlord with a lovely daughter. He locked her in his palace so she could not be seen by men who might fall in love with her."

Elsa inhaled the sweet fragrance of a single red rose on the climbing bush by the wall and moved closer to Ling.

"With only her old amah for company," he continued, "the

daughter was very lonely. She spent her days looking out the window and weeping."

"I wouldn't like that," murmured Elsa.

"Ah, but listen. Far away, among the cherry trees on a sacred mountain, lived a nightingale. Outside the girl's window was also a cherry tree, and when the tree was in bud, the nightingale would come perch on the branches and sing to the girl. The song was so lovely it opened her heart. Every day, the girl watched, and every day, the nightingale came to sing.

"One day, when the cherry tree was in full bloom, the nightingale came and plucked a blossom from the tree. The girl was enchanted with his charm and intelligence. She reached her hand out very slowly, so as not to frighten the bird.

"The nightingale hopped onto the girl's hand, and the girl took him into the room. She stroked his feathers and picked the flower from the bird's beak. And then something wonderful happened."

Elsa shivered with anticipation. "What?"

"A special magic from the cherry blossom turned the girl into a bird, a nightingale like her friend. Then they both flew out the window and lived forever in the cherry trees high up on the sacred mountain."

Elsa blinked back tears, and she touched Ling's hand. "That's the most beautiful story I've ever heard."

He seized her wrist in both his hands and pressed his mouth into her palm. His lips were very soft and warm, and Elsa felt as though dragonflies tickled her insides.

Gradually, she became aware that Miss Bergen was calling. In a daze, she pulled her hand loose and went to the clinic.

All day, Elsa didn't wash that hand. Whenever she thought about Ling, the story, and his kiss, her chest felt tight, and her stomach ached. She remembered Papa reading from the Bible about Joseph seeing his younger brother after years of separation, how his "bowels yearned after him."

At the time, she'd thought it was very funny, but now she wondered if this was what it meant.

The next afternoon, Ling limped through the gate, and Elsa ran into the front compound, calling his name.

He turned away to his own door without answering, but she'd already seen the cut on his lip and bruises on his cheeks.

"Tell me what happened," she demanded.

Ling shrugged. "It is nothing."

"Nothing! Then why is your lip bleeding?"

He snorted. "It will heal. And my enemies will eat bitterness."

Elsa stared at him, puzzled. Ling—her prince and champion—had enemies? "Were you in a fight?"

He postured and swung his fists at an imaginary opponent.

"Why?"

Ling's brown eyes flashed. "He who is different must bear the burden of his difference."

Elsa frowned, not understanding.

Ling laughed, a harsh bark. "Do not trouble yourself," he said, and then he hawked and spit a long, arched spurt. He wiped his mouth and said, "One must appease the spit god."

Elsa knew the Chinese believed anger and resentment could cause sickness. Tsao Po-Po had told her about a spit god who invaded the throats of men and had to be kept happy by their cleansing out the anger.

She wished she could get rid of all her jumbled-up bad feelings, too. Cherky's death, Mama's coldness and strict rules, Lihua's marriage problem. Red soldiers, bandits, the cheese man. Jasper's drowning. She'd prayed every night but still couldn't help remembering, and worrying.

Elsa juiced up as much saliva as she could, hoping to imitate Ling's magnificent stream. Only a little spray popped out, and this time Ling's laugh was real.

That evening she practiced spitting, aiming into the chamber pot. Mama came into the bedroom and saw her. She shook Elsa by the arm and said that was nasty. "Nice people don't spit."

"But Ling does it!"

Mama looked hard at Elsa, then said, "You see entirely too much of that boy."

Mama wouldn't approve of the spit god, either. Elsa sighed. She'd have to cleanse her feelings some other way. But she wouldn't stop seeing Ling.

SEVERAL DAYS LATER, THE clinic floor was dirty. Miss Bergen said, "Our houseboy is so unreliable. I wish we could find someone else."

Elsa's pulse raced, and she pretended to think. Then she said, "Choi's son, Ling, is a good worker."

"Oh," said Miss Penner. "I'll speak to Pastor Meier about him."

The next morning when Elsa reported to the clinic, the nurses were beaming. Ling had been at the door when they'd come to open up. He'd swept the floor, washed the windows, and comforted the crowd of waiting patients. All day long, he interpreted when the people didn't understand, and even held their arms for vaccinations.

Elsa watched him carry in boxes of medicines and cart away piles of dirty bandages. She saw trust in the people's eyes, respect in the nurses' manners.

Her heart swelled with pride. It was wonderful to have Ling for a friend.

Chapter 16

MAY AND JUNE PASSED QUICKLY. Elsa's legs grew longer, and if she stretched her toes, she could reach the pedals of Papa's bicycle. Papa taught her to ride around the tree-lined paths in the back compound, and feeling the wind in her hair and the power in her muscles was just as thrilling as swinging. But she always turned around halfway to the gate so she wouldn't see Jasper's grave.

Inside the house, Tsao Po-Po sewed steadily. A whole row of new clothes hung in Elsa's wardrobe, and her dresser drawers bulged with new underwear and pajamas. The pages of the school catalog curled at the edges and opened flat to the activity pages from her constant dreaming.

Then, in the middle of July, Papa called Elsa into his study.

Papa's study was his private place. He said it was where he wrestled with the devil and argued with God. No one ever went into it uninvited, not even Mama.

The walls were bare except for embroidered mottos that said "Trust in the Lord" and "Go ye into all the world." Beside a crammed bookcase stood shelves made from slabs of polished wood balanced on crates, the boards cluttered with open books and loose papers. In the middle of the room was a bulky, unfinished wooden desk—a sad substitute for the beautiful lacquered desk that Papa had sold in Shungtau—and two rattan chairs for visitors.

He motioned Elsa to sit down in one of the chairs, and she was surprised to see Mama sitting in the other, her eyes narrowed and her mouth twitching.

Elsa half expected the devil to peek out from under the desk, but all she could see was a worn-out toe of one of Papa's black felt slippers.

Papa was writing in an account book; bits of wrapping paper with scribbled figures and sums had been stuck here and there among the pages. He looked up and said, "Your mama and I have been talking things over."

That sounded ominous, and Elsa sat up straighter. She must be in terrible trouble this time.

Her mind swept through the day. Could it be the spitting? Her messy room? She'd broken a dish in the kitchen last week . . . It couldn't be the imaginary friends; she hadn't played with them for a long time.

Then Elsa caught her breath, knowing it must be her friendship with Ling, and her stomach twisted with dread.

Papa stared down at the account book, fingering its pages. "Fu Liu and I went to see Wang Hsien-sheng."

Elsa frowned, confused. "Who?"

"The man who bought Lihua."

The pain in Elsa's stomach eased; she took a gulp of air and let it out slowly. She wasn't in trouble, after all. It was only Lihua's problem, and Papa would say he'd taken care of it. He was the *mushih*, the missionary everyone respected. He could do anything.

She waited, smiling.

But Papa didn't smile, and he still didn't look at her. "He is not willing to release Lihua unless her father pays back the engagement money, the *ting chian*."

"Why doesn't he pay it?"

"That's the problem. He doesn't have it anymore."

Elsa felt her chin wobble. "Why not?"

"He said he bought a little land and some seed. That he made a bargain and must keep it."

Her friend was doomed. The ache in Elsa's stomach came back and crept up to her throat. She pictured a crotchety old woman, Number One Wife, beating Lihua for not scrubbing the cooking pots clean enough. Number Two Wife dressed in brocade, sneering at her. And Lihua in ragged clothes, her hair straggly, her pretty face crumpled and twisted with despair. "Isn't there anything you can do?"

Papa cleared his throat. "Maybe." He glanced up, his eyes sad and drooping at the edges.

Elsa stared at him. What was he trying to say?

"We could buy Lihua back."

"We? How?" Compared to the small, bare Chinese huts, their long brick house was a palace. But Mama always sighed over the household accounts, saying they would have to be very frugal until the next mission-board check came. They had to save carefully to buy books and holiday treats.

Papa looked at her strangely, his eyes almost begging. "The tuition fund." He folded and unfolded his hands. "That's why I called you in here. This would affect you the most."

Elsa felt as though somebody had dropped a wheelbarrow load of bricks on her. The pictures in the school catalog flashed before her eyes. The friends she'd picked out, the teachers who would smile and say her lessons were perfect. All her new clothes. Parties, hockey games, skating on the lake. A library filled with new books. And Ling close by at the university.

But if she had all that, Lihua would be sold forever into slavery, with no way of getting out.

Lihua had talked about her father's opium problem. He'd probably lied and spent the *ting chian* on his habit.

Elsa's face burned with anger, and a rotten, bitter taste of hatred and frustration boiled up into her throat. *What kind of cruel father would sell his daughter for opium?* It wasn't fair; it just wasn't fair.

Papa talked on, but Elsa barely heard him through the darkness of her own thoughts. "The wedding is set for next month. We must move fast." He reached out to her, pulling her around the desk and onto his knee. "It's hard, I know. But it's the right thing, the only thing we can do."

How could the right thing hurt so much? She knew that missionary life was one of sacrifice. People left their country and their families to spread the gospel. Mama spent a lot of time teaching the women, and Papa would even give away the clothes he was wearing if someone else needed them.

But they were grown-ups, and they had chosen to be missionaries. It was different when it was her life they were talking about.

Elsa squeezed her eyes tightly shut until she felt her whole being turn inside out. She thought again about the boarding school, the friends she'd have, the games and plays—and Lihua scrubbing pots and weeping.

She sighed. How could she enjoy herself, knowing her friend was suffering? "I can't let Lihua marry that old man."

"That's my girl," said Papa. "I knew you'd understand. As we grow up, we can't always do what we want." He gave her a hug and set her on her feet. "We'll save up again for next year, and maybe more donations will come in." He smiled, his eyes still sad. "Time will go fast."

Until now, Mama had been quiet. Now her glance flicked from Elsa to Papa, her eyes glowering, her mouth again twitching. "So it's decided?"

Papa raised his eyebrows at Elsa, and she nodded slowly.

"Only for one year," said Papa, his voice pleading. "I just don't see any other way."

Mama marched out of the room, not looking at them.

SEVERAL DAYS LATER, AS ELSA worked at the clinic, she glanced out the window and saw Ling strut through the front gate. He had asked for a few days off, and now her heart thumped to see him again, and her fingers tingled as though she'd leaned on her hand too long.

He gave a little skip and threw his cap into the air, catching it on the way down. But by the time he walked into the clinic, he acted just as usual. His face was calm, yet all afternoon as they worked together, his eyes sparkled, and his mouth fought a smile.

After the nurses left for the day, while Ling cleaned up, Elsa stayed on. She asked him, "Why are you so happy?"

Ling straightened up from packing a crate. He looked shocked. "Happy? Why do you ask?"

"Because I know you. Something good happened. What is it?"

"It is bad luck to talk about happiness. The evil spirits might snatch it away."

"Christians don't believe that. Papa says it isn't true."

"One cannot be too careful."

"Well, I saw you jumping around when you came through the gate." Elsa edged herself up onto the nurses' desk and crossed her arms. "So you have to tell me about it. I won't tell anyone else."

Ling opened the door, poked his head out, and spat. This time it was just a little spurt into the flower bed. He looked around and shut the door again. "There was an examination in the village last week."

Elsa thought of the tests in her correspondence courses. Long pages of questions always ending with an order to write an essay on something. Her lip curled up on one side. "Do you *like* exams?"

Ling shrugged. "It was very difficult. Many students failed."

"Did you fail?"

Ling picked up a packet of bandages and tossed it at her. It landed in her lap, and she flipped it back.

"Well, did you?"

He came close and whispered in her ear, "I received the highest score. I have been approved for university study."

Elsa yelped with delight. She jumped off the desk, grabbed Ling's hands, and pranced around him, turning him about. "I knew you were smarter than all the rest! I just knew it! You're going to be a doctor!"

Ling pulled his hands away and placed them on her shoulders, forcing her to stand still. He looked into her eyes. "You think that of me? Even though you are American, and I am Chinese?"

"Of course!" Elsa stared at him. "What's that got to do with anything? I'm so proud of you I could just—" She took a deep breath, threw her arms around him, and hugged him tightly.

She felt his hands on her back, at first lightly, then with an answering pressure. His cheek was against hers, so smooth, so strong. Her stomach fluttered, and she felt warm all the way down to her toes. Love and pride swelled in her chest until she could hardly breathe.

Then she remembered. He would leave, but she had to stay home.

How could she bear it? She shut her eyes and squeezed him so fiercely she could feel his ribs against her chest.

Suddenly, the door crashed open, and Mama shouted, "What are you doing? Elsa, go to the house immediately."

Ling's arms dropped, and he bowed his head.

Elsa stepped back and faced her mother. "I was only—Ling just passed—" Then she remembered she'd promised not to tell anyone his good luck.

Mama's face was purple. "Did you hear me? Go to the house. I'll talk with you later."

Elsa looked at Ling, but he had turned away. Slowly, she walked out of the clinic and down the gravel path. Why did Mama have to come just then? And what would she do to her, to Ling?

Mama didn't come to the house for a long time. When she did, she knocked at the door of Papa's study and went in. Elsa heard voices but couldn't understand what they said.

When they came out, Mama's eyes were red, and Papa's mouth was tight. He started to say something, but Mama shook her head. Instead, she told Elsa to go to her room. There would be no supper for her that night—and no more work at the clinic. Instead, Elsa was to stay inside and double up on her study course.

Elsa stared at her mother. "Why?" She thought of the warlord's locked-up daughter weeping at the window.

But all Mama would say was, "You know very well."

The rest of that month, Elsa read her lessons over and over. Animals of Peru, American Constitution, the life of Benjamin Franklin, multiplication of fractions—none of it made any sense. She could think of only two things: what was Ling doing, and what was he thinking about?

Automatically, she filled in blanks on her work sheets. What difference did it make whether or not the papers were correct?

When the last assignment was finished, Papa mailed the packet and congratulated her on completing the eighth grade. She would receive her diploma when the papers had been checked.

That was her graduation.

The next day, Mama told Elsa she could report back to the clinic.

Elsa hadn't seen Ling for several weeks, and she rushed into the building.

The floor was dirty, and boxes of supplies stood unopened.

Elsa stared open-mouthed at the nurses. She asked, "Where's Ling?"

Miss Penner was looking through the medicine bottles on the shelf and didn't turn around. "He won't be working here anymore. We have a new boy."

The new boy, Ho Shao, swept the floor, but he left dust in the corners and under the chairs. When the people were vaccinated, his face turned greenish, and he hurried outside to vomit.

Every day, the nurses had to remind him what his duties were. He giggled and nodded, but the next time he had to be told all over again.

Elsa curled her lip. It wouldn't take long before they'd ask Ling to come back again.

She waited, but Ling didn't come back. Each time she asked about him, the nurses were suddenly too busy to answer.

A week later, after all the patients were gone and Ho Shao had left for the day, Miss Bergen closed the clinic door and told Elsa to sit down at a table.

"I have something I want to show you," she said as she opened an anatomy book and set it in front of Elsa. She showed Elsa pictures of a naked man and woman and told her what all the body parts were for.

Elsa looked at the man's picture, thought about the cheese man, and felt ill. Why was Miss Bergen telling her this?

"My dear," the nurse said, "all men are the same."

Elsa looked at Miss Penner, who nodded her head. "They only want to take advantage of you. To do terrible things to you. You must be very, very careful."

Elsa wondered how they knew this. Did they know about the cheese man? Had someone done terrible things to them, too?

"It all starts with a hug and a kiss," said Miss Bergen. "You can't trust them. Not even the boys."

Boys? Suddenly Elsa understood. They weren't talking about the cheese man. They were saying that Ling— No! Ling was her best friend. He would never do anything to hurt her.

She slammed the anatomy book shut and marched out of the clinic. For a long time after that, she couldn't look the nurses in the eye.

It would be hard to face Ling, too.

But she didn't have to. Days went by, and still she didn't see him. Finally, she asked Tsao Po-Po if she knew where he was.

"Gone away," said the woman. "To Peking."

Gone away? He'd left for the university without saying good-bye?

Elsa went into her bedroom, took out the chamber pot, and spit until her mouth was dry and only air puffed out.

When she came out, she found Tsao Po-Po sitting on a low stool in the sewing room, darning stockings. Elsa sat down on the floor in front of her and leaned her elbows into the beloved lap. "I wish I didn't have to grow up."

Tsao Po-Po slipped the gray wool sock out of the darning heel and folded it with its mate. "That is the way of life."

"Does it come suddenly?"

"No. One day you will look back and think, 'I am old. When did it happen?'"

"Why didn't Ling say good-bye before he left for the university?"

"He did not go to university."

"He didn't? Then where—"

"They say he apprenticed to a bookmaker. Will learn a trade. No time for school now."

"But he'd just been accepted. He was so happy!"

Tsao Po-Po squinted, guiding a long gray thread into the eye of the needle. She was quiet for a while.

"Not happy now," she said at last.

"Why didn't he go to the university?" Elsa asked. When Tsao Po-Po didn't answer, Elsa persisted. "Will he go later?"

The woman shook her head. "They say students have one chance only."

Elsa thought back to the last day she'd seen him. He'd tried to hide his feelings for fear the evil spirits would snatch his joy away. But she'd made him tell. And now he was gone.

Could it be true? Had evil spirits really taken away his happiness? If that had happened, it was her fault.

Then she remembered. *Mama!* Mama had been furious and hadn't come back to the house for a long time. It all fit. Mama had sent Ling away.

Fury boiled up inside Elsa's chest, and she could hardly breathe. She couldn't remember getting up and going to her room, but suddenly there she was on the bed.

Everything nice had been snatched away from her: Jasper, her imaginary friends, Fu Liu's nieces, Cherky, the boarding school, and now Ling.

But it was even worse for Ling. His whole future was ruined.

Elsa punched her pillow until feathers puffed out of the corners. "How could you, Mama! How could you!"

Chapter 17

THE AUGUST SANDSTORMS ARRIVED in cold, violent gusts. Elsa stared gloomily out her bedroom window, watching furious gray swirls flatten the petunias in their circular beds. Now that she had finally been allowed a little more freedom, it was too uncomfortable to go outside.

But there was more than sand in the air. She'd heard a lot of whispering—from Mama and Papa, the workers, and people attending the mission services—about glorious victories for the Nationalist army, Communist guerrillas leveling another of Chiang's fortresses, the Japanese taking city after city, the Communists defeating the Japanese. Nobody knew what to believe.

Papa went to the train station every day, but very little mail came through. The last newspaper had reported that the Communist and Nationalist armies had combined and forced the Japanese back. The next day, a telegram from Reverend Moffat had said, "Japan takes Peking."

But all of this was far away. What mattered most to Elsa was that Ling's life had been destroyed.

She'd kept her anger bottled up long enough. Mama was in the dining room preparing for the women's Bible class, but Elsa barged in, unable to hold back anymore. "Why did you send Ling away?" she asked. "He had just—"

Her mother's lips tightened. "That's between his father and me. It was for the best. When you're older, you'll understand and thank me." She closed her Bible, stood, and left the room without meeting Elsa's eyes.

Resentment boiled through Elsa's veins. She wasn't a baby. Thirteen was old enough to understand anything!

She followed Mama into the kitchen, wanting to force an explanation. But at the stove, a scowling Fu Liu shuffled a lump of dough between his palms, and three long, gray ropes of oat noodles slithered down, coiling into a steaming cauldron. As Mama approached him, he spit on the floor and ground the splotch with his foot.

Mama gasped, and Elsa held her breath. He'd never dared to do that before, not in the house. She forgot why she'd come there, and waited for her mother to fire the man. To her amazement, Mama didn't say anything.

The man growled, "My brother is very angry. Better Lihua marry old Wang, and have a rich home. Mushih should not interfere."

"It was wrong for you to betroth her to an old man," said Mama.

At least Mama and I agree on that, thought Elsa.

But Fu Liu shrugged. "Better to marry than starve." He reached for the cleaver, bobbing the shiny square knife up and down through the celery and cabbage on the chopping board. "No food to buy." Deftly he scraped the chunks into the sizzling cauldron. The pantry door stood open, and Elsa was shocked to see how bare the shelves were. Only a sack of flour, some jars of canned tomatoes and green beans, and a few tins of meat remained.

Mama asked, "Where have all the provisions gone?"

Fu Liu grumbled, "Foreigners eat too much." He whipped the frying vegetables viciously with two chopsticks.

Only two weeks before, Elsa had seen the cupboards nearly full. She didn't think the three of them could have used up all that food. All along, he must have been dipping into the pantry for his own use. Now it looked as if he'd sold food by the sackful.

Elsa waited for her mother to scold him, but Mama only said, "Go ask in the country. Surely you can find some food to buy."

"Nothing there. Many, many soldiers come through and tear out grain." Fu Liu slashed out with the cleaver, and Elsa was glad she was standing out of his arm's reach.

He added, "Steal pigs, goats. Kill them and feed the troops." Turning back to the stove, he cursed into the vegetables.

Soldiers? Here? Elsa remembered the sounds of gunfire at the Shungtau mission, her family's escape to the mountains, and coming back to burned buildings and ravaged fields. But Shungtau had been an important town. It couldn't happen here, in this remote little village!

She heard shouting outside and ran to the parlor. Papa opened the door, and she saw Choi, his face gray, his hands shaking. Behind him marched five smartly uniformed Japanese soldiers. They pushed into the house, and the commander announced in English, "This village is now under Japanese occupation, and you are under house arrest."

Papa invited the men into his office, and Elsa could hear the commander demanding credentials and shouting threats. Papa's voice sounded calm, and she couldn't understand his words through the closed door.

After a long time, while Mama had Fu Liu keep the noon meal hot, the commander marched out of the office, throwing Papa's documents on the floor. The other soldiers followed him, and they slammed out the front door.

Papa picked up his papers and asked Tsao Po-Po to go tell the nurses to box up the medical supplies and lock up. There would be no more clinic for the sick people of Little Goat Mountain.

From then on, shifts of Japanese guards marched in the front compound, shouting, laughing, and tormenting any Chinese in sight.

Only Choi was allowed to come and go with messages and mail. He reported beatings in the village, even torture and murders. Every day, Elsa heard of some workers and their families leaving, tunneling under the mud walls of their apartments and sneaking out at night. It wasn't long before most of the rooms lining the compound stood empty.

Mama didn't need to fire Fu Liu. One day he disappeared, and Tsao Po-Po took over the kitchen.

The days dragged by slowly, and it was hard to find things to do. Mama knitted stockings and an afghan and cried as she wrote in her journal. Papa spent a lot of time in his study, and their family prayers were long and earnest. Elsa begged Papa, and he persuaded the Japanese commander to let Tsao Po-Po move into the house.

After three weeks of house arrest, Elsa had read most of the books in the house, drawn several tablets full of pictures, and even revived the imaginary Mealy Fray and Crystal to play Chinese checkers with her. Now she fingered her bedroom drape aside and peeked out to watch the usual long afternoon shadows of the guards trailing through the front compound.

To her surprise, the yard was empty, and she opened the drape farther. The soldiers were probably in an empty apartment, smoking or playing cards. But most of the doors stood open with no movement to be seen.

Elsa went to Papa's office door, coughed politely, then called out, "Where are the guards?"

He came out quickly, smoothing his hair. She knew he must have been praying—his cheeks were flushed as if from the pressure of his hands. He went to the front door and opened it a crack, then held it wider, looking all around. Finally he slipped out, and she watched him go to Wu Shong's apartment. In a few minutes, the two went out the front gate.

Why hadn't he taken Choi? Elsa *had* to find out.

Mama was in the kitchen with Tsao Po-Po, but Elsa knew there would be no use to ask permission. Quickly, she sneaked out to the gatehouse and looked through the open window.

Choi wasn't at his desk, so she pushed the door open and called softly, "*Wei?* Hello?"

There were no bedrolls on the *kang,* no bowls on the shelves. Over the desk, the calendar with its picture of Jesus calming the sea hung crookedly, and the screaming disciples dangled above the waves.

Choi and his wife had deserted, too. How would she ever find Ling now?

She climbed up to the bell tower and looked out the window toward the village. It looked peaceful, as though nothing bad had ever happened. There were no soldiers, no dead bodies, and no signs of struggles.

Turning to leave the room, she noticed a scrap of paper on the floor. Picking it up, she saw it was Ling's drawing of the train station, with the tracks disappearing into the horizon. In the distance were a blur of the village and the spire of the Catholic church.

Holding the paper to her chest, she closed her eyes and breathed deeply. She felt Ling beside her; if she reached out, she could touch him.

She opened her eyes and looked around, but no one was there. She folded the paper and hid it in her *pow-dze* pocket, then went back to the house.

When Papa returned from the village, he looked puzzled. "It's like a ghost town. Most of the stores are boarded up, and few people are on the streets."

Elsa asked, "What about the Japanese?"

"I didn't see any."

"Then who's in charge?" asked Mama.

Papa held out his palms in bewilderment. "No one seems to know."

Mama stared at him, a smile dawning in her face. "Philip, this is our chance! Let's leave. Today, right now, before the Japanese come back."

But Papa shook his head. "How can we? Travel's still restricted, and we haven't received our papers."

There was a scratch at the door, and when Papa said, "*Lai!* Come in!" Wu Shong brought them a telegram from Shendong. Papa read aloud: "Moffat missing. Pray."

Mama slumped into a chair, and Papa put his arms around her shoulders. She moved away from him and asked, "He's been kidnapped. Is that what you want for us, too?"

Elsa went into the kitchen to find Tsao Po-Po. "Why would someone take a good man like Reverend Moffat?"

"Maybe for money; maybe to scare foreigners away," said the woman. "People are crazy now."

Pushing her knuckles against her mouth to plug the sobs, Elsa asked, "Will they hurt him?"

Tsao Po-Po hunched her shoulders. "Who can tell? If they don't get what they want . . ."

Days went by with no news of Reverend Moffat. The next time Papa went to the train station for mail, he came back with two Chinese officials and an American representative from the Peking consulate. He took Mama and the men into the study and closed the door.

Elsa put her ear to the door, but Tsao Po-Po flicked her hand. *"Buh, buh."* She nudged Elsa ahead of her until they reached the sewing room, which now was also her amah's room.

Elsa felt very tired, and her stomach ached. "I don't feel well," she said. "Would you please sing to me?"

Tsao Po-Po's eyes looked sad, and she pulled her lips tightly over her teeth. "Ai-yah, Eternal Virtue, my heart eats bitterness. I cannot sing." She began to weep, covering her eyes with her sleeve.

Elsa put her arms around Tsao Po-Po and suddenly realized she was taller than her old amah. "Don't cry. I'll sing to you."

But the woman only wept harder. When Elsa pressed her, all she would say was "Hard times, hard times. And more to come."

Elsa thought about all the hard times they'd been through. Red soldiers, bandits, Jasper's drowning, the Japanese. But God had protected them, and they'd come through all right. Even if they were low on food, they still had the garden.

She remembered acting out the Joseph story, how she'd wanted all the hungry people to be grateful and bow to her. Now, that seemed so silly. This famine was real, and she would have to be brave. It, too, would pass.

She heard doors open and shut. Looking out through the window, she saw the officials leave. Papa and Wu Shong walked out, too, going into the storerooms and bringing barrels and boxes into the house.

Elsa stared at the containers. The last time she'd seen them was when they'd arrived here from Shungtau. They couldn't go back there; not with the Communists in command. There wasn't any place to hide on Little Goat Mountain.

She went into the parlor and asked Mama, "Where are we going this time?"

Mama took a deep breath, and her eyes sparkled as she smiled. "California." She went into her bedroom and started folding clothes and bedding.

Elsa followed her and watched her hands working quickly. It had been a long time since her mother had smiled like that.

But California? That was in America! Elsa frowned and asked, "Why?"

Papa came down the hall with another barrel and answered, "The consul thinks it best that we go now while it's safe to travel. Don't worry, Dumpling. You'll like it there."

A shiver went up Elsa's spine, and her arms prickled. They were going to the other side of the world! She'd always known that Mama wanted to go back to America, but this news was too sudden, too definite. "When will we come back?"

Papa patted her shoulder. "I don't know. Maybe when things settle down. Right now, foreigners aren't welcome in China."

Elsa heard a sob, and turned to see Tsao Po-Po, tears streaming down her cheeks, taking down bamboo paintings and rolling them into thin cylinders.

"It's beautiful in California," said Mama, moving on into Elsa's room. "Nice houses and furniture, trees, lawns, running water, and electricity. Indoor bathrooms." She briskly folded Elsa's winter things and tucked them into the bottom of the box. "Wait until you meet all our relatives. You'll love having cousins to play with."

Elsa shook her head. Those relatives—aunts, uncles, cousins, grand-parents—they were all strangers, shadowy faces in small snapshots.

Mama went on, her arms moving in rhythm. "We'll be safe and happy. After all, America's our *real* home."

In shock, Elsa stared from Papa to Mama and clenched her fists. "No! *This* is our home. This is where we belong!"

She felt a love so fierce it hurt her chest. The big back compound, with its sandy paths where she could run free and wild. The syc-amores, tall now, standing in a row. Her swings. The church. The clinic. The front courtyard, with its little trees. The low, brick flower borders where she and Ling had sat so often. The gatehouse, with its bell tower.

Mama's voice, speaking to Tsao Po-Po, broke into her thoughts. "We must work fast. The *mushih* wants us packed in two days."

Two days! "What about our friends? The people? Ling?" Elsa said. Tears blurred her eyes. No, no, no! It was unthinkable. She couldn't leave China without seeing Ling, without saying good-bye.

Papa gave her a hug. There were tears in his eyes, too, and he wiped them away on his shirt sleeve. "Remember how it was in Shungtau? Now *these* people are afraid to associate with foreigners. We have to think about them."

Elsa bit her lip. Wouldn't somebody hide them? The church people, all the patients they'd treated—had they all turned against the mission?

"What about the nurses? Are they leaving, too?"

"We've discussed this with them. They'll come with us as far as Peking, and then stay at the consulate until their exit permits come."

"Peking?" Elsa jumped onto her bed and sat cross-legged, hugging her pillow hopefully. "Why can't *we* stay there? I could go to that school—" *And maybe I could find Ling.*

Papa shook his head. "No. Now that we have our visas, we must leave before they expire."

"Does Tsao Po-Po have a visa?"

Papa glanced at Mama, then said, "China won't allow its own people out. Just foreigners."

"Then where—?"

"She'll go along to Peking, too. The officials say she can work at the consulate."

Elsa pressed her face against Tsao Po-Po's, and their tears mingled. "How can I live without my amah?"

She looked over Tsao Po-Po's shoulder. Her mother actually looked happy! She *wanted* to leave China!

Then Elsa remembered something worse. "What about Jasper? We can't leave him here alone!"

Mama stopped smiling, and at first she didn't answer. Then she said, "Jasper is in heaven now. Only his shell is in the grave. You know that."

Elsa ran from the room and out the back door, breathing short, ragged gasps. She sat down on the swing and hooked her arms around the thick ropes, pulling them around herself to keep from exploding with despair.

The ropes scoured against her arms, and she clutched them even tighter, defying the pain. She pumped higher and higher, the wind whipping at her face and braid. She looked down at the garden, the trees, the empty stable.

The animals were gone, either sold or stolen. She wondered who had taken Empress.

Past the wall, Shiao Yangshan Mountain looked solid and friendly, and she thought of their picnics there and of the little stream she'd waded in. Until the rains came with that terrible flood. And Jasper . . .

She let the swing die down, slid off the seat, and trudged down the center path until she reached the last tree before the back gate.

Suddenly, as though pulled by a will not her own, she flung herself on the grave. Over and over, she repeated, "Dear Lord Jesus, let me stay in China with Jasper."

When she felt someone touch her shoulder, she realized she'd fallen asleep.

It was Papa, and he whispered, "I have good news."

Elsa sat up quickly, searching his face. "We're staying after all?"

He kissed her cheek. "No. That can't be. But we just got word: the Communists released Reverend Moffat. He wasn't harmed."

Her shoulders slumped. It *was* good news. But not good enough.

Chapter 18

THE MAJESTIC *EMPRESS OF ASIA* WAITED in the Tientsin harbor, idly puffing circles of black smoke into the sky. Hundreds of evacuees stood waiting on the pier, their faces tense and fearful. Many wept.

But not Mama. Her face smooth and calm, she sat on the *peshong*, pulled her journal from her handbag, and began to write.

Beside her, Papa stood quietly, and Elsa knew he was as sad to leave as she was. Maybe it wasn't too late to change his mind. Things had settled down now; maybe the danger was over. She started to ask him about that, but he turned away and checked the carry-on luggage again, patting his pockets to make sure of the tickets.

The nurses had come to see them off and had loaded them down with messages. "Don't forget to call my parents," Miss Bergen reminded Mama. "Tell them I'm fine and will come home just as soon as our visas come through."

Miss Penner smiled wistfully. "I hate to leave. We'd just learned to know the people. I wonder if the board will send us somewhere else."

Miss Bergen gave a crooked grin. "Sure. Probably someplace where we'll have to learn *another* language."

Elsa, sitting hunched on a suitcase, perked up. "If they send you to Mongolia, may I come interpret for you?"

Mama laughed, and Elsa stared at her. She hadn't heard her mother laugh for a very long time, and it sounded so different. Mama told her, "No, they could take Tsao Po-Po."

Elsa's head drooped again. She and her old amah had said tearful good-byes in Peking, where Papa had found a job for her taking care of the consul's children. Elsa felt the ache of longing and knew she would never again have such a loving friend.

A swarm of bare-chested coolies, pant legs rolled to their knees, wheeled huge cranes toward the ship. Sweating, grunting, shouting, and cursing, they hoisted trunks, barrels, and crates into the large nets, guiding the swinging loads up into the steerage gate.

The hold slammed shut, the purser signaled, and the passengers streamed up the gangplank. Elsa clung to the nurses, suddenly feeling closer to them than ever before. This couldn't be real—she couldn't be leaving China and everything she loved! But Mama handed her a satchel and nudged her into the moving crowd.

After Papa showed the purser their papers, a steward took them to their cabin down by the waterline, where foam was splashing up against the porthole.

Elsa explored the stuffy little room. Narrow bunks hung on each side; above one was a hammock. Three tiny drawers were built into the wall, and a hinged board next to them drew down for a table. There was a small lavatory, with a chain to pull for flushing.

It all looked interesting, but Elsa missed her own room in the long, brick house. And she needed to breathe fresh air. "May I go back on deck?"

Mama frowned. "Not yet."

Elsa persisted. "I'll be careful. I have to see China one last time."

Papa said, "What harm can it do?" He told Elsa, "Go on. I'll join you in a little while."

Elsa gave him a grateful smile and went into the hall, glancing through open cabin doors at the strangers settling in, but she didn't see a single Chinese face. She scurried up the narrow companionway, dodging the busy attendants.

On the deck, passengers lined the railing three and four deep. The coolies had left the pier, and only a small crowd of friends still waited. Beyond the dock, past the trees and cabbage fields, was the city of Tientsin. The very edge of China, now ruled by the Japanese.

Elsa went on until she came to the lifeboats swinging one above the other. Behind them was an open space where the railing ended. She crept to the edge and peeked over. Far below, filthy water sloshed against the ship's hull. Oily fumes mixed with the smell of fish and garbage. Orange peelings, bones, and empty tin cans bobbed with the waves, and seagulls dove for hidden treasure.

The steam whistle bellowed. Elsa jumped up and went to watch the sailors hoist the anchor.

A throng of passengers came back on deck, crowding to the railing. In the distance, Elsa saw Papa beckoning, and when she went to him, he pulled her close. Mama was already at the railing, and they all stood together, searching the straggle of people on the dock until they spotted the nurses waving.

Those on board threw rolls of streamers to the ones left behind, keeping one end of the paper ribbons, holding the bond as long as possible. Someone on the shore started singing, "God be with you till we meet again . . . ," and the people on the ship joined in, weeping.

It was the saddest song Elsa had ever heard. Tears rolling down her cheeks, she reached into her pocket and fingered the farewell gift that Tsao Po-Po had given her: one of the treasured hairpins with the head of a lion. "For luck," her amah had said. Holding the pin tightly and leaning against Papa, Elsa sobbed with him.

Then the engines rumbled, the ship rocked, and the steam whistle blasted again. Papa grabbed the railing, Elsa grabbed Papa, and someone shouted, "We're moving!"

The pier fell away; the streamers tore and sagged into the bay. The people on the deck still sang, "Till we mee-ee-eet . . . ," and waved until their friends on shore were but tiny dots along the pier.

Elsa felt a sorrow too heavy to bear. This was final. Her life was over. She was leaving China, her birthplace, her home, everything she loved, never to see it again.

When the dinner gong sounded, Papa took her hand, pushing through the crowd until he found the lower dining room. A heavy smell of grease and meat hung in the air. A waiter showed them to a table and set down filled plates.

Papa's face turned pale. "Oh no, I'm going to—" He got up and rushed out the door.

Elsa eyed her plate warily: pale thin noodles and little balls of meat in a strange-smelling red sauce. Vegetables mixed in a jumble.

Raw cabbage chopped into a sloppy dressing. Little black lumps in a dish of something that looked like rice but tasted sweet. If this was a sample of American food, she would rather starve.

With irritating cheerfulness, Mama said, "Eat your spaghetti, Elsa. It's good!" *Spaghetti.* Even the name was strange. But she tasted it, and it wasn't so bad after all.

For the rest of the trip, Papa stayed in his bunk. He held a paper bag handy and kept groaning. "They ought to build a bridge over the ocean. Nobody should have to endure this."

Mama said she didn't feel well either, and stayed with Papa in the cabin, knitting a sweater.

Elsa felt sorry for Papa, but she thought Mama was foolish to stay cooped up in the stuffy, sour-smelling cabin, just sitting and wiggling those long needles. *She* would walk around and get some fresh air.

In the corridors, other children scampered around, but when she spoke to them, they ducked their heads and didn't answer or said, "Mind your own beeswax."

She tugged herself up the companionways and wandered around the deck, balancing herself against the pitching of the ship. China had slipped away, and all she could see was rolling ocean. The whole world was made of water, and there was no other life.

She thought of Jasper, his tawny hair golden in the sunlight, his head bobbing as he ran beside her. His body, limp and soggy from the angry flood.

She leaned over the railing and watched the green waves slam against the ship, splashing white foam up toward her. What if— what if the *feng-shui* had swirled Jasper's spirit down the river and into the angry sea? Was he waiting there for her? How would it feel to slide into the water, down, down, down, so far she couldn't come back up?

Under the waves, the water looked dark and evil, ready to pull her in and never let go. Hypnotized by the monotonous surge of the waves, she leaned farther, farther.

Somebody touched her arm, and she heard a man's voice. "Better stay back, girlie. It's a long way to the bottom."

She felt as though she'd been torn out of an evil spell, and followed the man back to the companionway.

The next morning, Elsa avoided the railing. Instead, she sneaked up to the first-class decks and found children laughing and screaming, crowding around a playground with games and swings.

She thought of her big compound in Shiao Yangshan, the swings Papa and the *yahbah* had made. The wonderful feeling of wind whipping her hair and face.

When one of the swings was empty, she got on and stepped back, ready to pump herself high. But a woman grabbed the ropes and said, "What are you doing, a big girl like you? These are for little children."

Elsa hung her head and walked away slowly, not looking back.

Mama was wrong. She wouldn't like America at all. The food was awful, and the people were unfriendly.

As she walked back toward the cabin, a beautiful woman came out of a nearby door. Pale blonde hair swirled on top of her head, and two long curls dangled over her shoulder. She wore a shiny, tight-fitting green dress and smelled like flowers. She asked Elsa, "What's your name, honey?"

"Elsa Meier. Are you an actress?"

The woman laughed and smoothed her dress over her hips. Her nails were long and red. "You might call it that. Did you live in China?"

"I was born there. Did you?"

"Peking. For ages and ages. Have you been to America before?"

"No. Mama says it's wonderful, but I don't think that's true."

The woman leaned her head to one side, studying Elsa. "C'mon. I'll show you some pictures."

Elsa went into the woman's cabin. Perfume bottles and face-cream jars covered the shelves, and a beautiful red, filmy garment lay on the bed. The woman saw her looking at it and said, "That's a negligee. Do you like it?"

Elsa nodded, and the woman opened her purse and took out some photographs. One showed a big white house surrounded by trees and a lawn. Another had people in fancy outfits, their arms around each other, laughing, leaning against a long automobile.

Elsa ran a finger over one of the pretty dresses. "Is all of America like that, nice clothes and big houses?" she asked.

"Most of it," said the woman. "There are lots of stores, exciting things to buy, and plenty to eat."

"You mean like milk and honey, and streets paved with gold? Like heaven?"

The woman laughed. "I don't know much about heaven, but there's a lot of milk and honey if you know where to find it."

The dinner bell chimed, and Elsa said good-bye and ran to her cabin. She announced, "I've made a new friend!"

Mama looked up. "That's good. Is she your age?"

"Oh, no," said Elsa. "She's grown-up. She has fluffy hair and the prettiest clothes. Her room is all fancy and—"

Mama's lips twitched. "You went into a stranger's room?"

"She's only a few doors from here. She showed me pictures of America."

Mama looked at Papa. Then she said, "Elsa, listen to me. Never go into her room again. Don't even speak to her anymore!"

"Why not? She's nice!"

"You must obey me. When you are older, you will understand. Promise me, or you'll have to stay in the cabin for the rest of the trip."

"But—"

Mama planted her hands on her hips and looked at Papa. "Philip?"

Papa raised his head from his pillow and said weakly, "Your mother's right."

"Oh, all right," said Elsa, kicking a slipper across the floor. How would she ever make friends if Mama wouldn't let her talk to anybody?

That evening after dinner, Elsa and her mother took a stroll on an upper deck. Leaning against the railing, very close to a gray-haired man, stood the beautiful woman. She wore a purple dress, even tighter than the one she'd had on earlier. Mama had said not to speak to her, but she hadn't said anything about waving. So when Mama looked the other way, Elsa lifted her hand and smiled. But the woman looked past her as if she weren't there and kept right on laughing and talking to the man.

Elsa sighed. Even the friendly people didn't care about her.

Day after day, the ship bobbed and rolled. The air grew nippy, and Elsa pulled on her *pow-dze* when she went up on deck. By the time they'd been on the ocean three weeks, she knew her way around the ship. It was like a city built in layers; the halls were streets, and the cabins little houses. Time had stopped, and all the people were doomed to live forever suspended in this watery world.

One evening as she took her usual tour, a flash of white caught her attention. In the distance, in a group of people, stood a familiar dark-haired figure in black trousers and a white tunic.

"Tsao Po-Po!" she shouted and darted across the deck. "Tsao Po-Po!"

She threw her arms around the woman. In Chinese, she said, "You came after all!"

The woman drew back and stared at her. "Forgive me, dearie. Do I know you?"

Elsa looked up into the woman's face and realized her mistake. Now that she was close, she could see the woman wasn't even Chinese. Too choked to explain, she flung herself away and scuttled down the closest companionway.

Under the stairs, she found a crawl space and curled into it. Something poked her thigh, and she reached into her pocket and took out the silver hairpin. Tsao Po Po's song ran through her mind: *I hear the river flowing, and I must sail away. But my heart is sick with fear I won't return by day.* Huddled in the corner, clutching the pin, Elsa sobbed until she was dry and spent.

It was nearly dark when loud noises aroused her. People shouted and hurried past, up to the deck. "Lights, lights!" they yelled. "We can see land!"

Elsa stuck the pin back into her pocket and climbed up the steps. Crowding in among the passengers, she saw twinkling dots in the murky distance disappear and flash on again. Mama came up to join her, and said, "There you are! I was getting worried. I wish you wouldn't always wander away."

Together, they watched the lights on the shore until it was very late, and Mama insisted they go down and pack.

Later, Elsa lay awake in the dark cabin, listening to her parents whisper. They talked about all the relatives they'd meet.

Papa said, "For your sake, I hope your parents will be there."

"Even if they'd swallow their pride, they wouldn't come that far."

"I wish I could make it up to you."

Mama was quiet. Then she said, "You have. You've brought me home."

Elsa's throat ached. She didn't care who met them—they'd all be strangers in a foreign and unfriendly country. Pushing herself far under the covers and curling up into a cocoon, she whispered a final good-bye to Jasper, Tsao Po-Po, Ling, Empress, Mopsy, and all her friends in China.

THE TRAIN SCREECHED TO A STOP, ending the last segment of the long journey to Fresno, California. Elsa stepped out into the dusty September heat of the San Joaquin Valley.

No coolies with handcarts fought over their luggage. No vendors begged them to buy enticing food and wares. No Chinese in padded clothes bowed to them and welcomed them with firecrackers.

Instead, trucks backed up to the wooden platform, where a boxcar waited on a side track. Here, even the coolies were American! Men with huge hairy arms loaded stacks of crates, all the same size with pictures of fruit on the sides. On a nearby street, dozens of cars whizzed by, honking and squealing around corners.

A crowd of strangers with light hair and pink faces approached them, all talking at once in loud and shrill voices. Relatives, friends, and people from the first church Papa would candidate in, Bethel Mennonite in the nearby town of Riverglen.

Elsa heard a long list of names: Uncle George and Aunt Mary, Aunt Nettie and Uncle Silas, Grandpa and Grandma Meier, Mr. and Mrs. Bauman, an elderly couple named Hiebert, who would be their neighbors. All of them looked the same; she would never get them straightened out.

Mama and Papa hugged, kissed, and shook hands with everyone.

But Elsa stared at the splintered train platform and the dry weeds between the rails.

So this was America. Rickety wooden buildings. The smell of rotting fruit. Swarms of tiny black insects swirling in the hot air, getting into her hair and nose.

Where were the streets paved with gold, the lands rich with milk and honey? The big white houses, the people in party clothes?

She turned, thinking to climb back into the train, but Mama caught her arm and said, "Elsa, this is Regina Bauman. I'm sure you'll be good friends."

Regina was about Elsa's size but looked cool and tan in a green-checked pinafore dress. Her blonde hair hung to her shoulders in perfect golden curls.

She grinned at Elsa until the adults turned their backs. Then slowly, deliberately, she wrinkled her nose and stuck out her tongue.

Elsa drew back for a minute, shocked. Then she raised her chin and returned the compliment.

Part 2

Chapter 19

October 1938

IN HOT CALIFORNIA SUNSHINE, Elsa trudged the seven blocks home from high school, trying to stay in the shade of the sycamore trees lining the sidewalk. Her arms were loaded with books and draped with the hated brown coat that Mama had insisted she wear because the morning had been cold. What she wouldn't give to be back in Shiao Yangshan, running on the sandy paths of the mission compound in her Chinese *pow-dze* or flying on the swings, her braid swishing in the wind.

Each day here was an eternity of confusion and misery, trying to find her classrooms in halls with endless doors, pushing through crowds of students all jabbering at one time, using words that hadn't been in Mama's English textbooks. Watching out for two-legged signs on restroom doors—in China, all the girls had worn *kuhdze*, long pants—and remembering to flush.

Last week, someone had offered her a sip of cool drink from a bottle. It had been tasty, so she'd taken a gulp and then nearly choked when it made her belch, fizzing painfully through her nose. Yesterday, it had been trick gum that stuck to her teeth.

Today had been the worst yet. During the last period, the exercise class that everyone called PE, she had enjoyed the running and kicking game called soccer. She'd even made a wonderful score, kicking the ball into the net from a distance.

But the teacher had yelled, "You with the red braid! The goal is in the other direction!" and all the girls had screamed in laughter, pointing at her. How was she supposed to know they'd switched sides in the middle of the game? It was hard enough to remember which team she was on; everyone wore the same bloomers and white shirts.

Surely boarding school would have been so much better, with other missionary children and teachers who understood them. The catalog had listed chapel in the mornings and prayer with small groups in the evenings to help each other get through any problems. Here, even the few young people in church seemed to think she was odd.

Elsa turned the last corner, finally reaching her house, and pulled open the squeaky screen door.

"Don't slam the door," called Mama, but of course, it was too late.

Elsa sighed. "I'm sorry." It seemed as if she was forever apologizing. She found her mother wearing a cotton print dress covered by a big white apron and kneeling over the claw-footed tub in the bathroom.

"No matter how hard I scour, these awful rust stains won't come out," grumbled Mama, brushing a sweaty strand of hair from her forehead.

Elsa knew she should feel sorry for her, but she couldn't. It was Mama's fault they were here. If Mama had agreed to wait out the war in China, where they'd had servants, she wouldn't have to work so hard. Of course, it wasn't wise for Elsa to say that aloud; it would only start another argument.

In this farming community, from what she'd heard, the Mennonite women did all their own work and expected the pastor's wife to do the same. Floors waxed and buffed, fruit canned, and a week's worth of baking done on Saturday. Cakes, pies, and the all-important rolls—those odd-looking, double-decker things called *tvehbachs*.

Mama had acted so happy to come to America, but ever since they'd moved to the town of Riverglen a month ago, she'd done nothing but complain. The parsonage was shabby, the linoleum floors were worn, and the mismatched pieces of furniture surely were discards of the congregation.

Papa was glad to have a car, but Mama said the old tan Studebaker must have been one the dealer couldn't sell. She'd scolded him: "With all the churches available, why did you choose the smallest in the whole Mennonite conference? If you'd just looked around a little, you could have done better."

But Papa seemed content here. Elsa suspected he was happiest where the need was the greatest.

As she changed into a cooler dress, she heard a rustling sound at the front door and then a sharp knock. For a crazy moment, she waited for Tsao Po-Po to answer it. But then came a louder rapping, and Mama called, "Elsa, don't you hear that?"

Quickly, she buttoned the shirtwaist, threw back her braid, and went to the door. Three women stood on the porch, all in dressy outfits, with dark straw hats over hair pulled tight into buns—*schupses,* they called them—and old-lady lace-up shoes.

"Good afternoon," said Mrs. Bauman, looking sturdy and confident. "Is your mother in?" Elsa recognized her as the wife of the chairman of the trustees.

A tall, thin woman introduced herself as Mrs. David Loewen, president of the sewing circle. "How are you, um, is it Elsa?"

The third one was tiny, white-haired Mrs. Thesman, whom Elsa had seen with the man who led the Sunday school openings.

Before Elsa could think of anything to say, her mother came forward, smoothing her skirt, looking embarrassed to be caught in everyday clothes.

But Mama was skilled in politeness. She straightened her shoulders and held out her hand. "Come in, come in! So nice of you to drop by."

Mrs. Bauman ignored her hand and pulled Mama into a smothering embrace, and the others followed her example.

Before Elsa could duck out of the way, they caught her too, all talking at the same time: "We're so very pleased the pastor and you have come."

"An answer to prayer."

"Hope you feel at home by now."

Elsa watched Mama step back with an extra-bright smile, and she bit her lip trying not to laugh. She had never seen her mother show affection, not even to Papa, and especially not in public. But these people all seemed to hug and kiss every time they saw each other, the women standing so close while talking that their breath was all mixed together.

Mama went to the faded corduroy sofa, straightened the knitted afghan on the back, and picked up a book from the overstuffed chair. "Please, sit down. Would you like a cup of tea?"

The women looked at each other, and Mrs. Bauman said, "We'd rather have Postum, if you have some." Her eyes swept the room, resting for a moment on the *peshong*, which Papa now used for a footstool, and the nested lacquered tables beside the sofa. "My, how fancy. I hadn't noticed these when we helped you unpack. Did you bring them from China?"

Elsa listened to her tone of voice more than the words. Was the woman criticizing or complimenting? Still used to the hidden nuances of polite Chinese conversation, she hadn't yet learned to read the Mennonite mind and wondered if her mother could.

"From Tientsin," said Mama. "They were quite inexpensive." She'd mentioned once that Germans had a great respect for thrift, always looking for bargains and asking how much others had paid for things.

A lot of the church people had helped them settle in—they'd brought chicken casseroles and peach pies and swept, scrubbed, and unpacked until everything was tidy. But they'd also eyed each item as if pricing all the Chinese mementos Mama had collected over the years: cloisonné vases, rugs, handmade silverware.

Now Mama raised her eyebrows at Elsa and said pointedly, "You know where the Postum is, don't you?"

Elsa did, but she couldn't get used to being a servant in the house. Grudgingly, she went into the kitchen and searched through the shelves before finding the jar of instant coffee substitute way in the back. Mama would also want something for the women to nibble on. Last Saturday, her mother had tried baking those *tvehbachs*, but it now being Friday, there were none left. That was probably good, because they hadn't turned out as fluffy as the ones the women had brought over at welcoming visits, and most of the tops had fallen off. Instead, Elsa rummaged around, found some leftover sponge cake, and cut small pieces of that.

When Elsa went back into the parlor, Mrs. Thesman was saying, "I'm a little hard of hearing. When you and the pastor gave your testimonies, I didn't get it all." Her head tilted. "What did you say was your maiden name?"

Mama blinked, and Elsa watched her with curiosity. Mama never talked about her family. Would she finally describe them now? Why did these people think it so important to figure out everyone's background, who was related to whom?

She pulled apart the little lacquered tables, remembering conversations she'd overheard after church services: *"Ja, his uncle was a Friesen, first cousin to my grandmother on her father's side, one of the Nachtigals from Corn, Oklahoma."*

"Ach, what do you expect? She was a Knull on her mother's side; they weren't very refined, always a little bit prust."

The ladies watched Mama, practically holding their breaths, until finally she answered, "Carlisle." When they still stared, she added, "from Canfield, Indiana."

They mouthed, "Oh," and nodded, frowning a little. Mrs. Thesman's eyes seemed sympathetic, as though working out a way of acceptance for Mama's obviously non-Mennonite background.

Finally Mrs. Bauman asked, "But you were baptized into the church?"

Mama lifted her chin. "I joined Philip's church in Henderson, Nebraska. Soon after that, we left for China."

"Ja, well," said Mrs. Loewen, patting her on the arm, "I guess our mothers all hung our diapers under the same sun."

Mrs. Thesman's forehead smoothed, as though relieved that she would be allowed to accept Mama. "I heard you taught in the mission school? Arthur—Mr. Thesman—wondered if you'd be willing to take the intermediate Sunday school class."

Elsa eyed Mama again. This was almost as good as watching a Ping-Pong match. She could just see her mother leading the class, making them sit straight as the Chinese children, all loudly reciting Bible verses until they were memorized.

But before Mama could answer, Mrs. Loewen's eyes widened, and she nudged Mrs. Thesman. "Maybe the daughter could help with the primaries, too! Vera Hiebert said she needed a rest."

Elsa wondered if that might be a way to fit in. She could act out the characters in the stories—

But her mother tensed. "I—I'll need to speak with my husband first. Would you like some more Postum?"

Mrs. Bauman held out her cup toward Elsa. "I heard you had servants in China."

Didn't all missionaries? As Elsa went back into the kitchen, she listened for her mother's answer. "Life was so primitive—if we had hauled water and boiled laundry there wouldn't have been time for the Lord's work."

A score for Mama, thought Elsa. *Besides that, without servants we would have lost face to the Chinese.*

When the Postum was finished, the ladies rose. "Think about that class. Pray about it," urged Mrs. Thesman. "The Sunday school department needs both of you."

Mama stood at the window watching them get into Sophie Bauman's car and drive off. She sighed. Not turning around, she murmured, "How do they expect me to do all the housework, keep their pastor fed and well dressed and on time to all his meetings, and still have time to prepare lessons?"

For once, Elsa agreed with her mother. Maybe now they would get along better.

Chapter 20

March 1940

ELSA SAT UNDER A TREE ALONE, eating her sack lunch and watching the other students. They all clustered in noisy groups laughing and shouting, showing off.

She'd thought that after she'd survived her freshman year, the worst would be over. Those days, she'd worn the clothes that Tsao Po-Po had sewed and knitted for her for boarding school, and everyone had stared at her. One dress had zipper plackets on both sides of her waist, and the other had frog fasteners at the bodice. The sweaters were neatly made, but their colors were strange. Mama had bought her one American dress at a used-clothing store, but the next day at school, Elsa had overheard a girl whispering, "That dress she's wearing? It used to be mine. I always hated it."

All summer, Elsa had slaved in a fruit shed, cutting peaches for drying so she could buy material for stylish clothes. Today she wore a new suit she'd made—a green pleated skirt with a matching jacket—so she'd never again need to wear that ugly brown coat. Now that she was nearly through her second year, she knew her way around school and had learned what was expected of her. She'd even joined beginner's band with an old clarinet their neighbor Mr. Hiebert had lent her. That was the best class so far, as long as she didn't produce squawks that made the class giggle. Finally, she'd be just like all the others.

But no matter how hard she tried, she still didn't fit in. The kids—she couldn't see why they liked to be called little goats—all seemed to follow secret directions, know private jokes. She seemed to be the only one fumbling for clues, trying to say and do the proper things. She felt them watching her, waiting for her to make a dumb mistake so they could laugh.

Despite all the people around her, she felt lonesome. Even after all this time, she missed Tsao Po-Po's comforting arms, her generous love. Pretty Lihua with her smooth braid, and her sister, Shirhua. Ling, the most special boy in the world. There were a few girls here who whispered to her during class, especially if they didn't understand algebra or needed to know how to spell a word. But at lunchtime, they all hurried away to their tight little groups of friends.

At the beginning of this year, she'd made one friend—a Japanese girl named Tomiko, who liked to be called Tommie. But now even she and Tommie had quarreled and weren't talking.

Elsa sighed, folded her empty paper bag into her binder, and hurried to the school building. If she got to algebra early, she might get a front seat.

Her body hit a solid mass, and the crash sent her sprawling. Books and papers flew all over the sidewalk; her binder splayed upside down like a steep blue roof. On each side of it, she saw a huge black cowboy boot, scuffed at the toes.

Dazed, she stared at the boots; for an instant, she thought of her old imaginary friend Mealy Fray.

But this person had a deep voice. "Why don't you look where you're going, squirt?" Elsa's eyes traveled up long, hefty legs wearing dirty yellow corduroy pants. Above a wide leather belt, she saw a blue short-sleeved shirt, and thick arms crossed in front of a broad chest. This definitely wasn't her idea of Mealy Fray.

She scrabbled around, rescuing her books. "Why don't *you*?" She looked up farther—how tall was he, anyway?—to see a broad face and wavy blond hair, piercing blue eyes, and a wide mouth with a crooked grin.

He shrugged. "You ran into me."

She shook out her papers, trying to hide her embarrassment. "You could help me pick these up." *Ling would have picked them all up, smoothed them, and apologized no matter whose fault it was.*

"You're closer to the ground already." But he helped her gather the books, and when she'd stood and brushed herself off, he dropped them into her arms.

Then he squinted at her. "You know, you look like an elf in that green getup!" He strode away, his corduroy pants swishing.

Elsa grabbed up one last paper that had flown against the wall. Laughter rippled behind her, and she wished she were invisible. All her hard summer's work, all her careful sewing, was for nothing. She hated America, hated this high school, hated the boy who reminded her that she was still different from the others, like a goose in a flock of cackling chickens.

Elsa marched into the girls' restroom, looking twice at the sign to make sure. Inside the room at the wide mirror, three girls were applying lipstick and giggling. They all wore pleated gabardine skirts with coordinated jackets.

Elsa looked down at her own outfit, so much like theirs—except for the color. Why had she been so stupid as to choose green?

The second bell rang, and she ran to her classroom. It was just her luck that the only empty seat was near the back. But she hurried to it, glad that the teacher was busy writing on the blackboard and didn't notice her tardiness.

From behind her came a snicker, and her face grew hot. Tommie had said the boys who sat in the back of the room had nasty minds. Were they whispering about her?

She felt a sting on her right leg and rubbed the spot with the toe of her left shoe. Then another one, right above her bobby socks. Looking down, she saw two rubber bands on the floor. She turned to see where they had come from.

All the boys had their heads down, busily working on equations. All except one. Across from Elsa and one seat back sat the boy she'd run into outside. He was peeking over his propped-up binder, grinning that dumb crooked smile. Big block letters on the binder said *Morris Drake*. He mouthed, "Elf."

Elsa clenched her teeth. Would the teasing never stop?

From then on, she remembered to walk more slowly at school and to look around corners. She came to classes on time, sitting in the front of the room, her feet under the desk, skirt draped as far as it would go. If a rubber band came her way, it couldn't touch her.

A week later, at a time when the teacher's back was turned, a tightly folded piece of paper landed on her desk. She turned to see Morris Drake looking at her with that silly grin.

Why couldn't he leave her alone? She remembered Miss Bergen's anatomy lecture, and a chill rippled up her neck. *They all want the same thing.*

Without opening it, Elsa tore the paper into tiny pieces and swept them into her empty lunch sack.

For several days after that, Morris didn't bother her. At first she was relieved, but then she began to wonder what had been in that note. Why hadn't she peeked at it before destroying it? She began to sneak glances at him when he wasn't looking.

Morris was taller than all the other boys in the class. But he held his back straight and didn't slump like some of them. He didn't seem to have any special friends—just walked to and from class with his head up in the clouds, wearing that crooked grin as though he knew a private joke.

He was strange. Different from the other guys. Why hadn't she noticed him before?

She wished she could talk to someone about him. If only she wasn't still mad at Tommie.

Tommie had taught her so much. Americans didn't beckon palm-down with a clawing motion like the Chinese, she'd said; they turned their palms up and curled one finger.

They knocked at doors rather than scratching on them or standing outside clearing their throats. The people inside didn't shout, "Enter!" They just opened the door and said, "Hi! Come on in."

Kerchieh wouldn't do here. If she didn't accept an invitation right away, too bad—there'd be no more. And she should *never* use the standard Chinese greeting, "Have you eaten yet?" or ask older people their age.

At first, she hadn't told Mama about Tommie. Mama had been shocked enough to learn there were Japanese living in the area.

"You can't trust them! Don't you remember what they did in Shiao Yangshan?"

Then one weekend, Elsa's parents had gone to a conference. She'd stayed with neighbors and wangled a visit to Tommie's house. She and Tommie had experimented with hairdos, and before she'd thought about the consequences, Elsa'd let Tommie cut off her braid.

Mama had been furious! "You *know* that at baptism the girls in this church must promise not to cut their hair. You should do the same." It didn't matter, she'd added, that Elsa hadn't made that promise when Papa had baptized her in China. He hadn't made a lot of rules for the Chinese Christians because in their world, it was hard enough for them just to follow Jesus. "You," she said, "don't have that excuse."

Mama hadn't stopped with Elsa's chopped-off hair. She'd drawn the whole story out of her, including her friendship with a Japanese girl. At school, Elsa had tried to explain to Tommie about Mama's prejudice, and somehow that had been the end of their friendship.

Elf, indeed. Why had she let Tommie cut her hair so short?

During Easter vacation, Elsa sewed a new dress, a crisp cotton pique in the new princess style, nipping in at the waist, the skirt flaring out. The pattern of orange and lavender flowers reminded her of the nasturtiums in Shungtau, and she could almost taste the sweetness of their nectar.

She wore the dress the following Monday when she went back to school, feeling springlike and pretty, bravely smiling at everybody who looked her way. She was even bold enough to say hi to a handsome boy in her English class.

It was a beautiful sunny day, and Elsa's good mood lasted all through school. On the way home, she strutted a bit, feeling her skirt flip saucily against her knees.

"*FWEE-Fwoooo!*" A wolf whistle shrilled behind her.

Nobody ever whistled at *her*. But maybe, just maybe, since she'd worn her pretty dress . . . could it be that boy in English class?

"*FWEE-Fwoooo!*" There it was again, closer.

She wouldn't turn around. It was embarrassing if you looked and the whistle was for somebody else.

A bicycle skidded behind her, spinning to a stop just inches from the curb.

Elsa whirled around, clutching her binder to her chest.

"Oh," she said flatly. "It's you."

Chapter 21

MORRIS DRAKE STRADDLED AN old bike, his long legs trailing all the way down to the ground, his arm muscles bulging against the short sleeves of his shirt. He sat staring at Elsa with his strange half smile.

She'd thought she was rid of him. She looked around for somebody to call in case she needed help, but nobody was close enough.

"What do you want?" she asked, trying to keep her voice from shaking.

Morris cocked his head. "There's a long string dangling from your dress." He pronounced it *strang*.

A string? Had she forgotten to pull out the basting from the skirt of her new dress? She twisted around to find the offending thread.

"April Fool!" Morris whizzed off, bending over the handlebars until his knees nearly bumped his chin.

Exasperated, Elsa hurried on, taking a detour to the church to see if Papa was in the office. Maybe he could tell her what to do about that crazy boy.

It was a pretty little church, painted white, with a hand-stenciled sign saying Bethel Mennonite Brethren Church. It had a steeple, which used to house a bell, but the bell was gone now, and the space was now used to store old hymnbooks and Sunday school pictures. Sometimes, Elsa climbed the steep wooden stairs and looked out the tiny window. She'd shut her eyes, pretending to be in the Shiao Yangshan mission with the train station just beyond. Any minute, Ling would come up to ring the bell.

But when she'd open her eyes, all she saw in the distance was the Taft Grammar School and the Bright Haven Home for the Aged.

Now as she walked up the steps to the circular porch, she admired the lavender pansies and golden marguerites newly planted around the building.

Inside, the custodian moved from pew to pew, straightening the hymnbooks. He looked up and smiled. "You just missed your father. He left to visit Tante Krause in the hospital."

Disappointed, Elsa left the church. Then she saw Morris again, two blocks ahead, pedaling toward her. Walking faster, she prayed, *Please don't let him stop.*

It was no use. Again she heard that screech of tires, that circular skid. She walked on, ignoring him.

Morris trailed behind, pushing himself along with his big boots, one foot on the curb, one on the street. "That your church?"

Elsa shrugged, not looking at him. "Yes."

"You the preacher?"

She wrinkled her nose and turned to squint at him. "Of course not." What a dummy.

"Then it's not your church."

"Well, it is too," she said indignantly. "My *dad's* the pastor."

"Oh, a P.K."

"A what?"

"A P.K. Preacher's kid. Alias: *brat*."

Elsa turned and hurried down a residential street. "Look who's talking." At least she'd learned a few American phrases that weren't in a grammar book.

Morris followed her. "Yeah, well, I got me a good excuse. I'm an only child. You got any brothers or sisters?"

"Lots," she fibbed. "I've got seven brothers who can beat you up if you bother me, and a dog that'll eat you alive—what are you staring at?"

"There's a wasp on your collar."

Elsa scowled at him. Another April Fool's trick. Well, she wasn't going to be fooled this time. But something tickled right below her ear, and she reached up to brush it aside.

Fire stabbed her neck, and she stood as though planted in the sidewalk. Her mouth flew open, but she couldn't make a sound.

Morris threw his bike down and came toward her. "See, I told you. You wouldn't listen." He grabbed her hand and pulled her toward the nearest house.

What was he going to do? Her neck stung so badly she couldn't think. She felt like screaming but didn't want Morris to think she was a baby. Numbly, she watched him grab a hose from the lawn and turn on the faucet. She tried to pull loose, yelling, "What are you doing?"

"Hold still," he commanded. His strong hand clamped her arm like a vise, and her school books slid down and scattered on the grass. The hose squirted into a flower bed, and Morris dropped to his knees beside it, dragging Elsa down with him.

"Let me go!" she shouted. "Help! Somebody help me!"

"Hush up. I'm tryin' to help you." He picked up a handful of mud and slapped it on her neck. Brown slime trickled onto the flowers of her dress and ran down into her brassiere.

"There," he said. "Doesn't that feel better?"

Elsa struggled to get up, gulping in air to scream again, but Morris pushed her back down and clapped his hand over her mouth.

She stared at him in shock. What would this big maniac do next? Her mind flashed to the root cellar in Shiao Yangshan, the stifling hot breath of the cheese man. Now there was no *yahbah* to rescue her. Wasn't anybody home at this house?

Morris said something, but she couldn't take in the words. He kept talking, quietly now. "Keep your britches on. You'll be okay."

He knelt beside her, watching her, his face flushed and frowning and his arm holding her down. Slowly, he got up and released her, still watching her.

Elsa jumped up and backed away.

"Hey," he called. "Your books." He picked them up and offered them to her, but she couldn't move. Did she dare get close enough to take them?

He walked toward her, still holding out the books. She stepped back farther, taking no chances.

He looked at her with his half grin and said, "I told you to hold still. If you had, you wouldn't have got so dirty."

Then Elsa glanced down at her spattered clothes and gasped. The bodice was filthy and the back of her skirt was stained brown. "My new dress!" She tried to brush off the smudges but only smeared them worse.

"It's just mud," said Morris. "Good for stings. Guy back home, he died from a wasp sting. You gotta stop the swelling right away."

She looked at him doubtfully. "Well, how should I know? I've never been stung before."

"Not even when you were a little kid?"

"In China? Where I lived, it was too cold for wasps." *Why had she said that?* Now he would tease her like the other kids had.

But Morris didn't say anything. Elsa turned to look at him. This time *his* mouth was open.

Maybe he had been trying to help her. She asked, "What's the matter? Haven't you seen a red-headed Chinese before?" Funny, the wasp sting didn't hurt as much now.

He squinted at her, his head on one side. "You're not Chinese."

"Oh no? *Hao buh hao, Hsien-sheng!*" Inwardly, she shuddered. Why was she doing that? Her mouth seemed to be talking on its own. "*Wo jiao Yung-det.*"

She waited. But Morris just looked at her, so she asked, "Well, aren't you going to laugh?"

"What for? Was that a joke?"

"No, that wasn't a joke. I said, 'How are you, mister? My name is Eternal Virtue.'"

Then Morris did laugh. He threw back his head and laughed until tears ran down his cheeks, and his blue eyes vanished into two slashes under his bushy eyebrows.

Elsa grabbed her binder and books, hoisted them to her chest, and with all the dignity she could manage, stalked down the sidewalk toward her house.

Morris picked up his bike and trailed after her. "C'mon," he said between gulps of air. "I thought—I thought—you said—it wasn't a joke."

"It wasn't!"

"Eternal Virtue? A sassy little elf like you? I can't stand it." And he doubled up, laughing so hard that he dropped the bike and sat down on the sidewalk.

Elsa grinned in spite of herself. He wasn't laughing at her Chinese background; it was the name. That, she could accept.

She stopped and looked back at him. "My amah said it ought to be Eternal Mischief."

Morris exploded again, rocking back and forth. His voice came out in a weak falsetto. "Eternal Mischief. That's more like it. Oh, joy." Still laughing, wiping tears from his eyes, he stood and picked up his bike. Then he sobered and asked, "What's an amah?"

As Elsa walked slowly home, Morris beside her propelling the bike with his feet, she told him about the compound in Shiao Yangshan, Tsao Po-Po, the *yahbah,* and Fu Liu. Bottled-up memories flooded out, and she was surprised how good it felt.

Morris shook his head. "I'da never guessed it. You came all the way from China?"

"I don't like to talk about it."

"Why not?"

Elsa scuffed her shoe at a weed growing through a crack in the sidewalk. "Last year, I wrote an essay in English class. About the mission and all. The teacher made me read it aloud."

"So? Then it must have been good."

"I wish I'd never written it. Afterward, the kids asked me all kinds of dumb questions. 'Do you read backwards?' 'How do you say dumbbell in Chinese?' Stuff like that." She turned away, swallowing hard. She couldn't repeat that stupid rhyme they'd chanted: *Chinky, chinky, Chinaman, sittin' onna fence, try'na make a dollar outa FIFTEEN CENTS!*

Morris looked sympathetic. "What did you do?"

Elsa bit her lip, remembering. "I appeased the spit god."

"Come again?"

"The Chinese in our village believed that you had to appease the spit god when you were angry, or you'd get sick. So I spit."

"In front of the kids?"

"You know Regina Bauman? That giggly little blonde in algebra? Right beside her perfect saddle oxfords."

Morris laughed almost as hard as before. "You didn't!" He shook his head. "Eternal Mischief. That's you all right." Then he frowned. "Why her?"

They'd reached Elsa's front yard, and she leaned back against the sycamore tree. "Well, once my father invited her family over for *jaodze*—"

"What's that?"

"It's a special Chinese dish—little dumplings filled with meat and stuff. My mother and I worked so hard to make them. But they didn't like them. That day at school when everybody was teasing me, Regina said we ate pukey food. So I got mad and spit."

She sighed. It hadn't made her feel better. She'd been ashamed of her looks, her ignorance, her Chinese customs; and then she'd felt guilty for being ashamed of China.

Morris glanced up at the sun dipping toward the trees on the horizon. "Hey, I gotta go. Your seven brothers'll bust my head open and feed my brains to the dog."

Elsa shifted the books in her arms. "I lied. I've got a little wienie dog—a dachshund named Fritzie. But no brothers. Not . . . anymore."

"What do you mean?"

"Nothing. I don't want to talk about it." Elsa looked down at her dirty dress, and the wasp sting twinged. Suddenly, she realized how late she was and started toward the house. Then she stopped and looked back. "Why do you call me an elf?"

Morris shrugged and bit his lip. He looked down, and his face turned red. "Well, I just . . . I . . . you're so little. And kinda . . . cute." He spun his bike around and rode off.

What a crazy guy. Compared to Ling, he was big and clumsy. Mama would say he was crude. But he *was* easy to talk to.

She twirled around, letting her skirt flare, and ran up the steps to the porch.

Chapter 22

MAMA THREW OPEN THE DOOR. "You're late," she scolded. "Where have you been?" She looked past Elsa. Morris was still in sight, riding slowly, looking back at the house. "Who was that?"

Elsa started to walk past her, but Mama grabbed her arm, holding her in place. "Answer me!" Her face was a thundercloud, her lips tight.

Elsa shrugged. "A guy from school," she muttered.

Mama stared at Elsa's damp, tousled hair, then at the mud on her dress. "How did you get so filthy? You look like you've been rolling in a ditch."

Mama turned again, but now Morris was out of sight. "What were you doing with that boy?" she asked.

Elsa's face grew hot, and she shook her head. How could she explain that crazy guy? "N—nothing! He just—followed me home."

Mama took Elsa's other arm and shook her. Flecks of mud fell to the floor. "Don't lie to me! What did you do?"

Elsa pulled away. "I'm telling the truth! I—I got a wasp sting, and Morris put mud on it. That's *all!*"

"Morris, hmm?" She glared at Elsa, and Elsa dropped her eyes. In the back yard, Fritzie whined.

Mama gave Elsa another little shake. "That better be all. What will people think—the pastor's daughter flirting with strange boys?"

"I wasn't flirting. He just happened to be riding past." Couldn't she do *anything* without her mother getting suspicious?

"Just riding past? Do you expect me to believe that?" Mama flicked her hand at the stains. "I've been washing and ironing all day. Don't expect me to clean up after you, too. Take off that dress, and soak it in cold water." She glanced at the floor. "And sweep up this mud."

Elsa trudged into the screened porch, slipped off her dress, and turned on the water in the stationary tub. From inside, she heard her mother shout, "And from now on, come straight home from school. *Alone.*"

Resentment boiled in Elsa's throat—she could even taste it—and she made a face in the direction of the parlor.

None of this was her fault. She hadn't even wanted to talk to Morris. Why did her mother always make her feel so guilty?

Scrubbing viciously at the spots on her dress, she grumbled on. Mama never let her have any friends. It was Mama's fault she'd quarreled with Tommie. And Ling—

After nearly two years in America, she still missed Ling. She could see his face, smooth and glowing, his eyes sparkling. His foot batting the *jiandze,* never missing, his graceful hands flipping pebbles— scholar's hands, now probably rough from tanning boot leather. His life was ruined, and she would never again have a friend like him. All because of Mama.

Elsa looked down at the dress. Most of the stains had come out. She'd sewn it so carefully, and had loved wearing it. Now it would never be the same. Every time she wore it, she would think of Mama's suspicions. Why did that big clumsy Morris have to follow her home?

Then she thought of how he'd sat on the lawn, laughing with his whole body, his eyes narrowed into slits, and she bit back a grin. He had been fun to talk to. He'd actually seemed interested in China, in her as a person. That was more than she could say for any of the boys at church, the ones who Mama said were so very nice.

Like Joe Schmidt, whose father owned a packing shed. At a church party, she'd sat next to Joe, and all he'd talked about was hot rods and prize hogs.

Elsa threw on a robe, then took the dress outside and hung it on the line. Fritzie ran to her on his short little legs, and she picked him up, cuddling his ears against her face. "You'll never guess what happened today. . . ." He licked her face, and she let it dry in the air.

The next day in school, a rubber band snapped against Elsa's ankle, but she didn't turn. On the way home, she heard a familiar *"FWEE-Fwoooo!"* but kept on walking.

When she crossed the street, Morris's bike sped past her and then spun around in front of her, tires screeching, blocking her way.

Elsa sighed. "Not you again."

"Yeah, it's me. You deaf or something?"

She stamped her foot. "Leave me alone. I'm in enough trouble already."

"Trouble?"

"When my mother saw my dress—"

Morris leaned back and laughed, that big, roaring laugh that seemed to come all the way from his belly. "You sure were a sight, all right!"

Elsa scowled at him, and he sobered. "S'pose I explained to her— real sweetlike—about the wasp and all. Your mom could see I'm just a harmless Oklahoma farm boy."

Elsa stopped walking. "You're a—a—"

"Yeah, I'm an Okie."

Elsa didn't know what to say and stared at her feet.

Morris shrugged. "Doesn't matter. I'm used to it."

She'd seen them at school, had driven past their trailer camps. Boys in bib overalls, girls in faded dresses, wearing pumps with run-down heels like the shoes that came to China in those missionary boxes. Other kids avoided them, said they stank. If she was friendly with the Okies, her classmates would make even more fun of her, saying she was one of them. But Morris seemed different from those in the camps.

"You don't look like—" She stopped.

"We were lucky. My dad's got a steady job." They walked in silence for a while, Morris guiding his bike with one hand.

Then Morris asked, "Well, how about it? Shall I talk to your mom?"

"No!" Shocked, Elsa stared at him. Was he serious? It would only make things worse. "She was really mad. If she sees me with you again—"

"Okay, okay. I'll turn off before we get to your block. I've got a lot of algebra homework anyway."

Algebra? He was awfully big to be in that class. "Why are you taking that? You're not a sophomore, are you?"

"Senior. Flunked it twice. If I don't pass this time, I won't graduate."

Elsa bit her lip and considered. Math was easy for her. Should she offer to help him? She looked up at his face, so wide and round. Sort of innocent. As though his body had grown faster than his brains. Like a baby elephant clomping around in huge black boots.

Then she realized he'd spoken to her and was now looking at her, waiting. "What?"

"I said, 'How about going to the show with me Saturday night?'"

Elsa swallowed and her face grew hot. This couldn't be happening to her. Most of the Mennonite sins—drinking, smoking, cards—didn't tempt her. But going to movies—that one was hard to resist.

She turned away and dropped to one knee, retying a perfectly good knot in her new saddle oxfords. Her mind raced. Tommie had described the music, the scenery, the MGM lion's roar. Mickey Rooney, Judy Garland. Clark Gable—she'd hidden *Gone with the Wind* under her mattress, reading the book three times through before returning it to the library. If there was any way she could sneak out . . .

No. Her mother would find out. And Elsa would be doomed to hell. But it would be too embarrassing to tell that to Morris. Or that Mama didn't trust her with boys.

Morris had been nice to her. She couldn't hurt his feelings and say it was because he was an Okie.

He wheeled around on his bike, still waiting for an answer. She had to say something.

She gave her shoestring a final tug. Her back still turned toward him, her face down against her knee, she mumbled, "Um, Saturday? Sorry, I'm busy."

There was a whir of bike tires, then silence. Elsa got up, peeked over one shoulder, then the other.

Morris was gone. She went to the corner and saw him on the side street, riding away fast.

She should be relieved. Morris had gotten her into trouble, and she'd gotten rid of him for good. Now they were even, and Mama would be satisfied.

But he must have known she was lying. She *had* hurt his feelings.

Being an Okie, Morris must have been snubbed a lot. She knew how that felt. Girls passed party invitations right in front of her, without including her. That awful *Chinky, chinky, Chinaman* . . .

And now she'd snubbed him, the one guy who knew how she felt. Misery gripped her like tight string around a package. How could she make it right without him thinking she liked him? She had to ask somebody!

Tommie. No matter what, tomorrow she would make up with Tommie.

That turned out to be easier than she'd expected, and by the time school was out the next day, Elsa had told Tommie the whole story.

Tommie giggled and sang out, "Ooh, Elsa's got a boyfriend."

"Never. Not if he were the last—" She grabbed Tommie's arm. "That's him there."

Morris Drake sailed past, his head high, ignoring her. He paused at a water fountain and stooped for a drink.

Tommie grinned. She dragged Elsa to the spigot next to Morris, turned it on, put her finger on the opening to squirt him, and then dodged around the corner.

Morris jerked back, his forehead dripping. "Hey, cut that out!" He wiped his face and looked up.

His voice was cold. "Oh, it's you."

Elsa looked around frantically for Tommie, but she'd vanished. "I didn't—it wasn't me—"

Morris glared down at her, his crooked mouth set in a scowl. "What do you want?" His eyes were like shattered blue ice.

This was her chance to be nice. She thought hard. "Um, uh, how are you doing in algebra?"

He lifted a shoulder and let it drop. "Okay."

"Do you think you'll pass?"

"Prob'ly."

"Good." How could she keep the conversation going? "Um, did you know I got into the orchestra?"

"Yeah."

"It's fun. Do you play an instrument?"

"No." He turned as if to go.

She couldn't let it end like that. "Did—did you ride your bike to school today?"

Morris nodded, his lips tight. "Yeah. I don't have a car like the rich guys."

This was embarrassing. "Well, you don't have to be touchy about it."

He sighed. "Mighta known it. You're just like all the others." He strode to the exit and pushed through the double doors, not looking back.

Like all the others? Surprised, Elsa followed him out and watched him walk toward the bike rack. His boots left big footprints in the dust. She shouted, "Thank you!"

Morris turned and looked at her for a minute, his face grim. "Wasn't a compliment." He spun his bike around, jumped on, and pedaled away.

Elsa stood still, barely aware of the other students jostling against her, laughing, jabbering. *Just like all the others.* Until now, she would have given anything to be called that. But the way Morris acted, it was almost a curse.

The rest of that year, Morris didn't talk to Elsa. She knew he must have passed algebra, because in June he graduated with his class. From her seat in the orchestra pit, Elsa watched him march down the aisle of the auditorium, his robe flapping, his face solemn. Although she tried to catch his eye during the service, he didn't once look at her.

Papa was on the stage; when the ceremony was over, he gave the benediction. It was a familiar one; he'd often used it in church. But this time Elsa listened carefully to the words: "The Lord bless thee and keep thee. The Lord make His face to shine upon thee, and be gracious unto thee. The Lord lift up His countenance upon thee, and give thee peace."

Peace? Lately, the radio had been shouting about war. President Roosevelt had said he hated war and that he wouldn't send American boys into battle. But he'd shipped ammunition to Europe.

That didn't sound like peace. If America was no safer than China, her family could just as well have stayed in Shiao Yangshan.

She went outside the auditorium and stood under a moth-covered streetlight, waiting for her father. People hugged their graduates, laughing and shouting, forming giant shadows dancing on the school lawn. Happy families and friends, all loving each other.

Three people pushed through the auditorium door and walked quietly toward the parking lot. A short stout woman with gray hair strained into a bun, a lanky man in a worn blue suit, and Morris, unfamiliar in navy slacks and a sport coat, his graduation robe over one arm.

The woman patted Morris on the arm; he leaned down and kissed her. Elsa felt guilty for watching, peeking into his private life.

This would be the last time she'd see him. He had forgotten her, walked out of her life. There would be no more rubber bands shot at her legs. No more wolf whistles. She ought to be relieved, but she felt so empty.

THE SUMMER SEEMED ENDLESS. Mama put Elsa to work beating carpets, scrubbing woodwork and canning peaches, and it seemed all they did was bicker. Nothing she did was good enough. Papa told her not to argue so much, but finally he found her a job cutting apricots at a drying shed. That was boring, but it was a relief to get out of the house.

She was glad when school started again. The orchestra took up a lot of her time, and with Tommie's encouragement, she signed up for chorus, too. Now that she was a junior, she felt more confident and found it easier to make friends. But she and Tommie were still best pals, sitting together at every school program that Mama let her attend.

The following summer, Papa persuaded the trustees to let Elsa help him in the church office after school and on Saturdays.

Besides learning to type bulletins and reports, she learned that Papa had been hiding a lot of problems. The trustees wanted to cut his gas allowance, and there was talk of limiting the conference trips.

There seemed to be two factions in the church, and they were squabbling over little things such as what color to paint the basement walls, which Sunday school manual to order, and whether buying an organ would be too worldly.

But Elsa knew the problems went deeper. Papa didn't always agree with the conference rules. When he spoke of love and forbearance, some of the church elders quoted the Old Testament prophet Samuel: "It is better to obey than to sacrifice."

That sounded like Mama's rule of life. When Elsa mentioned that, Papa said, "It's not easy for your mother. She's trying so hard to be a good Mennonite that sometimes she forgets it must come from the heart."

"But these church people—they were born Mennonite!"

"Ah, yes. But that's no guarantee of kindness. Some wear the rules like a cloak, thinking it's enough. What really counts is what's in the heart."

No one else's heart was as kind and gentle as her father's. He made Elsa feel confident, and she loved working with him. The pay was low, but typing was more fun than cutting apricots or packing fuzzy peaches, which most girls her age did during the summer. Here, if she finished her work on time, Papa let her go along on sick calls. He also taught her to drive.

And they talked. About the war in Europe. About China—the rain forests of Shungtau, the sandstorms in Shiao Yangshan. The rats, the *yahbah*, the Japanese occupation. How Papa's ivory-tipped cane with its hollow center had hidden enough money to get them to safety despite the bandit raid.

But when she mentioned Jasper, she saw hurt in Papa's eyes. She couldn't talk about the flood, and Papa didn't bring it up either.

One day, she asked, "Why did Mama send Ling away? He'd just qualified for the university; he wanted to become a doctor."

Papa looked at her, puzzled. "Your mother? She never mentioned that. You say Ling wanted to be a doctor?"

Obviously, Mama hadn't told him. Elsa changed the subject. "Do you think we'll ever go back?"

"I don't know, Dumpling. I would love to, but China's not the same now. Japan gobbled it up, province after province. General Chiang was so busy fighting the Communists that he had no strength left to stop them. Right now, foreigners would be an extra burden. Later, who knows?"

China didn't want them. They'd been in America for nearly four years now, and she still didn't feel at home. Where *did* she belong?

That evening, she took Fritzie out for a walk. It was the middle of July, and the sky was bright with stars. The night air was warm, but a cooling breeze carried the smell of orange blossoms. She breathed deeply, inhaling the fragrance.

A strange feeling overwhelmed her, infinitely sad yet unbearably sweet. Something waited for her, something unknown, wonderful but scary.

The feeling was so powerful she had to stop and lean against a lamppost, wiping away tears that wouldn't stop. Shaken, she pulled Fritzie away from his tree-sniffing and walked home.

Chapter 23

IN AUGUST, THE TEMPERATURE zoomed to 110 degrees. On the way back from a busy day of hospital visitation, Papa mopped his forehead with his handkerchief and asked, "How about a chocolate phosphate?"

"Sure! That sounds wonderful." Elsa parked in front of Grainger's Drugstore, glancing at the figure in a white cap and apron cranking down the awning against the afternoon sun. Then she gulped and sat up straight, her face turning hot.

Morris Drake worked there! She was embarrassed, confused, and could hardly breathe—and she was angry at herself for reacting that way. He meant nothing to her.

Suddenly, she realized that she was hot and sticky and her hair needed washing. "I changed my mind. Let's go home. I'll make some lemonade instead."

"What? You never pass up a chance for a chocolate phosphate! Come on. I'm thirsty." Papa stepped out of the car, slammed the door, and headed for the store.

Elsa lagged behind, hoping old Mr. Grainger would be tending the soda fountain. But by the time she slid onto the high stool, Papa had already given the order. And there was Morris behind the counter, his back to them, preparing the sodas. He turned and set the glasses on the counter. "Here you are, sir. That will be—"

Morris stared at Elsa, his mouth open, his eyes like blue headlights that wouldn't switch off. He was thinner now, his face not as pudgy, and a neat mustache decorated his upper lip. His hands groped for the tall glasses on the counter. Papa grabbed them just as they started to tip, sloshing puddles of brown foam onto the napkins.

Elsa shrugged helplessly. "Hi."

Papa looked from Morris to Elsa and back. "Do you two know each other?"

Morris gave his head a shake as though to clear it. "We've . . . um . . . run into each other at school." He reached for a cloth and quickly wiped up the mess.

Elsa remembered their first meeting. "With a crash."

Morris gave a little twitch of awareness, and then started laughing. That special head-thrown-back, eyes-squinted, down-from-the-belly laugh.

Elsa couldn't help laughing, too, and covered her reddening face with her hands.

Papa smiled and sipped his phosphate. "I don't know what the joke is, but it must be a good one."

Elsa gasped for breath. "Tell you about it later." She turned to Morris. "This is my dad. He's the preacher."

Morris wiped his hands on his apron and reached out to greet Papa. "Pleased to meet you, sir," he said. "You'll have to pardon my clumsiness. I haven't been working here long."

The doorbell jingled; more customers came in, and Morris moved away to help them.

On their way out, Papa slapped the money onto the counter, and Morris called, "Thank you, sir. Come again."

Back in the car, Papa turned to Elsa. "Okay, Pumpkin, tell me about this young man."

Forty-five minutes later, they drove into their driveway a few blocks away. "The fact that he's from Oklahoma isn't important," said Papa. "He seems to be a decent, mannerly boy. Does he go to church?"

"I don't know. I think so." Morris was polite, and he'd never teased her about China. "He's not Mennonite though."

"There *are* other Christians."

Elsa looked at Papa sideways, from under her eyelashes. For

a Mennonite preacher, he sure was tolerant. "Mama doesn't like him."

"She's never said anything to me." He eyed her for a long minute. "You just let me handle Mama."

Elsa didn't see any reason to bother Mama about this. Knowing where Morris worked wouldn't make any difference in her life.

That fall, when she was a senior, Elsa joined the church choir. It seemed better than sitting with her mother in the congregation like a dutiful little child. When she learned she'd be singing next to Regina Bauman's mother, it was too late to back out.

One Sunday in October, the choir sang an anthem and sat down in precision. Elsa carefully arranged the pleats in her robe to cover her knees and settled her hymnbook and music folder. Mama would scold her if she sprawled.

She glanced over the congregation. In a back pew sat some visitors—the woman short and stout, the man tall and thin. They looked vaguely familiar.

Then she looked at the person next to them. Intense blue eyes stared at her, and a mouth smiled crookedly.

Elsa closed her eyes in despair. It was starting all over again. How could Morris do this to her?

The hymnbook slid off her lap, and her robe inched apart. She picked up the book, and her folder fell instead. When she stooped to retrieve the music, the choir director motioned to rise for the next number.

Elsa scrambled to her feet and hid her burning face behind her music.

The choir sang, "Alleluia, alleluia," and Elsa prayed silently, *Dear Lord, don't let my voice crack.*

She could feel those compelling blue eyes beaming at her, and she struggled to keep her mind on the hymn. "Sing praises, sing alleluia."

Like steel to a magnet, her gaze pulled back toward Morris. Slowly and lazily, he winked. In the middle of a long and meandering "A-a-a-men," Elsa was horrified to hear herself giggle.

Sophie Bauman stared down at her with frowning eyes, such a contrast to her full, vibrating lips. Elsa forced the insistent laughter into her stomach, where it shook and bubbled until she had to chew her tongue to control it. Mrs. Bauman jabbed a sharp elbow into her rib, and Elsa choked down a cough.

She didn't dare look at Mama. But if she faced the other way, she'd see Morris. She stared at her feet.

Gowns rustled, the choir sat down, and again, she'd missed the cue. She plopped down quickly, her robe splaying open, and she whipped it together carelessly.

Papa got up to preach. *Concentrate. Concentrate on the message.*

"And the Samaritan went by the wayside . . . ," Papa was saying.

She tried to picture the Good Samaritan and was shocked to see him with piercing blue eyes.

Eons later, the service ended. Elsa hung her robe in the anteroom and hurried out through the side door. She couldn't face Morris and hoped he would never visit their church again. Yet why did she feel so bubbly inside?

She ran home and shut herself into her bedroom. She had to get calm before Mama came storming in.

She heard steps in the kitchen and the clatter of pans. Then voices at the front door. First Papa's, then someone unfamiliar. And then that laugh.

No! It couldn't be. Not Morris, not here in her house!

Papa called out, "Rachel, I've invited guests."

She knew Mama hadn't planned for company this Sunday. Would one chicken be enough?

Mama's voice called sweetly, "Elsa, would you come here, please?"

At least the scolding would be postponed. In the kitchen, Elsa helped Mama peel more potatoes. Then Mama said, "Let's go greet the visitors."

Go out there and meet Morris's parents? "No, Mama, you go ahead. I'll—" Elsa looked wildly around the room. On the counter, a head of lettuce stood next to a bowl. "I'll make the salad."

Mama's lips twitched, but she nodded. "Turn down the potatoes when they boil." She dried her hands on her apron and went into the living room.

The salad was a masterpiece, decorated with sliced cucumbers and radishes. Elsa carried it to the dining room table, being careful not to trip on the rug.

Through the open arch, she saw the Drakes sitting in the parlor, talking with Mama and Papa. Morris stood at the Chinese nested lacquered tables, looking at the pictures grouped around the cloisonné vase.

Oh, no! One was an old snapshot of her with a long braid, another with her hair chopped short. Elsa tried to slip back into the kitchen, but Papa spied her.

"Come and meet the Drakes, Elsa. They visited our church this morning."

As if I didn't know. Elsa's feet seemed weighted with rocks, and she had to force them forward. Morris turned around, but she couldn't look at him.

Mr. Drake smiled down at her with the same crinkling eyes that Morris had, and Mrs. Drake shook hands with Elsa. Her hands were fat and puffy but a little rough. She looked into Elsa's eyes as though searching for something.

As though she knows about me! Morris hasn't mentioned me to her, has he?

"And you know Morris," Papa was saying.

Elsa forced a little smile and a nod, not meeting his eyes. Then she excused herself and edged back into the dining room. She'd die before she shook his hand.

At the table, Mr. Drake and Papa traded jokes, and Mrs. Drake talked quilting with Mama. Elsa let the conversation swirl around her and tried not to spill or make eating noises. She glanced at Morris, who was busily attacking a mountain of mashed potatoes. He hadn't taken any of her beautiful salad.

Papa pointed his chin at Morris. "We met this young fellow at the drugstore a few weeks ago," he told Mama. "He's a good worker." He turned to Mr. Drake. "Where's your home church?"

"We went to a community chapel back home. Here we've joined the First Baptists—figured they stick pretty close to the Word. But we thought we'd visit around a bit." He winked at his wife, and Morris reddened.

Elsa wondered what the difference was between Baptists and Mennonites but didn't want to ask.

Papa smiled and nodded. "Have you lived here long?"

"Two years in March," said Mr. Drake. "Our farm in Chanakee just up and blowed away. Nothing we could do but move on and try to find work."

Mama passed around slices of lemon pie. "And did you?" she asked.

Mrs. Drake laid her hand on her husband's arm. "Harlan's a good fix-it man," she said. "He got him a job in the furniture store, delivering stuff and repairing the trade-ins."

Mr. Drake beamed. "I like the feel of wood. 'Course, I never had any training. Morris here is going to junior college, taking shop, learning the tools and all. Make a good carpenter, if he don't waste all his time takin' pitchers."

Morris grinned, and Mrs. Drake explained, "We give him a little box camera for his birthday, and he like to go crazy, snapping here, there, and everywhere. You can't do nothin' without him taking a shot of it."

After dinner, the men went for a walk, and Mrs. Drake started stacking plates. She motioned to Elsa. "You kids run along. I'll help your ma with the dishes."

Mama would never allow it. But Mama was already in the kitchen, and Mrs. Drake shooed Elsa with a chubby hand. "Go on, scoot."

Elsa stared after her in panic. What would she say to Morris? Her knees felt like Jell-O, and she had too many hands.

Morris bit his lip, his eyes squinting. "Had a little trouble with your hymnbook this morning, huh?"

Elsa groaned. "I thought I'd pass out before the service ended."

"That lady next to you, she about had fits."

Elsa thought of Mrs. Bauman's plump, vibrating lips and couldn't help giggling.

Then she heard barking from outside. Her knees became solid again, and she started for the back door. "Come on. I'll show you my dog."

Chapter 24

PAPA BOUGHT A SECONDHAND girls' bike for Elsa, and the next Sunday afternoon she rode with Morris to a small park beside a river several miles out of town. It was warm for November, and the liquidambar trees were still brilliant with red and golden foliage.

Morris snapped a picture of her leaning against a sycamore, and then they sat in the shade and talked. School, her senior year, his junior college classes. His job at the drugstore, her work in the church office. They talked about their churches, and Elsa learned that if you dug down past all the rules and customs, Mennonites and Baptists were a lot alike.

She told him about her childhood: the spools and blocks; Cherky, the cricket; picnics on Little Goat Mountain; and the rained-out Fourth of July. How much she had loved and depended on Tsao Po-Po. But she didn't tell him about Jasper.

Morris had moved a lot—from Oklahoma to Texas, then Arizona, finally ending up in Riverglen.

Elsa asked, "Do you like it here?"

Morris glanced at her and flicked a piece of bark into the river. "Now, I do."

They sat in silence for a while. Elsa felt an airy little tickle in her chest as though she'd ridden over a bump in the road too fast.

She'd been leery about going out with Morris. He was nice, better looking now than in high school, and a lot of fun to talk to. Papa liked him. But actually being on a date with him—that was a whole different feeling.

Morris reached for his wallet and drew out a picture. "This was my home back in Chanakee."

In a bare yard stood a square-frame house with no porch, just two steps leading directly into the door. On the steps sat a small boy in bib overalls and bare feet. Elsa leaned forward to see if she could recognize the little Morris. Then she stiffened. His arm had slipped behind her, and his head bent close.

She didn't dare look at him. Maybe he was only bracing himself for balance. No—she could feel his hair tickling her forehead. *What if he tries to kiss me? Do I want him to? Would it be a sin?*

Her chest felt tight, and her breath came in shallow gasps. What should she do? Her mind raced wildly, and she remembered Miss Bergen's anatomy book. The cheese man.

She forced herself to glance back at the snapshot, and said, "It's . . . very nice." Then in one motion, she handed the picture back to Morris and ducked out of his reach. "I've got to go. There's a church supper."

Morris sat watching her fumble with her bike. He asked, "What about next week?"

She couldn't look at him. "What about it?"

"Will you ride with me again?"

And go through this again? But she didn't want to hurt his feelings. "Maybe. I'll let you know."

Elsa led the way home, riding fast and welcoming the cool breeze on her hot face. Why had she acted so silly? He must think she was awfully dumb.

When they reached her house, Morris wheeled ahead and turned, grabbing her handlebars. He cocked his head, forcing her to look at him. "I'd really like to see you again next Sunday."

She nodded. "Okay." Maybe by then she'd have sorted out her feelings.

But the next week was Thanksgiving weekend, and Grandpa and Grandma Meier and all the aunts and uncles and cousins came down from Sacramento. Elsa had to visit with them and help with the meals. Uncle George brought a big boxful of snapshots from trips he and Aunt Mary had taken, and Elsa divided her time between their travel stories and playing with her younger cousins.

For a long time, Morris didn't call. When December came, the air crisp and the days short, Elsa decided he had given up on her. She wondered what would have happened if she hadn't slipped away from him that day under the tree—how it felt to be kissed, and if noses got in the way.

The next Sunday after church, Elsa helped Mama fix dinner. She fried slices of ham until they were crisp around the edges while Mama stirred gravy, thick and golden, from the drippings. The aroma, salty and pungent, was almost more than Elsa could stand, and she hoped Papa would be home soon. She quickly set the table, then went into the parlor and twirled the dial on the radio.

A football game, a sermon, a commercial: "Ivory Soap: it floats!" The New York Philharmonic. Then an announcer broke in, his voice loud and breathless. "Ladies and gentlemen: we interrupt this broadcast . . . Japanese attack on Pearl Harbor . . . stay tuned for further developments . . ."

Mama rushed into the room, her face white, her hand over her open mouth. "The Japanese!" she whispered.

The orchestra music came back on the radio, but soon the announcer broke in again. "Japanese aircraft invasion . . . dive bombers . . . U.S. battleships sunk . . ."

Elsa stared at her mother. America was being bombed? She could still remember the battle in Shungtau: the shots and explosions, the terrifying escape up the mountain, the bandits on the river. And later, Japan's capture of Shiao Yangshan and the house arrest.

Through the window, she saw Papa hurrying up the walk, his red curls disheveled and his face puckered as though he was crying.

"Have you heard?" He pushed through the screen door without waiting for an answer and crouched by the radio.

"The bombing?" Elsa asked. "Just now. Where's Pearl—?"

Papa motioned for silence, his ear next to the speaker. He shook his head. "We're in for it now." Mama stood behind him, shivering, her hands twisting together.

Elsa felt a hard lump in her throat. America was supposed to be safe! Where would they go now?

Then Mama turned to her. "You see now why you shouldn't associate with Japanese people? They could very well be traitors."

"Tommie has nothing to do with this bombing! She's as American as we are." But Elsa could see her mother wasn't convinced.

At school the next day, Tommie was pale and nervous. Some of the other students eyed her as though she were the enemy, and Elsa didn't know what to say to cheer her up. But she was determined to stand by her friend, no matter what.

After the last bell, Elsa walked slowly to the drugstore. The sun shone from a cloudless sky as if nothing bad had happened, but her stomach was in knots. Morris looked surprised to see her, but as he took her order for an ice cream cone, he seemed miles away. She wondered if he was still mad at her.

She sat on a stool, licking the strawberry drips and watching him mop the counter over and over, even though it was clean. Finally, she asked, "You heard about the Japanese bombs?"

He nodded. He took hot, sparkling glasses from a rack and set them on a shelf.

"That's all the teachers talked about today," Elsa continued. "But they said not to worry. Our army will win this war."

Morris's eyes focused on Elsa. "Our army?"

She frowned. Didn't he understand? "Well, Roosevelt declared war, didn't he?"

"Yeah. And you know what that means? All us guys will be drafted. *We're* the army."

Elsa stared at him. Some of the young men from her church were in alternate service in the forestry, and one had fled to Canada to avoid the draft. She hadn't realized that Morris— "The regular army?"

He looked at her as though she were dense.

She started to explain. "Mennonite boys go CO. That's—"

Morris waved that aside. "I know. Conscientious objectors. They're classified as 1-O or 4-E. But that's not for me. I couldn't let others do the dirty work for me just so I could live in peace." He glanced at her. "No offense."

Elsa shook her head, dismissing the barb. "I guess if everybody went CO, the Japanese would take over, and we'd have to get out of the country. That's what happened to our people in Russia. Only there it was the Communists, and they wanted our men to fight in *their* army."

"Russia? I thought you were from China."

"I am. But my dad's ancestors settled in Russia for a while. There were whole colonies of Mennonites until things went bad and they escaped to America."

"Now it's starting all over again, huh?"

Elsa nodded slowly. Only this time, there was nowhere to escape. Her appetite gone, she slid off the stool and dropped her unfinished cone into the trash can.

On the way home, Elsa thought of the soldiers in China, and the Japanese guards. She'd always believed they fought because they were wicked and liked to kill. She'd never thought of them as real people with lives of their own. But this war changed everything.

She pictured Morris in uniform. Shooting a gun, being shot at, getting wounded. Maybe even killed. She felt more afraid than ever before.

Chapter 25

THE WAR RAGED ON. TOMMIE STOPPED coming to school, and when Elsa called her, she seemed reluctant to talk. But finally she said her mother was sick with worry. With all the restrictions on Japanese people: how far they could travel, and what they could do, it seemed best for her to drop out. Elsa missed her a lot, and was concerned about her, but she was even more anxious about Morris.

Every week, the newspaper listed men who were drafted. So far, Morris was still free, and Elsa hoped he wouldn't need to go.

When he'd finally earned enough to buy a shiny, black Ford V8 coupe, he asked Elsa on a real date—to attend a church social with him—and this time she agreed. Mama was aghast. Elsa overheard her say to Papa, "With a boy—an outsider—alone in a car at night? It will surely lead to trouble."

Papa's voice was calm and reassuring. "She's nearly seventeen, and we can't hold back time. Morris is a good boy; I trust him."

If Papa trusted them, Elsa thought, she would do her best to deserve that trust.

After that, they spent a lot of Friday nights together at school plays, ball games, and church programs. And each time Morris came to pick Elsa up, he promised, "I'll bring her home by ten sharp. . . . No, ma'am! No monkey business."

But somehow, there was always a little extra time to drive into the country and park under a sheltering tree. They talked—he was still so easy to talk to—about anything and everything: school, his car, favorite foods, books, radio programs.

Elsa knew very little about radio. Papa listened to news, and Mama liked *Hymn Request Time* and sermons, all other programs being too worldly. But Morris told Elsa about *Henry Aldrich* and *Fibber McGee and Molly,* as well as *The Shadow* and *I Love a Mystery,* and Elsa realized there was a fascinating new world on the airwaves.

"Your mother's . . . pretty strict, isn't she?" said Morris.

"Strict?" Elsa nodded slowly. That was an understatement. Although some Mennonite leaders had started to overlook the jewelry, cosmetics, and shorter hair of the more daring young women, Mama refused to relax her rules. Elsa's hair was down past her shoulders now, and the girls at school had showed her how to curl the bangs and ends with bobby pins, just enough to make them look naturally wavy. Mama had objected at first, but had since admitted the result was smoother than before.

Morris looked sideways at Elsa. "She doesn't like me, does she?"

"She . . . ," Elsa sighed. Was there anyone her mother did like? "It's not you, exactly. She's always been suspicious. She has this high standard, and nobody can measure up to it. Especially me."

"Are all Mennonites like that?"

"My father isn't. Sometimes I wonder how the two ever got together. But see, Mama wasn't raised in that culture. She seems to think she has to . . . to prove herself. And that if I'm not perfect, she'll look bad to the church."

Morris nodded, grinning. "Eternal Virtue. Well, my folks think the world of you."

"They're nice." Morris and his parents seemed so relaxed together, his father always joking, his mother hugging and accepting. Despite the friendliness of the church people, Mama still didn't like to show affection, and if she ever showed approval, Elsa would be amazed.

"My dad wants me to be a cabinetmaker when I'm through college," said Morris. "But I like working at the drugstore. Mr. Grainger's taught me a lot. He says it's a good business to be in; people will always need medicine. Especially now with the war and all."

War. It was always there, a thin stream of worry running through Elsa's mind. If she wasn't careful, it would cut out a channel and flood all her thoughts.

She sat carefully on her side of the car, but Morris sprawled across the seat, his arm lying across the back rest, his hand toying with her sleeve, her collar, her hair. Every touch felt like electricity, and once when their knees grazed, she jumped. She tried to act calm so he wouldn't think she was naive, but her stomach felt hollow, and her heart did somersaults.

One evening, he reached over and brushed his fingertips over her cheek. "You're so pretty." His voice was just a whisper; she wasn't even sure she'd heard him correctly.

She froze, not looking at him, not breathing. When she finally glanced up, his face came closer. Then his lips touched hers—gently, softly. She felt a pain in her chest so unbearably sweet she had to close her eyes.

All the warnings of Mama and Miss Bergen faded away, and she moved from her side of the car and into Morris's arms.

It wasn't until the next day that she realized . . . noses hadn't been any problem.

ON A TUESDAY EVENING IN March, Elsa sat at the dining table, working on a chemistry report. It was late, and her parents were already in bed. She'd rolled up her hair, each flat little circle crossed with two bobby pins.

Suddenly, the familiar *chug-chug-chug* of Morris's Ford sputtered in the driveway. Startled, Elsa jumped up and looked out the window. Mama only allowed her out on Friday evenings and never this late.

She ran to her room, quickly tied on a bandanna, and slipped out the front door. Embarrassed for him to see her this way, she asked, "What are you doing here?"

Morris stood under the sycamore tree, his face sober and his jaws flexing. "I was just driving around. I had to see you." He turned away and fumbled in his shirt pocket.

Dread formed a hard knot in Elsa's throat. Something was very wrong. A dim light went on in the Hieberts' bathroom next door, but she ignored it.

He took out a folded piece of paper and handed it to her.

It was too dark to read, but he recited it from memory: "'You are instructed to report to military duty at Camp Barkley, Texas, on Monday, April 27, 1942.'"

Shivers ran up Elsa's arms, and she stared at the paper, wishing the words would disappear. She whispered hoarsely, "For how long?"

"I guess till the war's over. Couple of months, years . . ." He shrugged, his palms turned out.

So this was it. They'd both expected the notice, but still the printed words felt like a death sentence. "Texas. That's awfully far. Can you come home sometimes?"

"Maybe. That's just for basic training. Then, who knows? I might be shipped out."

"Out?"

"Overseas. Wherever there's fighting."

Elsa scanned his face, memorizing each plane and angle. If he left, would she ever see him again? She put her hand on his arm and looked up into his eyes. "Oh, Morris!"

His other arm drew her close to him. His mustache whispered over her cheek, and his mouth searched hungrily. A warm bubble curled its way down to her toes, and her knees felt weak.

He kissed her again and again, his lips moist and eager. Her bandanna slipped off, and some of the pin curls came undone. But she didn't care. Helplessly lost in a spell, she melted into his embrace.

Then Elsa became aware that Fritzie was barking, and suddenly a blinding light flashed over them. Morris stepped back, drawing her behind the tree.

Papa stood on the porch steps in his robe, peering into the shadows. "Elsa, are you out there?" His voice was a husky whisper.

Elsa pulled loose and ran to him. "Oh, Papa, Morris has been drafted! He has to leave in a few weeks!"

Morris stepped out of the darkness behind the tree, and Papa went to him. Putting his hand on Morris's shoulder, he said, "I'm sorry. Just now when your life is starting—it's not fair."

Elsa looked at him gratefully. Papa was so understanding. He had never put pressure on Morris to be a conscientious objector like the Mennonites. But what would Mama say?

"I'll be praying for you," Papa continued. "Stay close to the Lord.

I wish I could tell you it won't be hard, but that wouldn't be true. It'll make you tough. Just don't let it turn you bitter. And God willing, you'll come home safely."

Morris nodded, biting his lips. "Thank you, sir."

Papa turned to Elsa, standing at his shoulder. "Better say good-bye now. Mama's getting nervous." He went inside, turning off the porch light.

Elsa tied her bandanna back on more securely. Suddenly she felt shy and confused.

Morris kissed her once more, quickly. Then he was gone. The scent of orange blossoms drifted over in the breeze—sweet, power-ful, painful. Was this love? Nobody had told her it could feel so good yet so awful. She remembered the evening in July, when she'd felt such an exquisite but disturbing yearning, and knew that she would never again be the same.

ON FRIDAY MORNING, APRIL 25, Elsa stood next to Morris at the train station. Not caring who saw her, she leaned back into his embrace while he nuzzled the top of her head with his chin.

During the past month, they'd spent all their spare time together, and one afternoon, she'd even ditched school to drive with him all the way to the coast.

At Morro Bay, they'd taken pictures of each other frolicking in the waves and hunting for seashells and hermit crabs. Morris had found a perfect sand dollar and given it to her for a keepsake.

In the shadow of the sturdy Morro Rock, they'd spread a blanket for their picnic lunch; afterward, Morris had stretched out on the blanket, closed his eyes, and taken a deep breath. "Boy, this is the life."

Elsa sat beside him and tickled his nose with a seagull feather. His eyes opened, shining with such passion she had to turn away in painful ecstasy.

But he pulled her down, crushing her to his chest. His kisses were sweeter than ripe peaches, and the war was far away.

Now, at the train station, he held her tightly, caressing her arms.

Through her blur of tears, she could see his mother nearby, wiping her eyes, his father pacing the platform.

Papa stood next to them, giving words of comfort. Then he came and patted Morris's shoulder. "Keep the old smile smiling. Remember, you're not alone. God goes with you."

Morris nodded. "Thank you, sir." Elsa buried her face against Morris's chest, the cramp in her throat not allowing her to speak.

Papa went on through the crowd of recruits and their families, shaking hands and giving encouragement, and Elsa felt proud of him. For Morris's sake, she wished Mama had come too, that she didn't hate soldiers so much.

Mama had said, "I'll pray for his soul," but Papa had replied, "His soul is fine. We'll need to pray for his body."

Now Elsa felt the vibration and thundering of the approaching train and heard the lonely howl of its whistle. The crowd surged forward.

Morris hugged his parents and kissed Elsa, lifting her off her feet. He said, "Be sure to write, you hear?" Then he ran down the platform and disappeared.

The train, satisfied with swallowing up Riverglen's finest young men, began moving again. Elsa ran alongside, searching the train windows. Where was Morris? She had to see him one last time.

Bodies hung out the windows, arms waved, and boys shouted. None of them was Morris. Elsa felt crushed as a broken shell on the seashore. She stopped and started to turn away when she heard a shrill wolf whistle.

She whirled back. In the last car, Morris hung out of a window, frantically waving both arms. "Good-bye, Eternal Mischief! Good-byyye!"

The train shrank until it was a little black dot between converging lines. Then, it disappeared.

Chapter 26

Dear Elsa:

I bet you wondered what happened to me. We spent thirty days rolling and heaving on a troop ship. It's a relief to be on land again. We've been here three weeks now, but it seems like three years. I can't believe it's winter at home. Everything here is ████████. Today we marched twenty miles through the ████████. You should see my blisters.

Tonight, the USO is going to give us guys a show, but I don't know if I can keep my eyes open long enough to watch.

Tell my folks I'm fine, except I had a cold last week. That's why I didn't write.

The food is lousy. I'm hungry for good old home cooking.

Yours truly,
Morris

ELSA LEANED AGAINST THE MAILBOX and sighed. Finally, she knew he was all right, even if the letter had been censored and she had no idea where he was.

Morris was such a sweet guy. She missed him so much. But he'd never said anything about his feelings toward her—whether he missed her a lot or wanted to be with her when he came home. His letters were so unsatisfying. Almost—she hated to admit it—almost boring!

As boring as the rest of her life. Most of the Mennonite young people had left, the boys going to civilian public service jobs in forest conservation, at dairies, or as aides in mental institutions. A lot of the girls hired out as housemaids in big fancy houses in Fresno or Visalia, so she had hardly anyone to sit with in church.

Junior college was no better. Many of the teachers had either enlisted or left to work in the defense plants. Sports were out; all the good athletes had been drafted. The orchestra director went into the Marine Corps, and there weren't enough musicians left in school to bother with finding a replacement for him.

Worst of all, Tommie had left town. In May, her family had been rounded up with other Japanese and sent off to an internment camp somewhere in Arizona. Mama said her dad was a spy and that the police had confiscated a two-way radio in their basement.

Elsa knew that was just a vicious rumor. She and Papa had gone to the bus station to see Tommie and her family off, had seen the hurt and bewilderment in their eyes, and had cried with them. They were loyal Americans; they wouldn't do anything to hurt this country.

There was also talk about German Mennonites and their resistance to the draft, but so far, no one in their church had been arrested.

If only there was something interesting to do. She'd seen pictures in the newspaper—girls wearing coveralls in defense plants, working punch presses or operating cranes. Inspecting ships and planes. Some working in canteens, cheering up soldiers with doughnuts and coffee. But stuck here in Riverglen, there was absolutely nothing she could do to help win the war.

She gradually became aware of the tantalizing aroma of Mama's oven-fried chicken wafting out from the kitchen. She tucked Morris's letter into her pocket and went inside. Papa, in his easy chair reading, glanced at the envelope peeking out of Elsa's pocket and gave her a thumbs-up sign.

Mama saw, and her lips twitched. "You wouldn't be so cheerful if you heard what the church people are saying."

Papa raised his eyebrows. "Now what?"

"They're wondering how you can shepherd a congregation if you can't control your own daughter." She wiped her hands on her apron. "It's all over church. Elsa skipping services to run off with a soldier.

Quite a testimony for a girl whose father preaches nonviolence." Her voice was harsh.

Elsa knew what she meant. Five months ago in September, right after basic training and just before being shipped overseas, Morris had been given a two-week leave, and she'd spent every possible moment with him. It had been a bittersweet time, and finally, she'd been able to tell him about Jasper.

She shrugged. It wouldn't help to defend herself now.

But Papa frowned. "He's a fine young man, Rachel. More upright than some of the men who went CO. Honest, hardworking—"

"Tell that to the council," said Mama. "They're the ones who give the vote of confidence. With elections coming up next week . . ."

Elsa looked from Papa to Mama and back. Surely the council wouldn't vote Papa out for something *she'd* done! "That's not fair! They wouldn't be so narrow-minded, would they? If it were Joe Schmidt instead of Morris, we could smooch on the church platform, and the people wouldn't care."

Mama gasped, her mouth staying open, her eyes cold.

Elsa thought of Morris's strong arms around her, his soft kisses, the smell of his clean, crisp uniform and a faint whiff of Old Spice. The half-teasing look in his eyes while he warbled along with the car radio, using his own version: *"Don't sit under the sycamore tree with anyone else but me. . . ."* Even if the whole church whispered about her, she wouldn't give him up.

Then she saw the worry wrinkles around her father's eyes, the sad little smile at the corners of his mouth. If the church did let him go, what would he do? Everyone knew that Mrs. Bauman's brother was looking for a pastorate—he'd snap up the job in a minute. *Oh, Papa, I don't want to hurt you. But I love Morris so much. What'll I do?*

ON SUNDAY, PAPA PREACHED about tolerance. The Lord had visited with the Samaritan woman at the well, even though her lifestyle was unacceptable, and the disciples had been shocked. When soldiers came to Jesus for guidance, did He tell them to leave the army? No. He told them to do the best job they could, to be obedient and honest.

From her seat in the choir loft, Elsa scanned the congregation. The men in dark suits, unsmiling, arms crossed over their chests, women in knitted shawls and last year's drab felt hats. Their expressions were polite and attentive, but now and then they glanced at each other.

Were they convinced, or was Papa's message too liberal for them?

Beside her in the choir, Mrs. Bauman smoothed her robe, picking off an invisible bit of lint. Her husband, Ezra, chairman of the trustees, pursed his lips as though he were spitting out a bitter raw olive. Elsa saw them look at each other, disapproval in their eyes. Had Mrs. Bauman started that gossip about her?

After the business meeting the following week, Papa came in quietly. Elsa, listening from her bedroom, held her breath, but she couldn't understand what was being said. When she couldn't stand it any longer, she went into the living room. Her parents sat close together on the sofa, Papa's arm around Mama, Mama wiping her eyes.

Papa smiled at Elsa. "Well, we won't have to move."

"The vote?"

"Ninety percent. Better than I'd hoped."

She ran to him and hugged him. "But Mama . . . I thought . . ."

Her mother shook her head. "His raise was turned down again. The Baumans have a lot of influence." She looked at Elsa meaningfully, as though it were her fault.

"Don't worry," said Papa. "We'll manage."

Elsa knew he'd been yearning for a set of expensive commentaries. If she'd wear her old jacket another year, maybe she could afford to get him one or two volumes for Christmas. At least he hadn't lost the church on account of her.

The next week, on Friday, December 18, Elsa stood beside her mother at the kitchen sink, gingerly squishing hamburger and bread crumbs through her fingers. She looked out the window; it was growing dark and beginning to sprinkle.

Mama chopped onions, bobbing the cleaver the way Fu Liu had done. "Papa's late tonight," she said.

"He had a lot of calls to make."

Mama scraped the onions into Elsa's mixture. "Why didn't you go along? You could have kept him on schedule."

Elsa slapped the mounded meat into a pan and shoved it into the oven. One of Papa's appointments had been with Ezra Bauman. She was sure it was to smooth out any hard feelings the man might have after the elections. Papa was good at that, but she just couldn't face the Baumans, resenting them as she did. She might have added sparks to the flame.

Mama stared at her, waiting for an answer, but Elsa turned away, pretending to concentrate on the radio news blaring from the living room.

"Naval victory off Guadalcanal, heavy Japanese losses . . . British Mosquito bombers attacking German tanks . . . President Roosevelt offering reassurance . . . Gas rationing limited to three gallons a week . . . Chew Wrigley's Gum."

The clock struck six-thirty. Papa was never this late. What was keeping him?

"Set the table and start the potatoes," said Mama. "I'm sure he'll be here by the time they're done." She went into the parlor and sat down with her knitting.

Spicy fragrance from the meatloaf filled the kitchen, and Elsa's stomach growled. She set two places, pretending it was her own future home, then guiltily added the third. Tapioca pudding waited in the refrigerator, and she poked out a quick taste with her finger. With sugar rationed, dessert was a rare treat.

The sudden jangle of the telephone made her jump, and she ran to the living room to answer it. "Hello? Yes, I'll get her. . . . Mama, it's for you."

When Mama put the receiver to her ear, her face turned gray, and red spots shone on her cheekbones. Her mouth worked soundlessly, and Elsa wondered what was wrong.

She took the receiver from her mother's limp hand and listened. "Down the road from the church . . . car skidding . . . drunk driver . . . to the hospital . . ."

Elsa spoke through numb lips. "Yes. All right. We'll be right there." It couldn't be true. Papa in an accident?

She turned to Mama. *Something must be done. Why doesn't Mama tell me what to do?* But Mama stared into space with dull eyes, not moving.

The potato water bubbled over and sputtered onto the hot burner, and Elsa turned off the gas.

The hospital. How will we get there? She looked out the window; it was raining hard now, the bushes whipping in the wind.

The neighbors. Elsa phoned Mr. Hiebert, and a few minutes later, the white-haired couple was at the door. She grabbed her mother's purse and led her to the car.

Maybe it was only a little accident. Papa would be sitting in the waiting room, an ankle bandaged, a few cuts on his face. He'd smile at them; they'd hug him and then take him home.

But Papa wasn't sitting up. He lay pale and still on an examining table, his red hair matted with blood. Tubes crisscrossed his face, and a respirator hid his mouth. He was covered with a blood-smeared sheet, and his strong hands lay limp and helpless.

Elsa leaned weakly against the wall. Papa was dying, and it was all her fault. She should be the one lying there.

Two orderlies lifted Papa onto a gurney. One of his arms swung loose, and a man flipped it back up as though it belonged to a rag doll.

Mama moved with the gurney, and Elsa followed, walking as in a dream. She watched dully while the orderlies bumped Papa's gurney head-first through swinging doors into surgery.

A nurse led them into the waiting room, the same place where Elsa and Papa had sat many times comforting other people. Now the room felt strange, the few visitors one-dimensional, like pictures on a wall.

The wait seemed endless. Mama sat stiffly at the edge of her seat, motionless as a stone. Mr. Hiebert called the church people, and they came and went, murmuring their concern.

Elsa heard words, but they meant nothing to her. Someone brought coffee in a thermos jug. She didn't like coffee, but she welcomed the hot, bitter jolt.

Finally, the doctor came in and said her father wasn't awake yet, but they could go see him.

Papa lay with his eyes shut, breathing harshly in uneven gasps. He'd been cleaned up, but crusts of blood still streaked his face. His head was completely covered with bandages. Several tubes emerged from under the sheet, leading to bottles on the floor, slowly filling with dark red liquid.

Chapter 27

LATE THAT NIGHT, ELSA STILL SAT at Papa's bed. Mama stood on the other side, stroking his forehead, squeezing his hand, asking over and over, "Philip, can you hear me?" Elsa couldn't remember seeing Mama show that much affection to him. Why hadn't she acted that way while Papa was well, while he could appreciate it?

After a while, Papa's eyes did open halfway, then shut again slowly as though he were far away and it took too much effort to return. His chest rose and fell, each breath a choking struggle. Elsa breathed deeply, as though that would encourage him to come back to her.

He would be all right. He *had* to be. Papa was strong. All her life, in China and now in America, he'd been her strength. She'd never be able to survive without him.

Suddenly, he opened his eyes wide and whispered, "Rachel."

Elsa jumped up, and Mama bent over him, her hands cradling his cheeks. "Yes, my love, I'm here." She leaned closer and kissed Papa on his parted lips.

Elsa felt as though she were standing on holy ground and didn't belong there, but she couldn't turn away. She glanced at Mama, but her mother didn't seem aware of anyone else in the room.

"Just rest now, dearest," Mama went on. "Save your strength. You'll be better soon."

Papa murmured, "Elsa?" Mama caressed his face and kissed him again, then turned aside, looking down, a slight blush on her cheeks.

It was so wonderful to see Papa wake up, but hearing his weak voice sent a flood of guilt over Elsa. "I'm sorry, Papa," she moaned.

"It's all my fault—I should have gone along. I can't do anything right! First Jasper, now you—"

Her father rolled his head side to side on the pillow. "No—not your fault. Promise . . . promise me. Don't blame yourself. Just . . . both of you . . . take care of each . . . each other." He groped for Mama with his other hand. "Maybe . . . it's just . . . my time."

Mama clasped his hand in both of hers. "No, don't say that! I won't let you go."

She kissed his fingers, and he mouthed the words: "I love you, Rachel."

Mama glanced at Elsa, then moved her face close to Papa's. Elsa heard her whisper, "I love you, too, darling. Sleep now. You'll feel better in the morning."

He shut his eyes, and Mama still caressed his forehead, his cheeks, his limp arms. Papa relaxed, his breathing labored but more even.

Hours passed. Every so often, a nurse came in and checked his vital signs, and still he slept, murmuring, groaning, sighing.

Now that the crisis seemed over, Elsa went out into the hall. She peeked into the waiting room and saw the Hieberts sprawled on the chairs, sleeping. She walked past a janitor swishing his mop, shoving along a metal bucket. Then she heard a rumble, and from around a corner hurried an aide pushing a supply cart full of linens, leaving two even streaks on the wet floor. Moans came from one room, a hysterical cackle from another. Somewhere, an oxygen tent hissed.

Despite all the times she'd visited people in hospitals with her father, she'd never realized how noisy it could be at night. She wondered how patients could sleep through all that.

A little radio at the nurses' station played quiet music, and one of the nurses looked up as she passed. "Is everything all right?" she asked.

Elsa nodded. "My father woke up for a bit, but he's sleeping now."

"I'll check on him in a minute," she said. "As soon as I finish charting."

When Elsa went back into the room, Mama was sitting beside the bed, asleep, her head resting on Papa's leg.

Papa wasn't breathing as heavily now, and Elsa was relieved. Except—something didn't seem quite right. She touched his cheek, and it felt cool.

"Papa?" she whispered. Then a little louder, "Papa?" She leaned her cheek against his slightly opened lips but felt no breath at all.

"Papa!" she shouted and reached over to shake her mother's shoulder. "Mama, wake up! Papa, he's—he's—"

Her mother jumped up, felt Papa's face, and screamed. "Philip, Philip! Oh, no! Oh, dear Lord, no! Please, God, don't let it be!" Frantically, she breathed into his mouth.

Elsa pressed hard on the call button, and the nurses came running. They yanked the bed curtain around him, nudging Elsa and her mother out of the circle. A doctor rushed in and slipped behind the screen; Elsa could see their forms moving around.

She leaned against the wall outside the door, staring at her mother and praying silently, *Please, dear Jesus, don't let my papa die.*

But when the doctor finally opened the curtain, he shook his head. "I'm so sorry. We did all we could. The injuries were too severe."

Mama went to the bed and touched Papa's face. Then she slumped over his body and wept in ragged sobs. After a while, a nurse took her arm and led her out, and Elsa followed, her head swirling. This wasn't real. There had to be some mistake.

The Hieberts were now awake and met them in the hall. "He's gone," sobbed Mama, and they hugged her, crying with her.

Elsa moved away, feeling numb and cold as stone. A tic jumped in her eyelid, and she reached up to rub it. Maybe if she stayed in the waiting room, the nurses would come tell her Papa had recovered after all. But Mrs. Hiebert put an arm around her, and Elsa's feet moved automatically until she found herself back in the car.

FOUR DAYS LATER, ON TUESDAY morning, Elsa listened as ministers, mission-board members, and furloughed missionaries eulogized their friend, Pastor Philip Meier.

Relatives had come from all over, many of whom she'd never met before. People jammed the church pews, lined two deep along the walls, and spilled out the front doors.

Just like Shiao Yangshan at Christmas. She thought back to those days, wishing she could move time back. Life had been so happy there.

Until Jasper died. And Ling left. And Tsao Po-Po couldn't go along. Now in America, the country that was supposed to be so wonderful, people were still leaving her. Everyone who cared about her: Morris, Tommie, and now her dear Papa, her champion, her ally. She was all alone.

Next to her, Grandma Meier whispered, "Go ahead, let it out. It helps to cry."

She wished she could cry. But the funeral didn't seem real; she was numb, separated from her body, watching the scene from somewhere else.

They buried Papa in the cemetery right outside of town, under an oak tree. Then everyone surrounded her and Mama, saying how much they'd loved and appreciated Papa. The Hieberts patted her on the back, and she thanked them for their help. Even Ezra Bauman, who'd surely voted against Papa in the trustees meeting, nodded and shook her hand.

The church had prepared a meal in the fellowship hall: ham, potato salad, and canned peaches. Cakes of every shape and flavor. People seemed relaxed now, chatting and joking over their coffee cups.

How could they laugh at a time like this? Even Mama, listening to someone tell a favorite memory of Papa, had a watery smile.

Uncle George brought over relatives to meet her. "Your third cousin once removed—remember that picture we sent you?"

"I can tell you're a Meier. You have your papa's red hair."

"Be glad he didn't suffer long."

Elsa felt heat flood her body. How could she be glad? And what did they know about his suffering? They hadn't been there.

But one after the other, the people hugged her, smothering her in their embraces.

"Be brave," they said. "Your mother needs you."

What about my *needs?* She watched for a chance, then slipped out of the building and walked aimlessly through town, block after block.

At one of the houses, she heard a radio playing. "General Eisenhower pledges speedy victory in Europe . . . Be patriotic: collect metal and bacon grease . . . Wash your clothes Rinso bright."

How strange that the world still kept turning. Didn't they know that Papa was dead and life had stopped?

Exhausted and shaky, Elsa found herself at home and went into Papa's office.

Books covered his desk in untidy piles, and papers lay all around as if he were still studying for a sermon. On a nail in the wall hung his cane, his faithful traveling companion in China. Elsa took it down and stroked the polished wood, the smooth ivory tip. She thought of its secret, the hollow inside where he'd tightly stuffed the paper money. She unscrewed the tip and poked her finger into the cavity.

How clever of Papa to outsmart the robbers. He'd always found ways to take care of his family. Who would take care of them now? She replaced the tip and hung the cane back on its nail.

Going into her own room, she took from her closet the commentary volume she'd bought for Papa's Christmas gift. She set it with all his other books and papers into a neat tower in the center of the desk. Then she sat down in his chair and stretched her arms out, encircling the stack. Laying her head against the books, she whispered, "Papa, Papa, what will I do without you?"

The only answer was the ticking of the clock in the empty parlor. The rhythm lulled her, and words formed in her head. *God be with you till we meet again.* That heartbreaking farewell song at the pier when they'd left China. *Till we mee-ee-eet.*

Outside, Fritzie whimpered, then howled, as though he sensed death. Finally, Elsa was able to weep.

Chapter 28

ON THE FIRST OF FEBRUARY, Elsa came home from school to find her mother packing their clothes and the treasures from China in grocery cartons. She knew they had to move out of the parsonage; the church needed to get it ready for the next pastor. But looking at the boxes brought back an ache of memory, of leaving Shungtau, leaving Shiao Yangshan, leaving her beloved China. If only they could go back there now! But with Papa gone, that could never happen.

"Where are we going this time?" she asked, dreading the answer.

Mama carefully wrote "towels and bedding" on a box, then looked up. "I've found a job."

Elsa froze. Had her mother been hired at the junior college? So many of the men teachers had been drafted. What if she'd have to take classes from Mama? For a moment, she was a rebellious child again, sitting in the mission house classroom, watching Mama's red pencil mark all her mistakes.

"I'll be clerking at Schaeffer's Dry Goods store," her mother said. "The pay isn't much, but I'll get a nice discount on clothes and furnishings. And Mr. Schaeffer told me about a woman, Mrs. Weston, who has a one-room apartment with a hot plate at quite a reasonable price, so I went over and rented it."

Elsa's breath of relief changed to a gasp. "One room?" Mama and her crammed together—how would she ever get any privacy?

"Mrs. Weston will go down even lower if you help with the yard work," her mother went on. "The best part is that it's walking distance from the church and stores. I certainly can't afford to buy a car."

This was too much. How could her mother do all this without even discussing it with her? Didn't her opinion count for anything?

Elsa heard Fritzie whining outside and went to get the little dachshund. "Will the landlady let me keep him?"

"No, she won't take pets. But Mr. Hiebert said he would take it."

Elsa cuddled the dog's long ears against her cheek and blinked back tears. It was bad enough to lose Papa, and for Morris to be shipped overseas in the middle of the fighting. With Fritzie gone, all that was precious to her would be lost.

Her mother sighed. "Oh, Elsa, don't be a baby. You can live without a dog. It'll be a relief not to hear that constant whining and scratching. It might be a bit crowded here, but I'll be at work and you're in school all day. And if we're very careful with money, maybe I can save up for a bigger place."

A month later, with all their things stuffed into the apartment's closet, drawers, and under the double bed, Elsa looked around the room and sighed. The only familiar things were the cloisonné vases on the dresser, the Chinese rugs on the linoleum floor, and the nested lacquered tables. Even the *peshong* was hidden under their hanging dresses, covered with a runner.

It would never be home—not without Papa. He'd been gone nearly three months, and she wondered if she would ever get over the ache in her heart. Morris's letters were so widely spaced that each time between the letters she became convinced he'd forgotten her. Sometimes, it seemed life wasn't worth living.

She finished her meatless chili-bean supper, cleared the few dishes off one of the little tables, and slid the table back over the others. As she ran water into the tiny sink, she glanced at her mother.

Mama leaned back in her chair, her feet soaking in a basin of Epsom salts. Her ankles were swollen from standing, and Elsa had a fleeting memory of the terrifying escape into the mountains about Shungtau, waking up the next morning to see Tsao Po-Po rubbing salve into Mama's feet. She wondered if she should offer to do that now. Maybe that would put Mama into a better mood.

But before she could ask, Mama said, "There's still some daylight. Mrs. Weston says the victory garden needs weeding and watering."

Mrs. Weston loved flowers, too, and her beds of petunias and red verbenas bloomed happily. Elsa needed to study for a chemistry test, but she was glad to go outside and breathe the fresh air. She crossed the patch of lawn, passed an orange tree loaded with fruit, and got a trowel and hoe from the small shed at the back of the yard. If she worked hard enough attacking the weeds around the cucumbers and cabbages, maybe she could forget her problems.

ONE EVENING AFTER PIN-CURLING her hair, Elsa lay on the bed, studying. In a chair next to the kitchenette, her mother sat knitting, her feet propped up on a small wooden step chair.

Every evening, it was the same. She could almost count the minutes until Mama started complaining. She'd heard variations of the same theme dozens of times:

"An old man came in asking for long underwear. Imagine that—in the middle of May! . . . They had the most beautiful voile, but after the woman had me cut five yards, she didn't want it, and we had to put it in the remnants . . . "

"Mama, I'm studying. There's a test tomorrow."

Her mother sniffed. "Pull your dress down over your knees. No lady sprawls like that." Her needles clicked on, filling the silence. Then, "Put some vinegar on that sunburn. I heard that—"

Without a word, Elsa gathered her books and papers, took them with her into the bathroom, and locked the door. Before long, she heard pounding on the door.

"Are you finished? I need to take a bath."

Elsa went back to the bed, opened her health book, and tried to memorize the parts of the digestive system.

Before long, Mama came out of the bathroom in a nightgown and robe. She looked at Elsa's book. "Why are you staring at that naked body?"

Elsa sighed and turned the page. "It's for my final. We have to—"

"You don't need that to be a good secretary."

A formation of planes droned loudly overhead, saving Elsa from answering. She had no intention of staying in the church office if

Mrs. Bauman's brother became their new pastor. She put away her book and rummaged through the dresser drawers for stationery.

Mama turned around. "What are you looking for?"

"V-Mail stationery. Where did you put it?"

"You must have used it up. It's shameful, all those letters you write. A nice girl wouldn't chase after soldiers that way."

Elsa's scalp tingled. She closed her eyes and breathed deeply. How much more would she have to take before she exploded? Her voice came out louder than she'd intended. "Morris isn't just any old soldier. He's as decent as any Mennonite boy. Why do you always—"

She stopped. Mama's eyes had filled with tears. *Oh, no. Not again.*

Mama's voice trembled. "You wouldn't talk back like that if Papa were here."

If Papa were here, there wouldn't be a problem. Without him to smooth things out, Mama had become more critical and sour than ever. With a tight throat, Elsa muttered, "You said life would be better here in America. Why didn't you just leave me in China with Tsao Po-Po?"

Mama blew her nose and didn't answer.

There was no reasoning with Mama. She could twist any words into an insult. *Papa, Papa,* Elsa cried silently, *why did you have to die and leave us like this? Why weren't you more careful?*

Later, with the lights out, she lay rigid in the double bed she shared with Mama, trying not to touch her mother's body. She thought of the little huts in China where people had even less space and privacy—the *kangs,* where whole families slept together. She'd envied them, thinking it was so cozy. Now she wondered how they survived.

She couldn't stand this much longer. Something had to change.

Maybe she could run away and get a job in a defense factory. But even Papa wouldn't have approved of that. His last words were that she and Mama should take care of each other. *Oh, Papa! Without you, that's impossible.*

As soon as school let out that spring, Elsa went to work in a peach-packing shed at the edge of town. In the stall ahead of her worked a girl named Lillian, and during breaks, she and Elsa relaxed together. Lillian had a car and soon began driving Elsa to and from work.

It was nice to have a girlfriend again. When the fruit didn't come in fast enough and they had some hours off, they window-shopped and lined up to buy nylons and bobby pins and chewing gum. Lillian persuaded Elsa to shave her legs and showed her how to use just enough Tangee lipstick to make her face light up.

Then a heat wave hit, and peaches ripened so fast they had to work evenings, even some Sundays. On an especially sweltering afternoon early in August, the packing-house machinery broke down, and the foreman said it would take several hours to fix.

It was five o'clock; Mama wouldn't be home from work for at least another hour. Elsa invited Lillian to the apartment to rest.

The windows were shut, and the room was hotter than outside, so Elsa plugged in a fan and turned it on. Lillian pulled off her shoes and dress, letting the breeze hit her bare arms and legs, so Elsa did the same. They lay on the bed in their slips, eating saltines and listening to the radio. First the war news: a battle in the Aleutians, bombings down in the Solomons. Then the *Easy Aces Comedy Hour*, and they laughed so hard they didn't hear the door open.

Mama's face was red, and her lips twitched. "What's going on here?"

Elsa jumped up and put on her dress. She introduced Lillian and said, "We were just cooling off, waiting to go back to the shed."

Lillian fumbled with her tie-back sash, then held out her hand. "Pleased to meet you, Mrs. Meier."

Mama ignored the hand and barely nodded, her eyes narrowed.

Lillian glanced at Elsa, her eyebrows raised, then looked at her watch. "We ought to get back." Elsa tied her shoes and quickly followed her out before her mother could scold her.

In the car, Lillian said, "Your mother doesn't like me, does she?"

Elsa looked away. She remembered Morris asking the same thing. "It's not you; it's me. She's so afraid I'll do something wrong and embarrass her before the church people."

"I don't get it. What kind of things?"

"Oh, wearing makeup and jewelry. Dresses too short. Going to movies, playing cards. Even radio programs."

"Sounds pretty narrow."

"Yeah." Elsa sighed. "It's not like I want to go out and get drunk or anything. It's just—it'd be so nice to be normal. Like everybody else."

Long ago, Morris had said, *You're just like the others. . . . It's not a compliment.* Was it wrong to be like the rest of the world?

Lillian looked puzzled, and Elsa told her, "It wasn't so bad when my father was the pastor. He wasn't like that at all. He was . . . tolerant. Now, I feel like everybody's watching me, hoping for things to gossip about."

"Doesn't your mother stick up for you?"

"Huh! You'd think she wrote the Ten Commandments."

In the evening after work, Mama told Elsa, "That girl's a bad influence on you. Lolling around on the bed, half naked—"

"We didn't want to get our dresses wrinkled! It was so hot—"

"But on the bed?"

Elsa shook her head. "Where else could we rest? Sitting on our two straight chairs? We didn't do anything wrong. Good heavens!"

"Elsa—that's sacrilegious! See? That's just what I mean. You're even picking up bad words. You're not to see her again."

Elsa groaned. Why did her mother make her feel so dirty? "Mama, I work with her."

"People say you've been running around town with her, giggling, acting foolish. Wearing paint on your faces."

Elsa puffed out her breath. Other young women in church had started using makeup. Why did she have to be the most virtuous?

She eyed her mother, ready for bed, nightgown buttoned to her chin.

Eternal Virtue. In China, names were considered self-fulfilling. Mama must have hoped for a saintly daughter. But this was America, and Elsa knew she'd never fulfill her Chinese name.

She bit her lip to keep from saying that aloud. Going to the little kitchenette sink, she dampened her hair and wound it into pin curls.

The next day, Lillian asked her, "How can you stand it, day after day, crammed in that little room with your mother?"

"When my father died, I promised him I'd take care of her."

Lillian frowned. "She's in good health, isn't she? Seems like she could take pretty good care of herself. Surely he didn't mean for you to live with her all your life."

"What else can I do?"

"Go away to school. Get a teacher's credential. Anything!"

Elsa wrinkled her nose. "I don't want to be a teacher. I've lived with one too long."

"Something else, then. A librarian, accountant, bank teller—with so many men gone, there are all kinds of jobs out there."

Elsa remembered helping in the Shiao Yangshan clinic and dreaming of working together with Ling. "When I was a little girl, I wanted to be a nurse."

"Well, there you are. Be one."

Elsa shook her head. "I don't have the money for nurses' training."

But the next week, Lillian helped Elsa apply for scholarships to several nursing schools. They filled in Mama's small income, saying there was no way she could help with expenses.

Three schools accepted her application, and the Langford School of Nursing offered her a full scholarship, including a weekly allowance. It would be a three-year program, with two weeks off in the summer.

Elsa didn't know how to tell her mother. Finally, on a Monday less than a week before she was to leave, she said, "Mama, I can't live like this anymore. I'm going away."

Mama stared at her. "What do you mean, going away?"

"I'm entering nursing school. In Shelburne, near Los Angeles."

"Los Angeles?" Mama made it sound like a den of iniquity. "No. I forbid it."

"I'll live in a dorm. They have strict rules." Elsa explained about the scholarship, the high standards of teaching.

"You can't just run off and leave me all alone." Mama's eyes filled with the expected tears.

Elsa steeled herself. "I have to. Before we both go crazy. It's all settled; they're expecting me."

"You promised your father—"

"I'm not deserting you. I'll write every week."

Mama eased herself into a chair. "When?" Her voice was weak.

"I leave this Saturday. Do you want to help me pack?"

Mama didn't move. "How . . . how did you know what to do, who to ask about this scholarship?"

Elsa didn't want Lillian to be blamed. "I got help. The school office had forms to fill out. Mama, it's time I took responsibility for my own future."

Chapter 29

September 8, 1945

ON THE WAY TO HER ROOM IN the Langford dormitory, Elsa stopped by the nursing matron's office to pick up her mail.

She shuffled through it quickly before climbing the stairs. The next month's work schedule, a catalog for medical instruments, a letter from Mama. In the room, she looked through the envelopes more carefully. Still nothing from Morris.

It was eight o'clock on Saturday evening, and the dorm seemed empty with her roommate, Fern, and many of the other girls out on dates. In the little cubicle she and Fern shared, she switched on the desk radio, rubbed her aching shoulders, and let the romantic lyrics of the *Hit Parade* soothe her body and spirit. If only she were hearing the words from Morris instead of Dick Haymes!

It had been a long, hot day, endlessly applying steaming packs to young polio patients. Dinner had been a quick bite taken at the nursing station—a ham sandwich, for the first time since meat rationing had been relaxed.

Now Elsa gratefully pulled off her sweaty uniform, flung it over a chair, and threw herself on her bed. Opening the envelope from Mama, she thought of the day her friend Lillian had come to the apartment to cool off. Good thing Mama couldn't see her now!

This will be a short letter because I am very tired. Tonight I attended Mrs. Thesman's birthday party, given by her daughter. Anna is so good to her and comes to see her every day.

Elsa sighed. She knew that had to be a poke at her for not being a dutiful child. But Anna Thesman was a fortyish spinster with no life of her own. Elsa wondered: if she hadn't left, would she have ended up like that?

I still can't see you as a nurse cleaning bedpans and being among all those germs. You've never cared about other people's feelings. Are you doing this just to spite me?

Elsa had worked hard at the classes and nursing skills, not to spite Mama—although to fail would have been to lose face—but for her own fulfillment. The hours were long, the work hard, and the equipment old and worn since all new materials went to the war effort. But for the most part, she'd been happy. She knew Papa would have been proud of her, now into her second year of the three-year course.

It had all been worthwhile when a child said in a wondering tone, "I didn't even feel that shot!" and when a grieving family thanked her for giving them comfort.

I hope when you come to your senses and move back home you'll be able to get a job better suited to you. Morgan's Department Store is advertising for clerks . . .

Elsa looked out the window at the three-story brick hospital with its red-tiled roof. Tall palm trees circled the grounds; on the other side of the highway, the town of Shelburne nestled against purple mountains.

This was home now—more so than Mama's apartment had ever been. But she only had one more year to go, and then what? Moving back to Mama was unthinkable.

She'd gone back to Riverglen only once—the Christmas after she'd left. Although the apartment wasn't quite as small as her dorm room, she'd felt stifled. She was a different person now, but Mama hadn't changed at all.

At church, the new minister—not Mrs. Bauman's brother after all—had been kind and the people friendly, but most of the young people were still gone. Regina Bauman had married Joe Schmidt and gone to work as a waitress in Placerville, near the CPS forestry camp where Joe was stationed.

The girls who remained giggled about fashions and hairstyles and complained about sugar rationing. Elsa had witnessed terminal illness, tragic accidents, the death of children. On affiliation to the veterans hospital, she'd tended discharged soldiers with missing limbs or with minds that couldn't accept the horrors they'd seen. She felt ages older than those silly girls back home.

Some of the Langford students talked about becoming army nurses. Elsa wished she had the nerve to sign up. She imagined herself near the front lines, bandaging wounds, assisting in surgery, whispering comfort to lonely men.

But the church wouldn't approve, and Mama would disown her. As much as Elsa wanted freedom, she wasn't sure it was worth the price of ostracism.

Keep your eyes open to all the dangerous influences around. Communism can creep up on you and deceive you.

Mama, fiercely Republican, had believed that President Roosevelt was not only a Communist but the Antichrist as well. When he'd died, she'd written that it was a hoax and in three years he'd be back with all the horror of Armageddon.

Elsa had been terrified at his death. Would the leaderless country now lose its hard-won toehold in Okinawa, its precarious advance across the Rhine? But the war had ended after all, and servicemen swarmed home to make new lives with the help of the GI Bill passed while Roosevelt had been in office. Mama couldn't be right.

Don't be led astray into dancing or movies. It may seem innocent fun, but one step in the wrong direction will lure you onto the wide path to destruction.

Her mother would have been horrified to see Elsa jitterbugging with soldiers at the USO on her free evenings, or kicking in a conga line on the main street of Shelburne when Germany surrendered.

Her love of stories and drama had prompted her to find out just why the church banned movies. Some she wished she hadn't seen, but many were as innocent as a Sunday school story. Still, she'd prayed that the theater wouldn't burn down during the show, with her name listed as a fatality for all the Mennonites to see.

You haven't written much about your soldier friend. Have you finally broken off with him? I told you he would only bring you grief.

Elsa put the letter down and rolled onto her stomach, wishing her mother hadn't brought that up. She hadn't heard from Morris for several months and imagined him wounded and suffering like the men in the veterans hospital. Maybe even killed. She'd prayed so hard every night and throughout the day, and had wondered if God heard her.

She'd even written to Morris's parents, but his dad said not to worry. Morris wasn't much of a writer—she'd known that already— and if anything had happened, they would have been told. But she still imagined all kinds of possibilities, including a new girlfriend somewhere in the Pacific zone.

They hadn't made any commitments to each other, but in his last letter, he'd written, *"Remember that time in Morro Bay? When I get home, we'll go again. Do you still have the lucky sand dollar I gave you?"*

The sand dollar lay wrapped in tissue paper in the little wooden treasure box on her desk. She often took it out and held it against her cheek. It soothed her more than Ling's smooth little rubbing stone had.

Now, listening to Frank Sinatra croon about remembered kisses, thoughts of that sunny afternoon at the beach washed over her. The look in Morris's eyes, his eager kisses . . .

Her body tingled. He was so sweet, so tender—yet strong and dependable. Like Morro Rock. He did love her; she knew he did. Just the way Papa had loved Mama.

Then why hadn't he written? Was he missing and the War Department hadn't gotten around to notifying his parents? Had she been mistaken about his intentions? Could Mama be right about that?

Nearly every day, students and teachers proudly introduced their discharged sweethearts and husbands. Elsa tried not to be envious, but she couldn't help being angry at the war, the enemy, God—maybe even at Morris himself. And now Mama.

She skimmed over the rest of the letter—*"Shun evil and stay pure"*—and shook her head. Why couldn't Mama just come out and say, "Don't fool around with men"?

She'd flirted with soldiers at the USO. All the girls did; it was their patriotic duty. Most of the boys had been polite and decent, missing their sweethearts back home. A few had been lonesome enough to steal a kiss in a dark corner of the room, and there'd been a corporal from Texas whom she might have considered if she weren't in love with Morris.

But there'd also been Douglas. Though she'd made it plain she wasn't available, he'd attached himself to her like flypaper. Last Saturday night when the band had drifted into romantic melodies and the couples had switched to slow dancing, he'd gotten down-right fresh. She'd slapped him hard—there was even a red blotch on his cheek afterward—but he'd still had the nerve to ask her to go see *Casablanca* with him the following week. She'd turned and left without dignifying his question with an answer.

Rolling over on her bed, Elsa slid Mama's letter into her desk drawer. The evening stretched endlessly before her, and she wondered whether to study, clean the room, or put on her pajamas and catch up on sleep.

Sleep was winning when a monitor popped her head through the door. "Someone here to see you!"

Elsa's spine prickled. Would Douglas never give up? "Tell him I'm not in. Tell him I'm sick. Or dead. Just get rid of him."

But the messenger had already left. Elsa pulled her dirty uniform back on and marched down the stairs, not bothering to comb her hair. She burst into the lounge, glaring. "You've got a lot of—"

Her mouth went dry, and her anger evaporated. Across the empty room, a tall soldier leaned against the door frame. He took his cap off, showing a stubble of blond hair.

Elsa's heart turned a handspring. Morris was back, he was here with her, and he was gorgeous!

Lean and muscular, his face tanned, he smiled with that familiar crooked smile, drowning her with the love in his eyes. With a few long strides, he closed the space between them.

Elsa's knees wobbled, and the last bit of energy drained out through her toes. She tried to smooth her hair, straighten her uniform. "Why didn't you tell me you were coming?"

Morris said, "Hush, woman. First things first." His kisses were gentle, loving. His soft lips, muscular arms, strong eager body, all felt wonderful. Vaguely, Elsa was aware of other students peeking through the door, but she didn't care.

She led him to the couch, her head spinning with his intoxicating sweetness, and they sat down together. She touched his hands, his arms, his face, making sure he was real—alive, safe, and healthy. He'd come all this way just to see her.

Morris whispered, "I've missed you so much, my China doll, my darling little elf."

Elf. This time it sounded beautiful. His clear blue eyes shone with an adoration so powerful that her body went limp from the wonder of it.

"I've been bragging to all the guys—showing them your pictures." His voice was husky.

"I waited and waited to hear from you. I thought—"

"Couldn't write in the trenches. We didn't even know the war was over until we got back to the base. I wrote as soon as I could. Didn't you get that letter?"

She shook her head, unable to speak.

"You must have been worried sick. It was one big snafu—guys leaving, the rest of us waiting to be notified. Probably that's why the mail didn't get through." He cupped her chin in his hand and looked steadily into her eyes. "I'll make it up to you now. You'll see."

Elsa never knew she could feel such joy—joy so intense it hurt.

Morris still hadn't said he loved her, but she knew he did. And she loved him.

A YEAR LATER, ELSA AND MORRIS were married in a simple Mennonite ceremony, the Bethel church transformed with roses and baby's breath from Mrs. Weston's garden.

They walked down the aisle together, hand in hand, while the pianist played "Savior, Like a Shepherd Lead Us."

Elsa wore a long white crepe dress she'd sewn herself and held a bouquet of yellow daisies. Tsao Po-Po's silver hairpin held a veil that reached Elsa's fingertips. She was floating, an imaginary person only pretending to exist.

Was she really the same girl who had come from China? It was hard to believe that when she'd met Morris, she'd thought he was a pest—following her home on his bike, skidding around so she'd be forced to look at him.

It had taken a war to make her realize what a wonderful guy he was. She still felt the thrill, the miracle of seeing him safely back. When his last letters had finally arrived, three of them at the same time, she'd read of the joy and hopes he'd been holding back, and realized, even early on, how deep his love had been.

When they reached the front pew, Elsa saw her mother sitting primly regal, and her happiness lost a little of its glow. Mama still hadn't accepted Morris, hadn't forgiven him for serving in the military, for daring to enroll in a school of pharmacy in Los Angeles, so temptingly near Elsa's school. She wouldn't credit Elsa with enough maturity to make her own boundaries and rules, and she hadn't bothered to come to the nursing school's graduation.

Mama had said they didn't deserve to have the wedding in the Mennonite church. But Elsa and Morris had talked to the pastor, testifying to their faith, and the pastor had said he'd be glad to marry them. Now Mama was angry at the pastor, too. For once, Elsa was thankful that her mother was too proper to make a fuss in public.

Elsa looked up at Morris, so handsome in his navy blue suit, a lighter blue tie matching his sparkling eyes. His crisp blond curls had grown back, and a tiny spiral escaped down his forehead.

His eyes met hers, and she felt radiantly alive. He squeezed her hand, and she knew their love was the only thing in the world that mattered.

They stepped up to the platform, facing the waiting pastor. Standing there, Elsa heard the soloist sing, heard the rise and fall of the minister's long sermon, made the right responses. She and Morris knelt, murmured their prayers, then rose, and finally turned to be presented to the congregation.

Mama sat unsmiling, and her mouth gave a slight twitch. In time, Elsa thought—surely in time—Mama, too, would realize how wonderful Morris was. But if not, it would be Mama's loss. Not hers.

In the opposite pew, Morris's parents sat beaming, Mr. Drake giving Morris a thumbs-up sign. They seemed more like family than her own mother.

Elsa smiled at Mrs. Weston, Tommie and the handsome husband she'd met at camp, Fern, her old friend Lillian, her grandparents, uncles, aunts and cousins, and a few other relatives she'd met at Papa's funeral.

Papa. Tears pricked at her eyes. If only Papa were here. Then the minister raised his hand over their heads.

"The Lord bless thee and keep thee. The Lord make His face to shine upon thee, and be gracious unto thee . . ."

Papa's favorite blessing. The minister went on, but instead, Elsa heard Papa's voice. "The Lord lift up His countenance upon thee, and give thee peace."

She felt Papa there on the platform, sharing in their precious experience. *Peace.* It was real, and God would be with them.

From a church tower blocks away, chimes struck eight o'clock. "*Yi, er, san, si, wu, lui, chi, bah.*"

The perfect number. It had finally happened. She was happy and beautiful. She was Eternal Virtue. Maybe now, she and Mama could become friends.

Part 3

Chapter 30

October 1956

MORRIS AND ELSA'S APARTMENT IN Los Angeles wasn't much bigger than Mama's, but Elsa loved it. This was the closeness she'd yearned for when she'd thought of whole families sleeping together on a Chinese *kang*. Waking up next to the man who treated her like a treasure, coming home from her work at the hospital in the evening to tell him all about her day, helping him with his studies at the school of pharmacy—this had to be what heaven was like.

After Morris graduated, he'd taken a job at a large pharmaceutical house in the nearby suburb of Creston. Elsa kept working, too, hoping they could save up to buy a house.

But one night she came home to find Morris staring soberly at the floor and tapping an envelope against his chin. "What's the matter?" she asked.

He turned to her. "What would you think of moving back to Riverglen?"

Elsa swallowed hard, a heavy weight settling onto her chest. How could she, after all these years, settle back into that town of so many memories? The awful high school days, surviving through the war, Papa's accident—and through it all, trying to please Mama. No! It was impossible.

"Mr. Grainger wants me to take over his drugstore. He'd like to retire." Morris handed her the letter.

She read it carefully. Not only was this a job offer, but it also held a possibility of someday owning the store. She imagined Morris dispensing the bottles of pills, explaining their effects to the customers, being a respected businessman in the town. Now, he was only one of many workers, but at a little store like Grainger's, he would be the boss.

"My dad and mom would love it, I know," he said slowly. "And housing is a lot less expensive there. But would you be able to stand living near your mother again?"

Elsa leaned over his shoulders, hugging him. He was always so considerate of her feelings. She knew if she refused, he would turn the offer down. "I guess I'll have to do a lot of praying about that."

He pulled her around and onto his lap. "Maybe after being apart this long, you could start all over. You might find your mother easier to get along with."

Elsa sighed. "That would be a miracle."

"We wouldn't need to live that close to her. And if you want, we could join my folks' church."

She thought about that. Mom and Dad Drake had generously taken her into the family. With them, she could be herself—not on guard all the time, afraid she'd say or do the wrong thing. But wouldn't that be allowing Mama to restrict even her church attendance? Maybe they could visit both, and see where they fit the best.

A month later, she and Morris made their decision, and she wrote a postcard to Mama: "Moving back to Riverglen. See you next spring!" As she dropped it into the mail, she hoped they weren't making a terrible mistake.

April 1957
ELSA EXAMINED THE KITCHEN TABLE. For the first visitor in her first real home, everything must be perfect. The blue-checked cloth hung evenly all around, the forks and knives were straight, the napkins—real linen—were threaded into ceramic napkin rings. In the exact center, three pink camellias floated in a shallow glass bowl.

The little radio on the counter played a lilting tune, and Elsa hummed along. This time, Mama wouldn't be able to find fault. Today would be the start of their adult friendship.

Carefully, she spooned tuna salad into two scooped-out tomatoes nestled in lettuce on her best salad plates.

Through the window, she could see a hummingbird dart from the ornamental pear tree to the feeder on the patio, take a sip, and flash back to its nest. The birds seemed to enjoy their home as much as she and Morris loved theirs.

They had been right to come here. It had taken a while to find the perfect house, but Morris's parents had seemed happy to take them in until escrow closed.

At the Mennonite church, several people had greeted them politely, but there was an unfamiliar minister and many newcomers she didn't know. Few remembered Papa, and Mama's friends eyed her with suspicion.

The people in Dad and Mom Drake's Baptist church greeted them with hugs, smiles, and a big church dinner. Elsa had been so touched she hugged them all back. Best of all, her high school friend Tommie, with her husband and two small children, attended here. She and Tommie had kept in contact with Christmas letters, but now could have a wonderful time renewing their friendship. It hadn't been hard to decide to attend there, visiting Mama's church on special occasions.

Elsa was sure that Mama thought her leaving the Mennonite church was the same as backsliding. Although she had pointed out the similarity of their beliefs, both stemming from the same Anabaptist movement, and the fact that she still highly regarded the Mennonites and their traditions, she could tell her mother wasn't convinced. Maybe today she could explain how she felt.

It was nearly noon, and Mama would arrive any minute. Elsa snapped off the radio, opened the preheated oven, and popped in a pan of rolls to warm.

When the doorbell rang, she took a final look around the room, smoothed her newly permed hair, and opened the door, smiling warmly.

"Welcome to the Drake mansion," she said. It would be fun to play hostess to her mother.

Mama stood in the doorway unsmiling, her eyes roving around the living room. Suddenly, the house that Elsa was so proud of, and had worked so hard to set in order, seemed shabby.

Why was it that Mama always made her feel inadequate? "I don't have any pictures up yet," she said lamely.

Mama nodded. "That would help." She walked through the living room, sniffing. "Is something burning?"

Elsa dashed into the kitchen and snatched the rolls out of the oven. The bottoms were too brown, but they were still edible. She tilted the pan into a cloth-lined basket, and two rolls dropped on the floor. Quickly she snatched them up and dusted them on the dishtowel. They wouldn't be dirty; she'd just washed the floor this morning.

But Mama was watching, so Elsa put them aside. Morris would gladly eat them at dinnertime.

She filled the waiting glasses with iced tea. "Everything's ready. I hope you're hungry." Gesturing to a chair at the table, she sat down on the opposite side.

She asked Mama to say grace, hoping for a blessing on her and the house, too, but Mama only murmured thanks for the food.

Then Mama tasted her tuna salad and asked, "What kind of mayonnaise do you use?"

"Home Pride. Why?"

"Next time get Salad Mate. It isn't quite so sour."

Elsa took a sip of iced tea and didn't answer. Morris *liked* this kind.

Mama refused a roll, and left her tomato untouched. "Don't you know I'm allergic to tomatoes?"

"No," said Elsa. "You never told me that. I don't remember you not eating them."

Mama put her napkin on the table. "Well, now you know."

Elsa stared at her plate. Would she never please her mother? Deliberately, she buttered a second roll.

After lunch, Elsa showed Mama the rest of the house. The spare bedroom was still filled with unopened packing boxes, but the master bedroom was neat, and she'd found time to sew curtains for the large window—forest green leaves twining through tiny orange flowers on a pale yellow background. Tommie had helped her pick out the material, but she knew better than to mention that.

"I haven't finished the bedspread yet. It'll match the curtains.

And then I'll make solid-colored cushions. Probably orange—I've always loved orange. It reminds me of the nasturtiums in Shungtau. Remember them? They climbed up the side of the veranda. I liked to suck the juice from the spurs."

Mama didn't seem to be listening. She fingered the curtains, examining the gathers, while Elsa held her breath, waiting for the criticism. "It's good work." Elsa exhaled slowly so Mama wouldn't notice. "But I think yellow cushions would match better."

Elsa led her mother to the living-room sofa and showed her a picture album from the years in Southern California. "This was the apartment house where we lived, and right up here"—she pointed to a third-story window—"was our room. It had a little kitchen in an alcove and a small living-dining area."

Mama glanced at the pictures and pushed them aside. "Elsa, why did you come back? It doesn't make sense—after all those years of study, to quit a good job and end up in this hick town."

Elsa looked down and smoothed her skirt. Maybe it was too soon to say anything. But Mama was waiting, her eyebrows raised.

"Mr. Grainger has some long-range plans," said Elsa. A partnership. Maybe eventually us buying the store."

Mama's lips twitched. "You'd really be committing to this town. Doesn't Morris have any ambition?"

"We like a small town. It's a good place to raise a family."

Mama looked sharply at Elsa. "You're not—"

Elsa blushed. "Due in November."

Mama shook her head. "You just don't know what you're in for, moving here. How could you fall into the same trap that I did?"

Elsa stared at her. "Trap? Mama, what on earth do you mean? Morris and I have a good life, careers we enjoy, and a promising future. What more could we want?"

"No. It is a trap. You do what he wants you to, and you do it for him. And then you're caught living in the same little box for the rest of your life."

Elsa closed the picture album and stood up. "Morris and I love it here. And here, we feel needed. Can't you understand?"

"I understand you all too well. Ever since you were a baby—"

Elsa put her hands on her mother's rigid shoulders and looked into her face. "Mama, I'm not a baby anymore. I'm a married woman. I love my husband, and I want to please him. I cook the food he likes, I use the mayonnaise he prefers—"

Mama sniffed, and her eyes filled. "You never listen to any suggestions for improvement."

Elsa sighed. This wasn't working. Why had she thought it would? No matter what, Mama still viewed her as a naughty little girl.

But this time, she refused to let Mama's convenient tears make her feel guilty. *How sad*, she thought. *Mama doesn't even understand the love, the happiness that Morris and I share.*

WHEN CRYSTAL WAS BORN, Elsa saw an amazing change in Mama. Her mother oohed and aahed into her granddaughter's pretty little face, gasped when tiny fingers curved around her hovering thumb, and marveled at the fuzzy head burrowing into her shoulder, finding just the right spot for comfort.

The next Mother's Day, Mama stood beside Morris's parents as Elsa and Morris dedicated their six-month-old baby at the Baptist church. She joined them all for lunch afterward, as pleasant and polite as anyone could wish. Although she glanced with tight lips at Elsa's pinned-back hairdo and brightly flowered spring dress, she didn't comment.

But there was one thing Mama did not like.

"*Crystal* is tableware!" she scolded. "Why did you name her that? Why not Christine, after my mother? Now that's a refined, cultured name, a good way to start a life."

Christine? Elsa hadn't even known that was her grandmother's name. She'd always loved the name Crystal, but she knew she'd better not admit that she'd used it for one of her favorite imaginary friends.

When Morris shortened the name to Crys, Mama didn't fuss anymore. As long as she didn't see the name spelled out, Elsa figured, Mama could think she'd had her own way.

As the baby grew, Elsa tried to point out how much she favored Morris—her sweet disposition, wide blue eyes, and the wispy hair that promised to be golden curls.

But Mama disagreed with that, too. "No. She's the image of Jasper."

Elsa had to admit that resemblance. Like him, Crystal was born to cuddle. It was obvious that the loss of her little brother was still a spike through Mama's heart, and despite Elsa's promise to Papa, remorse again flooded through her.

Now her mother visited often, usually when Morris was away at the drugstore. She sang songs and recited nursery rhymes that Elsa had never heard, played pat-a-cake and peek-a-boo, and the baby cooed and gurgled for her. Each time, Mama brought a gift—a pretty little dress, an educational toy, or a book—her face smooth and happy as she helped Crys's tiny fingers touch the bow and tear open the shiny paper.

Elsa was jealous of every moment the baby was in Mama's arms, but she told herself their bonding was building a truce of sorts between her and her mother. Although they didn't always agree on how the baby should be fed, clothed or disciplined, now they could usually work out a compromise.

Elsa and Morris had planned to have more children, but Crystal's birth had been a difficult one, and the doctor advised Elsa against it. Regretfully, she tried to make it up to Crystal by arranging playtimes with Sunday school friends, and later, schoolmates.

Morris kept busy at the drugstore with plans to modernize the building. Finances were tight, so when Crystal started second grade, Elsa went back to work at the hospital. From then on, Mama kept Crys after school until Elsa's shift was over. With her grandmother's constant drilling, the girl couldn't help but get top grades.

Even when there was no longer any need for child care, Crys often visited her grandmother, and soon it was obvious that they had developed a special, loving relationship. One that didn't include Elsa.

But that didn't keep Crys from being sunny and affectionate at home, and Elsa tried to swallow her bitterness. As the years passed, Elsa enjoyed her daughter's accomplishments in school— music, drama, and sports—as well as her spiritual growth, but her resentment of her mother grew. Sometimes she felt like lashing out at Mama, but knew that would only make things worse. Instead, at

Morris's suggestion, she volunteered at Crystal's school and took part in the parent-teacher club.

Crystal breezed happily through high school, surrounded by a crowd of friends, occasionally dating a boy that even Mama liked, and staying active in the church youth group. When she finally graduated as a popular valedictorian with several scholarships, Elsa remembered her own childhood battles, and couldn't help being proud of producing such a perfect daughter.

But Mama wasn't satisfied. According to her, Riverglen couldn't provide a decent education.

"No community college for my granddaughter," she announced. "She needs to attend the best university. Stanford, Duke—maybe even Harvard."

Elsa sighed. "You don't understand, Mama. Even with the scholarships, schools like that are way beyond our means. Morris is doing well at the drugstore, but he's had to put most of our income back into the business. Maybe after two years of general ed here, we can think about a university."

"No." Mama wagged her finger against Elsa's protests. "It's you who doesn't understand. We need to think about her future. She must move in the right circles and meet young men who will become doctors, lawyers—maybe even someone high in government. Smart as she is, she could have a career of her own." Mama hesitated, then rushed on. "I didn't tell you this, but long ago when Crys was a baby, I took out some college insurance for her. By now, it should be enough."

Elsa stared at her in disbelief. How could Mama afford this on her small salary from the dry goods store? Thinking back, she slowly realized that her fashion-conscious mother had worn the same suit for several years, only changing the veils on hats, the buttons and trim on blouses. She'd always thought that Mama dieted to stay slim, but now she suspected she'd scrimped on food, too.

Elsa knew she ought to appreciate all those sacrifices and hoped her thanks to Mama sounded sincere. But no matter how much she prayed about it, resentment twisted around her heart like a strangling vine.

She thought back through the years. First her mother had sent Ling away. Then, as if her struggles to adjust to America weren't bad enough, Mama had disapproved of her only high school friend, Tommie. Her packing-house pal, Lillian. Mama had even tried hard to push Morris out of her life. Did she now plan to take Crystal away from her, too?

Several weeks later, while Mama was visiting, Crys surprised everyone. "I've been accepted by Barton University. A small college in Chicago. I know it's not Ivy League, not even very well known, but it has the best studies in social science."

A small college? *Social science?*

Crystal nodded. "I'd like to get into counseling, work with people with problems. Life has been so easy for me; I need to give something back. I believe that's what God wants for me."

Mama was horrified, and Elsa was sure she would cancel the college insurance. She didn't know whether to be happy or sad for her daughter's sake.

But Crystal didn't seem worried. She showed the brochures and catalogs to her grandmother, with all the good references, high ratings, and lists of courses needed for a solid career in social work.

After fuming several days, Mama finally gave in. "I've asked around," she said. "That line of work does have possibilities. It could even lead into a position in government."

Finally, Elsa and Mama agreed. No matter what Crys decided, she would be the best in her field.

Chapter 31

May 1980

THREE YEARS LATER, WITHOUT WARNING, Elsa and Mama's fragile truce shattered.

Home from school at the end of her junior year, Crystal's words echoed in the dining room: "I'm quitting college."

Across the table from her, Elsa sat stunned. Last night, she and Morris had been so happy to see their daughter. All the way home from the airport, they'd talked about her classes at Barton, the things she'd done in Chicago, what had been going on in Riverglen while she'd been gone. Morris had told her the pharmacy had been so busy he'd hired an assistant manager.

They'd arrived home late, hugged again, and gone to bed, telling Crystal to sleep in while Elsa and Morris went to work.

Now, the work day over, they'd enjoyed the meal that Crystal had fixed and had been relaxing around the table, eager to continue their happy reunion.

Crys took another bite of apple pie, then gestured with her fork. "The people at El Seco taught me more than any textbook could. All year, I've been thinking about them, and I'm convinced I can't waste any more time just reading textbooks."

Along with other volunteers, she'd spent the previous summer at a relief station, passing out supplies to needy families. In a dusty little village deep in Mexico, they'd lived in tents, chopped firewood until their hands blistered, and cooked over an outdoor spit. Besides bringing the gospel to the needy, they had taught them skills that made them self-supporting.

Elsa had been proud of her daughter's willingness to serve and knew that Morris was too. But quitting school? She frowned. "What about your senior year? Your degree?"

"Next year's mostly fieldwork anyway. What better place to do it? Besides, Ruben says I have more insight than any counselor he knows."

Morris set down a forkful of pie and pushed the plate aside. "Ruben?"

"Dr. Valdez. I've told you about him—we worked together in El Seco. He—we've been corresponding. A lot. You ought to see him minister to those people. I've never known anyone so dedicated." Her face beamed, and Elsa sensed that her daughter was attracted to more than his dedication. "The people trust him. They look to him for cures, for miracles. To them, even an aspirin is a miracle."

"Dr. Ruben Valdez." Elsa remembered the name. The man who had talked Crystal into volunteering last summer instead of coming home and helping Morris in the drugstore. "But I've always pictured him as an old man."

"He's thirty-three."

"Is he . . . a Christian?"

"Oh, yes, Mom! He loves the Lord just like I do. He puts his faith to work."

Morris cleared his throat. "And he's persuaded you to give up everything you've worked for?"

Crys finished her last bite of pie before answering. "Dad, that settlement in El Seco—you have to see it to understand. All those poor people, all the suffering. That's what made me decide."

"What does Greg think about this?" Elsa watched her daughter's face. The boy Crys had dated in high school and during college vacations now seemed part of the family.

"He's coming home from Stanford next week. I'll tell him then."

Morris's cheeks sagged a little. "He's a fine boy. We'd hoped you two would get married someday."

"No. We're good friends, but our goals are in opposite directions. He's all finance and politics, and I—well, my future is to help people."

Elsa said, "You might feel differently when you see him again."

Crys shook her head. "We were never in love. Not like you and Dad. With you as an example, I can't settle for less."

Elsa glanced at Morris, and he winked at her. Despite what Mama said, she'd never regretted marrying him. He was her anchor, her happiness. Of course, she wanted Crys to have the same thing. But this was so sudden, so impulsive—Crys couldn't know what she was doing.

"Crys." Morris reached across the table and took her hands. "I'm glad you feel that way about marriage. But give Greg a chance. He's grown up a lot in the past two years. I know he thinks the world of you." He turned away and blew his nose, and Elsa knew he was hurting. He and Greg had become good friends. He'd even mentioned taking the boy into the drugstore and putting his aggressive ideas to good use.

Crystal sighed. "I thought you would understand."

Elsa couldn't believe this change in her daughter, this child-woman she loved so much. She thought back to Crystal's growing years—the wild cheering at her volleyball games, applauding at her piano recitals, swelling with vicarious glory when she charmed audiences in drama productions. She was so bright, so capable.

The worst was, what would Mama say? After grooming Crystal all these years, preparing her for acceptance in the right circles, all the financial sacrifices—why, with Greg's promising political future, Mama had decided that Crys could rise up to head the federal Department of Health and Welfare, developing programs and making policies. All Mama's hopes were tied to the balloon of Crystal's future. Now, for it to just drift away . . .

Elsa knew that Mama would blame her for this, and it would be one more black mark against Morris. She got up and started to stack the dishes. Morris left the room, his pie unfinished, and she heard the back door close. Her heart ached as much for him as for herself. She took the dishes to the sink and stared out the window.

She felt Crystal's hand on her shoulder. "Think of it as missionary work—like Nana and Grandfather in China. Nana said—"

Elsa turned around abruptly. "You told your grandmother about this? When?"

Crystal reddened. "This afternoon, while you were at work. I would have told you last night, but the time just didn't seem right."

Was any time right for news like that? Elsa went back to the table and sank into her chair. As much as Crystal's decision hurt, the fact that she'd gone to Mama first hurt far more. "What did your grandmother say?"

"She—" Crystal sighed. "She wasn't too happy. But after we talked awhile, she said it might be possible to get an extension on the insurance payments, so I could go back later." She shrugged. "If I decide to."

"She didn't try to talk you out of it?"

"Oh, yes. But I explained it all to her."

"And it was all right with her?"

"Well, she said something strange. About the sins of the parents being passed down from generation to generation. I'm not sure what she meant by that."

Elsa knew. Mama still hadn't forgiven her for marrying an outsider to the church. Now Crystal was following in her steps by getting involved with this Dr. Valdez. The people of El Seco definitely didn't move in the right circles. "Is that all she said?"

Crystal set her father's pie aside, then started to rinse the other plates, loading the dishwasher. Droplets of water splashed onto the window and tracked down the pane. "She said she would talk to you about it."

Elsa could hear it now: *If you had trained her right . . . if you had been a better example . . . if you hadn't encouraged her to go to Mexico last summer . . .*

Through the window, she could see Morris vigorously chopping weeds in the garden. That was his way to release emotions. She wished she had an outlet for her own. Crystal followed her gaze. "Dad's pretty upset, isn't he?"

Elsa scrubbed the already clean table. "What do you expect? We've given up a lot to help you through school." Even with scholarships and Mama's insurance, there had been many extras. Barton University was expensive.

"You know I appreciate everything you've done. But Mom, I

thought you of all people would understand. All my life, I've heard how you loved China, how you didn't want to leave."

Shiao Yangshan, the big sandy compound. Tsao Po-Po. The yahbah. *Going along with Papa to the outstations. The clinic, all those people waiting for help. Ling.* It had nearly torn her heart out to look through the train window and watch the compound wall disappear in the distance.

And the hard adjustment to America. If only Mama had helped her instead of criticizing, it could have been so much easier.

Even after Papa died, when all they'd had was each other, Mama had held her at arm's length yet never let go.

Like an echo to Elsa's thoughts, Crystal said, "Sometimes I think you just don't want to let go of me."

The remark stung like the snap of a wet towel, and Elsa felt tears gathering behind her eyes. She wasn't like Mama. Was she? Did Crystal feel stifled?

Yet even the tears were like her mother's; they'd always been Mama's best weapon. Sick at heart, Elsa turned away and blinked them back.

Crystal closed the dishwasher and turned it on. "Mom, you and Dad raised me right. Now you need to trust my judgment. Don't worry—I've prayed about this and feel at peace. And when you meet Ruben, you'll see that he's right for me."

Elsa wiped the drops from the window. If only she could get rid of her tears as easily and feel at peace. "Give me time. I need to think about it."

Chapter 32

FOR SEVERAL DAYS, ELSA WORKED extra shifts at the hospital to avoid the dreaded talk with her mother. It also kept her from arguing with her daughter.

She felt guilty for being away so much, but Crystal said she had plenty to do, what with shopping, reading, and visiting friends. Elsa knew that her daughter also wrote many letters to Ruben and remembered those years she and Morris were apart. Did Crystal really feel the same way about her Mexican doctor? Even if she did, she couldn't know what kind of life would be ahead if she married him.

The morning of her day off, Elsa entered the kitchen to find her daughter and Morris already at the table, drinking coffee and reading the newspaper. Crystal looked up and tapped the page. "Mom, you should read this."

Elsa leaned over Crystal's shoulder to see the headline: "College Professor Gives Talk on China Trip."

"What?" she shouted. Hurriedly, she pulled out a chair and sat down next to Crystal to scan the article.

For the first time in a generation, groups of selected people had been allowed to tour certain cities in China. They had gone to schools, hospitals, the Forbidden City, the Great Wall, and much more.

When Elsa finished reading, Crystal told Morris, "You ought to take Mom on a trip like that. It would really bring back memories for her."

Elsa stared at her daughter, jolted as though she'd just grabbed the end of a live wire. She saw herself standing on the balcony of the Shungtau mission house, looking down at the rice paddies, the Han

River, and the green mountains beyond. Grown-up or not, she'd climb the chestnut tree . . .

No, that was impossible. Long ago, she'd heard that the red-tiled mission had been demolished by the Communists, and the chestnut tree had burned down to a stump. There'd be no use to go there. But the Shiao Yangshan mission with its mud-walled compound, the gray brick house—that might still be standing. She could walk to the village, talk to the people in their mud huts with pigs and chickens running in and out, rooting and pecking among the melon rinds. She'd eat hand-rolled noodles fresh from the pot. Pickled carrots. Ginger cookies.

Elsa sighed. What was she thinking about? Morris's profits went back into the store, and most of their savings had gone toward Crystal's education. "We can't afford a trip like that," she said.

Crystal persisted. "When's the last time you two had a vacation?"

Morris handed back the paper. "We go every year—"

"Sure. San Francisco, Seattle, Memphis. Wherever your conventions take you, right?" Crystal shook her head. "Business trips. You sit in meetings, and Mom takes a tour bus with other pharmacists' wives."

"You make it sound so boring. We've had great times. With all expenses paid." He finished his coffee, kissed them both good-bye, and left for work.

But the article kept nagging at Elsa. Old memories crept out, flooding her mind, drowning her in emotions: Fu Liu with his insolent sneer and wickedly sharp cleaver; his pretty nieces, Lihua and Shirhua; the swings, the stable, the open-scroll wall between the yard and the graveled front compound leading to the gatehouse; the bell tower.

Elsa shook her head. That part of her life was over. The adjustment had been too hard. It had taken a long time, but she was happy now. Morris had filled the emptiness of her life. Even if they could afford it, it would be too painful to dredge up the past. "No. It just isn't possible."

Morris worked hard at the drugstore, often into the night and on weekends. Even his hobby, photography, had been turned into a sideline, supplying picture postcards for the store.

But Elsa couldn't get China out of her mind. As she loaded the dishwasher, she wondered if any of the church people still lived in Shiao Yangshan. While wiping the table, she thought of Wu Shong and his wife, Sen Ying, Mama's helper at all the women's classes.

The next day, as she sat at the nurses' station studying the charts, an Asian family passed by. Their teenage son reminded her of Ling— his slim build; his smooth, clear skin and dark sparkling eyes; his self-assured swagger.

For a moment, she closed her eyes, feeling again the bittersweet emotions of her girlhood. Those first stirrings of young love, the sorrow and despair when it had been flung away and trampled like melon rinds tossed to the pigs.

From deep in her heart an ache surfaced, and she realized it had never left. Part of her had stayed in China. Going back might serve as a closure.

But how could they manage it, and how would she convince Morris?

Two days later, Elsa had an idea. Excited, she grabbed her purse and walked the eight blocks to town. The sun shone warm, and white clouds floated in a friendly blue sky. A breeze ruffled the leaves of the ornamental pear trees shading the front walk. In every yard, roses, pansies, and larkspurs shouted with color.

At the drugstore, she pushed open the glass door, and the chimes tinkled. The two salesgirls, busy with customers, smiled at her. Dick Ellis, the assistant manager, stood at the counter studying a catalog with a cosmetics salesman. In the back, behind a window partition, Morris moved among his vials and paper scoops.

The place had changed so much since the days when he'd worked at the soda fountain. Spacious aisles wound past shelves stocked with a variety of health and beauty preparations and gift items.

The snack bar was long gone; in its place stood a locked case filled with photographic equipment. On the counter, a rotating display showed his scenic postcards: Yosemite, the Sequoias, Crystal Cave, Morro Bay.

Morris looked up from his work and saw Elsa through the glass. He smiled, motioning for her to come into his private domain.

Elsa's spine tingled. After all these years, his eyes still sparkled when he looked at her. Could she blame Crys for wanting the same thing? She slipped past the little wooden swinging doors and into his embrace.

She took him to a Mandarin café for lunch. Pagodas, dragons, and lotus flowers decorated the walls; lacquered screens set with pearl fans stood next to the counter.

Seated, Morris looked around and rubbed his chin. "Okay, doll. Now tell me what's on your mind."

He knew her better than she knew herself. "That article about China . . . the more I think about it—"

"It's really calling you, huh?"

"Imagine seeing the Forbidden City, walking on the Great Wall." She toyed with her napkin, not meeting his eyes. "Maybe even the Shiao Yangshan mission."

"I've been thinking about it, too. I know it would mean a lot to you."

Elsa waited, hardly daring to breathe. Morris liked an orderly world where things fell into place and life followed a routine.

He dipped a prawn into mustard sauce and chewed it thoroughly. Finally he said, "It would take some doing."

"I know we don't have the money. It's probably a dumb idea."

Morris spoke slowly as though weighing each thought. "I hate the idea of Crys dropping out of school. But if she's determined, that would be one less expense. And our credit's good. . . . But it's not just the money. There are conferences, sales promotions, the equipment fair—"

Now was the time to show her hand. "Think of the picture post-cards you could make for your display. You could work up a slide travelogue like the series the Kiwanis put on each year. Nobody's done one on China."

Morris cocked his head, and his eyes widened. He nodded slowly and smiled at her. "Did you have a certain time in mind?"

Her heart leaped. "Not yet. Maybe we can work around those conferences."

On the way home, Elsa stopped at a travel agency and picked up some brochures. The sun shone warm on her back, and the breeze felt refreshing. She passed a beauty parlor, a department store, and a car agency, but her mind saw little mud-brick shops with brown oil-paper in the windows. Women with black braids down their backs, men with shaved heads. Toddlers in split pants. Coolies squabbling over prices, grunting as they heaved huge crates onto their backs. Vendors shouting their wares of camel's wool blankets, caged crickets, and lunches packed in little sandalwood boxes.

All the smells—pork crackling in hot oil, moon cakes, sesame candy. *Jaodze*—how long had it been since she'd had *jaodze?* She must get that recipe from Mama.

Turning around, she walked to Mama's apartment.

Her mother, who was ironing a blouse, looked surprised. "Well, look what the wind blew in! Why didn't you tell me you were coming?" She adjusted the blouse and ironed another section.

Elsa automatically smoothed her hair. "I was on my way home from town and decided to stop by to borrow your old cookbook. You know, the one with the *jaodze* recipe.

"Why? You're not going to all that trouble to make them, are you? You're always saying how busy you are. Too busy to attend church. No time to come here."

Mama knew she worked in the hospital every other Sunday. Elsa shrugged. "I'm here now."

"Well, the cookbook is somewhere in the *peshong*. It's out in the shed now." Mama finished the blouse, hung it up, and took a pillowcase from a waiting stack.

Elsa looked at the neatly hung clothes, the folded sheets and tea towels. The unironed items looked almost as smooth as the ironed. "Do you mind if I look for it?"

Mama sighed. "Oh, all right. I thought you'd outgrown your obsession with China." She turned off the iron and set it on end, then reached for a set of keys dangling from a nail. Elsa followed her to the shed, ignoring her mother's muttered, "Got better things to do . . ."

The trunk smelled of mothballs and stale ginger. Its silk lining was smudged and frayed from dampness and age. Inside were wall hangings rolled into cylinders, Mama's picture albums, a straw mat.

Papa's Mongolian fur cap, his ivory-tipped cane. Elsa caressed each memento, aching with love for the one who had used them. Now that she was an adult and had her own home, maybe Mama would trust her with some of the treasures.

At the bottom were books: Shakespeare, Papa's Bible, the commentaries. The cookbook. Elsa picked it up and leafed through it. "This makes me so hungry for real Chinese food. . . . Did you know some Americans visited China recently? It was in the paper."

"I knew that President Nixon went there back in '72 . . ."

"Yes, but now these were ordinary tourists. Teachers, doctors, nurses. They went through schools and hospitals."

Mama narrowed her eyes. "I hope you don't get a crazy idea like that. No telling what could happen in that Communist country."

Elsa lifted her chin. "Morris and I *are* going. This summer, if we can get a booking."

"What? First you let Crystal drop out of school, and now you want to chase off across the world to a political hotbed. Have you gone berserk?" She started to pack the things back in the trunk, her lips twitching.

Elsa sighed. In her excitement about the trip, she'd forgotten about the talk with Mama she'd been avoiding. "Crys made her own decision. I . . . trust her judgment." She was surprised to hear herself say that and hoped it wasn't an awful mistake.

"If you were a better example—" Mama stopped short, staring at a small, flat box she'd just picked up. "My crochet hooks! I wondered where they were." She fumbled with the clasp.

Elsa reached for it. "Here, I'll open it for you."

Their hands collided just as the box opened, and the metal hooks scattered.

"Now look what you've done! You're as clumsy as ever." Mama gathered up her precious tools.

One hook had snagged into the silk lining at the side of the trunk, and Elsa carefully worked it loose. She noticed a rip in the faded material, and felt to see how bad it was.

Her fingers met a strange bulge between the lining and the metal frame. A circular shape about three inches in diameter, like a small embroidery hoop. Elsa pushed the object toward the slit to work it out. Her heart skipped a beat. Could it be?

"What are you doing?" asked Mama.

"There's something in here . . . I don't believe it!" She held up a pale green jade bracelet. Carved dragons wound around its curve. "No wonder the bandits didn't find it! Mama, remember that night?"

Mama took the bracelet and slid it onto her thin arm. "How could I forget?" She turned her wrist back and forth, admiring the beautiful jade.

Elsa stared at the delicately carved dragons and relived the terror: the bandits gesturing with bayonets, ransacking the baggage; the men chopping off her doll's hair and viciously slashing Jasper's teddy bear to shreds; their fury at not finding the matching bracelet.

Mama took the bracelet off. "I can't wear it. Those heathenish dragons—a pastor's widow—what would the church people say?"

Elsa could almost hear Papa. *They're too big for you now, Dumpling. But someday Mama will pass them on to you.* "I'll wear it," she said. "I've always loved the set."

Mama shook her head. "I've got a better idea. It's good jade. When Crystal marries Greg, I'll give it to her for a wedding present."

Elsa opened her mouth, but no words came out. How could Mama hurt her like that—and worse, do it through Crystal?

Then she also realized—Crys hadn't told Mama everything. Not about the breakup with Greg and not about Dr. Valdez.

Elsa turned and started out of the shed. *She* certainly wouldn't tell her mother. Nor would she give Mama the satisfaction of seeing her hurt.

"Wait."

Elsa turned. Had her mother changed her mind?

"Don't forget the cookbook. Isn't that why you came?"

Chapter 33

IT ALL WORKED OUT. Morris juggled his commitments, and the travel agent was lucky enough to find two cancellations on a China trip for the middle of July.

Two days before departure, while Elsa was in the bedroom packing the suitcases, the phone rang. When she answered, there was silence on the other end, and she repeated, "Hello?"

Morris's voice sounded strange. "I don't know how to tell you this."

She clutched her throat and felt her pulse throb. "What's wrong? Are you sick?" She edged to the side of the bed and sat down.

"No. But you will be. Bad news. There's—I can't go to China with you."

Elsa shrieked, "You *what?*"

"Dick just quit. Someone offered him more money."

Elsa felt a flash of anger. Some loyalty! Couldn't the man hold on until Morris could afford to give him a raise? "What about the salesgirls?"

"Shannon's already left for the trade fair. There's only Margaret, and I can't leave her alone in the store. She's too new on the job."

China was slipping away again, just as the compound walls had vanished from the train windows. "Can't Mr. Grainger fill in for those three weeks?"

"He's in bad shape. They took him to the hospital with a stroke last night."

"And there's nobody . . . ?"

Morris sighed. "I've already gone down the list of everyone who ever worked here. I just don't know what else to do."

Crystal, listening at the door, now asked, "Something wrong at the store? Anything I can do?"

Elsa asked Morris, "Could Crys fill in?"

"Normally, yeah. But not since we computerized the system. There are just too many changes since she last worked here."

Elsa didn't answer.

"This doesn't mean you can't go." Morris sounded forlorn, and she knew he must be just as disappointed as she was.

"By myself?" All the joy, all the excitement had drained from her.

"Well, you could take Crys. Her passport's current."

"It wouldn't be the same." She'd counted on showing Morris the rice paddies, the clinics, the apothecaries.

"She'd be good company for you. Who knows? It might even give her time to rethink her plans."

Elsa twisted the phone cord around her fingers. "You're absolutely sure you can't get away?"

"I've tried everything. I would even close shop for those three weeks, but there's a group of pharmacists coming in to see what we've done—Dick was supposed to handle that. Aw, doll, I'm sorry. You know I don't want to hurt you."

But it did hurt. Her heart felt like a chunk of lead. She turned to Crystal and tried to smile. "How soon can you get packed?"

THE 747 SQUEALED AND THUMPED to a landing at the Shanghai municipal airport. Elsa stared out the plane window, holding her breath.

In a few hours, she'd traveled all the way across the world—enough time to reconcile leaving Morris behind, but not long enough to adapt to China. Ready or not, here she was. Anticipation shot through her, intense, pounding, excruciating.

She hadn't known what to expect. In 1938, the ocean liner had left a huge dock with hundreds of coolies swarming, shouting, loading cargo. But here, outside the plane window, was only an empty, playground-sized stretch of tarmac with two cars parked in front of a squat gray building.

She squinted through the late afternoon sun, searching for the China of her childhood. *Coolies bending in the rice fields. River water lapping against a sampan.*

Then she saw it, just beyond the runway: a lush, green vegetable field nestled against the very edge of the tarmac. Workers stooped among the plants, pulling weeds. In a nearby ditch, a wallowing water buffalo submerged itself, its nose snorkeling for air.

From jet airplane to beast of burden, the new and old China joined in a unique embrace.

Crystal leaned against her, straining to see through the window, and Elsa shifted to make room. They'd been lucky to get the visa changed; there had been frantic phone calls and a mad dash to San Francisco to straighten it all out.

She thought briefly about the jade bracelet and swallowed the resentment in her throat. Crystal didn't even know about it. No matter what, Elsa was determined that Mama wouldn't spoil her relationship with her daughter. Especially not on this trip.

The front passengers started out the hatch, and Crystal pulled down the hand luggage. "This is it, Mom."

Elsa gathered her belongings, took a deep breath, and followed her daughter toward the exit.

The humid Shanghai air engulfed her. At the same instant, she smelled a mixture of oil, garlic, cabbage, bamboo, damp earth, and night soil. Yes, this was China.

The tour group gathered off to one side of the plane, their clothes already clinging with perspiration. Most of them jabbered and laughed, and Elsa could hear Crystal laughing with them.

"You mean this little bitty field is the main airport for a city of eleven million?"

"Nobody warned us about the smell."

A heavy-set man named Clyde shouted, "Oh, look—can you believe this—they're using a tea kettle to fill the oil tank! Grab the camera!"

For them, this was just another adventure. For Elsa, it was a journey into her innermost soul. She closed her eyes, lifted her tear-streaked face to the sky, and whispered, "I'm home."

THE JING AN HOTEL WAS FOUR stories high, a square building with a half-circle of steps leading up to a plain wooden door. Two armed guards came out of a small gatehouse and waved them into the driveway.

It wasn't the Holiday Inn, but their third-floor room had real beds covered with flowered spreads, and a private bath with a standing flush toilet. Elsa couldn't help thinking about the escape down the Han River, washing up in its muddy water, and drinking tea boiled from the next dipperful. Mud huts in Shiao Yangshan, families sleeping in rows on their *kangs*. The long, brick mission house with chamber pots under the beds and an outhouse in the back compound. Then, she'd thought it was a normal way to live, and Papa hadn't seemed to mind—he'd always accepted whatever came his way. But Mama was so fastidious—how had she managed?

Next to the window was a desk, and Elsa pulled out the rattan chair and sat down. Under the sill whined a small air conditioner, and she gratefully cooled off her feet. Through the window, she could see the locals walking down the sidewalks, and she longed to go talk with them. But it was time for dinner.

Downstairs in the dining room, the evening meal was ready. She and Crystal met the other tour members for sweet and sour fish, slivered duck with bamboo shoots, eel in garlic salt, and sliced pickled carrots, with a last course of winter melon soup. Everything was tastier than the chow mein back in America.

In the center of the table stood a cluster of bottles—orange soda and *pijiu*, Chinese beer. Elsa tried the soda but found it lukewarm and too sweet. Clyde, sitting across from her, fanned himself with his napkin. "Better take the beer," he said. "It'll kill the bugs."

Just then the waiter came with hot tea, and Elsa held out her cup. "Ah! Just what I needed."

Crystal stared at her. "Hot? Isn't this humidity bad enough?"

Elsa felt wise in remembered Chinese customs. "You'd be surprised. It'll actually cool you off. The idea is to be warmer inside the body than outside."

But this was not the same as the tea bags in America. Each cup had a log-jam of twigs and leaves floating on top. Someone asked, "How do you drink this?"

"You smile." Elsa demonstrated, straining the pale green brew through her teeth. "You have to slurp; that's a sign of enjoyment. And afterward, you belch to show your appreciation."

The others looked at her dubiously, then changed the subject to the scenery on the way to the hotel. Every available inch had been cultivated into vegetable fields, creeping to the very edge of the two-lane roads. Large factories with smokestacks spewed black smoke to the sky. There had been very little traffic: a few army trucks and some garden tractors pulling trailer loads of long, stringy vegetables. Bok choy; or maybe it had been spinach.

And all the bicycles! When they'd entered the city of Shanghai and the streets widened into tree-lined avenues, the bikes multiplied into a sea of shiny wheels. The bus honked, snorted, and nosed its way through the jingling mass.

Elsa felt a stab of deep regret. Morris would have enjoyed seeing that. His old bike was still dear to him; repainted and polished, it provided recreation and exercise whenever he had time.

After dinner, the Chinese tour guide, Rose Lee, pushed her over-sized glasses higher on her nose, consulted her clipboard, and laid out some rules. Drink only bottled water, buy only from authorized stores, stay with the tour group at all times.

Elsa winced. With so many restrictions, how would she find the real China?

Then Rose announced the next day's schedule: tours through the Longhua Pagoda and the Children's Palace, dinner at a famous up-town restaurant, and on to a performance by the Shanghai acrobatic troupe. "It will be a busy day. Tonight you must rest and adjust to the time change."

The other tour members started up to their rooms, but Elsa held back. Crystal tugged at her arm. "Come on, Mom. You didn't sleep on the plane. You don't want jet lag tomorrow."

Elsa grimaced. "I'm wide awake. China's out there on the streets, waiting for me."

"What are you saying?"

"Let's take a walk. Just around the block."

"Mom! You heard Rose. We can't go off on our own."

"I can still remember a little of the language. If we run into problems, I'll ask questions."

Crystal reached for Morris's camera, but stopped short. "What if we get mugged?"

"Don't be silly. These are my people."

Chapter 34

ELSA STARED IN WONDER. The Shanghai sidewalks presented a strange new world. The entire block consisted of identical, two-story, wooden apartments connected as though rolled out with a rolling pin. Women leaned against open doorways, and red-scarved children sat on stoops, playing games or working in textbooks.

Along tiny balconies on the second level, laundry was threaded lengthwise on bamboo poles, sleeves and legs hanging, dripping like giant shish kebabs on a barbecue pit.

Although it was eight o'clock in the evening, the stream of cyclists hadn't lessened, and the sidewalks swarmed with pedestrians. Most were solemn young people in white cotton shirts and navy trousers or skirts, the men with American-style haircuts, the girls with bobbed hair, plastic shoes, and knee-length nylons.

Elsa looked around, bewildered. Where were the Chinese she remembered?

Then she saw an old woman push through the crowd, carrying a small, three-legged stool. She wore old-style baggy black trousers ending at her calves and a white tunic with diagonal frog fasteners. Her gray hair was drawn back into a tight bun, and her cheeks sloped into thin lips barely covering her large teeth.

Tsao Po-Po! Elsa started toward her, then stopped short. When she'd left Shiao Yangshan, her amah had looked this woman's age—fifty, maybe sixty years old. By now—if she was still living, which was unlikely—she could be around ninety.

The woman settled her stool at the corner, squatted down, and impassively scanned the people swirling around her. When she spotted Elsa, her eyes widened.

Elsa smiled and greeted her. *"Ni hao."*

Crystal aimed her Polaroid, and minutes later the woman was examining her likeness and beaming. While she was occupied, Crystal snapped another picture of her with Morris's Nikon.

Immediately, a crowd formed around Crystal, and another pressed around Elsa. Families flocked toward them from nearby apartments.

These looked more like her people, and Elsa felt a bond with them. She spoke to them, but they shook their heads and laughed.

Had she used the wrong inflection? She tried again, pointing to her face with her thumb. *"Ni hao. Wo jiao Mai Yung-det.* Hello, my name is Meier Eternal Virtue." She'd decided "Drake" was too hard to say phonetically.

Then the people realized she was speaking their language, and they laughed again, giving her thumbs-up signals.

Long-forgotten words came tumbling out. "Over there is my daughter. We are from *Meiguo,* from America. How old are you, what is your occupation, where do you live? Do you go to school, is that your baby, how old is he?"

They were full of questions, too, talking so fast she couldn't follow. But some of the young people spoke a little English, and with laughter and gestures, the conversation flowed.

All the years dropped away. It seemed as though her red hair had turned to Chinese black and she was one with the crowd in body as well as in spirit. She wanted to hug all of them and cry out, *I belong here!* Just in time, she remembered that such a burst of emotion wouldn't be *kerchieh.*

One old woman fingered the material of Elsa's blouse, another tweaked her arm, a third tugged gently at her hair. When someone stroked her watch and a child in split pants squatted to feel her sneakers, she realized it would be wise to move on.

Crystal wormed a path through her admirers and joined her. "I thought I'd never get away. You sure you know what you're doing?"

"They were just curious. I'll bet some of them have never seen Americans up close."

Just ahead, a sidewalk vendor stir-fried pork and vegetables and offered steaming rice from huge vats. A long queue of people stood with bowls in hand, waiting to be served. Others sat on the curb and nearby benches, tilting filled rice bowls to their mouths, guiding and plucking bits of vegetables and meat with their chopsticks. Inhaling deeply, Elsa revived the aromas and tasty meals of her childhood.

At the next street corner, she stopped, awestruck. In the middle of the intersection was a domed booth like a tiny gazebo. A white-gloved traffic guard stood at the door, manually changing the signal lights. He waved his arms as gracefully and importantly as an orchestra conductor, urging one group of bicycles forward, holding back others.

Elsa shook her head slowly. "I've never seen that before." She thought of Shiao Yangshan with its dirt street and foot traffic, with an occasional ox cart or donkey. Maybe Fung Choi pushing a wheelbarrow load of bricks. This certainly was a new China.

On the next block, a woman poured hot tea into cups on a makeshift table. She held one out to Elsa.

"*Dwah-shao chee-en?*" asked Elsa.

She felt a nudge from Crystal. "What are you doing?"

"Asking how much it is. Do you want some?"

"Don't you remember? We're not supposed to buy anything off the streets."

Elsa bit her lip. "But tea's made with boiling water. That'll sterilize any germs."

Someone handed an empty cup back to the woman, who then swirled a dingy rag into it before setting it with the clean ones.

Crystal raised an eyebrow. "Still want it?"

"I guess not." Elsa smiled ruefully at the woman and said, "*Wo buh-yao*. I don't want it."

Strolling on, Elsa peeked into a bakery where smells of sesame oil mingled with ginger and orris root. A stationery store displayed bins of calligraphy brushes and reams of thin rice paper.

Next door, a man wrapped powders and chunks of roots in twists of brown oilpaper. Bottles and jars lined the shelves behind him. Elsa asked what they contained, but she couldn't understand the man's answers.

"Too bad," said Crystal. "We could have brought Dad some exotic remedies for his store."

"Like ginseng and ground rhino horns?"

"Ah, ginseng," repeated the merchant. *"Hao, hao!"* Good, good. He grinned, flexing his scrawny muscles, and held out a gnarled root shaped like wizened old man.

Elsa laughed and fanned her palms. *"Buh-yao, buh-yao."*

When they reached the end of the block, Crystal gripped Elsa's arm. "This way. You said we'd just go around the block."

But Elsa had spotted a vendor squatting on the edge of the sidewalk, arranging embroidered goods on a blanket. After studying the display, she pointed to a brocade coin purse. *"Dwah-shao chee-en?"*

The woman held up three fingers. *"San yuan."*

Elsa pulled out her wallet, extracted one coin, and offered it to her.

The woman shook her head, still waving three fingers. Elsa started to turn away, and the woman shouted, *"Er yuan."*

"Come *on*," said Crystal. "We've got to go back."

Elsa took out one more *yuan* and traded the two coins for the little purse. "That's the fun of buying from vendors. Chinese love to haggle. Rose says we can't do that in the government stores."

Crystal shook her head. "Mom, you've already broken two of the rules. If I hadn't stopped you, it would have been three. What am I going to do with you?"

They returned to the hotel without incident and tiptoed up to their room. Crystal took a bath while Elsa perched on her bed, scribbling notes in her trip journal.

A movement on the other bed caught her attention. She turned, saw nothing amiss, and decided it had been her imagination. Then she saw, almost camouflaged by the rust-colored flowers on Crystal's spread, a four-inch cockroach.

A chill ran up to Elsa's scalp. "Crys!" she called, her voice quavering. Crystal, in her pajamas, brushing her teeth, didn't answer.

The creature stared at Elsa, not moving.

Elsa edged onto the floor and darted to the bathroom door.

"Crys, there's a humongous cockroach on your bed!"

"On my bed?" Crystal came out of the bathroom with a towel and flicked it toward the insect. The cockroach backed up an inch.

Elsa opened the door to the hall. "Maybe we can shoo it out."

Just then, Clyde happened to walk by their door. He stopped and asked, "Got a problem?"

Elsa pointed to the cockroach, still on the bed.

Without a word, Clyde came in, slipped off one of his loafers, and with the force of a lumberjack, smashed the cockroach. The limp carcass stuck to his shoe sole and left a stain on the bedspread.

"That's the last you'll see of him!" He scraped it into the wastebasket, slipped his shoe back on, and went on his way, brushing his hands together with a triumphant grin.

Crystal peered into the wastebasket. "Poor thing. He didn't have to kill it. Maybe it wasn't even a cockroach—maybe it was just a large cricket."

Elsa's mouth dropped open. A cricket? Suddenly she remembered her pet Cherky.

She looked at the remains again and shuddered. It was hard to believe she'd actually stroked a pet like that. No wonder Mama had threatened to step on it—she must have been deathly afraid of it.

The next morning, after a long bus ride through the streets of Shanghai, Rose Lee ushered the group into the Longhua Pagoda and started her narration. "This seven-story wooden structure is one of Shanghai's true antiquities, dating back to the Song Dynasty somewhere around the tenth century. It was restored in 1954."

Elsa started up the worn, uneven steps circling up to the next level. She thought about the abandoned temple near Shungtau where they had hidden during the Communist raids and mentioned it to Crystal. "That one was much smaller—only three stories high. We slept on mats on the dirt floor. Jasper and I ran up and down the steps. There was nothing else to do; your nana wouldn't let us go outside."

They climbed on up to the fourth level and looked out the parapet to the buildings below. There were Buddhist temples, a gift shop, and in the distance, a palace. Farther down the hill stood an orchard of peach trees.

Crystal snapped pictures from several angles. "Dad will love these. He's going to kick himself for not coming."

Elsa looked beyond the peaceful scene into her memories. *Shungtau burning, spirals of smoke far in the distance. Opening the balcony door just a crack—Mama's swift spank.* She shivered. Despite all the shooting, the anxiety, she hadn't fully realized the danger they'd been in. Mama must have been terrified—what if someone had spotted them? They would have been massacred like the missionaries in the Boxer Rebellion.

Rose Lee clapped her hands. "Now we go on to tour the Children's Palace, where China's most talented students are trained. You will see dances and hear a concert."

Elsa took one last look at the mountains and reluctantly followed the group back down the steps. No matter how good the students were, she couldn't enjoy dances and concerts when her heart and mind were back at the mission.

Chapter 35

ELSA SAT AT THE DESK OF HER hotel room in Wuxi, pen poised above her journal. "Was that Hangchow or Suzhou where we saw the brocade shop?"

She'd followed the group down aisles of ceramic factories, tea processing plants, and silk laboratories where workers spindled thread from live cocoons. Before each visit, she had to sit through lectures and briefings on the history of the products.

They'd visited model hospitals and schools; at day-care centers, well-rehearsed tots led them by the hand to see structured activities. She'd passed out balloons, and Crystal had blown them up for the delighted children.

Mao Tse Tung's picture still presided at a few entrances of public buildings, but at others, Elsa noticed large empty frames and wondered if his popularity had slipped since his death.

At Number One Friendship Stores, the other tourists bought extra luggage to hold their purchases of silks, paintings, and dish sets. Elsa had bought only a few souvenirs: a tiny jade gargoyle, an embroidered tablecloth, a delicate vase for Tommie, a calligraphy brush and granite ink box for Morris, and a brocade cushion cover for Mama.

Crystal had pointed out a set of bracelets—green jade, similar to the one that Mama had, very expensive now. But even if she could afford them, Elsa knew they could never replace the gift that Papa had bought. They'd only be a constant reminder of Mama's heartless decision.

Her best souvenirs would be the pictures. Crystal was always the last one on the bus, aiming one more shot, now of a pretty Chinese girl framed in a circular doorway, now of life-sized stone lions. A lovely garden with paths winding past little tea houses. A wooden bridge arched over a stream full of huge goldfish. Carp, Rose called them; Elsa thought them too gorgeous for such a common name.

Ahead of the crowds, the tour group had been ushered into air-conditioned trains with white lace doilies on the headrests of the upholstered seats. They'd been served tea and snacks by a polite and helpful steward.

It had all been very interesting and exciting, Elsa thought, skimming over her journal entries. But—"They're showpieces," she told Crystal. "The factories, the schools. They're especially chosen to show how China has progressed. I've seen the travel brochures. All the tourists come here."

Crystal, absorbed in listing her day's worth of pictures, murmured, "I think it's fabulous. Too bad for Dad, but I'm glad I could come. Can't you just enjoy it?"

Elsa shook her head. "I want to see the old China—*my* China. I want to walk on dirt roads, enter the mud huts, take a sampan down the river."

The next morning, Rose Lee took the group on a ferry ride down the Grand Canal. Although Elsa didn't ride in a sampan, she saw plenty of them; the waters were clogged with the curved boats, so heavily loaded with bricks and other cargo that they sank halfway into the canal. Some were lashed together in queues of as many as ten, using the leader's power. A few boatmen, naked to the waist, poled their crafts in the old-fashioned way, but most tended small motors.

The ferry wound through the city of Wuxi, chugging past brick factories and homes and stone stairways descending into the water. Elsa stood at the railing and waved to elderly women squatting on the lower steps, washing their dishes, clothes, or vegetables.

She shouted greetings to families in houseboats, remembering the Han River trip of her childhood.

The people waved back, mothers leaving their woks of savory-smelling vegetables to snatch up wide-eyed, open-mouthed toddlers and show them the foreigners. Older children played with kittens on a leash or supervised fishing ducks with rings around their necks to prevent them from swallowing their catch.

Elsa filled her eyes and soul with the taste and smells of China. But instead of satisfying her, it only whetted her appetite. She cornered Rose Lee in the cabin of the boat where the guide was consulting the bus driver.

"I want to take a side trip to Shiao Yangshan. The map shows it on the train line, only fifty miles from Beijing."

Rose looked up, frowning. "But Mrs. Drake, that is impossible. There is no time." She ticked off her fingers. "Next we go to Nanjing, then fly to Beijing. There we go to the zoo, see the Temple of Heaven, the Summer Palace. Also the Forbidden City and the Ming tombs. The Great Wall will take a full day. We will be busy, busy, all the time!"

The bus driver nodded. "Nothing to see in Shiao Yangshan. Sugar refineries, coal mines. Very dirty, very dirty. You do not want to go there."

Crystal had followed her and overheard the last words. She grabbed Elsa's arm. "Mom, we can't go off by ourselves! Especially now. I promised Dad pictures of the Summer Palace and the Great Wall."

Elsa sighed. This was her only chance—she would never be this close again. "I'll give up the Summer Palace and the Ming tombs, but I *must* go to Shiao Yangshan. You go on with the tour and take your pictures. I'll be back in time for the Great Wall."

Rose shook her head. "It is too costly. There is the matter of a guide—"

"Why? I can still speak some Chinese, and surely somebody there will speak English."

"Maybe, maybe not. But it is not permitted to go without a guide."

"All right, all right. I'll pay for a guide. When can I leave?"

All day, Elsa thought about that trip, hardly paying attention at the pottery factory and the Yangtse River Bridge in Nanjing, barely noticing the bucking and plunging of the cramped and overloaded plane to Beijing.

The night before she left, she went over the schedule in her mind. At 4 AM, she would meet Rose in the lobby and be introduced to her guide. They would take a taxi to the train station and leave from there at five o'clock.

Her excitement rose like champagne bubbles. It was really happening. She would see the old compound, the gray brick church, the long, nine-room house. The gatehouse, with the calendar picture of Christ and His disciples in the boat. The bell tower . . .

Crystal took the elastic band off her ponytail and raked her fingers through sweat-dampened hair. "I still think it's crazy, going off by yourself. What would Dad say?"

"Not by myself. I'll have an experienced guide. There's no danger; it's all carefully planned. I'll be there one night, staying in a guest house."

What would Morris say? He'd probably agree with Crys. But she had to do this.

Chapter 36

"*Dso kai!*" shouted tiny Mrs. Ko, jabbing a path through the crowd with her pointed elbows. "*Ta shir Meguo!* Make way, she is American!"

Elsa's guide had appeared frail and timid, not at all capable of protecting her charge. But now she fought like a tigress with a cub in danger, and the crush of passengers on the train platform loosened a bit.

Away from the regular tour, there was no special treatment. In order to get on the train, Elsa and her guide battled through the crowd that was getting off. Each step forward was countered by two steps back, like pawns in a giant game of chess.

Elsa remembered arriving in Shiao Yangshan long ago. She had been insulted when Mama insisted she stay close to Tsao Po-Po. Now she understood. What a rascal she'd been, running off into the crowd!

She shoved her overnight case forward and stumbled up the rusty train steps after Mrs. Ko, jostling through the travelers and baggage until, miraculously, her guide found empty seats.

Elsa hoisted her bag onto the sagging luggage rack and collapsed on the bare wooden seat. The armrest was broken, and a blackened ashtray stuck out from the wall. She had told Rose Lee it didn't matter if she had to take the hard-seat coach. "Just get me to Shiao Yangshan. I don't care how." But now, struggling for breath in the crowded and stuffy car, she wished she'd tried harder to get better accommodations. The seat felt sticky, and the floor was littered with apple cores, chicken bones, and blobs of dried spittle. Obviously, this old train was not intended for tourists.

Beside her, Mrs. Ko sat primly, her feet between her small worn suitcase and a large shopping bag. She wore a neat gray skirt, a white over-blouse, and metal-rimmed granny glasses. A navy jacket lay folded across her lap.

The train lurched forward. They were actually on their way! Suddenly the filthy car didn't matter. *Papa and the* yahbah *building the swings. Mama scolding Fu Liu. Tsao Po-Po sitting on her low stool, darning socks. Ling swaggering through the gate.*

Shiao Yangshan. Her home.

The train moved faster and faster, and soon they were out of the city. Elsa looked at her watch. How would she endure the anticipation for three hours? She took a deep breath and looked around at the other passengers.

In the opposite seat, a middle-aged couple stared at her. They wore old-style gray wadded clothes with frog closures. Between them lay a covered basket and a cloth bundle tied with twine. Above on the rack was a large crate with a picture of a treadle sewing machine.

Evidently, they were village people coming home from a shopping trip. Were they going to Shiao Yangshan, too? Elsa watched them share a bag of peanuts, tossing the shells onto the floor, and she felt drawn to them.

"*Ni hao,*" she said, leaning forward. "*Wo jiao Mai Yung-det. Ni kuei jiao?*" What is your name?

The man giggled nervously and bowed several times in short jerks. The woman's eyes traveled slowly from Elsa's face down to her white sneakers.

Mrs. Ko frowned, her lips a tiny snout. "Pay no attention. They are peasants—without manners."

Shocked, Elsa stared at the guide. How could the woman scorn the very people she'd come to see? She'd thought Communism had done away with class prejudice.

Deliberately, she smiled at the pair, and the man broke into a torrent of unintelligible language.

Elsa asked, "What did he say?"

Mrs. Ko folded her arms and looked out the window. "He speaks another dialect. It is not our concern." Whether or not she understood, she obviously wouldn't interpret.

Elsa spread her fingers, palms up, in the universal sign of helplessness. *"Wo buh-doong." I don't understand.*

The man laughed and bobbed his head again, and the woman covered her mouth and tittered.

Elsa gave up and turned her attention to the passing scenery. They had left the cultivated farms and were beside a wooded mountain. At the base, a little stream followed its contours. She felt thirsty and wondered aloud whether the steward would bring the usual pot of hot tea.

Mrs. Ko rummaged in the shopping bag and brought out a thermos of hot water and a packet of large green tea leaves. She dug again, produced two cups and a cardboard box, and announced, "It is the time to breakfast."

A squeaking, thumping noise made Elsa turn. A vendor pushed a metal cart down the aisle, selling something in greasy cardboard boxes. All around, people shouted and held out coins. Mrs. Ko opened her own box and waved the vendor on.

She pulled out *bao-dze,* boiled eggs wrapped in oiled paper, and a handful of dried peaches. Elsa ate the steamed bun and sipped the tea, watching the peasant couple. They had bought noodles, and the man ate first, picking up a hank with his chopsticks and slurping through pursed lips. Sauce dripped from his mouth, and he wiped it on his sleeve before handing the carton to the woman.

The food smelled like *yomein,* the coarse gray oat noodles Elsa remembered from her childhood. She peeled her egg, wishing she could have tried the vendor's food. She offered the couple some dried peaches, but the man belched loudly and shook his head.

Mrs. Ko quickly folded the oiled paper into the box and stowed it back into the shopping bag. "I understand you once lived in Shiao Yangshan," she said, leaning forward, forming a barrier between Elsa and the couple.

Elsa shifted uncomfortably. Mrs. Ko was more like a warden than a guide. How disappointing it would be if the woman wouldn't let her speak to anyone at the mission!

But she settled back and talked about the long, brick house in the large, mud-walled compound. The dust storms, the rats. Helping the nurses in the clinic.

Once she got started, she had to mention the earlier mission in South China—the big house with a wraparound veranda, the chestnut tree. Being raised by Tsao Po-Po.

Nostalgia wrapped around her until she could hardly breathe. Was it really true that soon she would be back in her childhood?

The train was climbing; they curled in and out of tunnels dark as a moonless night. Hoarse squawks came from the pot-bellied steam engine and echoed against the bare, rocky mountains.

When Mrs. Ko had run out of questions, Elsa decided it was her turn. "Where did you learn to speak English so well?"

Mrs. Ko's mouth turned up just a fraction. "As a girl, I attended a mission school. In Shanghai."

"Is that your home? Shanghai?"

"No, I came from Guren, an inland city."

"And you've kept up the language all these years?"

"I was a teacher of English in the university. Until the Cultural Revolution." Mrs. Ko glanced at the couple. The woman's eyes had closed.

"What happened then?" asked Elsa.

Mrs. Ko looked around, then leaned closer, murmuring into Elsa's ear. "I was sent out to the country to plant rice. For two years, I worked in the fields."

"Wasn't that hard work for a woman?"

Mrs. Ko's eyes squeezed shut for a moment, and she took a deep breath. She shook her head and swallowed. When she opened her eyes, they were moist. "It was very bad. We carried heavy pails of manure. I had much pain in my back. Very little sleep." She was silent for a minute, then smiled. It was the first time Elsa had seen her smile. "I could never do it right."

"Do what?"

"The rice. I planted the seedlings, row after row, bending all day, my hands in muddy water. The next morning, they all floated on top. The leader of the brigade made me plant again. He was very angry." Mrs. Ko smothered a giggle as though it had been a joke on him.

Elsa pictured the tiny woman, neat and prim in her suit, mucking around with the coolies, ankle deep in mud and night soil. No wonder she resented peasants. They'd probably been her overseers. "Did the leader beat you?"

"Many times. My rations were cut in half. Always, I was hungry. I was even put up for struggle sessions." She leaned closer, whispered, "Bowed to the waist, arms back, I stood before the crowd, even former students. For hours they cursed me, screamed that I was a class enemy, that I taught subversive subjects."

How humiliating that must have been, thought Elsa, horrified. "Couldn't you defend yourself?"

"I dared not. I feared being arrested, so I criticized myself, saying I had been lazy and ignorant but now knew better. My heart knew that was not true, but it seemed the only way to be released." Mrs. Ko looked down, her lips quivering. "I was more fortunate than some others. The leader sent me to another work unit. There I picked apples."

"Was that easier?"

"Very much so. For that, one does not stoop. Sometimes, I ate an apple. But I had to eat all the core and bury the stem very deep so no one would know."

Had Ling survived the Cultural Revolution? Slaving in the boot factory through the years, all the while yearning to study?

The train swayed on and on, hooting at intervals. They passed piles of rubble, then suddenly a large section of the Great Wall, high, wide, and majestic, came into view. For a while, they rode parallel to it, then dipped into another tunnel and left the wall behind. Looking back, Elsa watched it dwindle into the distance, straddling the crests and plunging into valleys like an endless roller coaster.

She felt a twinge of guilt for leaving Crystal, but it soon passed. Now they chugged over a brown sea of foothills. Below them, fields of millet and opium poppies shone golden in the early sun. Little mud houses dotted the countryside, some alone, some huddled together in a village. The few trees looked thin and frail as if apologizing for taking nourishment from the earth.

Across from Elsa, the woman's head had fallen forward, and the man snored. Mrs. Ko pulled a worn copy of *Tom Sawyer* from her bag and began reading. Elsa had also brought a paperback along, but didn't bother getting it out. She'd never be able to concentrate.

The train bore down onto a plateau. A stream trickled down a dry riverbed, coiled through yellow grass, then vanished into the retreating hills. The mud houses were closer now, some larger ones surrounded with walls, miniatures of the mission compound.

A shiver ran up Elsa's spine. The terrain looked familiar—had she been here on trips with Papa to the outstations? She strained for the first sight of the village of Shiao Yangshan, the tower, the church, her home.

Mrs. Ko looked up from her book and consulted her watch. "According to the schedule, we will be in Shiao Yangshan in twenty minutes." She slipped on her jacket, and Elsa realized it might be cool outside.

She took down her bag and got out a parka. "Then we should see Little Goat Mountain soon." Was she shivering from cold or nerves? She rubbed her hands together to control their trembling.

In the distance, under a canopy of black dust, she saw a dry, lumpy hill. Smaller than she'd remembered it but unmistakable. The head, the haunches. Little Goat Mountain. Somewhere in this valley was her home. Elsa pinched herself to make sure she wasn't dreaming.

The train slowed, screeched, and snorted to a stop. Outside was the sandy expanse of the train yard, and across from it, the Shiao Yangshan station, now without its alarm gong. Vendors milled around, and people came streaming from all directions.

Elsa peered at the crowd. There were no familiar faces. Beyond them, smokestacks spewed out dark billows of smoke, almost hiding the village.

Village? This was a city! Beyond the train yard, a paved road led toward a three-story building—undoubtedly the sugar refineries the bus driver had mentioned. Instead of ox and donkey carts, trucks filled with huge canvas bags backed up to an open boxcar, and workmen began heaving in the load.

Instead of crude shacks and mud huts, brick apartments and tall buildings lined the street.

Where was the bell tower? And where were the compound walls?

Elsa turned to Mrs. Ko. "Are you sure this is Shiao Yangshan?"

Chapter 37

THE SKY WAS THE COLOR OF ASHES, darkened even more by spurts of soot from the steam engine. A pillar of sand swirled along the edge of the train yard and eddied upward toward the mountain. Elsa felt the sharp pricks against her face and shivered in the chill air, grateful for her parka.

"Come," said Mrs. Ko, pushing through the crowd of vendors shouting and waving their displays of blankets and carved knives, their trays of dried mutton. "We must find your lodgings."

Still getting her bearings, Elsa didn't move. "The compound should have been right ahead. The bell tower was at the entrance, right about"—she stood on tiptoes to see over the crowd and pointed toward an apartment complex—"there!"

Next to the apartments stood a square brick building. *The church?* She started walking toward it, and Mrs. Ko trotted behind her, muttering under her breath.

But the building was no longer a church. There was no steeple, no ornately carved portico, no orange lacquered doors. Instead, a metal gate opened; men pushed an empty wooden cart up to the entrance and began loading boxes into it.

"That is merely a factory," said Mrs. Ko.

Elsa went to the gate and looked past the cart. Instead of benches for worshippers, the building held rows of long tables heaped with sections of leather, fur, and boots in various stages of assembly. Men and women sat on benches and at cobblers' machines, busily shoeing the nation.

Ling had worked at a boot factory—could he possibly be here? Elsa

256

caught her breath, searching the faces, but the workers all looked too young, many with the distinctive high cheekbones of Mongolians.

At the far end of the building, a raised area held more machinery and a desk. The platform! She could picture the pulpit, Papa behind it preaching. Tears blurred her eyes, and she leaned against the doorjamb.

She felt something bump into her back and startled back into the present. Four workmen struggled to push a loaded handcart past her.

Mrs. Ko cleared her throat. "Mr. Peng is waiting."

"Please," said Elsa. "Just a few minutes more." She pointed to a row of warehouses nearby. "The first room was our clinic, and workers and evangelists lived in the others. Our home was a long string of rooms farther back." She darted off, Mrs. Ko nearly running to keep up.

Elsa hurried down a dusty path between the buildings to an open-brick wall with a small wooden gate. In the front courtyard were the little circular brick enclosures where she and Ling had sat so often. They were empty, with no sign of the flowers and trees.

But the long mission house was unmistakable. Seven windows in a row, a door, then three more windows, each topped with a decorative pattern of curved bricks. To guard against curious eyes, Mama had hung thick curtains over the windows. Now they were bare, staring vacantly at the foreigner they had forgotten. Some were broken, the holes covered with oilpaper.

Elsa knocked at the door, wishing she could throw it open and call, "Papa, Mama, I'm home!"

The door opened a crack, and an old woman peered out. Seeing Elsa, she shrieked and tried to close the door, but Elsa's foot held it ajar.

Mrs. Ko pushed past Elsa and spoke rapidly in Chinese. The woman seemed to relax a little and answered the guide but kept staring at Elsa.

From inside, a small child poked his head between the woman's trousered knees and watched, open-mouthed.

"She thought you were Russian," said Mrs. Ko. "She says Russian soldiers came here many years ago. They were most cruel. Now the people are afraid of foreigners."

"I'm sorry," said Elsa, craning her neck to see into the house. Terrible things must have happened here after they'd left. "Tell her I mean no harm. I just wondered if I might come in for a bit. Only for a few minutes."

"Impossible. It is not on the approved list."

"But I need to pay respect to my old home."

Mrs. Ko frowned, but she hesitated, and Elsa knew she had made a good point—respect to family and ancestors was important to traditional Chinese.

The guide spoke again with the woman, then turned to Elsa. "She says many families live here now. She tends their children while they work in the factory. She is very busy, but you may enter." Mrs. Ko looked at Elsa sternly. "As you said, it can only be for a few minutes."

The woman led them into the kitchen, where she stirred the coals in the stove, then pulled a kettle forward to the heat.

The room had been redesigned for communal cooking. The cupboards built by the *yahbah* had been divided into family sections, each holding a few bowls, chopsticks, and cutlery. The stool Elsa had sat on to eat bits of Fu Liu's cooking was gone, as well as Mopsy's little bed under the stove.

The kettle hissed, and the woman picked it up and led the way down the hall into her apartment. Elsa counted the closed doors: dining room, parlor, Papa's study, Mama and Papa's bedroom, Jasper's room.

The door after that stood slightly ajar. Elsa's pulse raced. *My own bedroom . . . the shelf holding my books and treasures . . . Cherky's little cage in the window . . .*

But when she peeked in, she saw crowded together a double bed, a twin bed, and a dresser with a Playmate ice chest on it, and she felt sad—almost betrayed. There was not even a hint of her past life.

Mrs. Ko called her, and she saw the woman of the house had stopped at the next door and motioned for them to enter.

The old schoolroom. Elsa had a vision of her child-self doing sums at the table with Mama, red pencil poised, frowning over her shoulder.

Again her heart sank. Two double beds and a small table filled the room. Several toddlers lay asleep on the beds, and on the floor between, three little girls sat bouncing pebbles on the backs of their hands. When they saw Elsa, they stared open-mouthed and dropped the pebbles.

Chinese jacks. Just as Elsa had played with Lihua and Shirhua. She smiled at the girls, squatted down beside them, and flipped her own palms. One of the girls handed her the pebbles, but when she spilled most of them, they giggled with her at her foreign clumsiness.

The woman dropped tea stems into a thick white cup and poured in the boiling water. Shooing the children out of the way, she reached for a chair nested under the table and motioned for Elsa to sit.

Mrs. Ko looked at her watch and frowned, but Elsa accepted the teacup respectfully with both hands, raising it in a silent toast to the old home and its memories. The moment seemed holy, reverent, a spiritual connection with the past. Any minute, Tsao Po-Po would walk in, bringing a plate of ginger cookies.

Through Mrs. Ko, she asked the woman if she had known Tsao Po-Po and the other workers. "I know it's been a long time. Nearly forty years. I really don't expect any of our people to still be here. But I wonder if she might remember them, might know what happened to them."

The woman didn't recognize the names; she had been transferred here only ten years ago.

Elsa finished her tea and set the cup on the table. "Please, may I look out the back door?"

Mrs. Ko shook her head. "We must go now. It is very late, very late."

Loud shouts outside sent the woman and Mrs. Ko scuttling to the front door, and Elsa quickly followed them.

A stocky man stood in the entry. He wore baggy, olive-green pants and a tunic, and his short bristly hair looked as if it had been cut around a shallow bowl. When he saw her, he said in English, "Ah, Mrs. Dsake-y. I believe you come to the wrong house. I am your host, Peng Shih."

Mr. Peng frowned at Mrs. Ko, speaking again in Chinese, too fast for Elsa to understand. Then he turned back to Elsa. "I had expected you earlier. We have arranged extensive tours to the refineries and factories for your pleasure."

More tours and briefings? Not if she could help it. "Please," she told the man. "Don't trouble yourself. I don't need to be entertained. I would be happy to walk around by myself and see the people, the buildings."

Mrs. Ko sucked in her breath.

Peng Shih was polite but insistent. Everything had been planned. Elsa's visit had been approved only on the condition that she follow the prescribed agenda. Any deviation would be reported to higher authorities, and her visit would have to end immediately.

He stared at her, his eyes narrowed, and Elsa wondered if he thought she was a spy.

The swings, the stable, the tree-lined paths to the back gate. Disappointment washed through her. She'd been so close.

Chapter 38

AFTER THREE HOURS OF BOUNCING in an old truck, visiting a wool processing plant and a vast coal mine, and learning more than she wanted to know about China's exports, Elsa was glad to follow Mr. Peng into his walled compound.

She walked over a tiny arched bridge into a rock garden where a straggly juniper shielded a stone bench from the midday sun. A gravel path branched off to the surrounding buildings; Mr. Peng veered to the right and opened the door to a small guesthouse.

He bowed. "Here are your quarters, Mrs. Dsake-y. Your guide will occupy the room across the hallway. You will be summoned for the noon meal at twelve thirty."

Elsa's room held a high iron bed, a wooden chair, and a dresser. Above the dresser still hung the familiar face of Chairman Mao. She peeked through a curtained doorway and saw a tiled bathroom with a sink, a tiny shower stall, and a real porcelain toilet. Beside the toilet stood a filled bucket of water—for flushing, she assumed. It must have been a dry year.

Finally alone, she scrubbed the coal dust from her face and hands. Her bag had been brought in earlier, and she hung up the extra jeans and blouse she'd brought. Before she could decide whether to change now or after the next round of inspection, she heard a soft knock at the door.

A slim young woman with short bobbed hair stood outside. "I am Mei-Lien. The noon meal is served."

Mei-lien wore dull blue trousers and a tunic and looked to be in her twenties. She led Elsa and Mrs. Ko across the rock garden to a larger building and opened the door.

Straight rattan chairs lined the walls; between each two stood a brass urn and a square lacquered table. One table held a porcelain teapot and three covered cups.

Mr. Peng stood waiting; he indicated the chairs on each side of this table. "Please to sit."

Elsa sat down and looked around. On the opposite wall hung a straw mat—a painting of a branch of cherry blossoms. Two nightingales sat on the branch, one with its head cocked, as though questioning, the other looking down. At the bottom, a faint stain darkened the straw.

A vague memory nagged her. Nightingales. Cherry blossoms. Where had she seen a picture like that before?

Mr. Peng had taken the chair on the other side of the table and now gazed at Elsa. "I am told you lived in this village as a child?"

"Yes, my parents were missionaries here until 1938. Were you here then?"

His lips twisted. "My home was in Beijing until 1970. At that time, I was reassigned to this place." He hawked loudly and spit into the brass urn.

"Would you know if any of the people from that early time are still around?"

Mrs. Ko, seated in a chair nearby, coughed a quiet warning, but Elsa refused to look at her.

Mr. Peng shook his head. "Very unlikely. During the sixties, there was much change. Whole villages were relocated."

Elsa sighed. She'd been so hopeful for someone, anyone, from the old days. Not Tsao Po-Po, naturally, because with the Meier family gone, she would have had no reason to come back here. But Wu Shong and his wife; Fu Liu, the cook; the *yahbah;* or the gateman Fung Choi and his family. Had they all gone without a trace?

Desperation made her brave. "Is there a register somewhere, a list of all the people? I might recognize a few names."

"That is not possible." Mr. Peng stood up, went to an inner door, and clapped twice.

Mrs. Ko leaned toward Elsa and murmured, "It could be dangerous for them if a foreigner sought them out."

Elsa hadn't realized that. She didn't want to get anyone in trouble.
But she had come so far. There had to be something she could do.
"There have been so many changes," she told Mr. Peng when he returned. "I am amazed how the village has grown. It's such a big city
now. I'd like to walk down the streets and visit the stores to see all
the improvements." *And to see if I recognize anyone, anything.*

Mr. Peng bent his head. "I will be happy to escort you this afternoon on our way to the sugar refinery."

Mei-lien came quietly in and out of the room with plates of sliced
cucumbers, melons, and thinly sliced dried mutton and bowls of
gray noodles in a savory sauce—*yomein!*

After tasting the noodles, Elsa gave Mei-lien a thumbs-up sign.
They were as good as she remembered.

When the meal was over, the young woman brought in a plate of
small wrapped candies. Elsa tasted the mixture of honey, sesame,
and crushed peanuts and closed her eyes in ecstasy. *Christmas church
services, Papa on the platform, the sanctuary packed so tightly with
bodies that people even leaned against the walls. Bare tree branches
decorated with colorful paper chains and flowers. Singing—each one
to their own tempo. Children reciting poems and Bible verses. Finally
the gifts of fruit and sweets—sticky sesame candy wrapped in brown
paper.*

She looked up to see Mei-lien refilling her cup of tea, and Mr.
Peng staring at her, talking on and on about the excellent production
record of the refineries, the superior craftsmanship at the boot factory. "And we have a feast planned in your honor tonight. The most
industrious and deserving workers and leaders will be there. This is
indeed an important event."

"A feast?"

"It will be held in the labor hall. At that time, you may speak with
the people." Mr. Peng beamed as though he were handing her the
award of the year.

Would anyone there remember her? After what the man had said,
she doubted it. Elsa took a last sip of tea and set the cup on the table.

"Now you must rest," said Mr. Peng. "The tour will begin at two thirty."

Back in her little room, Elsa frowned at the clothes she'd hung up. She hadn't expected a formal affair, but they would have to do. At least the blouse was pretty.

Her watch showed one fifteen. If she didn't rest, she'd have just enough time. Quietly, she opened her door.

Immediately, she heard bedsprings creak, and Mrs. Ko peeked out of her room. Her hair was slightly tousled, and she wore no glasses. "Mrs. Drake, what do you need?"

Elsa sighed. She couldn't get anything past her warden. But determinedly, she stated, "I'm going into the city. Right now."

"Mr. Peng's orders—"

Elsa felt sorry for the woman. She would be accountable for her charge's actions. But if there was to be any time alone, it would have to be now. "I will be fully responsible for any violation. You may come with me, or I will go by myself. If need be, I can ask directions. But I am going."

Swallowing a yawn, Mrs. Ko said, "This is most irregular. Mr. Peng will be offended."

Elsa didn't answer, and finally, Mrs. Ko said, "If you are determined, I cannot let you go alone." She smoothed her hair and reached for her glasses.

Bless you, Mrs. Ko. Maybe you're not a warden after all.

They slipped through the gate and started down the street, passing an old man pushing a handcart piled high with bricks. His neck muscles were thick and strained as he leaned his shoulder to the hand bar.

Vendors sat dozing over their displays of folded paper animals, leather belts, little carved figures made from bleached bones.

In an open-air market shaded by cloth netting, skinned rabbits hung by their hind legs, and live turtles tried to escape from straw baskets.

At a greasy table, a butcher wielded his cleaver on large hunks of fat and bloody mutton. Bits of wool still clung to the legs, and flies circled around.

Elsa gulped. She hoped that wouldn't be the menu for the evening's feast. If Morris were here and saw that, he'd never eat Chinese food again.

Stringy green vegetables lay in heaps on the ground. Women haggled over the price of a handful, while in slings on their backs, babies slept or watched placidly.

Elsa studied the faces. They all belonged to strangers. Was it true that the whole village had been relocated? Was there possibly a section of the old town still standing somewhere among these newer buildings?

She greeted a few of the women, but they shied away from her, shielding their babies as if she might harm them.

Elsa told the women, *"Shiao Yangshan shir wo di chia."*

The women snickered and shook their heads, pointing to Elsa's feet.

Elsa was surprised to hear Mrs. Ko laugh too. "So sorry, Mrs. Drake. You just told them Shiao Yangshan was your toenail. You must say it like this: *chia*, with an upper even tone. Then it means home." She explained the mistake to the women.

Soon Elsa was surrounded with people, all staring at her and fingering her clothes and hair. She tried to talk to them about her childhood, and Mrs. Ko interpreted for her but also told them that Elsa was a guest of the city and staying in the house of Peng Shih. The women became quiet again, backing away, frowning, mumbling to each other.

Elsa asked, "What's the matter?"

"They are afraid of Mr. Peng."

Maybe she hadn't taken the man seriously enough. Would he arrest her for leaving her room without permission?

But this was her only chance, and she pushed away her apprehension. "Please—tell them I once lived in that long house south of the railroad station. I was very happy here as a child. Tell them my father was Mai Mushih; ask them if they know Fung Choi, Fu Liu—"

But the crowd melted away, looking back at her, their faces unfriendly.

Elsa felt wounded. Couldn't they understand she belonged here? Depressed, she wandered on past the stores.

Then in a window display, she saw an assortment of handmade toys. Brightly lacquered clay birds with blue tail feathers hung on strings from a bamboo frame. Just like the ones Papa had given her. Whatever had happened to them? She couldn't remember seeing them after leaving China. Had Mama thrown them away?

She went into the store and poked at a shiny red bird, sending it swinging. *"Wo yao mai naiguh,"* she told the woman behind the table. "I want to buy that."

When Crys married and had children of her own, they could learn how their grandmother had played.

Elsa picked up a little wooden clown on a stick and pulled its string, laughing when its jointed legs jumped. She added the toy to her purchase and started to leave, when she noticed some tiny cages on the next table. When she peered into one of them, eyes like black pinheads stared back at her.

Cherky? The creature's shape was very different from the one that had been on Crystal's hotel bed. She realized it wasn't a cricket Clyde had killed, and she was glad.

"I had one like this when I was little," she told Mrs. Ko. "I loved it very much. But now . . ." She shook her head as they went out into the street.

"One changes as one gets older," said Mrs. Ko.

"Is that good?"

"I believe so. Nature changes. Trees grow, rivers alter courses, mountains shift. That is life, and we must accept it. How else would we have progress?"

Elsa looked at her guide in wonder. "You're quite a philosopher, Mrs. Ko."

"No. But I accept what must be."

"Even if bad things happen?" Elsa thought of all the troubles the woman had gone through during the Cultural Revolution and of the problems that might still lie ahead for her.

"Yes. They will pass. If we trust and wait."

Elsa stopped and looked into Mrs. Ko's face. "Do you believe in God?"

The woman glanced around. "I do. Yes. When times were hard, I often doubted. But when it seemed I could live no longer, I received a little more strength. I believe that was a special gift, a blessing."

Elsa nodded. God's gifts came just when they were needed and not a minute before. Like this walk.

They started back on the other side of the street, passing small, older-looking buildings: a barber shop, a clinic, a noodle factory. In the distance beyond the last building and across the railroad tracks, Elsa could make out the old church and was sad for the desecration.

They paused beside a small fabric store, and Elsa peeked through the door. Bins along one wall held thread, needles, and buttons. Bolts of dull blue fabric were piled on the floor, along with rolls of funeral white. A table was covered with red brocade—bridal material. A tiny, shriveled old woman sat on a low stool, sewing a jacket of the red fabric. She looked up at Elsa and sucked in her breath with a hiss.

"Ai-yah!" She put clawlike fingers over her eyes. *"Meiguo kwei!"*

Mrs. Ko looked from the woman to Elsa. "She thinks you are an American ghost."

That much Elsa had understood. But . . . "Why a ghost?"

The woman rose, teetering on small feet and swollen ankles. Her sewing fell to the floor as she chattered, pointing to Elsa.

Mrs. Ko interpreted, "Long ago, she has seen red hair like that."

A chill ran up Elsa's spine, and she entered the store. "Would she remember Pastor Meier? *Mai Mushih, ni gee-duh Mai Mushih?"*

Eyes fixed on Elsa, the woman picked up the fallen garment. Her mouth was clamped shut, her lips trembling.

Who *was* this woman? Elsa repeated, *"Ni gee-duh Mai Mushih?"*

A tear crept down the woman's cheek, and she nodded, whispering, *"Shir duh, Mai Mushih. Ni shir shei?"* I remember. Who are you?

Time stood still; they were the only two people in the world. Elsa answered, *"Wo jiao Mai Yung-det.* I am Meier Eternal Virtue."

The woman reached out and took Elsa's hands into her own and looked up into her eyes. *"Shir Yung-det."* It is Yung-det.

Chapter 39

THE WOMAN REACHED UP AND stroked Elsa's cheek. *"Wo jiao Sen Ying,"* she said.

Sen Ying, Mama's teaching aide! Elsa remembered her as being polite and friendly, but unlike her husband, Wu Shong, a quiet figure in the background. Now she was the only link to the past, and Elsa felt as if she'd found her best friend.

She drew Sen Ying close and hugged her, but the woman pulled loose, staring fearfully at Mrs. Ko.

"Buh hai-pah, buh hai-pah," Elsa told her. *"Ta pung-yo."* She hoped she was right, that the guide was trustworthy and there was nothing to fear.

Sen Ying went to the doorway, looked out into the street, then closed the door. Pointing to the stool, she told Elsa to sit, but Elsa was too exhilarated.

Her package of toys had spilled out, and Sen Ying rolled them back into their wrappings. She pointed to the bird—but it was not until Mrs. Ko interpreted that Elsa understood. When they'd left for America, Mama had given Sen Ying Elsa's toy birds for her own little children. "She says the children played with them a long time until the birds crumbled apart," added Mrs. Ko.

So Mama hadn't thrown them away. She'd put them to good use.

Sen Ying asked, *"Mai Mushih, Mai Tai Tai, hao buh hao?"* She smiled to hear the answer that Mama was well, but when Elsa told her about Papa's accident and death, her eyes filled with tears. "The *mushih* helped us. He cared. He was a good man of God."

Elsa was avid for news of the Chinese Christians. Where was Wu Shong?

Sen Ying seemed reluctant to say, but Mrs. Ko ferreted out the story. Both of their sons had joined the Red Army, and she'd never heard from them again. Because of that, Wu Shong had been opposed to the Communists and refused to give in to them. In the fall of 1945, he had been arrested and dragged out of their home. He died in prison. No one knew exactly how. Sen Ying was sure he had been tortured.

Tears streamed down the old woman's cheeks, and she wiped them away with the back of her hand.

Elsa wept with Sen Ying, rocking with her in embrace. Wu Shong had been Papa's best helper, a good, faithful Christian. What a terrible ending for someone who had never hurt anyone.

When she could talk again, Elsa asked, "What about Fu Liu?"

Sen Ying spat thinly on the wood floor and scuffed the drops with her foot. She spoke in a deep guttural tone that seemed to come from the depths of her soul, and Mrs. Ko interpreted. "He was evil. A traitor. It was he who betrayed Wu Shong."

Elsa remembered Fu Liu's insolence those last days, how fierce he'd looked wielding his sharp cleaver, and she shuddered. He'd probably been plotting against them even then. "You have suffered so much. How you must hate the Communists."

Sen Ying wiped her eyes and nodded. "I hated for a long time. But no more. Now my heart is at peace."

Elsa gazed at the woman in wonder. How could anyone forgive such awful crimes?

"Your father said," explained Sen Ying, "if we do not forgive, bitterness eats our heart, and it never heals. I prayed for a long time, much hate. Fu Liu was a very bad man. But God helped me forgive." She stroked Elsa's hand. "I am old. Soon I will see your father and Wu Shong in heaven. That makes me happy."

Elsa wondered if Fu Liu had betrayed Wu Shong to get back at Papa. He'd been so angry when Papa had rescued Lihua from marrying that rich old man. "Where are my friends, Lihua and Shirhua?"

"Shirhua—I do not know. But I hear Lihua studied to be a nurse."

A nurse! Just like me. How good to know Fu Liu hadn't turned around and spitefully sold the girl to a different rich old man. The rescue had been worth the tuition money if Lihua had been able to do something worthwhile with her life. "There was a *yahbah*—"

Sen Ying shook her head. "Poor man. The Red Army . . ." She drew her hand sideways across her throat. "No use for *yahbahs*." She whispered, "I am happy that your family escaped. Otherwise, it would have been very bad for you." Sen Ying stroked Elsa's hair. "Your mother is my friend. Much joy we had together. But it was very hard for her. So much fear. All around bandits, soldiers, disease. The Japanese army was very cruel."

No wonder Mama hadn't trusted Tommie and her family. To her troubled mind, they were still the enemy, and she'd never been able to accept them as Americans.

Sen Ying was still reminiscing: "And Little Tiger, the drowning. Great, great sorrow. Mai Tai Tai was never the same after that."

Elsa thought back, reliving her own tearing grief and guilt. If something like that had happened to Crys, how could she have gone on living?

As a child, she'd seen her mother as old, harsh, and domineering. But how old had Mama been then? Thirty, thirty-five? Sen Ying said she'd been a frightened young woman. Trapped in a country she didn't understand, trying to protect her children from constant dangers—only to lose her beloved Jasper in such a senseless way. Yet still going on, pouring out all her energy into the women's classes because duty demanded it.

Mama and Crys—both dedicated to their commitments. They were a lot alike; no wonder they'd formed a bond.

"The Christians—the church people—are they all gone?" asked Elsa. "Are you the only one left?"

Sen Ying glanced out the window and whispered, "Many are still here. We meet in homes. Always we remember what Mai Mushih and Tai Tai teach. We tell others; they believe too. But we must be careful, be secret."

Mrs. Ko looked at her watch. "It is two fifteen. We must go back to our quarters."

Elsa asked Sen Ying, "Will you be at Mr. Peng's feast tonight?"

The old woman laughed. "I am only a little potato. Mr. Peng invites important people to banquets."

Elsa remembered that derogatory term, *little potato*. She patted Sen Ying's shoulder and said, "To me, you are an important person." She sighed. "There's so much more I need to ask you. And we leave early tomorrow. Tell me, what happened to Fung Choi and his family?"

"Fung Choi and wife were forced to work in the millet fields. Choi was a labor leader, very respected."

"Are they still living here?"

"Aiyah! Cholera came to the village. Both died. Very sad, very sad."

From out on the street, Elsa heard a high voice calling her name.

Mei-lien! Now she *was* in trouble. She quickly looked through her handbag for something to give Sen Ying for a keepsake.

Nothing seemed right. Then she found the little brocade coin purse she'd bought on the street that first evening in Shanghai. She hated to part with it, but since it was Chinese, it wouldn't be suspect if Peng should find out about this meeting.

Sen Ying started to protest, but Elsa had no time for *kerchieh*. She pressed it into the woman's hand. But she couldn't leave without one more question. "Choi's son Ling—what happened to him?" She glanced out the window as though the mention of his name would bring him here.

Sen Ying shook her head and spoke in bitter tones. Elsa didn't understand any of the muffled words.

Mrs. Ko said, "Fung Ling joined the Red Army and fought in the hills."

Elsa's stomach lurched. Ling, a Communist? He must have changed a whole lot. "Did he—was he married? Does he have a family?"

"I do not know, I have not seen him in many years."

"Where is his home?"

"They say Tienjin. He is an important man now."

Elsa wondered what he had done to be important. Had he also

been a traitor to the church people? Had he joined the Reds out of resentment for the punishment Mama had given him?

The door opened, and Mei-lien looked in. "Come quickly," she said. "Before Mr. Peng learns you are missing. He is ready to leave for the refinery."

"*Hao, hao,*" Elsa told Sen Ying formally, running her hand over the red brocade. "*Wo yao jayguh.*" *I want this one.* Handing Mrs. Ko some money, she said, "Tell her I want four yards of this. I'll meet you at Mr. Peng's."

THE LABOR HALL WAS A LARGE, brick building at the other end of the city. Dismal gray walls were relieved only by three windows on each side and a large picture of Chairman Mao at one end. Long plank tables had been set up on the bare cement floor, and servers laid out plates of melon seeds and peanuts and tall green bottles of clear liquid. Bowls and chopsticks stood ready for the feast.

A crowd of Chinese waited in the room, straddling the backless benches or standing with a foot hiked up to a bench. Some squatted on the floor. Mr. Peng escorted Elsa and Mrs. Ko past them to a table at the far end.

Elsa was exhausted. Her early train ride, all the obligatory tours and lack of rest had caught up with her. The excitement of seeing Sen Ying, sorrow for Wu Shong, and the disappointment about Ling was almost more than she could bear.

In her mind she had known she wouldn't see Ling, but her heart had hoped. To hear he'd turned to Communism was the final blow.

She turned her attention to the labor hall and had a strange feeling of déjà vu.

It must be her imagination. This building was on the opposite side of the city from her old home; it probably hadn't even been built when she was a child.

She looked carefully at the faces. The people stared back curiously but blandly. If anyone recognized her, they didn't show it.

Mr. Peng stood and held up his hand. He had changed to a gray, Mao-style suit and looked the part of a leader. About a hundred people settled into their seats, ready for the festivities, and latecomers hurried in to join them. Most of them, men and women, were wearing loose trousers and tunics in drab colors. A few young men sported Western-style turtleneck shirts and smoked American cigarettes, squashing them out in ceramic ash trays.

The program started; many people made speeches, and others proposed toasts.

"Long live the great and beautiful country of America!"

"Long live the People's Republic of China!"

Shouts of *"ganbei!"* the Chinese "bottoms up," echoed through the hall.

Waiters bustled around, refilling everyone's thimble-sized bowls of fiery *maotai* liquor, and the cheers went on.

"The great, glorious, and correct Communist Party of China!"

"The mighty workers!"

"Friendship between the nations!"

"Long live Elsa Dsake-y, who honors us with her presence!"

The floor became littered with cracked watermelon seeds and peanut shells. Someone turned on the lights, bare bulbs dangling from the ceiling, and Elsa looked through the windows at the contrasting darkness. *The windows*—there was something different about them. They were larger than usual for that area, rectangular but domed at the top.

Russian built? No, that didn't seem right. She started to ask about it, when she noticed a design in the panes. A vertical line of frosted glass, about four inches in width, divided the panels. Near the top, a horizontal one. A cross? In a Communist labor hall?

Suddenly she realized. *The village next to Shiao Yangshan, a long-ago rainy night. Cots set up in rows; people camped all over the room. Nuns serving hot tea and* bao-dze. The Catholic church! The city had grown until the church in the neighboring village had also been absorbed.

Like her father's mission, the building was still intact, but the trappings of religion had been removed. No statues in the window ledges, no altar, no holy water. Just the crosses in the windows, hidden unless one looked at them a certain way. Elsa smiled to think the Communists probably weren't even aware of them. They hadn't removed the most important symbol of Christ.

The room had grown silent, and the people stared at her. Mrs. Ko said, "You must give a speech."

What could she say to these people of Shiao Yangshan who were not of her village? Would they understand her thrill at coming home? If only Morris were here to give support and help her think clearly.

She hadn't come to see these strangers; still, they were Chinese. They'd allowed her to visit, honored her with this feast. She stood up, raised her *maotai* in a toast, and motioned for Mrs. Ko to interpret.

"I thank you for this feast of celebration. This is a very special evening for me. Many years ago as a child, I lived in the long, brick house east of the village. My parents were missionaries; my father's name was Mai Mushih.

"I love China. I loved the village of Shiao Yangshan, now an important city. I had many good friends here, and I was very sad when we moved to America." Elsa could almost hear the song phrase, *till we mee-ee-eet,* and she blinked away tears. The wrench of leaving flooded back to her, and her heart swelled with the emotion of returning, of meeting Sen Ying.

She wiped her eyes and cleared her throat. "Now your country and mine are friends again, and I have come back to visit my old home. It is a great joy for me to be here, and I thank Mr. Peng and all of you for this privilege. It is a very good thing for our countries to be friends. We can learn much from each other."

Many heads nodded.

"Your country has made great progress," Elsa continued. "I see many new and modern buildings and factories. Thriving industry, modern airports. Fine schools and universities for your eager and bright young people."

She didn't mention the desecration of the churches; what would have been the point of criticizing, of making them lose face? She was here at last. And just being here, she felt restored. Maybe someday the churches, too, would be restored.

Elsa sat down, the people applauded, and the food came. An elaborate, fourteen-course meal: hummingbird tongues, mushrooms and white fungus, sweet and sour rabbit, Mongolian mutton—*from the open-air market?*—long, green vegetables in sauce, tiny strips of melon. Elsa nibbled politely, tasting everything, barely touching her lips to the *maotai* for the ongoing toasts, and soothing the sharp bite with tea.

Turtle with bamboo shoots, mushu quail. And then—a huge tureen of dumplings. Her self-control vanished. *Jaodze!* Real, authentic *jaodze* as made only in Shiao Yangshan! Filled with ground mutton and onions and boiled—not fried or steamed as others made them—then smothered with bean threads and sprouts and chunks of pork. There was red vinegar and soy sauce to add, and *lahdey*, the hot pepper sauce. She dipped a chopstick into the *lahdey*, very carefully, letting only two drops fall into her bowl. She looked around to see if anyone was watching, but they were all busy eating and talking. Except for one man at the far end of the table.

An older man with thick gray hair and black-rimmed glasses. Their eyes met, and the man smiled and nodded, raising his *mao-tai* cup.

She lifted her cup in answer, ate another *jaodze*, and took a sip of tea. The man still stared, and she wondered if he might be a government official checking up on her. Servers carried the last course away. Conversation became noisier, and people left their places, some coming to Elsa and offering their good wishes. The gray-haired man also approached her, his thin face sober.

Mr. Peng rose. "May I present Mr. Fung of Tienjin."

"Fung?" repeated Elsa, her throat so constricted that she could barely speak. "Are you related to the Fung Choi family that once lived in this village?"

The man nodded, his mouth pursed as though he were enjoying a private joke. "I am. Do you not remember me?" He spoke in flawless English.

Elsa looked through his glasses into glowing brown eyes. Her heart leaped into her throat, then plunged into her stomach.

The man slowly shook his head. "The full-blown rose is even more lovely than the bud."

She clutched the edge of the table and tried to keep her voice steady. "Ling?"

"The same. And you are Yung-det. Eternal Virtue."

"You still remember my name!"

"One does not forget a friend."

Chapter 40

IN MR. PENG'S ROCK GARDEN, a full moon shone through the juniper branches. Elsa sat beside Ling on the stone bench and thought, *This isn't real.*

She'd dreamed of meeting Ling but had never expected to actually sit beside him in the moonlight.

Behind his black-rimmed glasses, Ling's eyes sparkled. What was he thinking? Long ago, they had been close friends, but how did he feel about her now? There was so much she wanted to ask, but she didn't know where to start. Her throat tightened, and the words wouldn't come.

Then he whistled softly, a familiar, plaintive tune. "Do you remember? *'I hear the river flowing, and I must sail away—'*"

Elsa picked up the song. "*'But my heart is sick with fear I won't return by day.'* Tsao Po-Po sang that to me. I loved the melody, but the words made me feel sad."

Ling nodded. "I feared you had gone away forever, but now you have returned."

"I have returned," she mused. "That sounds fateful."

"It is fate. We were meant to meet again."

Elsa felt a rush of tenderness. After all these years, he still cared. His eyes searched hers, but she looked away. Smoothing a wrinkle in her sleeve, she wondered how to keep the conversation light. "I—I don't understand. I heard you lived in Tienjin. How did you happen to come to Shiao Yangshan on this particular evening?"

Ling smiled. "For a long time, I have followed news from America. First we were told that foreigners were destructive to our system and banned from our country." He paused, then flung his hands out dramatically. "Suddenly, your President Nixon comes to China, and our leaders say Americans are our friends. I say, let them visit our cities. And one group came, then another. I waited, wondering if perhaps the red-haired Yung-det might be drawn back to her home."

Her pulse raced. "But how did you know I was here?"

"I am inspector of factories in this region. I travel to many cities and villages. I tell my comrades: if they learn of Americans coming here, they must report to me."

"So Mr. Peng wrote you? He told me he didn't know anyone who lived here then."

"Not Peng." Ling hawked and directed an arc of spit over the next boulder.

That shocked Elsa a little. He'd seemed so cultured. She remembered admiring that skill when they were young and Mama's disgust when she'd copied it. Now it didn't fit with Ling's dignified manner. He must not be on good terms with her host.

He glanced up at the dark and silent window of Elsa's host and spoke softly. "No, it was not Peng. I have contacts in many places. Two days ago, I heard you were coming here." Then he smiled, his eyes glinting. "It suddenly became important that the sugar refineries be inspected. I arrived on this afternoon's train. Here, my friends informed me of the feast."

The tightness in her throat had released and talking was easier. "Then Mr. Peng invited you?"

Ling's lips twisted. "Let us say, I was able to make arrangements."

Elsa waited, but he didn't explain. She wondered if he'd threatened to give the refineries a bad report or bribed the officials, and she shook her head in amazement. What an incredible number of strings he must have pulled to be here tonight. And just to see her.

Looking at him, she could still see traces of the young boy she'd admired so much. "Do you remember the day I fell and cut my knee? You took me into your home and put some of that black salve on it."

"And then you asked to see the bell tower."

"You had some drawings up there—trains, people . . ."

Ling smiled. "I tried to hide them from you, but I was not quick enough. I was afraid you would laugh."

"Never. I loved your drawings; they were very good. After your parents left Shiao Yangshan, I went up to the tower and found the one of the station. I still have it."

He drew back in amazement. "You kept it all these years?"

She nodded and repeated what he'd said after the feast, "One does not forget a friend. . . . Do you still draw?"

"Not for many, many years. My father did not approve."

Elsa asked Ling about his parents, and he confirmed what Sen Ying had said.

"It was very hard for them during the war years. My father was strong, but my mother was not accustomed to field work. When the cholera epidemic came, her body could not resist it. Shortly after that, my father was also stricken."

"But you didn't get sick?"

"I was not there. Much later, I learned about it."

"I'm sorry." She remembered Ling's mother only as a shadowy figure in the background. But Fung Choi was still vivid in her mind, the man who had welcomed them at the train station, had pushed Elsa to the village in the wheelbarrow, had led them to the Catholic church on that awful, rainy day. She felt a deep sadness for her good friend who'd worked so faithfully for Papa.

She knew it must have been painful for Ling. She, too, knew the sorrow of losing a father; how much worse it must be to lose both parents even when they were far away, whether physically or emotionally.

She could see the gatehouse, Fung Choi at the desk registering visitors in his big ledger. The *kang* in the back room. The wall hanging . . .

She turned to Ling. "Remember that story you told me—the legend of the cherry blossoms?" He'd sat beside her just like this, had kissed her hand, and she'd adored him with all her childish heart.

"Cherry blossoms?" He frowned into the distance, his foot sliding side to side like a pendulum in the dust.

"You know, the girl who talked to the nightingale?"

Ling's face creased into a smile. "Ah, yes, the beautiful princess who became a bird and flew away with the nightingale into the mountains." His face colored a little. "You remember that?"

"A picture on Mr. Peng's wall reminded me. Birds on a cherry branch. Wasn't there a wall hanging like that in the gatehouse?"

For a moment, anger flickered in Ling's eyes, but then his face became serene. "Many things were confiscated during the Cultural Revolution. All was done for the good of the people."

"You mean it's the same picture? Are you sure?"

He gave a wry smile. "There is a stain on the bottom of the panel where once I clumsily spilled tea."

"Why don't you claim the wall hanging?"

"Ownership is not important. Here, many people can enjoy it."

Elsa frowned. If that was her picture, she would march right in and demand it back. But that was not the Chinese way.

They went on to talk about the mission, the clinic, the good times they'd had working together. Then for a while, they sat in silence.

Ling cleared his throat. "Your parents—they are well?"

She told him about Papa's death, about Mama now living alone in her little apartment.

Ling nodded, his eyes sympathetic. "And you? Is your life in America good?"

Elsa stared into the shadows, remembering the early adjustments, the teasing from her classmates. "Now it is. I had a terrible time at first, getting used to the different culture." She shook her head slowly. "Then I met Morris, my husband. He was—*is*—so gentle, so understanding. He helped me fit in, showed me it was all right to be different." She described Morris's clear blue eyes, his crisp, blond waves. His tall, muscular build.

"What is his business?"

"He's a pharmacist."

Ling looked puzzled, and she added, "He owns a drug—an apothecary—store. But he also sells gifts, cosmetics, costume jewelry. Cameras. He's especially interested in photography."

"He must be very tolerant to let his lovely wife come here alone."

"He knew this trip was important to me. Our daughter came

along, but she stayed in Beijing to take pictures for him. What about you? Do you have a family?"

He smiled. "A fat little grandson. Just so high—" His hand grazed his knee. "He tries to walk but staggers as though drunk."

It was strange to think of Ling as a grandfather. "Does he live in Tienjin, too?"

"No, our son married a girl from Datung. There he is the overseer in a sewing machine factory."

Elsa nodded, grinning. "Which you inspect often."

His eyes twinkled in response. "Very often. Otherwise, they have much trouble with breakdown of machinery."

"Tell me, how did you learn to speak English so well?"

"Bo-li—my wife—knows many languages. She tutored me."

"Where did you meet her?"

Ling shifted and leaned against the backrest. "We were cadres together in the Red Army. We fought together in the mountains. Now she is an interpreter for the Russian consulate."

It didn't sound very romantic. Elsa was ashamed of herself for feeling relieved. "When did you join up?"

"Long before that. I was sixteen years of age. I ran away from my apprenticeship."

"Only sixteen? In the army?" That must have been soon after she'd left China. A breeze rattled the juniper leaves, and Elsa shivered. She'd forgotten how cold the evenings were in the north, even in the summer.

"As youths, we ran errands for the soldiers. It was a great honor. Much better than making boots."

"But wasn't there a lot of violence, killing? A young boy like that—"

"It was for the good of the country. To liberate the people."

"And you stayed on as a soldier?"

Ling's mouth became a straight line, and his eyes glittered. "It was necessary to root out the corruption of the warlords. I was proud to help." His voice was harsh, his expression fanatical.

Shocked, Elsa studied him. This was not the Ling she remembered. Had he enjoyed the violence? Morris had hated the war. Even now, he wouldn't say much about the horrors he'd seen. "I heard about Wu Shong, that he'd been tortured and killed."

Ling shrugged. "Wu Shong was thought to be part of the foreign domination. Perhaps that was a mistake. At that time, there was much turmoil. But now everything is better. Religion is self-governed. People have jobs and food. The country is progressing. You see that, do you not? You mentioned it in your speech at the banquet."

Yes, she'd mentioned it. China had progressed in many ways—people were working, and there were no beggars to be seen. The clinics they'd visited were giving affordable treatment. But at what price? Young boys hating, killing—faithful Christians like Wu Shong murdered . . .

Elsa pulled her thoughts back, realizing that Ling was still speaking: "I hear you went into the long house—the workers' apartments."

News traveled fast. He must have spies everywhere. "It was quite a shock. I'd expected some change, but not that much. The tower gone, the church a factory. All those people living in our house."

He smiled. "You Americans use much space."

"I had hoped to see the back compound. But Mr. Peng came, nervous and upset, and insisted that I leave immediately. He almost threatened me."

"Our government prefers that visitors tour only approved areas."

"I just wanted to walk around the grounds. Now there's no more time," she said sadly.

Ling rubbed his forehead and cleared his throat. Finally he said, "It is against regulations. But I know your intentions are harmless." He paused. "I am told that at five o'clock in the morning, Peng goes to the labor hall and performs tai chi exercises. Rise early and go to the grounds at that time. *Only* the grounds. Do not enter the house, and do not disturb the people."

Elsa reached over and pressed his hand. "Thank you. I'll be careful. I loved that big back compound. The swings, the stable, all the trees . . ."

"Your front courtyard had beautiful flowers around each tree. Every day when I arrived from school, I looked for you there."

Elsa asked, "Remember when you'd had a fight and came home all cut and bruised? You said you had to 'bear the burden of your difference.' I always wondered what you meant. How were you different?"

"You do not remember? No, my head had been shaved then. My hair had not been black, as most Chinese are, but brown. No doubt a Russian ancestor or two. My friends would not let me forget. They jeered at me, said I was part foreign devil." He sighed. "Ah, yes. It is not always pleasant to be different. But that was my burden, not theirs."

"You're not different now."

"My hair is gray. And in Communism, all are equal."

"Even the Christians?"

Ling shrugged and raised his hands, palms out. "Let us not waste precious time with disagreement."

Elsa searched for something neutral to say. "This morning at the long house, I saw children playing Chinese jacks. It made me think of Lihua and Shirhua. Remember them? Fu Liu's nieces who came over to play." She almost shared her relief at Sen Ying's good news about Lihua, but realized that mentioning the woman might endanger the secret church. Instead, she asked, "Have you seen them since then?"

"No. After I left home, I broke all ties with the mission."

After he left. How he must have resented Mama! Elsa didn't want to risk more tension, but she had to ask. "You were so bright, so good in your studies—did you ever go back and finish school?"

Ling's face darkened. "That was not possible." He spit again, a short, sideways spurt.

Now she had spoiled the whole evening. She studied Ling's expression, his mouth bitter, and his eyes full of hatred. Did he resent her, too? "I'm so sorry. I'll never forgive my mother for what she did, sending you away like that. I wish I could make it up to you."

Ling turned to her, looking puzzled. "Your mother? I do not understand."

"She . . . didn't approve of our friendship. That day you passed your entrance examinations and we were so happy, I watched her go to your house. After that, I never saw you again."

"True. She came. She told my father it was not right for us to . . . be together."

"And then she sent you away."

Ling laughed, a short, hard bark. "No. That was my father's doing. He was very angry with me. But that does not concern you."

"Of course it does. I need to know!"

Ling looked down, the tip of his shoe drawing lines in the dust. "He . . . felt I had disgraced our family and made him lose face. We were lowly servants; you were distinguished foreigners. He beat me right before your mother and told me I must leave. Your mother begged for him to allow me to finish school."

"Mama? She stuck up for you?"

"She said I should leave the clinic and go away to school. But my father would not listen. He had always scorned my love for learning. This was his excuse to make me give it up."

Elsa's mind whirled. Choi had been the one?

Ling rose and walked toward the gate. He leaned his head against it, his hands balled into fists.

Elsa went to him, wanting to reach out and ease his pain, aching to embrace him in long-lost friendship but afraid he would misunderstand.

He turned around, his face contorted, his mouth working. "I had only the greatest respect for you. But my father would not believe me. I was not to speak to you again."

"Why didn't you go to Papa? He would have straightened things out."

"I could not. I was not allowed in the compound again."

Elsa went back to the bench and sat down. She had to think this through. All these years, her resentment had been built on a false impression. Had she been wrong about other things, too?

Choi. She'd thought he was so kind and wise. How could he have ruined his own son's life?

Confusion and anger mingled with a deep sadness for Ling, for the despair he must have felt, for the scholar he could have been. For the barrier she'd put between herself and Mama, for the lack of communication that kept them from reconciling. She put her hands over her face and wept.

She felt a warm breeze at the back of her neck and reached up blindly to feel Ling's face. He seized her hand and pressed it to his lips, and the years rolled back.

She was a child again, sitting on the brick flower border in the mission compound. A young girl feeling the first stirrings of love and the promise of unknown joy.

"Do not be sad," said Ling. "Life goes on. *Muh yu fadze.*"

The moon ducked behind a cloud, and the wind quickened. Elsa swallowed hard and turned away. He was right. There was nothing they could do about it now.

Despite their affection, she and Ling had little in common. Too much time had passed; too much had happened. Years ago, being a missionary daughter had given her prestige. She had spoken Chinese fluently and thought that made her one of them.

But she'd never belonged here. She'd never needed to submit to the disciplines of a true Chinese, the acceptance of *muh yu fadze,* taking whatever fate brought.

She still couldn't accept it. Even though Mama hadn't intentionally ruined Ling's life and crushed their budding friendship, there was still the matter of her constant criticism. And the bracelet.

Ling rose, and an impassive mask slid over his features. "It is very good to see you again. We are still friends?" He held out his hand.

Elsa shook it solemnly. "We will always be friends."

"Good-bye, Yung-det. Eternal Virtue. May you have long life and good health. I shall remember this visit fondly."

He kissed her on the forehead, then walked away, head high, his slender shoulders erect. There was a hint of youthful swagger in his stride.

As he stepped through the gate, he turned and raised his hand in a silent salute. Then he was gone.

Chapter 41

IN THE CHILL GRAY OF PREDAWN, Elsa made her way toward the old church. Early morning workers, opening its metal gate, turned to stare at her.

She went on, passing the warehouses—the old clinic, the apartments—and finally reached the long house.

Window after window reminded her of another life. Papa's office, where she'd given away her tuition to save Lihua from a life worse than death. Jasper's room, where she'd acted out stories with him and played with the spools and blocks. Her own room, with the shelf of books and treasures and Cherky's cage in the window. The schoolroom, where Mama graded papers with a red pencil. The workroom, where Tsao Po-Po had sewed her dresses, darned the family socks, and told her stories about dragons and dwarfs and magic bells.

Elsa sighed. How she'd love to go in once more, to fill her heart with memories. But she'd promised Ling not to bother the tenants.

The front door opened, and she felt a shiver of expectation. Papa? But a stranger stepped out, an old Chinese man scratching his ribs and hawking. He spit in the sand and fumbled with the drawstring of his pants.

Elsa slipped around the corner toward the back, trailing her fingers along the gritty brick wall.

Then she stopped and stared. The back compound was now a cluster of small mud huts, the first one right where the root cellar had been.

The root cellar! That cool cozy playhouse, the wooden spool families, her cat Empress—*the cheese man.*

For so many years, she'd pushed that experience to the farthest corner of her mind, refusing to look at its ugliness. Maybe now was the time to face it squarely, to conquer it once and for all.

She allowed the whole nightmare to sweep over her again. The sour smell of the man's breath, the rough feel of his hands. His high, lewd giggle.

She pressed her arms against her chest. Just that way, she'd squeezed Empress so tightly the cat had yowled and wiggled free, darting out the door. What if the *yahbah* hadn't seen it, hadn't realized there was danger and come to her rescue? The results could have been so much worse. But God had given the *yahbah* enough presence of mind to come, and she'd been set free. *Thank You, Lord,* she breathed, and released the memory.

Smoke drifted out of the chimneys, and Elsa could smell food cooking. She inhaled deeply, remembering that smell. The thin gray oat gruel she'd had for breakfast so many times. *Yomein huhu.* It reminded her that she hadn't eaten yet.

Looking more carefully at the houses, she noticed that one, next to the old well and washing cauldron, was made of wood and larger than the mud huts.

Could that be the old stable? It had to be. She thought of Mealy Fray and all her imaginary rides into the grasslands. *If I could bring him to life, would he still be the dashing horseback rider, or would he have aged to be a toothless, wrinkled old man like the one at the front door?* How she wished she could peek through a window!

Don't bother the people. Elsa hurried on, looking for more landmarks. The swings would have been between the first two huts. Now a fat sow lay in the dirt, nursing a dozen piglets. In a nearby melon patch, chickens pecked at rotting melon rinds.

She'd expected the rows of trees to guide her, but they, too, were gone. A dusty road streaked with cart tracks led toward fields of oats, millet, and sugar beets, and beyond them, Little Goat Mountain. *Picnics among the rocks, happy times wading in the friendly little stream. Until the flood.*

She felt weak, and her ears throbbed in unison with the thumping of her heart. She took a step back and nearly tripped. A circular piece of wood lay almost flush with the sandy ground. A tree stump, sheared down to the ground. A few feet away was another stump, and then another. She followed to the last one and walked east, counting her steps. "*Yi, er, san, sih, wu, liu, chi, bah.*"

It should be right here—the little mound where Jasper was buried in the shade of the wall. But the wall was gone, and all around, the ground was flat. She checked once more, looking back past the huts to the long house.

Where could the grave be? Surely no Chinese would have desecrated a burial place. She dropped to her knees on the ground, patting the smooth, dry earth, frantically searching for clues.

Painful memories seized her, swarmed through her mind. That terrible day, the flood, his death. And all her fault.

The pounding in her ears turned into the thundering roar of the water; the little stream changed into a horrible devouring monster . . .

Looking over the compound wall, seeing Papa in the distance walking toward the river. Running after him, Jasper following—"No, Little Tiger, you're too little!"

The huge swollen river, boiling, roaring, gobbling up chickens, ducks, goats, bushes, wooden beams from people's houses.

Then hurrying back—Papa, Reverend Moffat, Choi, Jasper, and me—and all around, those innocent-looking rivulets breaking loose to form a huge boiling ocean. Jasper—Oh, dear Lord! Reaching my hand out to him, screaming . . .

Jasper's head going under, surfacing again, his face pale against the muddy foam, his own screams muffled by the water's roar.

On her knees, searching for the grave, Elsa felt overwhelmed with despair. She'd been only nine, five years older than Jasper but not much bigger. What more could she have done to keep him from drowning? She remembered Papa's last words on his own deathbed: *No—not your fault. Promise . . . promise me. Don't blame yourself.*

Now she understood: along with their sorrow, her parents had suffered guilt, too. Papa, unfamiliar with desert floods, curious, not seeing the danger. Mama, knowing her rebellious daughter so well, yet too busy to watch her children closely.

"Oh, dear Lord, forgive me," Elsa groaned. "Forgive us all."

Papa's favorite blessing echoed in her mind: *The Lord lift up His countenance upon you, and give you peace.*

Peace. It swept over her soul, wrapping around her, filling her, soothing her. The guilt of a lifetime floated away, and she realized that she'd been forgiven all along. The only thing left was to forgive herself.

And Mama. All these years, she'd blamed her mother for Ling's problems, as well as for her own. She'd never understood, had never known what Mama had gone through. The fear. The loss. The guilt.

If Sen Ying could forgive Fu Liu for betraying Wu Shong, for causing his torture and death, Elsa thought, with God's help, she herself could forgive Mama the hurts of the past.

Her mother was who she was. Stern, righteous to the point of harshness—but demanding no less of herself than of others. She'd worked so hard to be a perfect missionary that she'd failed to accept the inner peace, the love of God, that overflowed to others.

Footsteps crunched on the sand, and Elsa looked up to see Mrs. Ko.

"Come," the woman whispered. "Mr. Peng will soon be home."

"My brother's grave—it's gone."

"Many floods, many sandstorms. Do not fret. He is in your Christian heaven." The guide stood with her hands folded, head bowed.

In heaven. Filled with warmth like a celestial embrace, Elsa imagined Jasper riding on Papa's shoulders, holding on to Papa's thick, curly red hair.

As they started back, Elsa stopped and looked around one last time. The long house made into apartments. A warehouse barely recognizable as the former clinic. The old church naked without its steeple and wooden doors, violated under the disguise of progress.

Behind it, black smoke from the refineries rose to the sky. In the east, the horizon blushed with dawn.

Elsa wiped away her tears. "Mrs. Ko, thank you for being patient with me. I'm finished now. Lead the way."

Chapter 42

THE TOUR BUS SWAYED AROUND the narrow, twisting mountain roads leading up to the Great Wall. Elsa looked out the window at a sheer drop into deep rock quarries. Beyond them were villages and small compounds surrounded by mud walls, just like the ones she'd known in Shiao Yangshan.

It was hard to shift from the emotions of the past day. At the Shiao Yangshan station, she'd looked back for a last good-bye to her beloved village, and had seen only an unfamiliar city. If it hadn't been for Ling and Sen Ying, her early life could have been erased like a mistake from a blackboard.

She'd spent the train ride back to Beijing lost in thought, and Mrs. Ko had been kind enough to respect her privacy.

Her feeling of peace still lingered, but underneath had come a new sadness. She now realized that all the experiences that had shaped her life had been seen through the eyes of a confused child. Leaving China, she'd felt ripped out of the warmth of her home, yet she'd never truly belonged there. She'd only been a foreign child in China, shielded from dangers and threats by a terrified mother. Hardships, poverty, and lack of sanitation—the lot of most Chinese—had never touched her.

As a child, she had cuddled in Papa's arms or run to Tsao Po-Po for comfort. Never to Mama. Mama was the teacher, the authority figure, someone she had avoided for fear of a spanking.

Had that been her fault or Mama's? Why hadn't they been able to communicate? Hadn't Mama trusted her enough to tell her the truth? Didn't she realize that a child's imagination invented fears far worse than reality?

With a few words, Mama could have explained what had happened to Ling.

Ling. Still attractive, still charming, but not the same Ling she'd left behind. Or had she really known him even then? He'd seemed so carefree, so nonchalant, a prince among his friends.

Now, she could see that Communism had taken his life in an opposite direction from everything he had been taught at the mission. It was obvious that underneath his charm he was hard and cynical, bitter against the "foreign corruption," which included everything Papa had believed and preached. And poor Wu Shong had suffered the consequences.

Ling hadn't come to the station when she left. Their good-byes last night under the juniper tree had been final, and she would never see him again. It was just as well. She, too, had changed.

"Is that part of the wall?"

Elsa turned to stare at Crystal sitting beside her in the bus. *Wall?* Oh, yes. The Great Wall. She glanced at the brick ruins on the next peak. "I'm sure it is. It goes on for miles and miles, and only the tourist parts have been restored."

"I wish you could have seen the Forbidden City. Fabulous! I could have spent a week just wandering around, imagining the emperors, the eunuchs, Empress Tzu Hsih, and all the intrigues. Too bad we have to leave China tomorrow."

Leaving China. How different it would be this time, thought Elsa. Now she understood Mama's eagerness, the smiles that had been so rare before that. This time, leaving really meant going home.

Crystal showed her a medallion she'd bought in the gift shop. A red cloisonné heart decorated with golden jasmines. It would go well with the red brocade that Elsa had bought in Shiao Yangshan. But she would give that to Crys later, after she and Morris had a chance to meet Dr. Valdez.

Elsa admired the medallion and said, "I have to tell you something. I found your grandmother's jade bracelet. You know, the one the bandits missed."

"You found it? When? Where was it?"

She told Crystal about looking for Mama's cookbook, the rips in the trunk lid lining. "I can still remember seeing them in the vendor's tray, trying them on. So smooth on the inside, on the outside etched with dragons curling around until they met face-to-face, sharing their precious egg. The problem is—now that it's found—she thinks it's too worldly for her."

Crystal beamed. "Hey, then maybe she'll give it to you."

Elsa didn't answer. How could she admit her hurt without hurting Crys?

But Crystal persisted. "What's the matter? You think she won't?"

Elsa bit her lip and took a deep breath. *Might as well get it over with.* "She's planning to give it to you for a wedding gift. When you marry Greg." She turned away, angry at her sudden tears.

"When I marry—" Crystal's mouth stayed open.

"You haven't told her, have you? About Dr. Valdez."

Crystal's face reddened. "It was bad enough breaking the news about El Seco. Ruben would have been too much of a shock right then."

"There'll never be an easy time."

"I know." Crystal wound the chain of the medallion around her finger. "She's always expected so much of me. She thinks I'm letting her down."

The story of my life, Elsa thought. *Join the club. "That's good, Elsa, but why don't you do it another way, take it a little farther?" "Why waste time with an Okie when you could be with that nice Joe Schmidt?"* Aloud, she said, "Tell me more about this Ruben Valdez."

Crystal's eyes glowed. "Oh, Mom, I can hardly wait for you to meet him. We think alike on so many things, have the same goals. I've never known any man so sweet, so gentle. Except for Dad, of course. When I'm with Ruben, I feel—complete. And when we're apart, there's a hollow spot in my heart and I count the hours until I see him again. I'm convinced that he's the man God has chosen to be my partner for life."

Just the way I feel about Morris, thought Elsa.

Crystal's smile faded a little. "If only I could convince Grandma of that."

"Oh, Crys," said Elsa. "In her eyes, you can do no wrong."

Crystal shook her head. "I just let her think that way because it means so much to her. She's—she's not as stern as she acts. Deep down, she's really kindhearted."

"I hadn't noticed." Elsa thought of all the times she'd taken Mama's bait, always snapping back only to find herself in a quarrel. By rising above the words, not allowing them to hurt her, Crystal had preserved her relationship with her grandmother while keeping her own independence.

Had that been Papa's way, too? She'd often wondered how he had managed to get along with someone so different from himself.

"Next time she criticizes, say something nice in return," Crystal suggested. "You'll see."

Elsa tried to imagine it. One thing was for sure: it would certainly surprise Mama.

A jolt of the bus threw her forward, and she braced herself against the back of the next seat. They had stopped in a gravel parking lot next to a fleet of other buses.

On one side, far down a cliff, lay the town of Badaling. On the other side, hundreds of tourists streamed up an incline.

The sky was overcast, and a brisk wind played with the scrub brush and gnarled oak trees. In a sheltered arbor, Rose Lee served box lunches and then herded the group up the stone steps to the stronghold. In the old days, she said, six horsemen could charge side by side on the wall. Elsa could almost hear the pounding hooves, the shouts, the twang of spears meeting enemy armor.

She and Crystal climbed higher and higher as the wall sloped over the mountain, following its contours. They hiked past several lookout towers until the ramp was too steep for comfort. Elsa stopped at one of the towers, gasping for breath in the thin air. When Crystal crawled hand over hand up a series of metal rungs to the top parapet, Elsa followed and peered over the brick fortress. Down below, she could see the Great Wall continuing into the distance, a giant serpent coiling over the vast stretch of mountain peaks. Surely, this was the top of the world.

The wind whipped her hair, and she felt a surge of exhilaration. It seemed only yesterday she'd been thirteen, leaving China, thinking her life had ended. She'd never dreamed that someday she would come back and stand here, feeling a whole person, looking at China as a foreign country. It seemed as though the fragments of her life had come together and formed a new pattern, like the changing design in a kaleidoscope.

She'd had to travel more than five thousand miles to find out who she was, where she belonged. And in the process, she'd become better acquainted with Mama.

It would be interesting to play Crystal's game of ignoring Mama's barbs. But maybe she wouldn't have to. After all she'd learned on this trip, she felt the courage to do what she could never do before: to sit her mother down and tell her, "This isn't right. We need to talk things through, woman to woman. Find out why we, two mature Christians, can't get along. Because if we don't do this, we'll destroy each other."

She knew Morris would back her up; he'd also felt the sting of her mother's rejection too many times.

She looked down at the wall again, saw the other tour members starting to leave, and turned to climb down the rungs of the parapet.

But Crystal aimed the camera at her. "Smile!" Crys squeezed back into a corner of the tower to get more of the wall for a background. "There. That's a perfect ending to Dad's travelogue."

Elsa took a deep breath. It was a good way to finish the trip to China. Someday, she'd come back again to see the Forbidden City, the Summer Palace. The tourist things. But for now, this was enough.

She took one last look over the mountains of China. "Okay. I'm ready to go home."

Chapter 43

MAMA CRACKED OPEN HER apartment door. "You didn't say you were coming over." Her hair was disheveled, and Elsa realized she'd interrupted a Sunday afternoon nap.

"I'm sorry to wake you up," she said. "I would have come sooner, but jet lag did me in."

Mama sighed. "Now that you're here, you may as well come in." She opened the door farther, then went to her dresser mirror and recoiled the knot in her hair. "You could have called first."

Elsa walked in and pulled out a chair for herself. "I know. I didn't realize . . ." There was that guilt feeling again. Even though she'd forgiven her mother, this would be hard. But she remembered Crystal's advice and forced herself to stay pleasant. "I just wanted to see how you were."

"As well as can be expected." Mama's lips twitched, and she smoothed her dress.

"I brought you a souvenir; I think you'll like it. After our pictures are developed, we'll have you over for dinner and give it to you. We'll have a slide show. I think Crys got some really great shots."

"She told me." Mama sat down on her bed, wrinkles of discontent lining her pursed mouth.

Stay calm, Elsa told herself. "I take it that's not all she told you." She watched her mother and waited for the storm.

Mama crushed a handful of bedspread, smoothing it out before she answered. "How can you let your little girl run off with that Mexican?"

"Hispanic, Mama." She kept her voice light. "Dr. Ruben Valdez.

From what Crys tells us, I believe he's a fine, well-respected Christian man, and they love each other very much. She's twenty-three, old enough to know what's right for her. At that age, you were a respected missionary and teacher, and not long after that, a mother."

Mama turned away. "That was different."

"You were so brave to give up everything, travel across the world far from family and friends—"

"Oh, yes, I gave up everything." Her mother's voice was bitter, and she still didn't look up. "My parents thought I was crazy for marrying your father. Didn't you ever wonder why we never saw nor heard from any of your Carlisle relatives?"

"Papa said there'd been some trouble. He said you didn't like to talk about it."

"They would have accepted him, given him the right connections. He was so handsome, so charming. He could have been anything he wanted. If he had to preach, he could have had a big, prestigious church."

"Papa?" Elsa couldn't imagine him kowtowing to rich people in a fancy building.

"But he was obsessed with China." Mama sniffed. "He even convinced me—told me wonderful stories, showed me pictures. Pagodas, lovely brocaded silks, formal gardens. Ponds with gorgeous lotus blossoms and goldfish. So I gave in, took all the right training, did all the right things. I thought it would be a romantic adventure."

Suddenly, Elsa realized what even Sen Ying hadn't guessed. "You never wanted to be a missionary, did you? That wasn't what you'd planned for your life."

Mama turned sharply to Elsa as though surprised she was there. "We visited churches and people's houses, asking for support. Begging for money as if we were paupers. My father said I'd disgraced him. He told me to choose: the missionary or my family."

"And you chose Papa." Elsa thought of her father's dedication, his special love for God and the people of China. If Mama didn't have that . . .

"'One term,' he promised. Five years. But it turned out to be fifteen. And all that time, my family never answered my letters. As far as they were concerned, I was no longer alive. And all your father's stories about China turned out to be fairy tales."

"But Shungtau was pretty, wasn't it? That big house with its red tile roof and white arches, the flowers, the green mountains?"

"Oh, yes, South China had spectacular scenery. Especially in the spring when all the wild orchids and camellias were in bloom. But what good was that when the war broke out?" Mama took a deep breath and blew it out. "When I heard all the shooting, the horrible shouts of killing—'*sha, sha!*'—I was sure your father had been murdered in those same beautiful mountains."

Elsa remembered that flight; she'd been so scared, too. "But God kept us safe and brought Papa back to us."

"I never felt safe after that. Never. That dirty little village up north, so far from civilization—I was sure there were bandits roaming the area. Your father and I worked out a code, dotting our *i*'s with circles, curling our letters a certain way, in case we got kidnapped. And all the sandstorms, and the rats . . ."

Mama glanced at Elsa, her face creased in disgust. "The longer we stayed in China, the more native customs he developed. And you were even worse. By the time we finally came home, I couldn't get you civilized."

Elsa felt as though a hand had squeezed her heart. She'd tried to forget how hard it had been to adjust, to be like other Americans. As a girl, she'd missed Shiao Yangshan with every fiber of her being, never realizing that her mother had hated it with as much passion.

"While on this tour, I took a special trip to the village."

Her mother's mouth flew open, but Elsa didn't stop. "I was amazed at the changes; it's grown into a big city." She described the mission now filled with factory equipment, their old home occupied by several families of workers. "The church people seem to have scattered, but I did find Sen Ying."

Her mother drew back. "Sen Ying? My Bible woman?"

Elsa told her about the fabric shop and the woman's greetings. About the terrible things that had happened, and how wonderful it was that the tuition money had given Lihua a chance for a good life. "She told me how hard it had been for you. I'd never understood why you were so . . . protective. Now I can. I'd probably be the same way if I tried to raise little children in a primitive setting."

Mama looked at her from under a furrowed brow. "You? You'd be out there mucking in the dirt with them. You would have been content to live all your life as a peasant in Inner Mongolia."

Elsa knew that was probably true, and she couldn't help laughing. "I was quite a brat, wasn't I? I just wanted to be free, to live like the Chinese."

"Sen Ying was a big help," said Mama, "but even she couldn't understand hygiene. I warned the women that lice carried diseases, that their children could pick up parasites sitting on the ground with their split pants. But they just shrugged and said the babies were content. *Muh yu fadze.*"

"Sounds like Tsao Po-Po. She let us do whatever we wanted." Even after all the years, the thought of Elsa's amah gave her comfort.

"That woman was far too permissive. But your father wouldn't let me dismiss her."

"You never liked her, did you? Why, Mama? She was such a good worker."

"You should have seen her when she first came to us—ragged, filthy, covered with sores and bruises from the man with whom she'd been living."

Feeling sick, Elsa stared at Mama. How could someone abuse her beloved amah! As long as she could remember, the woman had been gentle and loving. And always clean.

Mama nodded. "It's true. All she owned were her silver hairpins."

Elsa remembered those so well. The lion pin that Tsao Po-Po had given her as a farewell gift still rested in her jewelry box. "What happened?"

"Your father rescued her from that drunkard, probably saved her life. But in China that meant she belonged to him and he was responsible for her."

Elsa felt a stab of grief for Papa. That had been his whole life—showing God's love through his actions.

Mama shrugged. "I didn't think she could be trusted, but what could I do? We cleaned her up, deloused her, and put her to work."

"But she was my amah! You trusted her enough for that!"

"I had to. When you were born—prematurely—I was feverish with malaria and had no strength to take care of a sickly infant. By the time I recovered, months later, Tsao had nursed you into a healthy, lively baby, and you were so fiercely attached to her you wouldn't even come to me. By the time you could talk, you called her Po-Po, as if she were your real grandmother."

"And then in Shiao Yangshan, you wouldn't let her take care of us anymore." Elsa could still feel the pang of separation.

"It was time! You were so impressionable, and she wasn't a good influence."

Tsao Po-Po? "But she came to church, sang hymns, prayed. She was a Christian!"

"She'd said she'd accepted the Lord, and your father baptized her, but I never could be sure she was sincere. She always filled your heads with nonsense—dragons and moon kings. Evil spirits."

"Jasper and I loved those scary stories. But we knew that's all they were. Stories."

Jasper. Elsa thought of that last morning in the compound—the desperate memories, and then the assurance of God's love and release. "I—looked for Jasper's grave. It was gone."

"Gone?" Mama put a hand up to her mouth, and tears welled in her eyes.

"It was quite a shock not to find it. But there was no way it could survive after all the years of sandstorms and floods."

"My sweet little boy." Her mother closed her eyes and took a shuddering breath. "I didn't think life was worth living after he died. I blamed you, blamed your father, blamed everybody but myself. But I knew. That day I was more worried about what to serve our company than about what my children were doing." She shook her head slowly. "If only I hadn't pushed Tsao aside, she would have been watching Jasper, and he wouldn't have drowned. I was afraid of losing face—and instead I lost him." The tears slid down her cheeks, and she made no effort to stop them.

All these years, Mama *had* secretly shared the responsibility. No wonder she'd been so bitter; her emotions must have been trapped in a prison so strong no one could get in. Memories choked Elsa again, but this time with a difference. "I guess, in a way, each one of us had something to do with it. But we can't change what happened. We have to let go of our sorrow and guilt and give it over to God. That's the only way to have peace."

"So many years out of our lives." Mama's voice was flat. "So much hard work—and what good did it do? After we left, the Communists took over and completely destroyed Christianity."

Elsa touched her arm. "No, Mama. It wasn't destroyed. Sen Ying said the church just went underground, meeting in homes. Despite all the persecution, it's still growing. The people remember the things you and Papa taught them."

Mama stared at her, disbelief in her eyes. "You mean—it wasn't all for nothing? God was able to use us? Even me—in spite of the way I fought back?"

Elsa thought of her mother's passion for cleanliness, her strictness. There must have been a purpose to that, too. "Oh, yes, Mama. God doesn't let anything go to waste." She watched her mother digest the idea. Maybe now their relationship could heal.

Then she dared to add, "I saw someone else in Shiao Yangshan. Remember my friend Ling?"

"No!" Mama looked horrified. "You met him there?"

"He's an important man now, a factory inspector."

"I hope you didn't . . . do something foolish."

Elsa gave a short laugh. "You still don't trust me, do you? I wouldn't do anything to hurt Morris. . . . Ling told me something that shocked me. He said it was his father who sent him away. All these years, I'd blamed you. I'm sorry for that. But why didn't you tell me what happened?"

"I thought if I didn't mention the boy, eventually you'd forget him. That when we came to America, you'd grow up and marry a nice, respectable boy from church." Mama glanced sideways at Elsa and muttered through clenched teeth. "I bent over backward to obey all the church rules. I was more Mennonite than your father! I could have fit in, too—but you had to take up with an outsider."

Elsa felt as if she'd been slapped. Their talk had been so promising, from deep in their hearts. But what good did it do if Mama still hated Morris? What would it take for her to accept him?

She chose her words carefully. "Mama, we're very happy. Morris is a lot like Papa—kind, loving, and considerate. He's been good to me, good *for* me."

Mama shrugged. "At least he's American," she said grudgingly. "And I must admit he's a good provider. But Crys ..." Her tears started again. "What will people think?"

Elsa bit back a smile. Mama had been more influenced by China than she realized—still so worried about losing face. "Those who love her will be supportive. The others—well, it'll be *their* problem."

Mama wiped her eyes again and blew her nose. She stared down at the bedspread and drew little circles on the pattern with her finger. Finally, she looked up. "I've ... changed my mind. I'm not giving Crys the bracelet. Not if she'll live in that dirty little village." She pointed to a small box on her dresser. "You always liked it. Go ahead and take it."

Shocked, Elsa stared at her. Yes, she'd always wanted that bracelet. But not this way. Not without Mama's love and respect. Hot resentment boiled up, nearly choking her. "No, thanks," she said tightly. "Save it for someone you really care about."

Mama's face flushed. "What are you saying? That I don't love my own daughter?"

Elsa looked her straight in the eye. "I don't know. Do you?"

"Of course! I've always tried to be a good mother. But ever since you were little, you've turned away from me, running off to your father or the amah."

Elsa had tried so hard to keep this visit pleasant, but if she was ever to get close to her mother, she had to be honest now. "Their love was ... unconditional. No matter what, I could count on them. With you, I always felt I wasn't good enough. If I followed orders, maybe you'd smile at me, tell me I was bright. If not ..."

She'd already stayed much longer than intended and now got up to leave. "We're both grown women—both Christians—and I'd like for us to be friends. To forgive the past and start fresh." She waited, trying to catch Mama's eye, to see if the words had made any impression. But Mama turned away.

With a sigh, Elsa said good-bye and left.

Chapter 44

A WEEK LATER, ELSA SET HER dining table with her best dishes and flatware. Mama would find something wrong no matter what, but at least everything would look festive. She glanced into the living room where Crystal had set up a screen and projector and Morris was sorting through the slides taken in China.

"When I have more time," he told Crys, "I'll arrange these into a video, with each shot merging into the next. For tonight, we'll just use the best ones. Don't want to bore your grandmother."

Elsa didn't think that Mama would have any problems with boredom. Rather, it might be the memories of China, the fear and resentment she'd bottled up all these years.

When her mother arrived, she seemed quieter than usual. She nodded at Morris, accepted a hug from Crys, and touched Elsa on the shoulder without the usual criticism of her hair or clothes.

Elsa was puzzled but decided Mama was showing Chinese *kerchieh*. Mama had always prided herself on good manners in public—maybe she was still sulking from their talk the week before and trying to cover it up.

At the table, Mama ate sparingly of Elsa's tender pot roast but took seconds of the green bean casserole. She even accepted a piece of cherry pie and surprised Elsa by commenting favorably on the flaky crust.

This is more than kerchieh, thought Elsa. Sliding a glance at Morris, she saw that he, too, looked baffled.

Mama sat quietly through the slide show while Morris and Elsa commented on Crystal's good photography, pointing out the beautiful gardens, the little curved bridges over ponds of lotus blossoms and huge carp, the pagodas, and the majesty of the Great Wall.

When the pictures were finished, Elsa presented Mama with the brocade cushion cover she'd bought.

Mama thanked her. "It's lovely." Then she stood and picked up her purse. "And thank you for having me over. Dinner was very nice." She hesitated, and Elsa waited for the inevitable "but why didn't you . . ."

Instead, she was surprised to see tears in Mama's eyes.

"Elsa, you were right." Mama paused and cleared her throat. "It's hard for me to accept the fact that your choices have turned out well even though I didn't agree with them." She looked at Morris. "You're a good husband and father. I'm sorry I didn't admit it sooner. And Crys—I find it hard to accept your decision." Her voice trembled; she wiped her eyes and then hugged her granddaughter. "But you've always shown good judgment before, so I can only wish you God's blessing and hope for the best."

She opened her purse and took out a box. Elsa recognized it as the one that held the jade bracelet. Despite Mama's apology, disappointment flooded Elsa's heart. Her mother had changed her mind again and would give it to Crystal after all.

But Mama turned back to Elsa. "I know your father meant for you to have this someday. Please accept the bracelet." She held out the box in both hands, the polite, Chinese way. "Please. As a peace offering?"

Elsa looked into her mother's eyes. She and Mama were still worlds apart in their concepts, but this could be a giant step toward friendship.

She glanced at Morris, and saw him give the slightest of nods. Crys rested her chin on her fingers, palms joined as though in prayer. Elsa knew everything depended on her answer.

She smiled and accepted the gift, also with both hands. The polite, Chinese way.

Slipping on the smooth green bracelet, she slid an arm around her mother's tense shoulders and gave them a squeeze. "Thank you, Mama. I'll enjoy wearing it. Someday I'll pass it on to Crys, and she can give it to her own daughter when she has one. It'll be our tradition, to keep you and Papa and the memories of China alive in our hearts."